The
Atua Man

The
Atua Man

A Novel

John Stephenson

Hidden Cove Press
Kailua, Hawaii

To the mystic in each and every one of you ...

And to my wife, Sandra, a mystic and my muse.

Mystics gain information from a source other than the known senses. They perceive time as an illusion, they are aware of a fundamental unity to all things, and they perceive evil as an illusion that changes when one shifts one's field of perception.

– BERTRAND RUSSELL

"Is there a reality that cannot be altered by perception?"

– SANDRA KNIGHT

Contents

PART II

PART III

Prologue

London, November 2004

He hadn't slept for the past three nights. Something within him, something beyond his control, kept him from finding rest. It had nothing to do with his everyday problems. It wasn't his wife or son or occupation that kept him awake; it was his soul. It was his awareness that there was something greater than mortal existence available to humanity, and that "something" wanted to use him as its outlet. Again.

He moved his comfortable wingchair to a spot close to the leaded windows and sat down. He studied the pale moon that sent its dim light through the fog and put a silvery glow to the tall sycamores in his private garden. He was privileged and blessed, and he was insecure and fearful. He was reluctant to let go of what the world thought of as reality. Would he be forever lost to those he loved if he succeeded? Should he even try to break the physical bonds of the material world and enter the spiritual dimension? He was terrified that this next step in his mystical journey would be another deadly ordeal.

For many years he had not told anyone about the first time he had experienced the immortal, not even his best friend, David. Gazing at the November moon brought the incident to mind. He was eighteen, surfing his first big waves in Hawaii. He felt the same way then as he felt now, frightened yet excited. His first ride fulfilled his dreams; his second ride nearly killed him.

He had been caught in the impact zone. The breaking wave had ripped his board from his hand and had driven him into the coral and sand bottom. He panicked, but after a moment the same knowledge that was pushing him now, his *greater self,* had taken away the fear and brought peace. Very soon he had no more breath. He had no more strength. His body automatically began to inhale, and that meant that his lungs would fill with water and he'd die. But his lungs miraculously filled with air. He was breathing underwater and then he heard the words, "You are not yet finished here."

Jason St. John got up from the chair, shook himself as if he were still wet. He questioned the timing of the memory. Did it come to reassure him that he was safe, that he would be protected in this new exploration into the nature of reality? Or, was it a warning? His earlier initiations came through his desire for adventure. He no longer wanted that. More than ever he needed the peace that came in meditation.

He sat back down and looked at his hands resting on the arms of the chair. As he relaxed, he contemplated what Einstein called the fabric of time and space, the fourth dimension of reality. He could not yet put into perspective what he had seen and felt these past few weeks. He never did understand the significance of his trials until they were over. All he could do was push ahead and pray that he still had something to give.

He closed his pale green eyes to shut out the garden and the fog and the moon. He consciously stopped the river of thoughts and images concerning his daily life from entering his mind. He rested into the stillness that he had known since he was a boy. It was a silence that filled him with peace. In that state of being, the beliefs that defined him materially and dictated how he should live dissolved. In the womb of silence, which was how he thought of the darkness, he became "one" with the invisible fabric of creation. He found himself integrated with every molecule of life, an experience in which he was at once himself and at the same time "one" with all that existed.

And then came new images, esoteric images of a world in which the colors barely held together, and solid objects burst into stardust the moment they were touched. Everything pulsed and vibrated to harmonic chords that were so beautiful they made him weep with joy. He knew deep down in his soul that he was glimpsing the unseen reality behind what the five physical senses describe as real.

In this dimension he felt a power that could only be called divine, though he refused to use religious terminology to define it. The power he felt was beyond his comprehension, yet it was the essence of who he was. It was not a cosmic force, but the substance of all that existed.

PART I

Chapter 1
Stanford House, London

Tuesday Morning, November 2004

Barbara Buchanan, an African American woman in her early fifties, pushed her way through the mob fronting Stanford House, the Tudor Revival buildings in South West London that housed the offices, television studios, and residences that made up the St. John Ministries. It was ten to nine and Barbara was going to be late for the quarterly board meeting if she couldn't get through the crowd. She hated to be late.

She wondered what in hell had brought out this crowd. There had always been the curious in front of Stanford House waiting to catch a glimpse of their messiah, but this morning was different. Something was going on.

Tall and thin, her close-cropped hair salted with white, Barbara was stronger than she looked. She elbowed aside someone trying to stop her by grabbing the strap of her Louis Vuitton bag. That act nearly choked her. She pulled the purse to her chest and then felt the jacket of her new suit rip as another person tried to keep her from getting to work. Cursing under her breath, she fought her way up to the steps of the gated entrance only to be stopped by a policeman.

"I'm Barbara Buchanan. I work here."

"I'll need some identification, ma'am." The policeman crossed his arms and looked at Barbara skeptically.

Barbara reached into her bag for her wallet only to find it gone.

"It seems I've been pickpocketed. I'm missing my wallet."

The policeman nodded but didn't move.

Gary Howell stepped from the entrance to the stoop to get a sense of the crowd. He was tense, expecting the worst. In his mid-thirties, Gary wore a tailored suit, and stood with a military bearing. He had a Bluetooth earpiece in one ear, a mobile phone to the other ear, and a walkie-talkie in his hand. His muscles bulged under his suit as he twisted around, taking in the full scope of the hordes hoping to glimpse Jason St. John. Half of the crowd yelled, "Heal us!" while further back, separated by police barricade, protesters shouted "*Antichrist.*"

"Barbara! What are you doing down there?" Gary rushed down to the gate.

"I lost my wallet and this person won't let me in."

Howell tapped the policeman on his shoulder. "Let her in. She's one of our directors."

"She hasn't any identification."

"I'll vouch for her."

"And who are you?"

"I'm the bloody head of security and I'll have your boss on the phone in two seconds if you don't let her in."

The bobby stepped aside, and Gary opened the gate.

Tony Bass, the dapper, fiftyish CEO of St. John Ministries, leaned over the shoulder of a young technician anxiously scanning the array of monitors in his cubical in the St. John

Ministries security bunker. The numerous screens showed the crowds on the street, the entries and exits of Stanford House, and the hallways, public rooms and garages of the compound.

"There!" Bass pounded his pencil on the monitor showing a car pulling into the garage. "What time was that?"

"About six, I think. One of the kitchen staff."

"This is serious, you know," Bass said. "You have no idea of the threats we have against Mr. St. John's life. I wish you people would get it through your heads that if the world loses Jason St. John, they have lost one of the great prophets of all time."

Bass watched for a moment longer until another monitor drew his attention to the breaking news of ITV reporter Theodore Spencer.

"Oh fuck. Not him *again*."

Spencer, Britain's answer to Geraldo Rivera, had such a relationship with the camera that those watching him felt that he was their best friend and that whatever news he was delivering was drop-what-you-are-doing important. He had a rich baritone voice that made everything he said sound credible, and piercing eyes that assured his audience that he would get to the truth wherever it hid. He had perfect English, more hair than he deserved, and he looked no older than forty. He had probably looked that way for years.

Tony Bass walked over to the monitor and turned up the volume. "Four twelve-year-old girls, here at Royal Marsdan Hospital, all in the last stages of childhood leukemia, left the hospital this morning apparently no longer sick, but full of energy and joy."

A grainy video from the hospital's security camera popped on the screen showing the girls scurrying across the lobby with their parents running after them.

Spencer's voice went on under the video; "The children claim that the world renown healing guru, Jason St. John, cured them of their disease. In fact, one of the girls told her doctor that she saw Jason St. John in the hospital room..."

The monitor went back to Spencer, filling the screen with his face.

"Are you recording this?" Bass was glued to Spencer's image.

"What?" The security tech followed Bass's gaze to the television. "No sir, that's just the telly."

"Record everything. And call me immediately when you find video of Mr. St. John."

The television captured a shot of the mobs in front of Stanford House and then cut back to Spencer with school photos of the girls under his talking head. "Last night these girls were on their deathbeds. We are waiting to hear from the attending physicians as to whether or not the children were indeed cured, and that will take some time. There are many questions here. There is no record of anyone coming into the cancer ward. And yet one of the girls positively identified Jason St. John at the foot of her bed. Did she really see him, or was she hallucinating?"

Bass returned to the young tech and his array of monitors. "Run back the CCTV from Mr. St. John's apartment. I want to see what you've got from nine last night until six this morning."

The technician queued up the video from the camera outside the St. John apartment, reversed it until the time code read twenty-one hundred. The picture that came up was the richly paneled hall with plush burgundy carpet from the top floor of the building, but no sign of life.

Bass waited, hoping Jason St. John would slip out the door and run down the hall. He tapped his pencil again on the monitor while he waited. "Are you fast-forwarding?"

"No, sir. It's real time."

"Then speed it up, you idiot. I don't have all day."

Spencer's voice was still grating on Bass. "The St. John Ministries was established eight years ago to manage the worldwide rallies of Jason St. John. This latest appearance, if it's true, a physical appearance of Jason St. John when there is no record of him coming or going from the hospital, is unprecedented. The St. John Ministries has yet to comment. Tony Bass, its CEO, has not returned our phone calls."

Finally, Bass picked up his briefcase from the floor, gave the young tech a few taps on his head with his pencil before dropping it in his case, and took one last look at Spencer on the television. "I want to know the moment you have footage of Mr. St. John; you hear. The very moment!"

Bass turned and headed for the door.

"Mr. Bass," Spencer continued in the background, "the Wall Street *wunderkind* was brought into the organization as the ministry's first CEO. With his financial background, it's apparent to this reporter that his primary purpose is to manage the vast sums of money that have made Mr. St. John a billionaire."

"Friggin' little pit bull," Bass muttered under his breath as the door shut behind him.

He took the stairs two at a time up to the ground floor and entered the reception lobby. He loved this area. It held the short history of the St. John Ministries. There were citations and honors from hospitals and governments covering its walls. Recessed television monitors showed clips from *The Healing Hour* television program, and pictures of Jason with various heads of state, prominent religious leaders, and celebrities of all stripes—from entertainers to athletes to scientists and statesmen—filled the room. He pressed the call button for the elevator. Tony felt that he was responsible for much of Jason's celebrity and success. He was the one who built the ministry into one of the great metaphysical organizations in the world.

He stepped into the waiting elevator—lift, he said to himself, and punched the button for the third floor.

Lillian St. John ambled into the parlor of her top floor apartment and moved her husband's meditation chair back to its usual place next to the inlaid ivory side table. She had just awakened, and she stood in front of the tall leaded windows overlooking her garden to let the foggy light wash over her. Her youthful face denied her forty-three years—she was still a great beauty, and her auburn hair fell in loose curls to the middle of her back. Her English blue eyes showed the stress of living in a fishbowl prison. She shivered and sat in the wingchair next to her husband's, wrapping herself in her Frette throw, kept there for mornings like this. The oaks and sycamores in the fog reminded her of a Turner painting. She closed her eyes and began to meditate. Just as she approached the stillness that would bring her into a state of bliss, the sound of her front door opening startled her.

"J.J.?" she called but heard no reply.

Her heart began to race. She jumped up, pulled her cashmere robe tight around her slender body, and ran into the foyer.

"What in bloody hell are you doing?" she yelled, blocking Tony Bass from entering her home. Her blue eyes turning to ice.

"Where's your husband?"

"Get out!"

She tried to push him out the door, but Tony wouldn't budge.

"It's urgent," he told her.

"Are you serious? Who on earth gave you a key to our flat?"

Again, Tony tried to get past her, but she blocked his way.

"Standard security precautions. We have keys to every room in the compound."

"You will leave this instant!"

"He better be at the board meeting and I expect him to be on time. We all want to know where he's been."

"What is *that* supposed to mean?"

"You tell me, Mrs. St. John."

Thirteen-year-old Alex walked in from his bedroom. He had just awakened and was still in his boxers and T-shirt.

"Good morning, Alex. Your father still sleeping?" Tony's voice masked his anger.

Alex looked puzzled. "I guess."

Tony turned to Lillian; "Melanie arrived last night. You know how hard it is to get her to leave Kauai."

That remark annoyed Lillian. Though she and Melanie had become close over the years, there were still rumors about Melanie and Jason and their South Seas voyage that Lillian didn't like. For Tony to make a remark like that was insulting.

Tony ruffled Alex's hair and walked out. Lillian slammed the door after him and leaned against it.

"Why are you so mad, Mom?"

"Mr. Bass just totally overstepped his bounds."

Tony Bass opened the door to the ministry's boardroom a few minutes before nine o'clock and found Dorothy Delaney already there making corrections to the minutes from their last meeting and writing notes on the day's agenda. She was a generation older than the rest of the board and her white hair was tied in a bun that bounced when she wrote.

Sensing Tony's anger, she snapped her portfolio shut. "Good morning, Tony. Are you okay?"

"No."

"Tony, you mustn't let ego rob you of your peace." She closed her eyes to take a moment of silence. "Meditate with me."

"Don't preach to me, Dorothy, I'm not in the mood."

Dorothy took a deep breath and went back to her notes.

Dorothy recognized Jason St. John—J.J. to his close friends—as an illumined soul the first time she met him when he was fifteen. She had been a student of the noted twentieth century mystic, Dr. Solomon Green, and was editing one of Dr. Green's books when Jason had accompanied his mother to a party for Dr. Green that Dorothy had organized. What Dorothy saw was a young man radiating Spirit.

Prior to his passing twenty years before, Dr. Green had opened the way for the critical examination of the relationship between body, mind and spirit. In his heyday, he had invited scientists and theologians to redefine the nature of life. He took the esoteric from the custody of religion and put it into the general discussion about the nature of life and the universe. He envisioned a real-world mysticism that would lift people out of their limited concepts of life into the freedom of spiritual understanding. Now, Dorothy edited all of Jason's work, and knew from experience how great his gift was, and how uncaring and selfish the world could be.

Dorothy continued to meditate while Tony sat at the head of the conference table and admired his cufflinks. The chill in the room was broken when Barbara Buchanan rushed in at precisely nine o'clock. She checked her watch, took her seat at the large polished table, and said, "Where *is* everybody?"

Without waiting for a response, she dropped her bag on the floor, took off her jacket, and examined it.

"Darn! They ripped my coat. And I lost my wallet! I've got to stop all my cards." She looked at Tony and Dorothy and picked up on the tension in the room. "How long are we going to wait?"

Barbara was the Ministry's Vice-President of Operations and Media Outreach. Seven years ago she had been a well-known fundraiser for a private foundation supporting educational opportunities for poor children of color. She had survived an abusive husband, had raised two kids in the roughest part of Oakland, California, and had managed to earn a master's degree at Cal Berkley. She had first encountered Jason when he spoke to a group of young people suffering terminal illnesses at an Attitudinal Healing center in Tiburon, California. She left with a feeling of overwhelming love. Barbara hadn't told anybody at that time about her breast cancer. Indeed, the renown that her work had brought her made her uncertain as to how she should inform her colleagues of her condition, and often she had wondered whether or not they even needed to know.

Barbara had gone to Jason's talk in the hopes of obtaining guidance for her next step in dealing with her illness. She had received different opinions for treatment, but none gave her more than six months to live. After being in the presence of Jason, her doctors found no cancer at all. She credited the healing to Jason and within six months was working for him.

"What's happening outside?" she asked.

"I'll let you know when everyone gets here." Tony leaned back in his large leather chair and studied the hammered beam ceiling. The boardroom was a copy of the Great Hall at Hampton Court Palace. A carved stone fireplace dominated one wall and two Flemish tapestries of biblical scenes hung between paneled bookcases on another. This décor too, was Tony's idea. He needed to set the proper tone for the importance of the St. John Ministry.

Gary walked in closing a conversation on one mobile phone and then another.

Tony stood. "Did you find him?"

Gary shook his head no.

Following on Gary's heels was Melanie Graff, all six feet of her, perfectly coiffed and looking anxious. "What's going on out there? Even the Pope doesn't draw a crowd like this. People kept asking me if it's true. What are they talking about?"

Melanie was one of the original trustees and in the early days managed the money. Her history with Jason went back to his life-changing voyage to the South Pacific. She had been on that voyage but never talked about it. The newer board members knew little about her except that she was athletic and tan, and that she flew in from the island of Kauai every quarter for the board meetings. "Where *is* J.J.?"

Tony ignored the question and began the meeting. "Please disregard the agenda in your portfolio. We will dispense with committee reports and begin with new business. I don't know if you heard the news this morning, but it seems Mr. St. John appeared in a hospital ward last night around three a.m. and healed four little girls."

Tony loosened his tie and undid the top button of his immaculate white shirt, a gesture of stress in the usually cool and dapper CEO. He couldn't hide his anxiety, which was caused as much by the sick girl's claim that she had seen Jason at the hospital as it was by Theodore Spencer's grabbing hold of the story.

"How wonderful," Dorothy said.

"It's not the healing that's the problem. Our security shows that he didn't leave the compound last night. And according to all the cameras at the hospital, Jason never entered the children's ward. None of the nurses on the floor saw anyone enter or leave." Tony looked at Gary for confirmation.

"As far as we can tell, he has not left his apartment since yesterday afternoon when he went for a stroll in the garden." Gary spoke slowly, choosing his words carefully and giving the impression that English was not his mother tongue even though it was.

Gary was one of Jason's more miraculous cures. Within hours of the Humvee explosion in Iraq that had made him a hero for having pulled his crew to safety, he had suffered a seizure and was flown back to the states with traumatic brain injury. He couldn't speak. He had lost his motor skills and had resented his caregivers. He would rather have died than be dependent on others for the simple necessities of life.

His wife wouldn't leave his side and had found Jason's book, *The Undiscovered Land,* at the Walter Reed Army Hospital. Not long after reading it she took Gary to a St. John Healing Rally at the Verizon Center in D.C. The atmosphere of stillness in that stadium was so powerful that she felt the vise of physical limitations leave her husband. Soon thereafter Gary's speech and motor skills came back, and he was released from the hospital.

"Jason St. John hasn't left the compound since yesterday, yet he appeared at Marsdan and was seen by four witnesses who claimed that he healed them?" Tony informed his board.

"Actually, only one girl saw him." Gary consulted his notes. "But they all seemed to be healed."

"I don't believe it," Barbara interrupted.

"What don't you believe?" Melanie said.

"Nobody can just up and disappear. We all had to seek out Jason and be in his presence for a healing. People have to come to his rallies..."

"That's such a materialistic perspective, Barbara," Dorothy said.

"I'm sorry Dorothy, but I'm a realist." Turning to Tony, Barbara continued, "Why are we accepting that this actually happened without any investigation?"

"Because thousands of people out there believe it happened," Tony told her. "And because it's at the top of the news cycle. People believe what they are told by reporters like Theodore Spencer."

"Come on, Tony, this is post-Christian London," Melanie said. "People don't care."

"Then why are there thousands of people outside our ministry wanting answers?"

"Why not just tell them what happened?" Dorothy asked.

"Because we don't fucking know what happened." Tony was embarrassed. He hated losing his cool. He continued more calmly; "Because Jason is doing something that will destroy us."

"How do you figure?" Melanie asked almost hostilely.

"Reputation is everything in this kind of work," Tony informed her rather condescendingly. "The St. John reputation is untarnished, up until now. Mr. St. John has been open to the public and the scientific community, and they have recognized the fact that people have been healed. Jason has never claimed it was because he was someone special, or that he had some kind of supernatural power. And, by the way, where is he? He knows there is a board meeting this morning."

"You're not reading this very well, Tony." Dorothy stood and looked at her colleagues. "Jason is who he is. This is not about reputation, or how people perceive us. That's your fear, Tony. You can't stand in the way of Jason pushing the boundaries of perceived reality."

"I have... we have a fiduciary duty to protect this ministry," Tony said. "We can't let him destroy the gift he's given the world by performing some kind of magic trick."

"You think he's doing magic?" Melanie asked. She knew more about Jason than any of these people, except for perhaps Dorothy, and didn't like where Tony was taking the meeting.

"I don't care what you call it, but appearing out of thin air, in a hospital, and having four little girls cured of cancer who walk out full of energy, stretches the limits of credibility. If we aren't credible, we are nothing," Tony declared.

"How does pushing the bounds of physical limitation deny Jason's work?" Dorothy leaned on the table and glared at Tony. "Isn't omnipresence a core principle? Didn't Dr. Green say that there are those who can step out of the mortal concept of body at will?"

"Omnipresence is a transcendent principle, not a physical fact," Tony stated.

"Not for a master," Dorothy replied.

Tony paused, seeming desperate, waiting for support from the other board members. He wasn't getting it.

"What are you afraid of, Tony?" Melanie asked, shifting the focus. "Losing your job?"

"Don't insult me, Melanie. I'm doing this to protect this ministry; to protect Jason."

"I doubt that."

"All it would take to destroy us would be a little negative press," Tony responded. "Reporters will make snide remarks, and comedians will tell jokes about Jason, and soon his detractors will dismiss us… Jason as another quack in a long history of snake oil salesmen. We can't let that happen."

"What do you mean by that?" Dorothy demanded. "Comparing Jason to a snake oil salesman is disgusting. Jason follows a long tradition of revealing the truth. Enlightened people all over the world have seen the links between Jason and Dr. Green and Shankara. We are here because we all love *The Life and Teaching of the Masters of the Far East…*"

"I don't know where Mr. St. John is," Tony interrupted her, "and it has me worried. That's why we have to stop this nonsense right now."

"How do you plan to do that? Lock him up in the basement?" Melanie and Tony locked eyes.

"Jason is stretching his wings, Tony," Dorothy said, breaking the tension. She started to walk around the table like a schoolteacher in a classroom. "It's been done in the East for centuries, but it's also part of our tradition. The Roman Church has many saints who have defied physical laws…"

"Is this relevant, Dorothy?" Barbara interrupted.

Dorothy stopped opposite Barbara and raised her hand like a traffic cop. "This is an interesting story and something you should all hear."

Lots of eye-rolling went on around the table. Dorothy ignored it.

"It took place during World War II. A Japanese fighter attacked an American bomber preparing to land on a small Pacific island, and one airman made it out of the bomber before it exploded. He tried to open his parachute and the ripcord broke. He was plunging to his death when a grey-haired man with a long beard appeared next to him—falling just like the airman. Before they hit the ground, the saint grabbed hold of the flyer and guided him to the ground. He landed without breaking a bone. Nobody could believe it, but he was alive, and the rest of his crew died when the plane crashed. When he went home on leave, he saw a picture of the man who saved his life. It was Padre Pio. His mother had prayed to him to watch over her son."

"If he were doing remote healing, like Dorothy's suggesting," Melanie piped in, "he'd still be in his apartment and that would have only been his image that the girls saw. But if he appeared in some supernatural way at the hospital," looking at Tony, "well, that's a different story."

"Why would that be a problem?" Dorothy asked. "Isn't it our goal in this study to realize that we are not localized or confined? Didn't Jesus appear to the apostles after the Crucifixion?"

"It *is* a problem if he can just appear like some alien," Tony insisted. "I went up to his apartment and Lillian wouldn't let me in. And she seemed strange to me. People are afraid of aliens, and Far Eastern masters, or any other title you want to put on him. We cannot allow this to happen, Dorothy. We'll lose our audience."

Lillian still leaned against the front door of the apartment as if she were waiting for Tony's scent to vanish before doing anything else.

"Where *is* Dad?" Alex was almost as tall as his mom with long hair and the same green eyes as his father. Lillian gave her son a good-morning kiss and tousled his hair, which he hated.

"What do you want for breakfast?" Lillian took his hand and pulled him toward the kitchen / family room. Alex pulled away and ran ahead, and sat at the counter. He took out his Game Boy and started playing.

The family room was Lillian's space. The furniture was soft and overstuffed. Meals were served on the large country table, which was also used for Alex's art projects. The adjoining kitchen was state-of-the-art with a professional range and copper cookware hanging over a granite-topped island. Lillian grabbed a French porcelain mixing bowl from the cupboard and took a dozen eggs from the fridge.

"How about scrambled eggs?"

"I thought you were giving me a choice?"

"Not this morning. And don't take an attitude with me."

"What's going on around here?"

Tony had upset Lillian more than she was willing to let on, especially to Alex. She had never liked their living arrangements, which had been set up by the board, and still got aggravated with Jason for letting the organization control their lives to the extent that it did. Everything the board did, so they said, was for Jason's protection. Lillian had preferred to live in the country, but the board had insisted on the city. Lillian had thought the organization would be completely separate from their personal lives, but the board argued that was impossible. Jason *was* the ministry, they'd say, and without him in the midst of day-to-day operations they would not have the spark to keep the organization spiritually centered.

Now she worried that the board, Tony specifically, wanted to intrude even more into their personal lives.

Lillian broke eggs into the bowl. "Grab a frying pan for me, will you?"

Alex reached for a pan on the rack above him. "Why was Uncle Tony so angry?"

"I don't know. I thought your dad would be out here when I got up. He wasn't in bed. Go see if he's in his office."

Lillian took the pan from her son and put it on the stove. "What were you playing?"

"Tony Hawk. Underground."

Alex noticed a half a dozen eggs in the bowl, and his mother was ready to crack another. "Hey, I'm not *that* hungry."

Lillian put the egg back, poured some milk into the bowl, and started beating the mixture with a wire whisk. "I thought I asked you to see if your father was in his office?"

Alex got up and ran to the other side of the apartment. Lillian switched on the small television on the counter while vigorously beating the eggs when a news commentator came on-screen speculating about Jason's alleged appearance at the hospital the previous evening. She switched to another channel and saw another version of the same report.

"Oh my god," Lillian put her hand to her mouth as Irma, the housekeeper, entered the kitchen carrying two armloads of groceries.

"I beg your pardon," she said.

Lillian quickly turned off the TV. Irma squeezed by, out of breath and out of shape.

"Sorry for being so late. I thought I'd be back before you folks got up. It's a zoo outside."

Irma put her packages down and took the bowl from Lillian. "I'll take over."

She shooed Lillian from the narrow space between the island and the cooktop and dropped a cube of butter into the skillet.

She gave the eggs a few more beats before pouring them into the pan. She whistled tunelessly.

Lillian sat at the counter, mindlessly watching Irma and trying to make sense of the news that was on television when her attention was drawn to the back door and the blood drained from her face.

Irma reacted to Lillian and stopped scrambling the eggs. "Come now, missus, this *is* my job, you know," she said, thinking Lillian was somehow displeased with her.

Lillian saw Jason St. John, her beloved husband, his long blondish hair disheveled as if he had just stepped out of a strong wind, materialize a few paces behind Irma. He stepped out of a pale blue light like he was emerging from a cocoon! He motioned for Lillian to be quiet. His face was flushed, his clothes clung to his slender, thirty-nine-year-old body like iron to a magnet, and he stood there for a moment letting the energy drain from him, like it would after surfing an exceptional wave. Reaching back, he opened the door to make it look like he had entered normally.

Alex came running back into the room just as his father pretended to close the kitchen door. He had seen the last remnants of a crystal-like aura dissolve around his father's body. "Sick!"

"Are there enough eggs for me?" Jason asked.

Startled, Irma turned around. "Isn't that a bit childish for a grown man to sneak up on an old lady like that?"

"Dad, how did you do that?" Alex said, running up to him.

Lillian slipped by Irma and ushered Jason and Alex out of the kitchen. "What the hell is going on?" she whispered.

"That was awesome!" Alex exclaimed.

"Okay. Okay. Sorry I startled you. Family meeting in ten minutes; I've got to take a shower."

"I think I ruined the eggs," Irma said, watching the family retreat. She dumped them in the sink and began to put away the groceries, whistling again tunelessly.

"Here's what I think," Melanie announced to the rest of the board. "That girl *thought* she saw Jason. Maybe she thought of him before she went to sleep and dreamed he was there. It could have been Jesus Christ or some saint."

"That's our angle," injected Barbara. "Since there's no video record of Jason being at the hospital, we'll credit him for the healing but not for being there."

"I didn't know we were keeping score in the healing department," Dorothy said dryly, taking her seat.

Ignoring her, Barbara continued, "I just want to understand this because if I get it, everyone else will. That girl saw an apparition, and her belief in Jason's power to heal had a positive result. It's no different than if someone saw an image of the Virgin Mary in a moment of illumination and everyone with that person was healed. People will understand that, even if they don't necessarily believe it."

Barbara looked at each board member for a response. Dorothy and Melanie shook their heads.

"Why do we need to say *anything*?" Dorothy interjected. "We'll never control world opinion about Jason so why try?"

"You're losing me here, Barbara," Melanie said, talking over Dorothy. "Apparitions are just someone's fantasy. They aren't real. Jason can heal. That's real. I've seen it. But this other crap... I don't know. We're a foundation, not a religion."

"You're wrong, Melanie," Tony said. "People look to us for a lot more than healing. They want principles to live by. They want guidance. They want to believe that there is more to life than mundane human existence."

"You need to reread our charter," Melanie insisted. She got up, walked around the table, stretching her legs. She was a formidable presence. "Tony, we are here to explore the mystical nature of reality. We are more scientists than theologians, and I'm very skeptical of secondhand information."

"Then we need to find out if in fact Jason is remotely healing or manifesting himself through thin air. If he is doing either of these things, we need to stop him," Tony emphasized.

"How?" Melanie asked.

"You let me handle that."

"We will be voting on everything you intend to do," Melanie insisted.

"What we need," Barbara said, "is for Jason to go on television and explain to the world what happened. People trust him. He can put this whole incident in terms that reflect current popular thinking."

"That's good, Barbara." Melanie agreed; "Jason could go on television and make what the girl saw a point of discussion about what constitutes reality. Isn't that our main question?"

"That is a dangerous idea, Melanie." Tony wanted to squash it before it took hold. "First of all, for Mr. St. John to go out into the public at this time could endanger his life."

"That's a fact." Gary rarely said anything at the board meetings but had to now. "He has a lot of enemies and I don't have the resources to guarantee his safety in public."

"I like Melanie's idea," Barbara said. "Jason wouldn't be going out in public. We could film it right here and broadcast it live. We'd gain a huge audience and I'm sure Jason can explain what those girls saw with a lot more authority than any of us could."

"I move that we organize a televised symposium with Jason and the heads of the Anglican, Catholic, Jewish, and Muslim communities to discuss apparitions—their meaning and historical relevance," Melanie said.

Barbara seconded the motion. "What about some scientists?"

"I doubt they'd come; they don't mix well with religious leaders," Gary remarked.

"We need a quantum physicist, someone like Alain Aspect." Melanie ignored Gary's opinion.

"This is a bad idea," Tony warned. "If I call a vote and you two prevail, this ministry will implode."

"You must call for a vote, Tony. It's been moved and seconded," Dorothy said.

"Obviously, Mr. St. John will have to agree," Barbara stated.

Tony called the vote and the motion for the televised symposium passed with Dorothy, Barbara, and Melanie voting for it and Tony and Gary against.

Jason, his hair still wet from the shower, walked into the kitchen and sat across from Lillian and Alex at the country table. He wore his favorite sweats—long sleeves as always, and his shoulder length hair soaked his sweatshirt. Lillian had sent Irma home and was on her third latte. They all stared at each other not knowing what to think or where to begin.

"What can I say? I've been having these experiences for a few months now when I get up to meditate. They scare me, but something keeps pushing me to go further. I don't really understand it, and I'm not sure I can stop, having gone this far." Jason sat up straight, closed his eyes, and rested his hands lightly on top of the table. "Indian fakirs have been practicing this for centuries."

The room grew extremely quiet and Lillian closed her eyes too. Alex, knowing the drill when his parents meditated, sat up straight and tried to let his mind grow still. He attempted to find the spaces between his thoughts but failed. His mind was running too fast.

But Jason wasn't meditating. "Don't close your eyes," he said.

Alex and Lillian opened their eyes. They watched Jason's hands and arms slowly slip through the table onto his lap.

"That is so unreal!" Alex shouted.

"This scares the shit out of me, Jason."

Jason and Alex looked at each other and started to laugh. Lillian never cussed. But her fear was palpable, so father and son stopped short.

"I mean this will shatter everyone's concept of reality."

"Is that so bad?" Jason understood Lillian's reaction. "Even in the physical world there is more space than matter in what we see and feel. This first happened about six months ago. I was so at one in the Spirit that I opened my eyes to see if the world was still there and I noticed that my arms had blended in with the chair. Then a gentle voice said to me, just like in scripture, 'Fear not.' So, I just observed my situation and when I felt myself completely here, I lifted my arms out of the chair and everything was normal."

"It's horrible. Don't you see what will happen? Tony Bass is already wanting to dominate and control you."

"Did you really heal those girls?" Alex asked his father.

"Not like you think, Alex. Our ministry is about revealing the essential nature of life, and when that is experienced ..."

"For God's sake, J.J., get serious. This is not the time for a lecture."

"Do you have magical powers?" Alex asked.

"Last night was the first time I've actually gone anywhere. Before that it was just like I showed you."

"Jason! Enough! Now let's get practical about this. You can't tell anyone on the board."

"I thought Dorothy should know."

"Absolutely not! Jason, you don't realize how dangerous this is. Put the brakes on your impulses and think this through. Think about us. You already have half the world thinking you're Satan, so please …"

Alex looked lovingly at his dad. "That's no big deal."

"I would think that you would want to keep this secret," Lillian said.

"I don't know. I can't stop, Lillian. Whatever it is that is giving me these experiences won't let me go back. When a new reality is realized, it can't be undone. And if I can experience it fully, I can teach others to do the same."

"What if they don't want to go there?"

"Dad, can you teach me?"

"Alex, I don't want you to tell anyone what you saw," Lillian ordered.

"Mom …"

"I'm serious. Tell no one! This is the biggest secret you'll ever have to keep."

"Irma saw it."

"She did not, and you didn't either."

"I did, too! I saw that blue stuff around Dad and he pretending to come in the back door. And we just saw what Dad did!"

"Your mom is right, Alex. If you mention this to any of your friends, they'll think you're nuts."

"Most of my friends already think you're a freak."

"I'm sorry," Jason reached across the table and took his son's hand. Alex couldn't look his dad in the eyes. Jason was his hero and he didn't mean to make him feel bad. But it was true.

"Okay, here's what happens, Alex. I don't disappear. When I'm in that invisible state I'm pure energy. There are laws of attraction in this world, and when I have no physical limitations I go where I'm needed. At least that's my current rationale. I think there must be some receptivity to Spirit to draw me, some longing for peace. And love. Love always brings me back to you."

Lillian burst into tears and reached for Jason. "This whole idea of moving in and out of the material world like some kind of ghost challenges everything I believe. Is it spiritual? How can it further human understanding?"

Alex pulled his hands away from his father and moved closer to his mother.

Jason looked across the table at Lillian and Alex, their anxious faces wanting answers. "You need to understand this, please, both of you. I'm drawn into that energy as naturally as being drawn into the ocean. But like I said, I can't resist it. After you've surfed your first wave, it's hard not to ride another and another. If I could take the two of you along I would. It's the ultimate freedom. I'd love to teach you how to do it, Alex, but *I'm* not sure how it's done. I'm still a beginner. What I do know is that we all have an incorporeal body that is not restricted by time and space. I can be anywhere, not as a ghost, but as me. Those girls saw *me* at the hospital."

"Then you *were* at Marsdan," Lillian stated. "When?"

"About two or three in the morning, I guess."

"And how long were you there?"

"I don't know. Time isn't a factor."

"A minute? An hour?"

"Maybe a minute. Otherwise I'd have been there when the nurses came in."

"So where were you the rest of the night?"

Jason didn't want to tell her the deepest part of his experience. He thought of explaining the time factor with an analogy of space. One minute in another dimension could be like hours on Earth. But his wife and son, the dearest things in the world to him, needed the truth, even if it might upset them.

"Lillian, do you remember that dream you had a few nights ago where you said that you were with Dr. Green?"

Lillian got up and made another latte. She had told Jason that she had dreamed of Dr. Green, but that was all. Why would he bring that up?

"I don't think that was a dream," he continued. "I went there. I entered this wonderful room, filled with light, and all these people were milling about the edges. In the center was a circle of people sitting on simple stools. I was invited to sit in the circle. The Presence was indescribable. If beauty could be put into words, that's what I felt. And Dr. Green was in the circle. And you were there too." He hesitated a moment and then continued, "There is a greater purpose to us being together than we know. All of us."

Lillian sat back down at the table. Jason had described her dream perfectly, but she didn't want to give his actions any credibility—not with Alex present. What if she, too, had entered this other dimension, but thought it was only a dream?

What if something had happened to both her and Jason in that dimension, leaving Alex alone? "We've all got to be in this together," she said.

Tears streamed down Jason's face as he got up and embraced his family. "You two are what I love most in this life and I would never want to leave you alone. I don't know where this new—whatever you want to call it—will take me, but I'll never hide it from you. We *are* together; we'll always be together. But I agree. We have to keep this secret. Alex, you're as much a part of this adventure as your mother and me."

Alex nodded. He'd never felt so close to his parents as at that moment, but he didn't want to cry even though tears filled his eyes.

"I want to call Dave. He's the only one we can trust," Lillian abruptly brought them back to the problem at hand.

Jason looked at his wife, weighing her suggestion. Jason and David grew up together. David knew all there was to know about Jason. He'd seen him do things no one else had seen, and when Jason and David Walker went their separate ways, all those who had wanted to exploit what David knew about Jason got nothing. "Okay, if you can get him to come, he'll be our buffer between what we are doing and the rest of the world."

They all sat there for a moment, and then Jason got up. "Let's keep our routine as normal as possible." He looked at his watch. "Looks like I missed the board meeting. What about you? What about school?"

"I told Donny that Alex would be late today when you were in the shower."

"I don't want to go to school today."

"It would be better if you did, Alex," Jason said. "What class would you be in if you left now?"

"History, I guess."

"Well, get ready," he told his son; then to Lillian, "What time is it in Hawaii?"

"Ten hours difference. It's still last night there."

Jason turned to his wife. "Are you sure you want to bring David back into the mix?"

"Positive!"

Chapter 2
Honolulu, Hawaii

Monday Night, November 2004

David Walker ignored the phone and let the call go to his answer machine. He and his friends were in the middle of a passionate discussion about cultural colonization. The group was mixed; two couples were in interracial marriages, one couple was only a few years in the islands from the East Coast, and David's girlfriend was a native Hawaiian. The question they were discussing: Was it culturally proper for someone to make art using another culture's icons? What if you have adopted a culture, chosen to live and participate in it, follow its customs, enjoy its food, are you a thief if you expressed your art as a native when you are a different race?

The phone kept ringing. Finally, David excused himself and answered it. When he heard Lillian's voice he tensed. "Lillian, what's wrong?"

Lillian tried to keep the panic from her voice. She had not talked to David for seven years, ever since he had walked out on the ministry when Jason brought in Tony.

"Well," she said nervously, "we have a rather desperate situation here and I couldn't wait any longer to ring."

"What happened? Is Alex alright?"

"Alex misses you so much. Can't you just pop over to London? Right away?"

"You're not making any sense." David's concern turned to fear. "Did J.J. put you up to this?"

His feelings were mixed. This had happened before. Twice. And every time Jason called, it threw David's life into chaos.

"Dave, this is serious. Jason wants you to come. We're in a bit of a desperate situation and you're the only one we can trust. Here, I'll put J.J. on the line."

David waited.

"Hey, buddy." The familiar voice, the confidence, and the presence that demanded one to follow was still there in those two words. There was no sense of elapsed time; they picked up as if they'd never been apart. David loved the man. Jason was the greatest friend and teacher he'd ever known; yet in the past, every one of Jason's calls had brought pain and conflict. Jason had turned David's life upside down before, and David didn't want to be sucked back into Jason's world again, not after seven years of peace.

"Davy? You there?"

"Hi J.J." David's mouth was suddenly very dry. "Your timing is always impeccable. I have a house full of guests."

"Solving the problems of the world, no doubt. I wish I could be there with you at this moment."

"Fly on over. I hear you have a new G-5, or whatever they're called."

"Don't believe everything you read about me." His old friend's façade of invulnerability cracked, and David could feel the gravity of the problem through the line. "I could really use your help."

David knew that those were tough words for Jason to say. He's the one who's always helping others. Now he's calling for help.

"We kind of have a situation here at the Foundation …"

David had heard the news. He could guess the rest. Still, to get on a plane and go back to a world he had abandoned years ago needed a significant amount of thought.

"…You'd be doing me a great favor if you'd come back."

There was a long pause on the line and David finally said, "I've got some things to clear up here before I can get away. How can I reach you?"

"Don't call my home or the Ministry. I'll call this number and leave you instructions." Jason rang off.

David hung up his phone and walked out onto the lanai of his rented house in Pacific Heights. He looked out over a sleepy Honolulu. The lights at the Matson dock on Sand Island brighten up the western sky. He couldn't think about Jason's offer yet—everything with Jason carried way too much baggage.

David walked back to his party. The discussion had moved to the controversy of a white painter making pictures of dead civil rights marchers. In the politically correct world shouldn't those subjects be reserved for black painters? But whites were part of that struggle too.

Nani, David's girlfriend, brought up David's work. "So by your criteria, Eddie, Dave shouldn't make art about Hawaiian culture, or use Hawaiian themes in his sculpture."

"There are always exceptions. I think we're talking about exploitation more than expression," Eddie said.

"Why is it that only dominant cultures are accused of exploitation and cultural appropriation? Don't all cultures adapt and borrow what's new and make it their own?

"I like what Picasso said," David said. "Mediocre artists borrow; great artists steal."

David motioned Nani over and led her into the hall. "That was Jason St. John."

Nani knew very little about David's past and was surprised that the great guru would call her boyfriend personally. She didn't know what to say, and quipped, "So is he going to show up at the party?"

"No. But I think I have to break things up, now."

"Oh. I'll tell everybody to leave."

"I need to be alone, sweetheart. I'm sorry. Just have everybody go and I'll clean up." He kissed her and walked into his bedroom and shut the door. Nani tried not to look hurt.

Chapter 3
Stanford House

Tuesday Morning, November 2004

Tony Bass barged into Jason St. John's office suite in Stanford House like the FBI serving a warrant to a white-collar crime boss. He leaned over the secretary's desk, invading her workspace, and demanded from the startled young Mary Perkins' her total attention, even though she was on the phone.

"I need to know Mr. St. John's schedule right now?"

Mary put her hand up, signaling "just a moment," but Tony pressed the button on the phone—disconnecting her.

"I'm sorry, Mary, but it's been a stressful morning and I need this information immediately."

"You just cut Mr. St. John off."

"He's in there?"

Mary got up to block the door but she was too slow. Tony pushed her aside and burst into Jason's office, leaving the door open. Mary stood in the doorway and shrugged—what could she do?

"Sorry I missed the meeting. I was in a deep meditation that Lillian didn't want to interrupt." Jason said, looking up from behind his Art Deco desk. "And by the way, I'm changing the locks to all my private spaces—and keeping them private. If something like what happened this morning happens again, you can kiss your ass goodbye."

"I did disregard your privacy, and I'm sorry, but that's not why I'm here."

Jason leaned back in his Aeron chair, pulled out a drawer and put up his feet. He wore a starched white shirt with French cuffs, jeans and Italian loafers without socks. "Let me guess, it has something to do with that zoo outside."

Tony had met this kind of challenge before from executives about to be dismissed. They had always underestimated him thinking that because they had founded a company, they knew more than he did. But they hadn't seen the big picture. If they had, Tony wouldn't have had to be in charge. Jason was no different. If he didn't wake up to the situation he had created by healing those girls at Marsdan Hospital the way he did, it would be up to Tony to save the Ministry.

Tony walked over to the French doors and contemplated the colorful cyclamen blooming at the base of the chestnut tree outside. He then turned to face Jason. Now Tony had the light behind him and Jason couldn't clearly see his face and eyes. Jason knew exactly what Tony was doing. Jason tried not to react, and to keep an open mind.

"You seldom take meetings in here. How come?" Tony asked.

"This is my sanctuary. You should know that. Then again, maybe you don't."

Tony examined the room as if he hadn't seen it before. The wall of French doors brought the outside in. A conversation area with leather sofas and a surfboard used as a coffee table marked the center of the room. Artifacts from the Marquesas Islands filled the room. An overflowing bookcase dominated one wall, and a giant poster of a container ship plowing through a one-hundred-foot wave off San Francisco's Golden Gate hung behind Jason's desk.

Tony walked over to examine the poster.

"Awesome, isn't it? It keeps me humble," Jason said.

"I'll get right to the point." Tony looked back at Jason. "Did you personally appear before those girls at Marsdan hospital last night?"

Tony's eyes drilled into Jason's.

Jason thought about his answer while Tony waited. "This isn't something you need to know. It's got nothing to do with the administration of the trust."

"My job is to keep the Organization credible in the eyes of the world. If you're doing something to destroy our credibility, then it's something I need to know. In fact, it is my duty to know what you are doing and what you present to the world. And if it doesn't conform with the principles you teach, then I have to stop you."

"Stop me! How would you do that?"

Tony paused, using Jason's tactic. "That's not something you need to know."

"Tell me, then, why do you think my alleged appearing to those girls is inconsistent with my books, or my *Healing Hour*, or the principles I teach?"

"In many ways you're like the Pope, Jason," Tony said. "He can't do as he pleases either. He has to follow the constraints of his organization. If he decides that priests can marry or that homosexuality is perfectly normal and not a sin, people would leave the church in droves. The church would fracture and whatever message it had given the world would be discredited. If you can actually appear to people out of thin air, and show the world that bit of magic, you'll destroy everything we've built."

"And you think that would be a bad thing?"

Tony became livid. He walked back to the wall of glass that looked out onto the garden. "Why the fuck are we here, then? If you think our work and our devotion to you are worth so little, why should we stay?"

"Well, maybe you shouldn't," Jason said, and after a pause continued, "I've never asked for anyone's devotion."

Tony turned and faced Jason, who was still calmly seated at his desk. "I will not let you pull down this wonderful ministry that has taught people everywhere to accept spiritual healing. You've given the world all it needs to know about ending the suffering of disease. I don't think you have anything more to give. No one needs another Houdini. You, Jason, have become irrelevant to this ministry."

"What are you going to do, kill me?"

"Jason, you left the world years ago, and all anybody knows about you comes through this office."

Jason reached for the phone on his desk and hit the button for his secretary. "Mary, book a table at the club for lunch for Lillian and me, and see if there is a tee time available for us this afternoon. Thanks."

Tony spun around and quickly left the office, slamming the door behind him. In the reception office a cold calm came back to him and he looked at Mary with hard eyes. "Mary, you're fired. Please pick up your things right now and leave."

Mary shuttered in disbelief. She'd never known Tony to joke around like that before. "I beg your pardon?"

"Get the fuck up and leave right now." Tony speed dialed a number on his mobile. "Gary, bring up a new secretary from the media pool for Jason. Mary just quit."

"I bloody well didn't quit!"

"And bring security with you."

Within minutes an ISD detail arrived with the new secretary.

Tony signaled one of the ISD officers to come over to him. "Escort this woman from the building. She's to talk to no one."

The guard did as he was told.

The new secretary looked at Tony, confused. "Should I sit here?"

Tony nodded "yes" and called over the other guard. He pulled him aside and said, "Mr. St. John is exploring a new level of consciousness and is afraid he might do something in public that would compromise the Ministry. So, he doesn't want any outside interference. We don't want the public to know that we are pushing the envelope here, and because of this, we'll need extra security. If Mr. St. John ventures outside the Compound, please inform me immediately. Okay?" Tony touched the man's shoulder, making him feel like he's an important part of ministry's scientific work.

The guard felt proud as he took his place by the door.

Tony then leaned over the secretary's desk. "What is your name?"

"Deborah. Deborah White."

"Deborah, for the time being, Mr. St. John won't be receiving any outside calls. Please refer any that make it through the screeners to either Mr. Howell or me."

Tony smiled at the new secretary, confirming his order and walked out dialing a number on his Blackberry. "Gary, where are you? Meet me in your office in three minutes."

He stopped and looked back to Ms. White. "And cancel Jason's lunch at the club."

Jason pushed himself away from the desk and flopped down on one of the couches. He immediately got back up and paced around his office a few times before finally sitting calmly in one of his Eames chairs. It took a good twenty minutes of meditation to release the negative energy Jason felt from the confrontation with Tony. Jason wasn't entirely at peace, but at least he could think. This was the first time he'd fought with a board member and his mind was packed with competing ways to handle the problem. He couldn't believe that Tony was serious. Had Tony's ego been so threatened that he'd forgotten the purpose of the organization? Or perhaps he himself had reacted poorly. Perhaps this moving between dimensions was not a good idea and Tony was right. But it wasn't Jason's idea or desire to slip away from physical reality into another realm. It just happened.

Jason picked up the telephone headset from his desk phone and buzzed Lillian on the intercom.

"Jason! What's going on?" she answered irritated. "I can't get an outside line."

"Really? I was just calling to say I made reservations for lunch at the club."

"Fine, but I'd have to bum around Wimbledon because Alex has a rehearsal after school. Besides, I promised to take him to that indoor skate park."

"Did he get off okay?"

"Yes. Why?"

"Listen. Tony barged into my office a half an hour ago acting very strange. Now you can't get an outside line. I'll get back to you." Jason hung up.

He unplugged his laptop from the monitor and put it in a slim briefcase. He slipped his mobile in his pocket, and walked out smiling, but stopped short when he saw the ISD officer standing by the door and Deborah White sitting in Mary Perkins's chair.

"Who are you?"

"Deborah White, sir." The secretary was short of breath. She'd never met Jason St. John in person and the shock of moving from the secretary pool to this position was making her extremely nervous.

"Where's Mary?"

"I think she quit."

Jason realized what was happening and smiled. Tony worked fast. But then that's why Jason had hired him. "Is my car ready?"

Deborah looked at Jason and then to the ISD officer. She didn't know what to say.

"It's a simple question. You can just say yes or no."

The guard answered for her. "I'm sorry Mr. St. John, but per your own instructions and for your own safety we are not to let you off the premises."

Jason looked at the officer and laughed. He walked out of his office, into the grand foyer, and down the marble stairs. Taking out his mobile as he went, he called the garage. Nobody answered. He disengaged and scrolled through his favorites and hit Alex's number. A message came back to him that he had no service. Seething, he shoved his phone into his pocket and rushed into the parking garage.

In the garage Jason walked straight to the manager's office to get the keys to his Jaguar sedan, but the office was locked. Nobody was there. He strode through the gleaming basement filled with late model cars and SUVs and felt the eyes of the security cameras on him. As he approached the exit, two security men walked up to him. He waved to them and turned and jogged back to the garage office. He kicked in the door and grabbed the keys to a few of the cars in his collection, and then ran back up the marble stairs to the grand foyer. He suppressed a feeling of panic as he contemplated what to do next. Hearing the soft-shoed footsteps of the ISD officers climbing the marble staircase behind him, he took off for the compound's dining room.

Over a hundred employees worked at St. John Ministries on any given day, and the dining room was like a grand restaurant. Employees ordered from an extensive menu offering local organic food, all of it free. Tables were set with fine linens, and the servers were teenagers from all over the world who had an interest in spirituality and wanted to study English. Jason seldom dined here, and as a result the servers and diners stopped to stare when he rushed in. He paused at the entrance for a moment, looking around, he spotted Melanie and Dorothy at one of the tables, and hurried over to Melanie, startling her with a kiss, and then sat down.

"Do you two know what's going on?" Jason said, looking back at the door.

"Are you talking about this crap about teleporting, or whatever?" Melanie said.

Dorothy said to Jason. "Have you made another breakthrough out of the corporeal?

"Dear Deedee, always cutting to the chase."

"Quit stalling, Jason. If you are actually appearing elsewhere while still in your present body that's something we should know about. We're here for you, to support you in dispelling the illusion of material cause and effect. If the rumors are true, then what you are doing is extremely important and we need to be consulted so that the world knows the truth and doesn't feed on rumors."

"No. Tony's pulling some sort of power trip. Forget the other stuff," Jason said.

"If you're worried about Tony and his behavior, leave that to us," Melanie said.

"What do you know about Tony's behavior?"

"Just what he said at the board meeting—that what you are doing will destroy the Ministry."

"What did the rest of the board say to that?"

"There was no consensus," Dorothy stated. "But it feels like Tony and Gary are plotting something."

"Like making me a prisoner here?"

"Come on, J.J., they couldn't do that," Melanie said.

"Notice anything strange in here?" As if on cue one of Gary's ISD officers appeared at each door.

Dorothy and Melanie looked around and saw the guards.

Jason talked quietly and quickly. "My mobile has been deactivated. My cars are locked up, and there are guards at every entrance with instructions, supposedly from me, not to allow me off the premises."

"What a jerk," Melanie said.

"What are you going to do, darling?" Dorothy asked.

"Keep you two out of it. If Tony questions you, say this was just a friendly hello since I didn't make it to the meeting this morning."

"Yeah, why weren't you there? Were you actually off the grounds?" Melanie inquired.

"Don't answer that," Dorothy said. "I don't want to be a party to lies and that's not the issue right now. What's important is Jason's well-being."

"Thank you, Deedee. Melanie, will you lend me your mobile?"

"You mean cell phone?" Melanie teased.

"Whatever."

"Okay. But why?" Melanie slipped her phone to Jason under the table.

"I don't think they can block your number from in here and I need to talk to someone on the outside."

"The landline doesn't work?" Melanie asked.

"No, and Lillian is quite upset. Alex is at school... " Jason abruptly got up, dropping Melanie's phone into his pocket as he stood.

Two ISD officers walked over to the table and blocked Jason's way. "Mr. Bass would like to see you in his office," the sergeant said.

Deedee and Melanie pushed back from the table and stood facing the guards, too.

"I have a full schedule this afternoon," Jason said. "You can tell him that."

The guards didn't move. "He insists you come with us." The sergeant reached out to take Jason's arm but Jason pulled back.

"Are you serious?" Jason said in a loud voice. "You want to force me to go with you and expect me to drop everything because Mr. Bass ordered it?"

The dining room grew quiet and the guards got nervous. "We're not forcing you," the sergeant replied.

"Good," Jason started to walk away.

The other officer stepped in front of Jason and blocked his way.

Jason turned back to the sergeant. "Do you know what this is all about? Well, let me tell you. For some reason, Mr. Bass does not want me to leave the compound. I'm sure he wouldn't want the public to know that. So look around. Everyone here is a witness. They will be leaving at the end of the day and I'm sure someone will tell someone on the outside that Jason St. John is a prisoner in his own house. That's a big story. Big headlines.

Do you want to be responsible for that rumor? Do you want to answer to Mr. Bass for the way this was handled? If you don't, you will step aside and let me get on with my business."

The officers stepped aside. Jason kissed Dorothy and Melanie, and whispered to Melanie, "Keep the faith. I've called Dave to come back and help." A big smile filled her face and she gave Jason a long hug.

Chapter 4
Kensington, London

Tuesday Afternoon, November 2004

Old Brompton Road in South West London was a parking lot. Theodore Spencer drove his Vauxhall onto the pavement and stopped in front of the Drayton Arms Pub and Theater. Samuel Butler, Spencer's cameraman-slash-producer, thumbed through a street guide of London, flipping a couple of pages back and forth.

"I told you we should have used Cromwell," Butler said, referring to the major road that cut through Kensington.

"That would have been worse," Spencer answered. "We'll leave the car here and walk. It's only a few blocks." Butler got out of the car, slapped a press sticker in the window, and ran into the pub. He handed the barmaid his card. "Call me if the police come nosing around. We won't be very long."

"You're blocking the foot traffic," the girl said, looking at the Vauxhall sitting outside her front door.

Butler slapped a twenty-pound note on the bar as he rushed out. "Thanks." Grabbing his camera from the car, he trailed after Spencer.

"Don't worry, we're on a roll. Might even get a shot of the man himself coming out to bless the crowds," Spencer said.

Butler, sloppy, and bigger than Spencer, pushed the way through the crowd shouting "Press! Coming through!" When they reached Bolton Gardens, the street was packed. As they got closer to Stanford House the people chanted "Antichrist!" The two reached the barricades at the corner of Wetherby Gardens. The crowd surrounding Stanford House was even denser. The police had cleared the sidewalks surrounding the ministry buildings and tried to keep the streets on either side of Collingham Gardens clear for cars. They had little success.

Butler and Spencer squeezed through the Wetherby street barriers and crossed over to Collingham where a policeman stopped them when they got close to Stanford House.

"Has the messiah come out yet?" Spencer showed the cop his press credentials.

"I wish he'd bless them and send them all home," the cop said letting them in.

Butler hoisted his camera to his shoulder and pulled a focus on Spencer, who said a few "checks" into the microphone. Spencer then turned to an attractive woman in her mid-thirties and asked, "Are you expecting to see Jason St. John?"

"Yes. Oh, he'll come out. He always does."

"Are you here to be healed?"

"I've already been healed," the woman said. "But when he comes out you'll feel it. There's an energy he has that fills you with joy. That's why I'm here."

A loud male voice yelled from somewhere behind Spencer, "He's the Prince of Darkness!" Spencer headed toward a middle-aged, working class guy holding a sign proclaiming Jason St. John the antichrist. Butler followed with his camera.

"Theodore Spencer, Independent TV." Spencer got the man's attention. "Why do you think Jason St. John is the Prince of Darkness?"

"He thinks he's God."

"Has he said that he's God?" Spencer asked.

"Read his book. All he talks about is I this and I that. You too can heal. Get in touch with your inner God, or some such bull. These people all need to wake up."

Some of the antichrist crowd came in closer.

The man gestured to those around him. "Jesus is the only Son of God. Only Jesus can heal. That man is the beast, Satan here on Earth disguised as God, and he's deceiving the people. It's all in the Bible. He has the melodious voice. He has the friendly, loving eyes. He's gentle and kind. He's handsome and he charms people. With all of his money he's extremely powerful. I can't believe everybody doesn't see this."

Spencer nodded as Butler pulled a close-up of the man.

He's a false prophet and all those who follow him will be sorry.

"What's your name, sir, so we can use this on the air?"

The man turned away. "Can't use my name. Those people will come after me."

Chapter 5
Collingham Gardens, London

Tuesday Afternoon, November 2004

Tony and Gary sauntered beneath the tall sycamores of Collingham Gardens—the Ministry's walled oasis in the heart of the city. Tony was still keyed up from his confrontation with Jason, and Gary, his tight suit bulging where his cell phone and gun were, reassured him that his tactics were right for the situation.

"I've seen what mobs can do," Tony said. "All press is propaganda. It's manipulative and designed for one purpose, to make money from controversy. Jason has been smart. He invited the press to witness his first healing experiments and won them to his side. But he will flush that all down the toilet with one mocking statement from good old Teddy Spencer, that paragon of truth who always gets the last word."

The two men sat down at a bench framed by a large bush of bleeding hearts. The fog had lifted and the day had turned into a dull overcast repeat of the past week. The autumn leaves were almost gone and the trees and bushes seemed as dull as the air. An overflying jet bound for Heathrow briefly interrupted the pause in Tony's rant.

"I'm right," Tony said. "Not only was Lillian evasive and rude, Jason lied when he said he was meditating. He wasn't at the board meeting because he wasn't at the compound. Jason is going to destroy the ministry!" He looked back at the gothic windows of the St. John's apartment with a mix of envy and righteous fury.

"If he can disappear and appear somewhere else like something out of *Star Trek*, and certain people learn of it, he'll disappear forever," Gary said. "I can guarantee that he didn't leave the compound by any normal route. You know that our security is impeccable."

"You agree that we're doing the right thing keeping him out of the public's eye?"

Gary shrugged and got up. Tony followed him to the far end of the garden, out of sight of the compound. They sat on another bench in the middle of a small forest of plane trees growing inside the walls. The huge crowds in front of Stanford House and the hum of chanting voices seemed like a distant memory of another place. Here all was quiet and the birdsong reminded Tony of the simplicity of life.

"The thing is," Gary said breaking the silence, "the people I know would never believe something like this unless they saw it. But if they thought it was possible, they'd find a way to isolate him and learn how he does it."

"We have to control Jason for his own good."

"I don't like the television symposium that Barbara and Melanie are planning," Gary stated. He rarely gave his opinion on ministry policy, keeping his input to security issues, but he felt the day's events changed all of that. "My only hope is that it shifts focus away from whatever Jason is doing to something that can be easily explained to the people."

"What options do we have? We can't go back to being a foundation like Melanie believes. We're passed that already. This hospital thing brings us into the world of faith and belief," Tony said. "What if the Pope had done what he did?"

"We can only assume that Mr. St. John did it," Gary argued.

"Oh, he did it alright. If the public perceives that Jason St. John can appear out of the blue and heal them, then St. John becomes a god and our organization dies."

"If the Pope had done what Mr. St. John did, we'd all become Catholics," Gary said.

"And the Curia would declare him the Second Coming and kill him." Tony got up, walked over to a tall plane tree, leaned against it and looked back at his head of security, deciding if he should voice what he was thinking. "I know you keep abreast of the groups that could adversely affect Jason and our ministry, like the antichrist mob."

Gary nodded. "Part of my training is to know my enemy."

"And keep that enemy closer to you than your friends?

"Something like that."

We can't let the mob make Jason a martyr." Tony bent down and watched a beetle carry a leaf across the gravel path.

"What if the crowds grow significantly larger and more violent?" Gary asked. "Do we pressure him to cut back his appearances and not leave the compound for security reasons?"

"He won't put up with that," Tony stood and looked Gary in the eyes. "He's fighting every restriction already. Even if it's for his own good. Knowing Jason the way I do, the more we try to control him, the more reckless he'll become. He doesn't realize how much he is endangering himself and his family. He has that kind of a personality. He could even get killed."

Gary looked away. Having read Tony's body language, he sensed that Tony was confirming his own beliefs.

"This could be the beginning of a new religion," Gary said mostly to himself.

"You need a prophet to start a religion," Tony declared.

Gary nodded. He believed in Mr. St. John like he believed in Christ. Shouldn't that belief be more than a set of principles? Shouldn't you give yourself body, mind, and soul to your savior? Jason St. John *was* his savior; Gary would give his life for him. But would Mr. St. John do the same? All this spun around in Gary's mind as he stared off at the well-pruned shrubs and manicured lawn.

Interrupting Gary's thoughts, Tony continued, "And that prophet needs to go away before a religion can take hold."

Gary turned and saw fire in Tony's eyes.

"So, you'd replace the ministry with a religion?" Gary wanted confirmation that he wasn't alone in his thinking.

Tony projected humility. "If necessary. You can belong to a religion. If the organization remains *a nonprofit trust*," words spoken with an air of disdain, "all that Jason has given the world will die. Do you know why? Because there is no commitment from the people, there's no community—nothing. Everything will just fade away."

Gary sighed deeply. His mind spun. His training, his instincts, and his love for what Jason St. John had done for him collided with the reality of what Tony was proposing. Finally Gary said, "I'll put some things in motion. But we need some new ground rules."

"Okay." Tony realized how right he was about Gary. He got the same feeling in his stomach that he use to get when he began a hostile takeover.

"We're never to be seen alone together," Gary continued. "I won't tell you anything about my plans. You will have total deniability if things go wrong. I'll be the fall guy. If you try to interfere or manage what I'm doing, I'll resign from the board.

I think you're right, but from now on I'm solely responsible for Mr. St. John's safety."

"What about our current calendar? What about the board vote to create a TV forum to discuss apparitions?" Tony asked.

"That's all your area. I'll support you on the board as I always have, but with the increased crowds, which I think will only grow, I won't have time for anything but Mr. St. John's security."

"I need to expand the board," Tony said. "We need people who see things the way we do. Will you support me in that?"

"Absolutely," Gary said.

"And I need something on Theodore Spencer. He stuck his nose where it doesn't belong and I'd like it cut off."

"I'll see what I can dig up."

Gary walked away, pulling his Blackberry from its belt holder and speed dialing a contact.

Tony sat down on a nearby bench and tried to keep doubt from flooding his mind. He wondered if he could really pull this off. His passion was promoting the healing principles Jason had revealed to the world. To do that he needed a stable organization and Jason's actions were not helping. The Ministry will change one way or another, he thought, and Tony needed to direct that change.

Chapter 6
Southwark, London

Tuesday Afternoon, November 2004

The Reverend Cyrus Germaine sat behind his elaborately carved desk below a stained-glass window of Satan tempting Christ. Germaine was pastor of Hope Chapel in the Southwark area of London, and was known for his conservative evangelical beliefs and his controversial sermons. He was a powerful-looking man in his mid-forties with close-cropped blond hair. He was astonished when his assistant interrupted his sermon preparation that Tuesday afternoon to tell him that Gary Howell from the St. John Ministries was waiting to see him.

"What does he want?" Pastor Germaine asked.

"He wouldn't say."

The pastor thought a moment. "Tell him it's his lucky day and send him in."

Pastor Germaine didn't get up when Gary entered, but directed him to one of two chairs facing his desk.

"It's very kind of you to see me without an appointment." Gary took a seat.

"I'm always ready to convert the heathen," Germaine said without humor.

"I know I'm interrupting, so I'll get right to the point." Gary looked intently at the pastor and asked, "I'd like to understand what's behind all the Antichrist signs and protests in front of our ministry. You seem to be an expert on the Antichrist."

"You know him quite well. He goes by the name of Jason St. John."

Gary held Germaine's eyes until the pastor looked down. "I know that's what you believe, Cyrus, but theologically, what does the Antichrist mean?"

Pastor Germaine closed his eyes a moment to think. His voice took on a different timbre when he spoke. "The Antichrist is the Sinner masquerading as the Savior. The Bible has many references to false prophets, wolves in sheep's clothing… that sort of thing. What makes the Great Deceiver so insidiously evil is that he performs miracles and appears to be an agent of God, drawing people to him and away from true redemption—exactly what your master does. When the Judgment comes, all those who have been misled will suffer the agonies of hell. Can you think of anything more evil, or more sinister? Your whole ministry, and I use that term very loosely, is based on a lie that one day will be exposed, and for which the people will be punished. Would you like me to cite the biblical references for this?"

"No. I've read them. What about the children healed on the brink of death? That can't be evil."

"It's not only evil to take a soul about ready to enter heaven and shove it back into the world of sin, it's exceedingly cruel. Why are you asking me this?"

"I've tried talking to your people on the streets, the ones demonstrating, but I don't think they know why they're there."

"They're confronting the devil to save their souls. Eternal salvation is through Jesus Christ and only Jesus Christ." The pastor looked firmly at Gary. "I could save your soul right now if you would repent."

"My soul has already been saved." Gary shook his head, trying to keep to his point. "The world isn't going to end any time soon, so why not tone down your rhetoric?"

"Many of the signs have been fulfilled—one of them being the arrival of Lucifer." The pastor rubbed his chin.

"You're comparing Jason St. John to Lucifer?"

Germaine continued, "God's army defeats Lucifer and we enter the Rapture. The saved are separated from the damned and remain on Earth to live under the government of the Christ."

"Doesn't the prophecy predict that the Antichrist will be assassinated?"

Germaine jumped up and pushed away from his desk. "Nobody's going to assassinate your little medicine man."

Gary calmly replied, "The way you've been preaching, somebody might. People have a way of taking what you say literally."

"So *that's* why you're here." Germaine sat back down, confident in his righteousness. "I can tell you right now that I'm not changing my sermons. The Bible is very clear on the sequences of the End Times. But I am not advocating the murder of anyone."

"If it should happen, you could be culpable."

"I think this conversation is over. Thank you for coming, but I have a sermon to write and you've just given me some fresh ammunition."

Gary stood and leaned over the pastor's desk so that Cyrus Germaine could feel his breath. "My job is to protect Jason St. John, and I'm very good at my job, Cyrus. I just want you to know that."

Chapter 7
Stanford House

Tuesday Afternoon, November 2004

An ISD officer stood outside the St. John apartment when Jason walked up to his front door. He was expecting something like this. Really, Tony, Jason thought.

"Hi, what's your name?" Jason asked, knowing the young man was just following orders.

"Tommy. Thomas Parker, sir." Parker was in his twenties—tall and muscular, newly promoted, with curly blond hair. He looked like a sweet kid and Jason was surprised he was a security guard.

"Well, Thomas Parker, since we'll be seeing a lot of each other I want to be able to call you by name." Parker blushed when Jason said his name. And when Jason entered his apartment, he saluted.

Lillian got up from the kitchen table when she heard the front door open. She'd been on the Internet looking at dozens of sites claiming inside information about Jason's appearance at Marsdan Hospital and explaining how he'd done it. The ministry's site had gone dark, overwhelmed with too much traffic.

"You're all over the web with that stunt you pulled last night, and the Ministry's site is frozen." She drew him close and gave him a kiss, and then whispered in his ear, "What on earth is happening?"

He whispered back, "They want me penned up in here, out of touch."

"I think our apartment is bugged."

"I don't think so. I don't think they'd go that far."

"Perhaps they did it before we moved in, during the renovation. Perhaps the whole compound is bugged. Who knows?" Lillian whispered.

Jason held her tight and said in a quiet voice, "Okay. We'll be careful. They have guards in the hall and in the parking garage."

Lillian had tears streaming down her face. Jason hugged her and for the first time in his life he felt extremely vulnerable. He handed her the mobile phone.

"This is Melanie's. I don't think they can tap into it. I want you to call your father and see if you and Alex can stay with them for a couple of weeks," He whispered.

She looked at the phone briefly and put it on the table.

"Oh, they'd love that, but how are we going to get Alex up to Chester?"

He reached into his pocket and gave Lillian the keys he'd taken from the garage. "Just drive up there," he said in a very hushed tone.

"We're just reacting, Jason. We need to think this through; meditate." She put the car keys on the table next to the phone.

"You're right."

Hand in hand they walked over and sat in their meditation chairs. Jason quickly attained a complete mental stillness. Lillian closed her eyes and cleared her mind of the thoughts surrounding their situation. She tried to release the fear and speculation about what was happening.

Jason felt himself begin to merge with the fabric of life. slipping into the nonphysical dimension. Something in the back of Jason's mind prompted him to squeeze Lillian's hand.

Lillian opened her eyes and saw him dissolving into the atmosphere. He was like a digital photo that had been blown up and pixilated. She saw the spaces around the molecules, and what appeared to be solid looked like a holographic projection. She looked down at her hand in Jason's hand, and it was as ethereal as his.

"Jason!" she said loud enough to bring Jason back into the physical.

He opened his eyes, looked into Lillian's eyes and then down at their hands. They both watched their hands and arms come back to physical reality and spent a moment in deep silence and awe. And then they looked at each other's countenance and burst out laughing.

"Okay, now what?" Lillian said.

"How about some music?" He smiled, got up, pulled Lillian from her chair—they had not let go of each other—and he led her over to the kitchen table. He tuned the radio to a soft rock station, and she turned it a little louder than normal.

"You and Alex have to get away from me so you can't be used to force me to do something I don't want to do. Right?" Jason said.

"Okay. But you'll be a prisoner. They'll control what the world sees of you. How will we know what's really happening?"

"I'll keep Melanie's phone and use your computer."

"You think it will be safe?" Lillian opened the phone and jotted down the number on a scratch pad.

Jason shrugged his shoulders. "You'll be in the normal world up there and can get police protection if you need it. Tell them there are some issues at the ministry..."

"Dad will love that."

"Yeah, I know. You can play on his dislike for me. You'll have Alex's computer and your mobile."

"And Alex's mobile."

"So, we're good."

Lillian hugged Jason again, but this time without tears. "I guess I better get going."

Jason's mind was already elsewhere. "I guess I'll have to redo the trust," he said as Lillian left.

Outside her apartment Lillian walked quickly toward the elevator at the end of the hall. "I'm going to fetch Alex. Do you know if Donny's in the garage?" she said to Thomas as she hurried past.

Thomas Parker thumbed the button on his lapel mike and gave this information to watch captain. Just as the elevator door closed he called out, "Wait. Donny's not there!"

The elevator landed in the garage and Lillian looked at the collection of keys Jason had given her. She recognized the key to the Range Rover, the vehicle she and Donny usually used, and walked over to where it was parked. Two repairmen were fixing the door to the parking office that Jason had kicked in, and the regular guard was standing at the gated entry from the street.

Lillian unlocked the door to the Range Rover using the remote on the key, got into the black SUV, and started it. She immediately locked the door, adjusted the mirrors and seat, and looked to see if anybody was approaching her. The men working on the kiosk looked up briefly but immediately went back to work when they saw that it was Lillian. She backed out of the stall and drove toward the exit. Again, she looked to see if anybody was running toward her. At the security gate, Lillian waved to the guard and put her window down. "I'm going to pick up Alex from school," she said.

"Where's Donny?" the guard asked.

"I really don't know, but I'm late. I don't want Alex hanging around waiting for me," she said and the guard opened the roll-up gate. As soon as she cleared the gate she accelerated up the steep driveway onto Wetherby Gardens. She turned right, away from the barricades and the crowds facing Stanford House, and drove quickly down the empty street toward Earl's Court Road where she made a left and headed for the Thames.

Barbara hung up the phone and put on the large loop earring she'd taken off for her call. Her trademark was oversized jewelry, but it had its drawbacks. She was at her desk in the ministry's media center and buzzed for her assistant. The ministry owned a part of StarSatellite, one of Tony's first purchases. StarSat circled the globe with sports and news, but kept a third of its capacity for St. John Ministries programming. Hidden behind the Tudor parapets on the roof, unseen by the neighborhood, was an array of satellite dishes that kept the world informed of the St. John Ministries activities and programs.

Jimmy, a young Jamaican man in his thirties, leaned into Barbara's office and said, "We're back on line."

"Far out," Barbara said. Jimmy was about to go when Barbara motioned him closer. He smiled, and listened intently. "We're a go. I just hung up with Bishop Eastman and we've got our panel for the show. Get the word out that we will be live this Friday, prime time at seven o'clock GMT. We'll broadcast on all media. Build up anticipation on MySpace, Friendster, and the other social media platforms. Use the normal key words plus apparitions, sightings, Marsdan … whatever else you can think of to connect this to Jason's appearance at the hospital. And make up a thirty-second promo to run on *The Healing Hour*."

Jimmy nodded, still smiling, giving Barbara a thumbs-up as he headed back to his cubicle.

Gary Howell entered on Jimmy's heels, and he wasn't smiling. "You're really going through with this?"

"The board voted, and Jason agreed. What can I say?" Barbara looked back at her notes.

"Tony wants to add another person to the panel, the Reverend Cyrus Germaine of Hope Chapel in Southwark."

Barbara was stunned. "Are you kidding? He's the most hateful man I know. Racist, too!"

"We need a balanced panel, and Tony wants Theodore Spencer to moderate."

Barbara couldn't believe this. "I thought Tony hated that little weasel."

"He does, but who better to tell the world the truth about Jason, that Jason is a normal person like you and me, and that the world has nothing to fear from him or our ministry?"

"I thought we were going to talk about apparitions—the nature of reality, and how it can be misperceived."

"We're going to make sure the world believes that Jason was nowhere near Marsdan Hospital, and what that girl saw was an apparition."

"Okay." Barbara said skeptically. "You won't be able to control Spencer. I get the feeling you want to sabotage our program."

"You just keep to the script we give you and everything will go as planned."

Barbara swallowed Gary's condescending attitude with a smile of her own. "We've got that French quantum physicists interested but I doubt he'll sit in the same room with Cyrus Germaine."

"Fuck the scientist. Just make sure Germaine and Spencer get the invitations and passes they need. Everything else is arranged."

Gary left. Barbara followed him out and walked over to another cubicle. She leaned in to talk to a young staffer.

"Joyce, tell me, what's the word on Jason's appearing to those girls?"

Joyce pulled up the current data on her iMac. "Twenty-seven percent believe he actually did appear, thirty-two percent think the girls were hallucinating, and that consistent twenty-five percent believe it's just another sign that St. John is the Antichrist. The rest had no opinion."

Chapter 8
Kensington, London

Tuesday Afternoon, November 2004

Theodore Spencer stood on the corner of Wetherby and Bolton Gardens, having milked the crowd for their opinions about St. John's appearance at the hospital. He was waiting for Samuel to bring the car around when Lillian St. John, in the black Range Rover, raced out of the Ministry's garage.

Spencer grabbed his mobile and speed dialed Samuel. "Where are you?"

"Brompton, turning on Bolton now," came back Samuel's voice on the phone.

"Shake a leg. I just saw Mrs. St. John leaving the Ministry in a terrible hurry."

Samuel drove up a moment later, stopped, threw open the passenger door, and Spencer jumped in. "Go down Wetherby. She's in a black Range Rover."

Samuel turned down Wetherby and accelerated when another car, a Jaguar sedan, flew out from the Ministry's garage, forcing Samuel to slam on the brakes.

"What the ... Who's that?" Samuel asked.

Spencer thumbed through pictures of Ministry personnel in his notebook as Samuel picked up speed and followed the second car. "Looks like Gary Howell, their Head of Security, but I don't know who's driving. Head after both of them."

Lillian kept looking in her rearview mirror but couldn't tell if she was being followed. Her normal route took her along King's Road to Fulham High Street for the fifteen-minute trip to Alex's school. She had to assume that if Tony knew she'd left the compound, he'd figure out where she was going and would send a car after her. She needed to think and make some calls, not just rush ahead like the others might expect. She was only a couple of minutes from Putney Bridge and just beyond that was the Putney Exchange shopping center. She decided to duck into the shopping center to plan her next move

The traffic wasn't bad. She crossed the Thames just as the signal changed, and knew that would give her a couple of minutes on whoever might be following her. She turned into the shopping center and drove up to the rooftop parking.

First Lillian rang Alex's school. She knew Alex wasn't allowed to answer his phone while on campus, but she also knew that the school recognized Alex's need for additional security and in that way the school was very cooperative. She reached the Junior School secretary and asked her to pull Alex from his rehearsal and have him call her. Then Lillian called Sir William Boyd, their solicitor, and arranged a Skype meeting with Jason for the following morning. Lastly, she called Jason on Melanie's phone and told him of his appointment with Sir William. She didn't want to stay on the line for long and told him to check her MySpace page for more information. She reminded him that she left her password on the dining room table. A moment later her mobile rang.

"Mom," Alex said anxiously, "what's going on?"

"Everything's okay, just a little change of plans. I'm coming to pick you up early, but not in our usual place. You know that pub across the street from your school? On Woodhayes Road? Run over there and wait for me in the little courtyard."

"Why can't you just pick me up in front of the school?"

"Donny and Mr. Howell are probably on their way and I don't want you to go with them. Grab your things and go over to the courtyard now."

Alex heard his mother ring off. The secretary released him, and he picked up his backpack from the foyer, and left the school. He ran over to the pub on the far side of the little triangle park and hid behind an iron fence in the pub's courtyard.

A couple of minutes later Alex watched a Ministry Jaguar pull up in front of his school. Donny got out and rushed into the building. And then another car, one that Alex didn't recognize, drove slowly past the school and turned off West Side Common to park across the street from the pub. Alex then saw his mother pass the school and the Ministry's Jaguar. She didn't slow down but looped around the little triangle common, and pulled up in front of the pub. She stopped the Rover so that Alex could get in without being seen. Alex left his hiding place in the patio and jumped into the car. As soon as he was inside and buckled up, Lillian pulled away and headed back the way she came.

Spencer stood beside his Vauxhall, leaned on the open passenger door and watched Gary wait for Donny in front of the school. He didn't notice Lillian drive by.

"Isn't that the black Range Rover we were following?" Samuel hollered as Lillian accelerated up the road.

Spencer saw the SUV and jumped into Butler's Vauxhall yelling, "Go! Go! Go!"

"What's she up to?" Samuel asked, pulling away as fast as the old car could.

"That's what we're going to find out."

"Why would she pick up her kid at a pub and not at school?

Spencer smiled. He had a feeling that things were going to get juicy. "Like I said, we're going to find out."

Chapter 9
Chester, England

Tuesday Evening, November 2004

That evening, not yet twenty-four hours since Jason had appeared before the girls at Marsdan Hospital, Lillian sat in the parlor of her parents' home thinking how radically her life had changed that day. In the last ten years, since Jason had established the trust and made her, David, Melanie, and Dorothy trustees, Lillian had lost many of her friends as well as her freedom. Now she felt she was on the verge of losing her husband too.

The early days of the work had been thrilling. Jason would speak to thousands of people about his book and was able to lift many of them to the heights of spiritual bliss. With baby Alex strapped to her back, Lillian had seen her husband's effect on people, and she'd felt the love of the crowds and had witnessed so many people transformed and healed. David had been their only helper—he had done everything from rounding up volunteers, to managing the large number of people, to babysitting Alex when she and Jason had needed to be alone. Melanie was also part of the early days, although she seldom traveled with them. Melanie handled the tons of mail that came to Lillian's London flat and made sure the embryonic Ministry had enough money to operate. Dorothy stayed in the apartment and edited the transcripts from the rallies that would later become Jason's best-selling books. The detractors and hatemongers had yet to surface, and the need for a trust and a board of directors hadn't even been considered. Fame had not yet become a kind of prison.

Lillian questioned why she wanted David to come back. He had been in her life nearly as long as Jason. If circumstances had been different, she might be living in Hawaii with David instead of in Jason's fishbowl in London. She had noticed the look on Jason's face when she suggested they call him. Jason and David would always be best friends, but when Lillian was with the two men, their competiveness made her uncomfortable.

Nancy Harvey, Lillian's mother, came into the parlor and set two glasses of sherry on the coffee table along with a package of letters tied with a ribbon. "I found these when I was getting your room ready."

Lillian looked at the letters as if they were toxic. "Did you read them?"

"Of course. I'm your mother."

"I should have burned them years ago."

Nancy put her hand on her daughter's hand with a mother's love and the wisdom not to say anything. The ladies looked into the flames of a small fireplace.

"Dave is coming back," Lillian says softly.

"Is that a good idea?"

"It seems the only way out of this mess."

"Won't it stir up old feelings?"

"Oh, Mom, not at all. Jason caused this current mess just by being himself. It was my idea to call Dave. At first Jason didn't want to. I think he was more hurt when Dave left the Ministry than I ever was. Of course Jason thought David betrayed him, and in a way he did. Dave was the buffer Jason needed so that he could stretch his saintly wings. I don't think Jason ever realized how much he used David. I think Jason saw David as an extension of himself. I cringe to think where we're all headed."

"My poor darling. All I want for you is to be happy."

Chapter 10
Oahu, Hawaiian Islands

Tuesday Morning, November 2004

That morning, before dawn, David drove out to the North Shore with his nine-foot-six-inch Dick Brewer surfboard hanging out the back of his pickup. He had heard that a swell was coming in and the radio had confirmed it. He was tuned to Perry and Price, Honolulu's morning radio show for commuters. They played some music, gave the weather and surf reports, commented on the news, and warned of traffic tie-ups. David wondered if they would mention Jason. The Marsdan incident was the kind of story they loved to comment on.

He switched the radio off and put a tape in his cassette deck. He didn't want to hear about Jason. With the windows down and Leon Russell's *Back to the Island* blasting from his dash, David left the ever-growing Honolulu suburbs, passed Schofield Barracks, and motored up the grade through what used to be acres of sugarcane and pineapple fields. Now they were mostly fallow. He had a setting moon in front of him and in a few minutes he would be at Laniakea sliding across smooth walls of curling energy contending with a gang of kids young enough to be his children. He would be doing exactly what they were doing, getting connected to the sea before going to school, or work... or London for that matter.

David was the same age as Jason, taller, and now fifteen pounds heavier than he had been in his twenties. He had gray hair and needed glasses to read a menu. He parked his truck across the highway from the surf break. The beach came right up to the highway at that point and the only place to park was a patch of dirt along what had once been a cane field. The surf was perfect and only a few people were out in the water that early. A station wagon drove onto the shoulder across the highway from him and stopped, blocking his view of the waves. A pair of thirteen-year-old boys pulled their boards from the back of the car and ran off toward the beach. David could hear the adult who dropped them off shout after them to not be late for school. The scene reminded him of the August afternoon when he and Jason were that age, and the event that changed his life. It was the first time he realized how dangerous Jason could be.

☉ ☉ ☉

Pacific Palisades

Summer 1978

Jason and David were as close to twins as two people born of different parents could be. They had loved each other since the first grade. They grew up in a sleepy mountain suburb of Los Angeles called Pacific Palisades, noted for its movie stars and for being the home of Ronald Reagan. They went to the same schools, sat in the same classes, played baseball in the spring and football in the fall. They hiked the mountains, surfed the beaches that edged the town just below the cliffs, learned to smoke cigarettes in front of the Bel-Air Bay Club, and discovered girls.

They were Boy Scouts and developed a passion for Indian lore. Jason was more passionate than David, but that was how it was in most things. The boys became part of the ritual team of the Order of the Arrow, the national camping society of the Boy Scouts of America. They chose what Indian nation to emulate, learned the customs of that population, and made their costumes in the manner of their chosen tribe. They learned to dance and performed the "call out" ceremony that initiated those elected to become part of the society. These O. A. rituals were secret, and the young scouts had no idea about what would happen to them when they were pulled away from their fellow campers to begin their initiation.

The boy's lodge met once a week at Camp Josepho, which was considered the "West Point" of scout camps. Josepho was a loose collection of clapboard cabins centered in one hundred acres of valleys and mountains just beyond the multimillion-dollar estates of the Palisades Riviera. Jason and David would ride their bikes up Amalfi Drive, past the homes of movie stars, until the pavement ended. From there they would coast down the steep dirt road, hugging the side of the mountain, drop through half a dozen switchbacks, ford a year-round creek and end up in the central meadow of the camp.

At the beginning of that summer Jason had conned a park ranger into giving him a dead coyote that the ranger had trapped. Jason had a way of convincing people that his vision was the way things should be, and even then, the ranger was no match for thirteen-year-old J.J. This event became the talk of the lodge, and Jason turned his coyote into an outfit worthy of an actual medicine man.

Jason's headdress became the envy of all of the scouts in the lodge. They were amazed at how well Jason had skinned the animal and prepared the pelt. But then, Jason always had been resourceful. He knew where to find help and collect information. He put a pair of yellow glass eyes in place of the animal's dead ones. He bought a jaw set and tongue from a taxidermy shop that made the creature look alive. The coyote's body was a slick fur coat which Jason wore with pride.

One day in late August Jason and David were alone in the craft building at the camp working on their costumes. A bag of eagle feathers—so the package said—was in the middle of the table, and Jason was contemplating where to put a feather on his pelt. David was doing the same thing, choosing feathers to sew on his beaded breastplate. He had chosen to become a Sioux, where Jason had decided to follow the Zuni people who worshiped the coyote as a trickster and a healer.

"Do you think animals have souls?" Jason asked, as he envisioned the best place to put his feather.

"I don't know. Do you?"

"I think so. My dog meditates with us."

"Huh? Really?" David was more interested in making his breastplate perfect than in Jason's meditating dog.

"Have you ever tried to meditate?"

David looked at Jason as if he was asking him if he'd ever met an alien. "No. Isn't it a bit weird?"

David had never truly understood Jason's fascination with spiritual things. Jason's mother, Elizabeth St. John, had experimented with all kinds of spiritual teachings, and at that moment she was a Christian Scientist. David had gone a few times with Jason to the Christian Science Church because that's what buddies did, but he thought the service was boring and sterile.

Yet David envied Jason's history; it was completely different from his. David believed that Jason's upbringing made him much more self-assured. David felt totally conventional, a true Baptist. He never liked to stand out. For him, the good life was getting good grades in school so that he could go to college and escape from his family. It was riding a good wave, and having friends he could trust, and being noticed by a beautiful girl—although David was a bit shy and hadn't the balls to make the first move. That's what Jason did. He was always the first to do everything. Sometimes David thought he was destined to be the sidekick, the willing accomplice who would follow Jason just about anywhere and do just about anything Jason was willing to do. David really didn't mind. Yet, when it came to delving into the occult, and many people thought that Christian Science was a cult, it challenged David's beliefs and the morals that his family lived by. Jason's religion confused David. Sin and redemption existed for good a reason, or so the Bible said. That didn't mean he didn't like adventure, but unlike Jason, David liked to know what he was getting into before he jumped.

"Actually it's kind of cool," Jason said, assuming David was on the same thought wave as he was. "My mom has these tapes she listens to and we meditate together after school."

"But what does it do? Doesn't it mess with your mind?"

"No. I was reading Dr. Green's book on meditation and he said that when you meditate the mind becomes the place where you can experience God." Jason rattled this off as if it made perfect sense.

"Experience God!? Wouldn't I die if I did?"

"No, not at all. I'm not dead."

"You haven't seen God."

"It's not like you've been taught. Come on. Let me show you."

"I don't want to mess around with that stuff. What's it make you do, hear voices?"

"No, it's rad. It's like getting this feeling that, you know, it's really far-out. It's like getting high without the weed."

"I don't know."

Jason jumped up, crawled across the table where the boys were working, and grabbed David around the neck. He pulled him close and looked deep into his eyes. David's heart started pounding. He couldn't breathe. Suddenly Jason let go, got off the table, and began pacing the room.

"No! There is a way. I know it. I can show it to you." Jason stopped and looked at David again, close to figuring out how to share his passion. "You know when we're surfing and you just fall into the groove and everything you do nails it and you don't really think about it? You've done that, right?"

"Yeah."

"That's like meditating! You're experiencing the wave."

"I'm riding it."

"Don't be such a jerk. I've seen that look on your face. I know you've experienced that."

"Okay. So surfing is meditation." David went back to sewing his eagle feathers on his Sioux breastplate.

Jason didn't give up and sat down next to him, speaking right into his face. To David, Jason's voice took on the caliber of a radio commercial. David occasionally looked over to him as he spoke; "The way Dr. Green explains it, we commune with God through a still mind. That's why they meditate in India. Mom and I light candles after school before Dad comes home. I don't think she's even told him yet. I know it sounds kind of strange, but it's really amazing. Anyway, we sit on the floor and mom tells me to watch my thoughts and see if I can find the spaces between them. I pretend like I'm watching cars on the freeway, but instead of focusing on the cars I focus on the spaces between them. I did it once, just for a few moments, and I felt this incredible peace. Like the whole world had disappeared and there was nothing but me, but it wasn't me like I am, it was me without a physical body!"

David was speechless. But, there was something about Jason's intensity that made him subconsciously pay attention. Jason was always enthusiastic about new things. He threw himself into projects—like the boy's O. A. costumes—so this wasn't out of character. There was clarity in Jason's eyes and a passion in his voice when he described his meditation, which David hadn't seen or heard before. And as much as he didn't want to give in to Jason's enthusiasm, he was intrigued by what Jason was saying.

Jason picked on David's openness and pressed on. "Want to try it?"

"Why not?" Perhaps David subconsciously wanted to break out from the narrowness of his family's conventional thinking.

"Let's do this. Let's get into our costumes and put on our paint and go up to the high meadow," Jason said. "I know the Indians would have done this. They could get themselves into a state of mind where they could feel totally connected to nature."

David thought this was exciting, like another secret ritual. No one was around. They were on our own, two young braves preparing to face the wilderness and explore the furthest reaches of their thinking. David felt it was kind of hedonistic, completely anti Baptist, and he liked it.

"Let's do this all the way." Jason stepped out of his underwear and wrapped his loincloth around his waist. Watching Jason gave David another sensation. It made his nuts tingle. It wasn't like he'd never seen Jason naked before—they were practically brothers. But this was a different situation. They were becoming primitive and discarding conventional morality. David loved Jason as a brother, but he was attracted to girls. He had two older sisters and a father who never talked about sex. David thought his father was afraid of it, afraid of having to tell his son what it was all about. Or maybe he didn't really know.

David pushed those feelings aside, took off his street clothes, put on his costume, and followed Jason from the cabin. Jason locked the door, hid the key under the mat, and the boys headed off upstream to the high meadow. Neither one of them noticed the ranger watching them from his cabin.

The boys hiked in silence, skirting the creek. Jason led as usual while David's mind raced ahead. What if all this wasn't just playacting, kid stuff, and make-believe? What if Jason was tapping into some psychic realm, intent on brainwashing him? David laughed at that thought. If Jason could do that it had happened a long time ago.

The upper meadow was about a mile from the main camp and a thousand feet higher. Typical of the Santa Monica Mountains, the lower approach was a winding, narrow canyon cut through the mountains by a stream. The high meadow blossomed out from there into a pear shape field rising to within a few hundred feet of the ridgeline, which was covered in chaparral and sumac. The meadow grass was tall and yellow, as high as the boy's knees, and smelled of summer rain. The source of the creek was a spring in the middle of the meadow that, because of the summer storm, had grown to the size of a pond. The water was mainly clear, though not very deep.

As the boys entered the meadow, David had the sensation that he was leaving his childhood. He followed Jason to the spring, and the young "Indians" fell on their backs and looked up at the extremely soft but brilliant blue sky.

"I've got fuzz-balls floating in front of my eyes," Jason said.

"It's the atmosphere."

Jason sat up, crossed his legs, and faced David. "All of this," Jason gestured to everything around them, "is inside of you, you know. Nothing is really out there. It's all in your mind."

"Really? I don't see that."

"If we believed strongly enough," Jason continued, "we could put ourselves back in time and experience what Indian kids our age did when they went through their rites of passage. We could, you know."

David sat up and faced him. "Then let's do it."

Jason said, "Cross your legs and put your knees against mine. Put your hands on my knees like this."

David put his right hand on Jason's right knee and his left hand on Jason's left knee, making a cross. Jason did the same and the boys were completely entwined.

"Now stare into my eyes," Jason continued.

David held his gaze for a few seconds and then started to laugh.

"Come on. This is scientific. We might experience something outrageous."

"Are you going to hypnotize me?"

"No!" Jason replied emphatically. "We're each going to look deep into the psyche of the universe."

David met Jason's gaze again, and after a few breaths relaxed into the awkward position. David's back straightened. The cramping in his legs left, and he felt like he was floating. Jason's eyes were almost unblinking and at first David wanted to count the seconds between blinks, but some other part of him said, "Keep still." Jason was breathing deeply in through his nose and out through his mouth. David followed Jason's breathing and soon no longer saw him. David felt calm.

Both of the boys' breathing slowed into long, steady breaths. They fell into the same rhythm. Their heartbeats were in sync, and the pulsing of the blood in Jason's legs matched the beat in David's. David was no longer aware of his breathing. He was now looking through Jason, traveling further into the depth of his eyes until he was no longer aware of Jason's form. All David saw was the pasture in the mountains, pure and pristine. There was no time.

David lost his sense of self and merged with all that surrounded him—the pasture, the spring and even Jason. He felt the water push through the grass into his body. He heard the wind carry the song of the wilderness to every corner of his being.

Jason shuddered and let out a long sigh. David snapped back to what he thought was the present time and looked up. They were surrounded by Native American boys, about their same age, dressed in animal skins, with their bodies and faces painted like war paint. Some wore elaborate costumes decorated with feathers, shells, and quills. Others wore only simple loincloths. They seemed to welcome Jason and David back as if they were long lost brothers. David felt love fill the air. It made him catch his breath. Made his heart beat faster.

Then one boy, with greased black hair tied into braids, loosened his loincloth. He stood naked in front of Jason and David, and then moved with an animal grace, completely uninhibited and free. The other Indian boys followed his lead, dropping their garments and joining his dance. They beckoned to David and Jason to do the same.

David looked at Jason. Was this real? Was Jason seeing the same thing? Jason needed to go first. David couldn't do it alone. Then Jason started to move and as he did, David saw the head of his penis protruding from his loincloth and growing with the steady pulse of the throbbing dance. David started to get hard and tried to fight it.

Jason stripped off his costume and joined the dance. David watched Jason spin around, his hands reaching up to the heavens and his manhood growing as stiff and as large as a satyr in the company of virgins. The naked Indians acknowledged his arrival with erections of their own, dancing in celebration of life—in celebration of their maleness. David felt the elation and wanted to join in. He wanted to be free.

David tried to get up but couldn't. Something in his head said that this was sinful; that he wasn't allowed this kind of freedom. He wasn't supposed to get aroused by other men. He tried to justify his arousal by arguing that it was natural. Jason was there to encourage him, showing him how to drop his conditioning and dance. "Who said thou wast naked?" came the Biblical statement booming into David's head.

When he finally did get up, he was as stiff as Jason. The Indians had vanished and there was Jason dancing naked, alone. In a rash of guilt, he once more lost his enthusiasm. The mystical union he and Jason had been sharing dissolved, leaving only sin and the promise of punishment.

"What the hell are you boys doing up here?" came the ranger's voice, yelling from the edge of the meadow.

David ran into the spring and fell face down in the cold water. Jason confronted the man with a look of complete contempt. He wasn't ashamed or intimidated.

"Get something and cover that thing up," the ranger shouted. Turning to David he said, "Get the hell out of that spring!"

David didn't want to move. He didn't have Jason's confidence, and he was harder than a rock. He would rather die than expose what he didn't want exposed.

"Now!" the ranger shouted.

David reluctantly got up and his loincloth looked like it was stretched over a tent pole.

"So what have we got here, a couple of little queers? Well, let's see how this goes down with your parents. Come on. Let's go!"

◉ ◉ ◉

David shook off the memory and got out of the cab of his truck. He watched a fresh set of waves bend around the point. A handful of people were now in the water. The two boys he saw being dropped off were in the channel, paddling out to the break as the swells turned into breakers. A surfer caught the second wave of the set. It had a six-foot face—making it a three-foot wave in Hawaiian measurement—and the rider moved up and down across the face in quick moves, bouncing off the bottom and then rising to kick off the curl.

David was surprised that his childhood memories were still so vivid. Just thinking about going back into Jason's world flooded him with anxiety. Was Jason just manipulating him again? Would he even make a difference? He thought it ironic, since he tried to live in the now, as Jason continued to teach. Maybe he was more connected to Jason than he was willing to admit. Maybe that feeling could never be purged. Maybe getting off his duff and getting into the water would change things.

◉ ◉ ◉

Pacific Palisades

Summer 1978

A few days after the incident in the meadow, Jason and his parents, Phillip and Elizabeth, were at June and Donald Walker's house for their weekly bridge night. Donald was in no mood for bridge that night and he had been drinking. Things were not going well for the Walkers. Their oldest daughter was leaving for college, and that put a financial strain on Donald. But more than that, Donald did not approve of premarital sex and he knew that once his girl was away from home, she would succumb to peer pressure and do "it." Donald hoped that his wife, June, had educated her on birth control, but he didn't believe in that either. His middle daughter had just gotten her driver's license and was begging for a car, which she wasn't going to get. And now the son of his wife's best friend was corrupting his son. On top of that, his company was moving him to Orange County. Donald had just told his family that news the other day, and he was worried about selling his Palisades house and finding one as nice down there.

When the St. Johns arrived, Jason and David went into the den and the adults immediately sat down to play cards. Donald Walker insisted on dealing instead of cutting the deck first. Everyone brushed over that without making a fuss. After the bidding, which the Walkers won, Donald became the dummy and went in to the kitchen for another drink. June concentrated on playing her hand and made no comment. Her hope lay in her cards, and if she won the hand perhaps her husband would mellow and it would be a pleasant evening after all.

David hadn't talked to Jason for a few days and was desperate to know what had happened to him. But, at the same time, David wanted to eavesdrop on their parents. He had a bad feeling about the game that night. It was quiet in the living room; the adults must have been concentrating on their cards, and Jason and David looked at each other rather awkwardly from opposite sides of the room.

"Did the ranger talk to your parents?" David finally asked.

"That friggin freak. Did you see he was covered in tattoos?"

"Yea, probably a marine or something, but what did your dad say?" David wanted to know if Jason had suffered as much humiliation as he had.

"My dad wasn't home. My mom and I talked about it and she was pretty cool. I explained the whole thing, and she doesn't think there's anything weird between us."

"My dad hit the roof. You'd have thought I'd murdered somebody. What about your dad, didn't your mom tell him later?"

"Yeah, but he didn't seem concerned. Said he'd love me no matter what. That was a little weird."

"My dad was all over my mom and my sisters. He blamed them for making a sissy out of me. God, this is going to get all over town. If we walk down the street together people are going to calls us fagots."

"So what!" Jason truly didn't care. "You and I know that we aren't, so screw them. I don't care what other people think, and what they think isn't going to ruin our friendship."

"Yeah." David had a hard time keeping his voice from breaking. To David, Jason's loyalty and friendship was a great relief. They were best friends, so tight, and what happened in the hills just added a profound layer to his already burdensome, adolescent angst. David checked his impulse to run across the room and hug Jason. He was too afraid.

Back in the living room, Jason's parents deliberately projected normalcy, though the tension at the card table could be cut with a butter knife. June Walker kept giving Elizabeth St. John glances that telegraphed her distress. "Pray for me. Help me. How do I deal with this kind of situation and maintain harmony?" June pleaded silently.

Instead of addressing June's plea for help, Elizabeth retreated into her detached, Christian Science practitioner mode where she had no sympathy for "mortal mind" behavior—that human perception that there is power in material cause and effect. As with everything Elizabeth did, she went all the way. She went through Christian Science class instruction with the finest teacher she could find and was a member in good standing of the Mother Church, therefore she was eligible to practice spiritual healing. June relied on Elizabeth for spiritual support and secretly went to the Christian Science Church. She liked the peace there; so different from the hellfire of her husband's Baptist Church.

Elizabeth wasn't being rude to June, though it might have appeared that way. She was silently working to bring harmony into the situation. Her Christian Science teacher had taught her that one of the strongest tendencies of the so-called mortal or carnal mind was its love for sympathy. She could not be an effective healer and have any sympathy for "error," or wrong thinking.

Donald Walker came back from the kitchen with another bourbon. "Any religion founded by a woman," he said, referring to Mary Baker Eddy, "has no balls and should be relegated to spinsters and old maids." He pointedly looked at Elizabeth. "You're turning my son into a fairy!"

And raising his voice to June; "David's going to go to a real church, one with some discipline, some hellfire and punishment!"

"You don't mean that, Donald," June said emphatically, as if denying her husband's outrage would delay the impending embarrassment.

"I mean every word of it. I'm sick and tired of all this pretending. You think you're fooling me by going to Elizabeth's "church." Her religion might be fine for sick people, but I won't let you brainwash my son."

"Donald, that's the alcohol talking and not really you," June said weakly.

Elizabeth got up from the table and put her hand on June's shoulder. "Let's make some coffee."

"Coffee won't do any good. It's not going to change things." Donald stood up and blocked the doorway to the kitchen. "You haven't told them?" he shouted to his wife. "Your goddamn best friend and she don't know shit?"

Donald's language nearly knocked over the St. Johns. Elizabeth grabbed June's shoulder to steady herself. Phillip jumped from the game table, ready to defend his wife if the scene grew more ugly.

Jason and David came in from the den. They couldn't help hearing what was said. Jason looked at David, his best friend, surprised he hadn't been told. David shrugged, embarrassed. All of it was terribly depressing; moving away from his best friend, being forced to go to a fundamentalist church—what was next, military school?

"We better go and let the Walkers work this out in private," Phillip said as he put an arm around Elizabeth. Elizabeth stepped back from June and beckoned for her son to join them. Jason silently walked over and stood between his parents. Phillip had always dubbed them the three musketeers; it was how he thought of his family.

Standing together like that, David suddenly saw it. Nothing could ever come between them. They were invincible, too strong for bumpy emotional detours; Christian Scientists to the core, standing "porter at the door of thought."

Their circling of the wagons turned David off. In the volatility of his family there was a lot of affection along with the fighting. It seemed more honest, somehow. How smug Jason and his parents appeared to David. How perfect. Then

Jason gave David a subtle wave, and David knew that they would always be buddies. Not even Mrs. St. John's steel-trap mind could alter their destiny. As David watched his best friend walk away, clad in the armor of metaphysics and right thinking, he felt surprisingly free. They weren't done with each other; they were just entering a new phase of their brotherhood.

"I'll call you, Elizabeth," June said.

"Fine."

The Walkers moved to Costa Mesa the next week, and Donald had all of his kids at the Baptist Church that Sunday. David never knew if his mom had called Elizabeth to explain things. He felt sure that she did, and knowing Elizabeth, knew that she listened politely to June, careful not to give in to sympathetic mesmerism.

◉ ◉ ◉

David caught his first wave as the sun came up over the Ko'olau Mountains. A couple of teenagers tried to drop in on him, but his style of surfing dissuaded them. Riding a long-board was like sailing a classic yacht; it's graceful, elegant, and smooth in a world of quick, frantic action. The kids surfing with him started to respect his style and soon they were mixing ballet with hip-hop on the same wave. After a dozen or so waves the kids said their good-byes and paddled in to go to school. David spent the rest of the morning sitting on his board, away from the surf line and the ever-changing crowd, thinking about Jason's call. By the time it became too hot to sit out in the sun any longer David was close to his answer and paddled in.

Chapter 11
Stanford House

Wednesday Morning, November 2004

Jason sat at the large country table in the family room of their apartment in Stanford House staring at Lillian's computer. He read the MySpace chats from the night before that ranged from speculation that Lillian was having an affair to Lillian's bizarre activities with Alex and their drive to Chester. He loved how Lillian had outthought and outmaneuvered Gary and the ISD.

Melanie's mobile phone rang and slid across the table, almost falling off before Jason could grab it. He checked the caller ID—it was Lillian. He was glad to hear her voice,. "Everything alright?"

"Much calmer this morning. There's a car that's been parked across the street a couple of houses down with two men in it. I think they followed me and are still watching us."

"Don't go out unless you have to. Perhaps you could sic your dad on them."

"You have Sir William waiting. Do you need help opening Skype?"

"No. Thanks for reminding me."

Jason ended his call and opened up the Skype program on Lillian's computer. As soon as he did he got the message that Sir William was online waiting to speak with him. The camera was kind to Sir William; he was a tanned, athletic man in his early seventies with short white hair and a gold earring in his left ear.

He sat in a paneled office with flattering light, surrounded by bookcases filled with important looking law books. The image Sir William presented was one of wealth, wisdom, and the assurance of a professional who knew what they were doing.

"Sir William, thank you for meeting me like this." Jason spoke into the computer screen.

Sir William Boyd, a senior partner at the law firm of Norton, Boyd & Gladstone, saw Jason, a harassed-looking man, anxious and worried. Sir William and Lloyd Harvey, Lillian's father, had grown up together in the countryside between Chester and Liverpool. Sir William became Lillian's godfather when she was born in 1961.

"Jason, what's going on?" Sir William was concerned.

"I've been doing some things that the board doesn't understand and they want to stop me."

"Like appearing in a cancer ward out of thin air?"

"That's being distorted and I plan to give the world a complete explanation. But first I have to deal with my board. They're isolating me and want to silence me. Frankly, I think some of them would like to throw me in a dungeon."

Sir William thought about that for a moment. "Are you sure?"

"Yes. I'm afraid of what it's doing to Alex and Lillian. They had to escape yesterday. This is ridiculous."

"Can't we meet in my office?"

"No. This is the best I can do. Lillian made sure our internet is separate from the Ministry's."

Sir William opened a thick folder.

"Have I screwed myself completely?" Jason asked. "Can we redo the trust?"

"It will be difficult."

"Is it even possible?"

"Not so fast. Remember, you were off setting up healing centers in the far corners of the earth, and didn't want to be bothered with, as you said, the 'organization.'"

"I know. I know. Don't you have any secret clause hidden away somewhere...?"

"I'm afraid not. You let Tony Bass dictate what he thought would be an efficient board. That's what you wanted—someone to take the burden off of you so you could write, teach, and heal. I counseled you to be more engaged in the process and tried to put articles in the deed that would protect you, but you let Tony modify them so that the board has total control over you."

Jason groaned.

"As the settler, Jason, you were the only person endowing the trust. At that time no one else put anything into the trust. You were calling the shots. The original endowment was for the purpose of promoting universal healing. All your assets at that time were transferred from you to the Ministry, or the trust. They're the same thing. It's all very standard and Tony organized the trust into the various departments so that the Ministry could efficiently fulfill its purpose. You wanted the trust to exist in perpetuity and, against my advice, inserted that only a unanimous vote by the board could dissolved it. Upon your death the trust will support Lillian and Alex for the remainder their lives but not Alex's offspring. There is nothing we can do about that part of the trust."

"Are you saying that there is something else we can do?"

"I did my best to protect you, but you were not the easiest client to work with," Sir William said.

"I was thinking how close we all were. How we all had the same vision."

"Tony and I had our biggest differences about your future material," Sir William continued. "I argued that you should keep the rights to whatever writings, videos, and unknown breakthroughs you might discover in your future experimentations. In other words, anything you created or developed from that moment on, and all the revenues generated, would remain with you and not the trust. But you trusted Tony back then. So right now, you, and all that you create—your image, name, new discoveries—belong to the trust. Since it owns all of that, a majority vote by the board can forbid you from any and all public activity that has any connection to St. John Ministries."

"What if I simply quit? Retire. I could take the family and move to the States, back to Hawaii and live on the beach."

"How would you live?"

"I'd get a job of some sort."

"You couldn't teach, write, or heal without the board's permission."

"What if people were healed just by being in my presence?"

"Now you're splitting hairs. But I would imagine the board could demand that you stop and if that meant that you could not go out in public, they could demand that you remain cloistered. If they went that far we could fight that last demand in court."

"I'd buy a boat and take the family to the South Pacific."

"With what? You've got no money outside what the trust gives you."

Jason got up and paced back and forth before Lillian's computer.

"Jason, sit down," Sir William demanded. "I can't talk to you when you float in and out of the picture."

Jason laughed at the irony. "You have no idea ... So is there *any* way out?"

"I was able to add a few clauses in your favor. One—you, Lillian, Melanie, Dorothy, and David, as founding trustees, can never be kicked off the board."

"But David resigned, remember?"

"Doesn't matter. His seat is always there for him if he ever decides to return."

"Secondly, though members serve a life term, a director can be removed by a two-thirds vote if their actions are shown to undermine the purpose of the foundation, and/or if they abuse their fiduciary duty. And thirdly, your vote on the board counts as two votes. So unless Tony and his supporters can stack the board, you have a powerful say in what takes place."

"That's golden!" Jason says. "How did Tony miss that?"

"He didn't. He was going to walk and I told him to go ahead. I told him you really didn't need a trust, so he took control of what he could. Given what he's doing now, Tony may assume that you don't realize the control you have, given the lack of interest you've shown in the past."

"Do the other trustees know about that two-vote provision?"

"Yes, it's all in the trust deed. Do you know how the board is split regarding your current activities?"

"Four, maybe five would vote with Tony. If Dave comes back, the three of us, Lillian, David and I would be four votes. Deedee, I'd have to assume would be with us, and Melanie could be toss-up. I don't know. We could be deadlocked. What happens then?"

"I, or someone from our firm, would cast the deciding vote, following as close as we can the articles of the trust deed and the mission statement of the Ministry."

"What if I die?"

"The current board would control all the assets and Alex and Lillian would be taken care of according to the trust provisions."

Sir William then leaned into the camera on his computer and said, "If you die, and there is a body—or if you're killed, the provisions of the trust are very clear and it would be extremely difficult for Mr. Bass or any other board chairman to deny support for Lillian and Alex or force them to do or say anything they wouldn't want to."

"What if I disappear?"

"If you disappear, and nobody can find your body, Alex and Lillian would be at the mercy of the chairman. He could determine that you were still alive and run the Ministry according to his agenda, as it appears he wants to do now. He could force Lillian and Alex to go along with his program and they would have limited legal recourse."

"So until Dave gets here I don't have the votes to go against the board. And until I have the board's support my family is at risk."

"May I make a suggestion," Sir William says.

"By all means."

"I don't agree with all that you teach, and I absolutely recognize the incredible scope of your healing Ministry, but I would advise you to follow one of the principles you teach—the one about non-resistance. Don't resist Tony. He's a fighter."

"I'm not going to roll over and play dead."

"Then, I wish you the best of luck."

Sir William signed off leaving Jason staring at his own picture in Lillian's computer.

For the first time in his life, he felt trapped.

PART II

Chapter 12
Honolulu, Hawaii

Wednesday April 26, 1989

United Flight 195 touched down at Honolulu International Airport six days before the *Mataʻi* was to set sail for the South Pacific. David's heart raced as he left the plane. He hadn't seen Jason in seven years. He was twenty-four now, and felt he was ready to take on the world. He had a fine arts degree from Rhode Island School of Design and had been in the middle of his grand tour of Europe when he got J.J.'s telegram and accepted his offer to sail the islands of French Polynesia.

Walking to the baggage claim David had a lot of questions. Who was Jason now? Who was the man who had been his best friend as a kid? Would they still have that connection after the years they'd spent apart—in college, traveling, finding love?

Jason was waiting for David at the baggage claim, a flower *lei* hanging on his arm. David saw him first. Jason looked more rugged than David remembered. His hair was longer, falling around his neck in sun-bleached curls. He was tanned to a dark oak and stood looking at the crowd in that loose sort of way that physically assured men do when they are totally unconcerned with their bodies.

His face lit up when he saw David.

The men greeted each other with a strong hug and Jason gave David the *lei*. David was in sensory overload. The colors dazzled him, so pure and sharp. The air, even at the airport, was tinged with the aroma of damp earth and flowers—the plumeria fragrance would stay with him forever. And it was hot.

"You don't look like an artist," Jason told him. "I was expecting a beret, or maybe a severed ear."

"It was a New England art school, all hard chairs and plain walls. You know, art with a puritanical twist."

Jason picked up David's seabag and David followed his friend across the street to the parking garage where Jason's "North Shore Cruiser" awaited them. It was the most dilapidated, rusty, aging Toyota station wagon David had ever seen.

"You expect me to ride in *that*?" he asked.

"It's puritanical, like your education."

Jason unlocked the tailgate and lifted it with a mighty pull. His surfboard, a Hawaiian Islands Creation thruster, lay in the back. He threw David's bag next to it, careful not to scratch his board, closed the back and opened the passenger door for David. The door was dented and opened with a bang.

"You need to slam it shut," Jason said as he walked around to the driver's side.

Jason coaxed the car to start, got it in gear and they set off toward Waikiki where Larry Graff's yacht, *Mata'i*, which Jason said meant "fair wind" in Tahitian was berthed.

"Sorry about the air conditioning," Jason said rolling down his window. David did the same thing.

"How's it going with Larry?" David asked.

"I'm still on probation."

David's puzzled look spurred Jason to unload some of his feelings. "I thought Larry invited me along on this trip because of my sailing skills, but he treats me like I've never been on a boat before. It's been frustrating. I know it's my problem. I'm probably nursing a bruised ego, but I've got to find a way to deal with it."

"He sounds awfully petty."

"Larry was impressed with your sailing skills and your winning the Collegiate Ocean Racing Championship in Newport. But he was even more impressed by your exploits in that Newport to Bermuda race where half the fleet was damaged by a tropical storm."

"That wasn't a bright moment for me. We should've withdrawn and run for cover. I let the skipper talk me into going for it. We were lucky to come out in one piece."

"Maybe I'm being too critical. I mean I like Larry. He's smart. He has a good sense of humor. He's always teaching me things a cruising sailor looks for. It's a lot different than taking a catamaran in and out of Waikiki."

"That's right. You wrote me how much you liked skippering those boats."

"Larry has no respect for the beach catamarans. He's a blue-water sailor, and he watches every penny. If he can't fix something himself, or make a part, he'll find the best deal for what he needs."

"It's good he can fix things. We like that, don't we? Who else will be on the boat?"

"Nobody. Just Larry, his brother Byron and you and me. Byron arrives on Sunday. We leave on Monday."

"Byron's cutting it close—arriving a day before we depart."

"From what Larry's wife told me, Byron didn't sit back and live off his trust fund. He owns one of the biggest real estate firms in Florida, has his own yacht, and regularly cruises the Caribbean. I think he's doing this for two reasons. One, it will be hurricane season in the Caribbean, and two, he's never been to the South Pacific. But what do I know? I've never met the guy."

The traffic started backing up around the commercial piers just west of downtown Honolulu. The afternoon sun baked the asphalt, and the fumes from the string of cars and trucks slowly snaking their way toward Waikiki polluted the old Toyota. The roasting pavement softened the tires, and the smell of scorched rubber mingled with sticky scents wafting from the nearby pineapple cannery.

"So what's next?" The driving was frustrating Jason and his questions to David were so empty they were almost rhetorical.

"I'm going to sail the South Pacific," David reached over and gave Jason a playful shake. "You know, you and me? Buddies off on our dream adventure."

"This trip may not be all that we've dreamed about."

"Are you getting cold feet?"

"No. It has nothing to do with the sailing. There's something I can't put my finger on that keeps giving me this uncomfortable feeling."

"I don't believe it," David said irritated. "I was in Barcelona three days ago, very happy with my life. So, we shouldn't do this trip?"

"No, not at all. We *have* to do it."

"I don't remember you ever being ambivalent. You'd get some inner message and off you went, dragging me along with you.

"No, I have to do this trip and I want you with me. But I think there's a lot more to it than just sailing to Tahiti.

"Chill out. You've been dreaming of this kind of adventure forever."

Jason relaxed as he pulled off Ala Moana Boulevard and parked in front of a leeward slip not far from the Hawaii Yacht

Club. The *Mata'i* struck a noble bowsprit, like an accusing finger, out toward the high-rise hotels fronting the harbor.

"When Larry first got this slip here, he said you could see the mountains while having your cocktail on deck."

David surveyed what would be his new home for the next few months. Jason grabbed his friend's bag and his surfboard from the car, and the men crossed the street to the yacht. Jason tossed David's bag on the boat and put his surfboard down on the end of the pier. He stepped on one of the spring lines to bring the yacht closer to the pier, jumped onboard, and unlocked the main hatch.

"Permission to come aboard, sir?" David said mockingly.

"Fuck'n A."

"What's aft?" David jumped down into the cockpit.

"Owner's cabin. Off-limits. Leave everything here and I'll show you around."

"I want to change." David was sweating in his mainland clothes, and the afternoon sun bounced off the glass of the surrounding hotels baking all the boats. "It's hotter than I thought it would be.

"You'll get used to it."

David opened his seabag and found a pair of shorts to slip into. He looked anemic next to Jason. His legs were pale and spindly, and his bare feet looked frightfully narrow and white, like they'd been bound for years and had never seen the sun. He was taller than Jason, and his thin frame, mop of black hair, and white skin made him look like Ichabod Crane.

"Don't worry, you'll brown up fast enough." Jason said.

The *Mata'i* spanned sixty-three feet from the tip of her bowsprit to her taffrail. Ketch rigged with an owner's cabin aft of the cockpit, she was built specifically for cruising the islands of the South Pacific. She had a high clipper bow and a long sweeping strake that ended a classic wing transom, which gave her the appearance of speed even while she was at the dock. Resting on chalks on top of the aft cabin, under the mizzen boom, was a ten-foot wooden dinghy named *Mata'i Iti—Little Mata'i.* Mounted on boomkin jutting out from *Mata'i's* transome was an Aires self-steering wind vane.

Jason took David through the companionway, down three steps into the main salon. The wood paneling was painted a soft cream and had been rubbed to a satin finish. The cherry wood trim was varnished to a mirror shine. The decks were teak and honed as smooth as a baby's cheek.

"We're going to be up forward with Byron when he arrives," Jason said. "Larry has a few idiosyncrasies you should know about. One, there's no refrigeration. You might want to back out on that alone."

"I might. What else?"

"Well, look around."

David sat down on the settee behind a gimbaled table on the port side of the salon. Looking back to the cockpit he had a clear view of the large traditional spoke wheel mounted on a binnacle. He noticed the windows on either side of the salon. They were larger than on most modern yachts and were bordered with little red- and-white Tahitian print curtains. The windows were one-inch-thick Plexiglas that could be wedged against rubber gaskets inside their bronze frame during rough weather, but that day they were raised high to let in the trade winds. The frames also allowed the Plexiglas to tilt in at the top for ventilation on a wet day when water flowed down the deck. It was rather ingenious. Jason told David that Larry had invented the versatile windows.

On the starboard side of the boat, across from the settee and two steps lower, were the galley and navigator's station. The galley included an icebox, a sink, and a gimbaled alcohol stove-and-oven combination. The navigator's station had a chest-high chart table and an array of radios, but only one GPS.

"The guy's a ham," David said. "And I don't think he puts much stock in electronic navigation aids."

"Very observant."

"All those electronics and no refrigerator take off a couple of points."

"You'll find all kinds of Larry's little inventions on the boat."

David got up from the settee, checked out the navigation station, and then made his way to the forward cabin, a step below the salon. The main mast came through the roof there, penetrated the cabin floor, and was attached to the keel. There were three forward-looking ports where the salon ended and the forward cabin began. The high berths on either side of the hull in the forward cabin were filled with gear.

"Where do we sleep?"

Jason followed David into the cabin and pulled out a drawer from beneath one of the high berths. He sat on the thin mattress of the narrow bunk and patted it as if he were checking out a bed in a department store. "We might be able to clear off one bunk when we get more organized, but this is where you sleep. I prefer sleeping in the cockpit—unless it rains."

Running along the inside of the hull, above the bunks on either side of the boat, was a bookshelf filled with leather bound books and a short railing that resembled a classical Greek balustrade to keep the books from falling out in rough weather.

"Someone likes to read," David said.

"Larry lived onboard for years. I think he still thinks of this as his second home."

"How'd you two meet?"

"I met him at one of my mother's retreats a few years ago. I've never been at sea with him for longer than an afternoon, but he has a great reputation as a blue-water sailor and a navigator. Hang around the club or talk to any of the old-timers. They all know Larry and would sign on with him in an instant."

"I'm not questioning his ability as a sailor. If he meets your approval, that's fine with me. So far I've picked up that he's a demanding boss who expects top quality work on his boat for the best price. He's literate and has a modicum of taste. He likes people and wants to be in touch. He might be a little stubborn and set in his ways, but he's embraced a spiritual teaching, so he's working on tolerance, forgiveness, and brotherly love. Have I missed anything?"

"I think he has a crush on my mother."

"Really? How does that make you feel?"

"It doesn't matter. She handles it very well."

"What about your dad?"

"He passed on a little over a year ago," Jason said turning away.

"Oh, I'm so sorry."

"Mom was at the height of her lecture tours, and Dad never liked to travel. I think it put a lot of stress on him, especially seeing the level of devotion some of the students had toward mother."

"So what happened?"

"An aneurism; very sudden, on the golf course. He had his buddies and loved golf and the men's world. I think he was happy.

When they were home together they were like teenage lovers, but when mother was getting ready for a lecture tour you could feel the curtain closing between them and they both shifted gears. Anyway, Mother and I were in Dallas when it happened. She left in the middle of a class and I filled in. We decided that I should give the remaining sessions."

"Weren't people disappointed your mom wasn't there?"

"People felt the atmosphere and I think it showed the student body that the mystical message transcends personality and the belief of death." Jason said that as if he'd convinced himself it was true.

"Do you speak in your mom's classes now?" David asked.

"Sometimes I do the meditations, but here in Hawaii I stay in the background. Mother rented a condo on Diamond Head for a couple of months and will stay on while we're in the South Pacific. I think she'll eventually retire here."

Jason paused for a moment.

David thought it seemed rather sad. The St. John's—the three musketeers—were no longer all for one and one for all.

Jason quickly changed into his trunks, took an extra key from a drawer, and tossed it to David.

"Lock up when you leave," he said.

"You going somewhere?"

"Surfing."

"Want to get a bite after?"

"You go ahead. Walk along the beach to the Reef Hotel and you'll find a right-of-way into town." David had expected a little more companionship, some more reminiscing, and maybe doing something together, but that was Jason; you never knew exactly what to expect.

David followed his buddy on deck in time to see him throw his board off the pier and dive in after it. He paddled through the harbor out toward a break called the Ala Moana Bowl without looking back.

Going below, David found a flyer for Elizabeth St. John's "Living Without Fear" seminar in Waikiki. According to the flyer, she had been lecturing all week in the evenings in preparation for the private "closed-class" that began Thursday morning. Thursday, Friday, and Saturday would be intensive sessions designed to awaken the student to the nature of the Spirit within. David placed the flyer back on the settee, found a cool drink, and flaked out in the cockpit. He soon fell asleep.

The "Living Without Fear" seminar was based on the writings of the great twentieth-century mystic Dr. Solomon Green, whom Jason and David had met when they were fifteen. Dr. Green had died on Maui in 1984 and Elizabeth had been there for his funeral. Jason, who had been a junior at the University of Hawaii at the time, had chosen UH to be able to study with Dr. Green. Besides having had a mystical connection, Jason and Solomon had also shared a love for the Hawaiian culture – and all the Polynesian cultures for that matter. They had studied the *Kumulipo* – the Hawaiian creation chant. The Hawaiians traced their linage back to the gods, and the *Kumulipo* was that story – like Genesis was the story of Judo-Christian origins. Jason had immersed himself into the poetry of the chant. Dr. Green had recognized Jason's spiritual capacities, and invited Jason to collaborate with him on a book tracing the spiritual roots of the Polynesian. Both men thought the Polynesian people were originally a Semitic race, perhaps one of the lost tribes of Israel. The Polynesian languages had similarities to ancient Aramaic that could be traced through Taiwan and India back to the Middle East. But Dr. Green passed away before the book was completed.

Dr. Green's funeral attracted people from all over the world. His widow, Ruth, had addressed the crowds, assuring them that his message would continue to unfold. She introduced the handful of teachers Dr. Green had recognized worthy to carry on his work. Elizabeth St. John was one of those. She had left the Christian Science church in 1980, soon after meeting Dr. Green, and shortly became one his most sought-after lecturers.

That Wednesday night was Elizabeth St. John's final public lecture before beginning her concentrated three-day retreat. She sat in her hotel suite meditating, opening herself to the Spirit so that her talk would be from that Divine Source within, and not personal ego. Her face glowed softly, reflecting the peace and tranquility she was experiencing. Her light brown hair fell loosely to her shoulders, cut in a way to accentuate its natural waves. Her eyes, when opened, were a piercing pale blue, clear and direct. They spoke of tenderness and strength but revealed none of the suffering she had endured by taking over such an important man's ministry.

The knock on the door to her suite brought her out of her meditation. Marjorie Cummings, a plain woman in her mid-sixties, who had been Elizabeth's traveling companion for the last two and a half years, answered the door and brought Larry Graff into the suite. Here was a man Elizabeth could get involved with. He was tall and trim, and his ruggedly tanned body bore evidence of years at sea and a life in the tropics. His close-cropped silver hair gave him an air of distinction and authority, as if he could protect her from the violence of the world while at the same time understand its underlying cause and scientifically explain why it wouldn't touch her. Elizabeth enjoyed his company, but always held back in the presence of such raw masculine power dressed in the politeness of a fast-fading era. Larry was seventy-one and rich. His upbringing had been prep schools and Ivy League colleges prior to World War II. Elizabeth thought he lacked the crudeness of the typical rich American.

Elizabeth stood up as Larry bowed to her, gently took her hand and kissed it in the European manner. "Your devotees await, and I am more than honored to escort you into the hall," he said without a hint of pretense.

"Thank you, Larry. You're always so gracious when I come to Hawaii."

Larry was more than flattered.

"How's the preparation for your trip? I trust it's going smoothly."

Marjorie picked up Elizabeth's shawl, and followed them to the elevator. Not wanting to let an opportunity pass for a private moment with his teacher, Larry said, "Jason is beginning to think like a sailor. I'm proud to have had a hand in transforming him."

Elizabeth just nodded, not willing to be drawn into a full conversation. Her mind was already turning within so that her message that night would be spiritually based, not coming from human opinion. "He's starting to notice all the little things that constantly need to be done around the boat," Larry continued, "and does his best to take care of them. The month in the yard was good for him. We let him stay with us for ten days during the worst of the refitting, but he preferred being on his own, even if it meant staying on the boat with all the dirt and jets taking off overhead."

"Have you been paying him?" Elizabeth broke her practice of not engaging in "this world" before a class session.

"I've been keeping a log of his hours. Remember, our deal was that he would be working for his trip."

"I think you should give him some pocket money. Otherwise he's going to feel like a slave."

Larry covered his reaction well. "He's your son. You know him better than I do, but our agreement didn't include me paying him any money. It becomes so messy with taxes and all. Besides, he said he has some money."

"Larry, this whole trip is going to be an out-picturing of your consciousness. If you prepare properly, it will open your eyes to the wonders of the Kingdom. If not, you will face the brunt of material cause and effect. Do you meditate with Jason?"

"No. We haven't been together at those times."

"I'd ask him to meditate with you at any time."

The elevator arrived at the lobby and Elizabeth and her party quickly made their way to the ballroom. Most people were already seated inside the auditorium, silently waiting for the Spirit of God to fill the hall. A few people were milling about in the foyer, looking at books and the recorded tapes and CDs Elizabeth had for sale. When they saw her they quickly entered the ballroom.

Elizabeth could feel the love and peace flowing from the auditorium. What was it that drew all these people from the far corners of the planet to spend their days and nights with her in a hotel ballroom when the beauty of Hawaii stood just outside? She knew the answer and felt the Divine Presence, which was the real draw. There was more satisfaction, fulfillment, and excitement in this room than in all the attractions of Waikiki. She knew the Spirit of God, within each individual in the audience, was breaking through the constraints of human thought, and that knowledge gave her a bigger thrill than anything else on Earth.

Elizabeth chuckled to herself. If her followers ever caught the secret, a secret Elizabeth had been revealing all of her adult life to anyone who would listen, they wouldn't scurry away in fear or awe. Nor would they puff themselves up when they were seen with her. But alas, that secret was as hard to hold on to as a squirming child.

It certainly wasn't her personality that drew them to the workshop. It never ceased to amaze her when that feeling of peace came. She detached from all the pains, concepts, hopes, and desires of those around her. Her countenance glowed with an inner light and her fifty-one-year-old face became timeless and ageless.

Before entering the ballroom, Elizabeth stopped and turned to Larry. "If you want Jason as a talisman on this voyage of yours, you better recognize the depth of what he has to offer."

Without waiting for his response, she entered the ballroom, walked down the aisle with the grace and beauty of a runway model, and took her place at the podium. After a few more moments of meditation, when the silence filling the room virtually thundered, she began to speak.

It was dark when David woke up. He was hot and sweaty and a little disoriented by the slight movement of the yacht. It took a moment for him to remember where he was and why he was on a boat in Hawaii. In the last four months he had slept in dozens of beds, on trains, been in eight European countries, three in North Africa, and hitchhiked the Anatolian coast of Turkey. He'd been in every major art museum and gallery in Europe, seen the great ruins of long dead empires, felt a great presence in the

Hagia Sophia, and a deep peace in John the Apostle's cave on Patmos. It took a moment for him to remember why he was on a boat in Hawaii.

Jason had left a note: "Meet me at the Hau Terrace in the Kaimana Beach Hotel. 8:30 sharp!" Great. That meant long pants and shoes, not what David was in the mood for. But this was Jason's gig, so he locked up the yacht and set off for Waikiki.

Jason sat at a table next to the neoclassical railing that separated the Hau Tree Lanai from the sand. A grand hau tree made a roof over the terrace with its low hanging branches.

"How was the surf?" David asked as he sat down.

"Okay. How was your nap?"

"Good."

"I recommend the *opakapaka*," Jason handed David a menu. "It's a snapper; their specialty."

"What about you?"

"I've eaten. Lillian will be joining us for dessert."

"Who's Lillian?" Jason had not mentioned a girlfriend.

"You'll like her. She's one of Mom's students and helps edit her manuscripts. She's English. She's smart, studied acting at the Royal Academy of Dramatic Art, writes well, loves art. Did I say she's absolutely beautiful?"

"Are you in love?"

"Could be. You won't be able to take your eyes off her."

"You *are* in love!"

"Hey, what about you? You wouldn't travel all over Europe for months if you had a steady girl."

"I'm a patient man."

Jason was no longer paying attention to David. His eyes were drawn to the entrance by an invisible force and he rose to greet it.

David followed Jason with his eyes to the most beautiful person he'd ever seen. She stood at the top of the stairs like a goddess, her gaze dancing off the mere mortals dining below. She then floated down into the lanai like a cool breeze in the humid night. She wore a colorful Hawaiian-print blouse, unbuttoned to reveal a tanned chest and a bit of cleavage. She was perfectly proportioned and glided across the floor into Jason's arms. Suddenly they were the only people in the room. Jason pulled her narrow waist tight to his and kissed her deeply. It was a kiss reserved for lovers whose love was so exclusive that no one else existed in that moment. It was a kiss that made David feel like this romantic spot was destined to bring lovers together, heal all discord, and bridge the differences between people of every culture.

Maybe it would even bring David love.

Jason walked the goddess over to their table. David stood up, totally distracted by her presence, and Jason introduced his love to his best friend.

"Meet Lillian Harvey."

David had barely said hello when Jason continued, "How was the class tonight, as if I need to ask?"

Lillian radiated light. Jason gave her one more quick but telling kiss before he sat her across from David.

"Your mother was in top form today," Lillian said in her proper British accent.

"This is Dave Walker, my best friend."

David stood again and Lillian offered her hand without getting up. "Dave, so nice to meet you."

David smiled and took her hand gently. "J.J. never mentioned he had a girlfriend."

"J.J. and Davy ... I bet you two were holy terrors. Why do I suddenly feel like an outsider?"

"You shouldn't," David sat back down. "J.J. and I haven't seen each other for a few years."

"Davy was the terror. I was the good one," Jason said, smiling broadly.

Lillian ignored him. "I don't believe that." She smiled at David, sizing him up like she would a costar in a play. "I just wanted to say hello. I've got an early class with your mum tomorrow."

"Don't go yet. The coconut pie is out of this world," Jason was basking in her presence.

"That's what I've heard. Tell me Dave, do you follow a spiritual path?"

"I don't follow any religion. If anything, art is my religion."

Lillian then looked directly into David's eyes. "Didn't you and J.J. practice some sort of pagan ritual in your Indian lodge?"

Yanked from his heady intoxication with Lillian, David thought, *Oh my God, she thinks I'm a fag!* Flicking Jason an icy stare, David said to him, "I'll have some coconut pie ..." finishing the sentence in his head ... *to throw in your face.*

"I thought you and J.J. meditated together until you went to Orange County and became a Baptist! You see, J.J. has told me *all* about you." Lillian relished the surprise on David's face.

"I did keep *some* secrets, Dave," Jason said.

David was livid but chose to keep it hidden. Some things about Jason never changed.

"I like what Dr. Green says about lineage and background," Lillian murmured in her smooth voice, which caused one to lean in closer to hear every word. "That until we no longer identify with human parentage, race, nationality, and all that, we won't experience the fullness of Spirit."

"I guess I won't be trading on my name, then," Jason teased.

"I thought you and your mother were already a team," David replied.

"She's the main event. I just fill in as needed. Besides, I'm not sure I want to follow in her footsteps. There are plenty of people out there who want that kind of work and relish the guru business."

"You should take a close look at yourself and find out what your greatest talent is," Lillian said rather sternly, "and then follow it."

"Should?" Jason said. "Too many people have my life planned out for me. What I ultimately do with my life will have nothing to do with how others see me."

"I'm sorry, honey. It's just that you have such an incredible and unique way of explaining mystical principles that I can't imagine you doing anything else." She turned to David. "Every time we're with a group of people and the conversations turn to spiritual things, as soon as Jason says anything, people want more. And these are sophisticated people. I work in the entertainment industry, and I've introduced Jason to many of my friends." She turned back and faced Jason. "You can deny it if you want, but someday you're going to have to grow up and accept the challenge."

Jason looked at David, and then at Lillian, and then began to laugh. "So, I'm God's gift to the world. I guess I can deal with that."

His remark clearly annoyed Lillian. "I wasn't joking, Jason. Recognition is a very important spiritual principle. Look, you two have a lot to catch up on. I'm going back to the hotel. I want to keep pondering Elizabeth's lecture and keep it alive in my mind."

She got up and left, but before she reached the exit, she turned and walked back to the table like she was taking a curtain call. Every eye was on her, particularly David's. Her long legs and shapely body carried her across the room effortlessly and her silk skirt moved around her ankles like pools of sea foam. Her jeweled sandals and painted toes were like tropical fish in rhythm with the surge of the sea. Her auburn hair framed an English face kissed gently by the sun; her sea-blue eyes became oases in the sand. At least that's what David saw. She said nothing but bent down and kissed Jason passionately on the lips.

David then watched her vanish up the stairs and into the tropical night.

Jason chuckled, fully aware of Lillian's impact. "Don't worry, you'll get used to the heat."

Chapter 13
Waikiki, Hawaii

Thursday April 27, 1989

David was late to Elizabeth's class. Jason had wanted the two of them to go surfing that morning, but David wanted to take advantage of the opportunity to hear Elizabeth, now the renown Mrs. St. John. The two got into a tiff and Jason left for the North Shore. He wouldn't drop David off at the class, complaining it was out of the way.

David was pissed at Jason's attitude. It was like he was running away from something and didn't care how his behavior affected others. And it was a long walk to the hotel where the class was being held. But it gave David time to think. He didn't understand why Jason didn't participate in his mother's work in Hawaii. Was it because of Lillian? Or was it because of their pending trip? David felt a dynamic taking place that made him uncomfortable. David had never heard Elizabeth teach before and he was curious. He wondered if the few times he'd gone to the Christian Science Sunday school with Jason had affected him. On closer thought, it was Elizabeth who had impressed him. Her gentle power and ability to keep calm in the midst of chaos was something David wanted to learn. Was Christian Science really "a religion without balls" as his father had said, something to be purged of? Or did it reveal one of the basic teachings of early Christians—spiritual healing? Now, after seeing the religious art in Europe, David was ready to find out what mysticism was all about.

And of course, Lillian would be there.

When he arrived, the lady at the registration table outside the Stevenson Ballroom didn't want to let David join the class. He wasn't pre-paid. He wasn't on her list. And Mrs. St. John was already inside meditating.

"Then let's not waste time." David wrote out a check.

"Have you studied Dr. Green's books or heard Mrs. St. John's recordings? Those are the prerequisites for the class, and you must attend all the sessions," the woman told him. She had snowy white hair and a grandmotherly look, but her attitude was as stubborn as a bureaucrat.

"Yes to both questions," David lied. "And I've met Dr. Green. I apologize for being late. I just arrived in the islands last night and would love to be able to enter the room and join in the meditation before Mrs. St. John begins speaking." He tore the check from his checkbook and slipped it to her as if it were a bribe.

The ballroom was filled, and David scanned the crowd for Lillian. There she was, meditating in the back with an empty chair beside her. He slipped in and sat next to her. It was profoundly quiet, and Lillian didn't seem to notice him.

Elizabeth's session dealt with breaking down the barriers that prevented people from experiencing their spiritual heritage. She covered all the pleasures and distractions that divert one's attention from witnessing the activity of Spirit. David couldn't help but think she was talking to Jason out on the North Shore surfing perfect little four-foot waves. David presumed surfing was one of those distractions.

But then, to be fair, so would sailing, painting, and any other human activity. She went on to point out that there wasn't a wall between daily life and spiritual awareness. The goal was to come to the point where anyone could see the Divine in every experience. In doing that, what would seem evil and destructive would dissolve in the face of Spirit, for in Spirit there is no adversity, only love. There came a point where David no longer heard her words. He was enveloped in a profound peace, and when the session ended, Lillian gently nudged him back into "this world." She motioned to him and he followed her out.

They found a table in the shade of a coconut palm in the courtyard of the hotel and ordered fruit drinks. Lillian took David's hand and looked deeply into his eyes.

"I'm very glad you're here with Jason," she said seriously. "I haven't been able to get past his façade of spiritual detachment, at least since I arrived. I think this trip is a disaster. It's nothing but a lot of male ego bent on proving itself. Have you met Larry?"

David hadn't.

"A more pompous, arrogant, egotistical man I've never met. I'm sorry to say that right after such a beautiful lesson, but every time I see him, I shiver," she continued. "He's attending the class, you know."

"Wow. Strange..."

"I knew it was you when you sat beside me in class. I didn't want to interrupt my meditation to acknowledge you, but I was thrilled to see you there. J.J.'s told me all about you, well—you know that—but you've got to convince him not to go on this voyage. I can't bear the thought of what Larry might do when he's away from civilization, out to sea."

She took a breath. David didn't know how to respond. "He's cruel, David. Not many see it. I don't think Elizabeth does. But then she only sees the perfect and the true. I've known men like him before. The West End is full of them. They're very good actors; very good at burying that unpleasant side of themselves—

and I'm not talking about actors per se. There are men who have that dark side, and unfortunately, I can see it. I've met men the world reveres, and tremble at what they do when freed from the civilizing constraints of women and society. Jason has none of that. He's a true innocent, and that's part of what I love about him, but I don't think he can survive in the long run with a man like that. Larry will kill his soul."

A thousand thoughts jammed David's mind. They ran the gamut from suddenly and completely falling in love with her, to thinking that she was another off-the-wall weirdo, and the reason why he seldom attended these types of events. She let go of his hand and took a long drink of her juice.

"Do you think Larry has ulterior motives?" David asked.

"Not at all. I don't think Larry is aware of his shadow side; he's in such denial. He's a weak man, David. He's doing this trip to win his daughter. When she arrives, you two better beware."

"I appreciate your warning, but I don't think J.J. is going to back out now. He's made a commitment and knowing him, he never breaks his word short of death."

"I know. I just wanted to warn you because J.J. won't listen to me. I mean, he *does*, but with all of his spiritual awareness, he relegates all of this to fear and dismisses it. But he's going to have to face that man, and I pray he doesn't lose his life doing it."

David was taken back by Lillian's warning. Her revelation added another layer to the undercurrents of rebellion and resistance he was picking up from Jason. But from his experience there were always issues people were unwilling to bring to light. That Lillian was willing just made her more beautiful in David's eyes.

"I'm jealous" David said. "I've never seen two people so much in love, and so reluctant to just accept it and enjoy it."

"Don't tell Jason what I said... Or maybe you should. I know he loves me, but he's so independent and self-complete that sometimes all I can think of is to play hard to get. I've known him five years and knew at our first meeting that we would be married. That was three lecture tours with his mother and one girlfriend ago. But he keeps coming back to me. This time, though, I'm frightened."

"As Elizabeth said this morning, all we can do is let go and trust in Divine Love, which has always known our needs and fulfills them." Lillian's eyes welled up with tears with David's reminder of what Elizabeth said. It was all he could do not to reach across the table and take Lillian's hand.

"I love him too and I won't let anything happen to him."

"Oh David, I know. I feel like you're family. You really are Jason's brother, you know." With tears streaming down her face, Lillian got up and left.

David didn't go to the afternoon sessions. The morning lessons and his talk with Lillian had given him all he could handle. Impulsively, he rented a convertible at the hotel and drove around the island. When he got to the boat that evening, sunburned and tired, Jason was sitting in the cockpit playing his ukulele.

"So you played hooky, too," he said.

"Needed to think about what your mother taught this morning."

"Lillian got to you, didn't she?"

"We talked after the class."

"She told me. You know, this is going to be an incredible trip. I think it'll be one of those defining moments of our lives."

Jason looked at David with a certainty that David had seen many times before. It was the same knowing that David had seen when they'd been inducted into the Order of the Arrow. "Are you taking me on another rite of passage?" David asked his friend.

Jason laughed. "Which one stands out to you?"

"I guess your fifteenth birthday when we met Dr. Green."

◉ ◉ ◉

Los Angeles

July, 1980

It was a warm July afternoon and the first good swell of the summer had arrived at Malibu—the kind of wave every surfer dreamt about.

June Walker had driven David up to the Palisades especially for Jason's birthday—something they had always celebrated together. She had no idea that her son would be whisked off to some mystical guru. Birthdays for her boys—she looked at Jason as part of her family too—would be hotdogs on the beach and surfing. And David had no idea that he'd be a witness to one of Jason's early spiritual breakthroughs.

The boys sat in the back seat of Elizabeth's two-year-old Pontiac. Elizabeth's friend Gloria, the fourth person in the car, knew Dorothy Delany, Dr. Green's hostess in Los Angeles and the one who had arranged the party.

David constantly reminded Jason of the sacrifice he was making in the name of friendship by putting on a borrowed coat and tie from Jason and taking tea with some guru. "Will he be wearing saffron robes?" David whispered to Jason.

"Gloria hasn't mentioned robes, but I think he has a shaved head and wears a jewel between his eyes," Jason replied.

"I heard that, J.J." Gloria turned to give the boys a stern look. She was made up like she was going to the Academy Awards. Her raspy cigarette voice and don't-mess-with-me attitude contradicted the sparkle in her eye. "Actually, he's become an Indian sadhu and wears nothing at all. He's completely renounced this world and I want you boys to honor that. Whatever you do, don't stare at his nakedness."

"Gloria! That's taking it a little too far," Elizabeth chided.

"Have you ever met him, Mom?" Jason asked.

"You know I haven't, but I've seen pictures of him, and Gloria is totally out of line right now."

"You know we're not going into the presence of some exotic magician. Dr. Green reminds me of a studio head I once knew. If you let his reputation intimidate you, you'll miss what he has to offer."

"I didn't know you'd met him, Gloria," Elizabeth pressed.

"I've had letters from him, and I've heard his tapes."

"I say we just be ourselves and let J.J. enjoy his birthday." Elizabeth had pronounced the current attitude; she always set the tone, and it was amazing how willingly everyone followed along.

David looked over at his buddy and rolled his eyes. Suddenly this birthday party was losing some of its luster and it hadn't even started.

"Did you say Dorothy's apartment was on Franklin?" Elizabeth asked Gloria.

"Yes, between Laurel Canyon and La Brea."

They were winding down Sunset Boulevard and passed the Beverly Hills Hotel on their way from the Palisades to Hollywood. The car grew quiet as Elizabeth concentrated on her driving, taking the curves like a racecar driver. There was a purpose to her driving, as if the act of maneuvering a car through the hills, if done with total dedication, would bring all the passengers into the proper frame of mind to meet Solomon Green.

Dr. Solomon Green was, at that time, an internationally known author and teacher who had introduced mysticism and meditation to Western thought in post-World War II California.

His work had opened the door to the spiritual revolutions of the late 1960s that had unlocked the minds of young people to the possibilities of spiritual healing and a world living in peace. Dr. Green had a large following as a Christian Science practitioner, which meant that he was an effective healer and counselor, and when he began to present mystical ideas to his clients, the Church excommunicated him and sought to discredit his work.

Elizabeth was also a journal practitioner in the Christian Science movement at that time, and to meet someone with Dr. Green's reputation could jeopardize her standing in the Church. In the Christian Science religion, being a "journal practitioner" meant that Elizabeth had been "class taught" in the faith by an authorized teacher and had had numerous testimonies presented to the Mother Church in Boston verifying the healings she had performed. Her position as a leader in the local church, as well as her reputation as a practitioner, excluded tinkering with any other metaphysical or transcendental teachings. The intent behind that regulation, according to Mary Baker Eddy—the founder of the Christian Science movement in the nineteenth century—was to keep the faithful pure from conflicting thoughts so as to be the more perfect instrument of God's healing grace.

Elizabeth fully embraced the tenets of the church—up to a point. Her life was good. She had status in her church, was respected in the community, and loved by her family. She knew how to resolve most problems metaphysically, if not spiritually, and yet there was something driving her to explore new areas of spiritual thinking. Jason encouraged his mother's search. He wanted to know the secrets of life too! Mysticism and meditation were their current passions. They would secretly meditate in the afternoons when Jason got home from school. Today this sounds so common, so normal. But for a Christian Scientist to meditate like that, at that time, would be like a Jew celebrating Easter with a Virginia ham.

The church had very strict tenets against what Elizabeth and her son were doing. Any Eastern religious practices were not allowed. Theirs was a religion based on the scientific understanding of primitive Christianity and effective prayer. Their focus was to "have that mind which was in Christ Jesus." By developing that mind, they would be praying aright, and with proper prayer they could meet every human need with the same attitude as their "way-shower," Christ Jesus. Meditation, psychic phenomena, the occult, spiritualism, and contact with the other side were distractions from their purpose. All they needed to practice their religion was the wisdom of the Bible and the insights found in the writings of Mary Baker Eddy.

Christian Science is also an individualistic religion. Each member of the church is responsible for his or her understanding of the truth. All of this Jason understood. When his mother began listening to Dr. Green's taped lectures, things began to change. Jason and his mother meditated instead of prayed. They stopped using affirmations and denials—affirming the truth and denying that the problem was real. They sought the tangible experience of the presence of God, and that changed their concept of Mind. Thus, in the eyes of the church what they were doing was heresy.

David had seen Jason change over the fourteen months since his family had moved to Costa Mesa, and David wanted to know what Jason was learning. David quickly realized that the Baptist way was not for him. He wanted to be like Jason, unconventional and independent. But gurus? Masters? Whatever you called them; they were off the charts for him. That Jason even wanted to meet Dr. Green, rather than spend his fifteenth birthday surfing with his buddies, spoke volumes.

Dorothy's apartment looked out over old Hollywood to the city below. The living room opened onto a balcony filled with semi-tropical plants and palms. Viewing the city was like looking through a jungle to a dismal future. The day was smoggy, and the plants helped clear the air, even if they did make the living room dark. Dorothy's furniture was comprised of heavy Eastern European antiques, and as Dorothy met the St. John party at the door, her slender pale appearance, dressed completely in black, gave the impression of a saint having transposed herself into the city of the future but unable to abandon her familiar trappings from the past. She graciously brought her guests into the living room, where Dr. Green sat in a garnet colored wing chair. Half a dozen of his followers were seated in the room, and they all seemed to know one another.

David felt completely out of place. He started noticing Dorothy's art as a way to connect, but it heightened the foreign feeling he'd had when he walked in. Dorothy's taste tended toward early Renaissance religious paintings in dull gilt frames. By the looks of things, he knew it was going to be a very long afternoon. He nudged Jason to signal a wipeout, but Jason had locked eyes with Dr. Green and there was fire between them. David looked at Elizabeth and she too was locked into the silent communication with the master. For the longest moment no one moved or said a thing. Dorothy, ever gracious, waited for a barely noticed nod from Dr. Green before introducing her new guests.

Solomon Green looked like a Jewish jeweler from Sixth Street in downtown Los Angeles. He was short; his feet barely touched the floor when he sat. He had close- cropped wiry hair streaked with gray, heavy black-framed glasses, and a huge midriff. His coat was unbuttoned, revealing trousers that were belted halfway up his torso. He wore a floral print tie favored by old time movie moguls (Gloria was right) and a sparkling white shirt. He didn't get up when introduced to Jason, but he did shake the boy's hand with a firm, friendly grip.

"I understand it's your birthday, Jason," he said with a glint of amusement. "Can't imagine anything more delightful than being dragged before a bunch of old hens for a tea, no offense ladies."

"I did want to meet you," he replied.

"So we've met. Would you like to go now?"

"Not really. I heard there was a birthday cake here somewhere. Wouldn't want to miss that."

"Tell me, why did you want to meet me?"

"I like to meditate. My mom said it was your idea."

"That's flattering, but meditation is hardly my idea. The Orient has been meditating for thousands of years. What does it mean to you?"

"My mom says ..."

"No," Dr. Green interrupted. "I don't want to know what your mom has told you about meditating. I want to know what it means to you."

"I suppose it's like praying without talking," Jason said. Dr. Green had suddenly become animated. He no longer looked like an old Jew; his appearance changed with his attitude, which was full of life and curiosity. He was totally interested in Jason.

"Well, how is God going to hear you if you don't say anything?"

"He knows all. What's there to say? I think it's more important to listen," Jason said. The others in the room began to notice Jason. Dorothy sat on the arm of Dr. Green's chair and paid close attention to the exchange.

"Then meditating is listening?" Dr. Green asked.

"In a way. Is this a birthday quiz?"

"No, no. Mrs. St. John, come sit closer." An Asian woman who was sitting next to Dr. Green got up without hesitation and gave Elizabeth her chair. Dr. Green leaned over close to her and said, "Have you and Jason been practicing meditation as I outlined in my book?"

"In essence," she answered. "We light candles and bring out our meditating cushions. There's a beautiful view from our house and we sit looking at the view until we feel the silence..."

"No music? No mantra?"

"No. As you've said in your book, we watch our thoughts and our breath until our minds are still."

"Is this what you do, Jason?" Dr. Green turned suddenly to Jason. He tensed up. It was like being called on by the teacher after you'd already answered the question and you thought you were off the hook, but suddenly were not.

"Yeah, sort of."

"Well, do you or don't you? Meditation isn't a kind of, sort of, practice. Do you play a musical instrument?"

"The guitar."

"Do you practice?"

"Sort ..."

"No, no, no! Do you practice?"

"Yes."

"Every day?"

"Yes."

"Do you enjoy it? Are you good enough to get pleasure from it?"

"Yes."

"Good. Meditation should give you the same kind of feeling you get when you've figured out a new song and can play it perfectly."

Jason, who had been standing next to his mother, sat down on the floor in front of Dr. Green. David sat down too, leaning up against Elizabeth's chair. Elizabeth subtly put her hand on Jason's shoulder, gently relaxing him and signaling to him that this was not a contest. She had heard of this kind of teaching, but never witnessed it. In her experience, the teacher presented the material and explained it. Dr. Green seemed to be forcing Jason to articulate one of the deeper aspects of mysticism. Her son was just turning fifteen, a little young to face a learned master. But then Jesus debated in the temple at twelve. That must have been some bar mitzvah.

"What happens when you look out at your view? What goes on in your mind?" Dr. Green's tone was insistent, but kind. He really wanted to know. It felt like he wanted to get inside Jason and fill him with all the wisdom and truth of the ages.

"Well, I know the view so well. We watch the sun rise over the city and ocean every morning. But I know it so well that I start not seeing it. It's there, but it isn't. There's a point where I close my eyes, and then I'm more aware of my thoughts. That's weird, isn't it? When I'm looking at the view my mind is quieter than when I close my eyes."

"When you look at your view, what are you seeing out there?" Dr. Green asked.

"You mean the queen's necklace and the ocean?"

"Are you aware of what you are observing?"

"Of course I am."

"Where is what you are observing?"

"It's ..." Suddenly Jason paused as if a something was dawning within him. It was a look David had seen in geometry class. "I'm seeing what my mind expects me to see."

"Is it the truth?"

"Sometimes."

"Explain."

"It's not the truth when it isn't harmonious and perfect. But when it's beautiful and clear and you can see the sun rising behind Mt. San Jacinto, it's more like God."

"You still haven't answered me. Where is what you are seeing?"

Jason thought for a long moment before answering. David was totally stimulated by the exchange and had dozens of answers running through his head, also many questions. Was this a trick question? Why was Dr. Green harping on "where"?

We all know where the world is. What was he trying to pull out of Jason? Was he impressed? David thought everyone else was. Finally, Jason answered. "It's all inside of me."

A slight smile crossed Dr. Green's face. He turned to Elizabeth and tenderly patted her arm. "Keep meditating with him. You're doing a wonderful job and your boy is going to be well-equipped to handle the slings and arrows of this world."

Dr. Green got up and suddenly turned back into a Jewish grandpa. "Isn't this a birthday party? I'd like some cake!"

With that, all the ladies who had been hovering around him got up and brought out the food. Dorothy properly introduced herself to Elizabeth and Jason. She was impressed with Jason. And then the food arrived, not only a birthday cake for Jason, but cookies, strudels, tortes, and every variety of pastries. Then came the ice cream, not in cardboard containers, but already scooped out and frozen in crystal bowls. And then there were toppings for the ice cream: hot fudge, hot caramel, marshmallow, raspberries, and strawberry sauce. These old ladies knew how to throw a party. They also knew what Dr. Green liked, and his eyes lit up brighter than Jason's upon seeing the spread.

◉ ◉ ◉

David smiled at the memory. That had been a beginning of sorts, for both boys, and also for Elizabeth. Suddenly he was very glad he had come to Hawaii, and glad that he would be accompanying Jason on a new adventure. For what was life, after all, without an adventure with one's best mate?

Chapter 14
Ala Wai Yacht Harbor, Honolulu

Friday April 28, 1989

The next day Jason left again to surf the North Shore. The swell had been building overnight. He wanted David to go with him. "Be spontaneous!" But David had paid for Elizabeth's class and wanted to be there.

The lesson that second morning was about spiritual responsibility. Are we responsible for others? What is our attitude when we witness discord and suffering? David knew the principles that Jason lived by. There were only two: Don't accept what you see at face value and go surfing. Was Jason really that free? Or was he simply running away? David didn't get it.

David skipped the afternoon sessions again and went to the Honolulu Academy of Art, one of the most beautiful small museums in the United States. He was to meet Lillian there after the class. He was sitting between a pair of Chinese lions when he saw her get off the bus.

"That lesson this morning exhausted me," Lillian said as David got up to greet her.

They entered a tranquil world of courtyards and quiet galleries. Lillian loved the Hawaiian section, especially the feather capes and helmets.

"I think this is your real church," she told David as they stood in front of a Hawaiian *tapa*. "From what J.J. said you kind of abandoned religion when you moved away and became an artist."

"I don't know if I ever accepted religion in the first place. Doesn't man make God in his own image? Look at these gods." He moved along to a display of carved Hawaiian figures. "Could you worship one of these with any conviction?"

"So you've been an atheist all along?"

"Not at all. I've met Dr. Green, and there's always been something about Jason, and Elizabeth too."

"You met Dr. Green?" Lillian said, shocked.

"I went with J.J. on his fifteenth birthday."

"Don't you know how special that is?"

"I'm not too big on this guru thing."

"Are you aware that Dr. Green may have lifted you into a higher consciousness just by being in his presence?"

David was not sure what she meant by that. They walked through more courtyards and ended up at the café for tea, but it was closed.

"The waves must have been good." David and Lillian sat on the steps in front of the academy entrance waiting for Jason to pick them up. "It's probably the last swell of the season."

Lillian took David's hand in both of hers. "I hope I can see your work."

There were sparks in that gentle gesture and for a moment David felt a love he'd never known. How could Jason be so blind? You can't take this kind of love for granted or you lose it. You can't put any other love before this, like surfing, and expect it will be waiting for you. David pulled his hand away, fighting the physical attraction, and reminding himself that this was the love of a friend in Spirit. Still, he was very attracted to Lillian.

The security guard locked up the academy behind them.

"Jason's not coming. Let's go."

"You sure?" David said.

"I'm sure." They got up and walked through Thomas Square toward King Street to catch a bus back to Waikiki. There was a farmer's market at the *makai* end of the square.

"Are you hungry?" David asked.

"Famished."

"I'll cook you dinner," he said as he looked at the fresh tomatoes. "I learned this wonderful summer pasta recipe in Naples."

"I love Italian," Lillian said. They bought locally grown tomatoes, zucchini, and garlic, and there was even a stall that sold herbs and spices. In five minutes they had everything they needed for dinner except bread and pasta. They waited a while for the bus, but it was running so late that they decided to walk back to the boat. They passed a mom-and-pop store where David bought the bread and pasta. He noticed a nice bottle of Chianti that he thought about buying but he wasn't sure if Lillian drank. When he got up to the clerk Lillian had already bought the wine—same brand and everything.

"I don't know if you drink wine, but I can't eat Italian food without some Chianti," she said. David just smiled and nodded.

When they arrived at the boat, they were hot, and their feet hurt. The tide was out, and the deck was well below the pier.

"This is going to be tricky." Lillian looked at the gap between the pier and the boat. They put their packages down and David grabbed hold of the shrouds and stepped on a mooring line to bring the boat close to the pier.

"Jump on board when you can."

Lillian did, and as soon as she was on the yacht, she unhooked the lifeline. The problem was that David had shifted his grip from the shroud to the line and when it went slack he fell in.

"What on earth happened?"

David swam to the channel. "Over here!" He took off his tennies and threw them on the deck.

"You did that on purpose." Lillian smiled.

"Not really." He pulled off his jeans, rolled them in a ball, and tossed them up to the boat. They didn't make it.

"Try again," Lillian said. He did and she reached out to grab them. But she bent over too far, lost her balance and joined David in the water. David reached down and grabbed her, not knowing how well she could swim, and she came up laughing and hung onto David. He had to turn his gaze away for fear of getting too intimate.

"Just float," he said.

David tossed his jeans over the stern line, took off his shirt, and then helped Lillian out of her dress. They floated out to the middle of the channel. The water was clear and an azure blue. They looked back at *Mata'i* and noticed how she listed to port, the water just touching the white of her hull over the deep blue waterline stripe that divided the white of the hull from the rust-colored bottom paint. The yacht looked small from that angle. Her name was engraved in the wooden banner attached to the transom. Hanging over the transom, mounted on a pair of boomkins—short booms that protruded from each corner of the stern—was the Aries self-steering gear.

"That little piece of equipment," David said pointing to the Aries "will be a lifesaver."

"Then I shall bless it and remember it the whole time you're away."

Floating on their backs, their hands and feet touching, David thought he was in heaven. They stayed that way for what seemed like hours. David felt that Lillian was as content and fulfilled in that moment as he was. Supported by that beautiful warm water, nothing else in the world mattered. Without either of them saying anything, David felt a union and connection with her that would never leave him. He couldn't betray his trust to Jason, or to Lillian for that matter, and he fought to hold back the natural outcome of their touch.

"How are we going to get out?" Lillian asked him.

"Well, we could swim around to the beach and walk back."

"Not in our underwear. Besides I don't really swim."

"We could wait until the tide comes in and climb up on the pier."

"So when would that be?"

"At least two hours."

"Forget it." Lillian began to look a little concerned. "Come on. I'm getting cold and suddenly it's kind of creepy out here."

David took her hand and the two of them swam back to the boat and stopped under the aft mooring line. David took hold of the line, pulled it down and stepped on it. From there he could reach the taffrail and pull himself on board.

"I can't do that," Lillian said.

David ignored her, opened the cover to the dinghy, and brought out the boarding ladder. "Swim to the other side of the boat," he said as he hung the ladder over the side.

Lillian loved David's pasta dish. They lounged in the cockpit, enjoying a second glass of Chianti as the afterglow of the sunset turned the sky a thousand shades of pale until there was only the faintest glow outlining the Waianae Mountains. Their clothes hung on the lifelines, and Lillian wore an old *pareu* David had found below. David was in his trunks.

Jason walked down the pier next to the boat carrying his surf-board. He stopped when he saw them in the cockpit drinking wine.

"Permission to come aboard?" he asked. David couldn't tell if Jason was joking or mad.

"Come off it J.J. Don't be a jerk." Lillian picked up on J.J.'s attitude.

"I've always wanted to live in Camelot. The ending kind of sucked, though."

"David cooked dinner for me. Wasn't that nice? Get yourself a glass of wine and enjoy the last of the sunset with us," Lillian said.

Jason jumped on deck and stowed his board against the lifelines. He gave Lillian a long passionate kiss. "Don't mind if I do."

"I fell in the water trying to get onboard," David said to whomever was listening.

Jason got his wine and sat close to Lillian. "Was it fun?"

"Was what fun?" Lillian answered rather tartly.

"The Academy."

"I loved it. Are you going to surf again tomorrow?"

"Why? You want another date with Davy?"

Lillian took her dress off the lifeline and went below to change. "You're being ridiculous."

Jason moved over, sat next to his friend, and put his feet up on the wheel. "I don't know why I react like that. It was just the sunset and the wine."

"We did have fun today." David said, and immediately knew it was the wrong thing to say. They weren't kids anymore, and though they had more or less the same perspective on life, they were neophytes when it came to love and jealousy.

David thought that Jason was so detached from his emotions that he didn't really care about his relationship with Lillian – or his mother or with David for that matter. Was it Jason's basic lack of fear? It seemed to David to be callous. David never thought of Jason as being insecure about anything, but maybe Lillian was the one to change all that.

"Lillian is perfect for *you*," David told his friend.

Jason finished his wine. "Maybe too perfect. I've never had someone tell me what to do so much. She needs to scratch the word 'should' from her vocabulary."

"What do I need to scratch from my vocabulary?" Lillian said as she came on deck. She was back to being the protégé of Elizabeth St. John with that certain proper attitude and reserve that said 'I have many secrets and you better not get too close.' Somehow in a *pareu* that attitude had disappeared, and she and David clicked. Perhaps that was what ticked off Jason.

"Should," Jason said boldly. "Should, should, should. It's an ugly word and doesn't fit someone with your consciousness and beauty." He took her in his arms and hugged her and tenderly kissed her.

"You shouldn't be so charming," she said playfully, kissing him back on his ear. "I forget everything when I'm in your arms."

"Good night you two." David left in mock disgust and went below to tackle the dishes.

"Don't wait up," Jason called back as he helped Lillian off the boat.

They walked back to her hotel holding hands. Neither of them said much. They felt comfortable together. When they reached the hotel, she kissed him and turned away. "Not tonight, my love."

Chapter 15
Waikiki

Saturday April 29, 1989

On the last day of the "Living Without Fear" seminar, David was already meditating when Lillian arrived. She didn't sit next to him. Larry Graff escorted Elizabeth down to the platform. She sat behind a table covered with a beautiful brocade cloth and an arrangement of tropical flowers that cascaded down the front. In these last sessions, Elizabeth explained how, after a week of presenting mystical principles, she had to turn the students and their meditations toward the world to give the world peace and forgiveness. She taught that these meditations were gifts to the planet, and that serious practitioners of mysticism should do these three meditations every day.

"In the first meditation," Elizabeth said, "just meditate until you feel the presence of God. You should have no goal, no agenda, just the desire to consciously experience a sense of oneness with all life. When you feel that stillness you will have completed your first meditation for the world. Let's all do this now."

David tried to follow what she said. He did feel the atmosphere become incredibly still, yet he couldn't get the image of Lillian off his mind. He tried to do what Jason had told him when they were teenagers—find the spaces between the images and thoughts. That worked for a few moments and then Jason came to mind. *What a jerk*, David thought. *How could someone go surfing and abandon such an important spiritual gathering?*

The word "judgment" came to him and he realized how judgmental he was. Why should he care what Jason was doing? Then his mind went into the serendipity of being in a spiritual retreat, and discovering a part of himself he didn't know existed. Or perhaps it had always been there. Maybe Lillian was right and just having been in Dr. Green's presence had done something to him. None of this had been planned, that much was for sure.

After a long pause, Elizabeth began talking again. "Now in your second meditation, after you have felt the deep stillness of the Spirit, say to yourself, 'This realization of spiritual wholeness nullifies material cause and effect.' You put spiritual law into play, the law of one—one power, one life, and one love—and as you let go of judgment you will see your life manifesting the fruits of the Spirit. So again, let's all do this."

This time David felt the peace descend upon him more quickly.

"Now in your third meditation for the world," Elizabeth said, "attain your realization of the Divine Presence, and then recognize this: 'This realization of spiritual consciousness is opening the human mind to the Truth.' That is all. That is your prayer. That is your gift to the world."

Elizabeth closed her eyes and the depth of stillness in the room became such that David thought everything disappeared— the people, the room, and time. It was something he'd never experienced before. Others had mentioned it—this incredible sense of *being*, yet without any personal attachment. The idea of who he was began to shift. He was still David, but at the same time he was himself without any limitations – nothing to fear. When Elizabeth began to talk again David could barely hear her. Slowly he came back and focused on where he was.

"We cannot go to the world and tell it to be spiritual. Most people are not interested. We cannot tell the average person about the freedom that comes from the discipline of the soul, because they're not willing to put in the work required to experience spiritual fruitage. But our three meditations for the world will break down the resistance to spiritual things, and perhaps in some, instill the desire to know the Truth."

That was how the class ended. Elizabeth thanked the class organizers, her volunteers, and her audience for their attention and willingness to go with her into the consciousness of love. David just sat there, not wanting to get up. Lillian came over and sat next to him. She took his hand and squeezed it. David was quite moved by it all and tried to keep his emotions in check. He squeezed her hand back but couldn't talk. She hugged him, got up, and left.

Elizabeth was standing at the door, still receiving the gratitude and love of her students, when David slid out of his row near the back of the auditorium. He noticed a man standing at Elizabeth's side, drinking in the adulation that spilled off of her. He assumed that was Larry Graff. David joined the line, and when Elizabeth saw him, a big smile filled her face.

"Davy, how wonderful to see you!" She gave him a big hug. "Why didn't you let me know you were coming to the class? I thought you'd be out surfing with Jason."

David just smiled. He still felt like he couldn't talk, and Elizabeth realized what had taken place. She hugged him stronger and David felt her incredible love. Finally, she let him go.

"Larry, this is one of your crew, David Walker."

"It's nice to meet you. Hope Jason has made you comfortable

on the boat." Larry radiated manners and breeding. "I didn't know you were interested in spiritual things. Jason never mentioned it. I thought you and my brother were going to be the two skeptics on the voyage."

He took hold of Elizabeth's arm to escort her from the auditorium.

"Larry, why not include Dave and Jason in our dinner tonight?"

"Well darling, it wouldn't be possible. We'll have plenty of dinners together, won't we, Dave?" Larry patted David's head as he guided Mrs. St. John out.

That night Jason took David to a restaurant and bar that was right out of a Somerset Maugham novel. A collection of South Seas schooners and rotting live-aboard yachts were anchored off the wooden piers fronting the restaurant. The Honolulu airport runways were directly across the lagoon, and when the jets took off, they drowned out everything. The décor was Polynesian kitsch. Dried puffer fish with lights inside hung from the rafters. Posts of carved tikis held up a bamboo ceiling, and live orchid plants grew from the walls. Waitresses in their sarongs and leis moved through the rowdy clientele.

A Hawaiian girl showed the guys to a table near the musicians—a four-piece string band playing traditional Hawaiian music. The crowd was local and loud, singing along with the band. Most of the patrons were drunk. Jason ordered them *poke* and a couple of beers.

"I love this place," Jason said, "And the music is great."

"You don't bring Lillian here, do you?"

"She loves it. At least she pretends to. She felt obligated to go to Larry's party tonight with Mom or she'd be here instead of you."

The band finished their song and a tough looking older man, a Caucasian with a weathered face and thinning hair got up and rang a bell next to the stage. Everybody cheered. The exotic waitresses picked up trays of beer and began giving away drinks. They served the musicians first.

"We'll get another set. Good on Fat," Jason said, referring to the guy who rang the bell.

The musicians started up again -- they were as drunk as the audience. It didn't diminish their playing, though, it made them freer. They were joking, singing "naughty" lyrics—as the locals would say, and rousing the audience. Some girls got up and danced to the erotic lyrics, grinding and thrusting, causing roars of laughter.

"You know what they're singing about?" David asked.

"Not really," Jason said. "I think it's about sex."

David took a long pull on his beer.

"What's going on, J.J.? I'm getting confused."

"What'd you mean?"

"Oh, I don't know. You? Lillian? Your mother? Me?"

Jason took a swig of his beer. "It's complicated."

"Lillian loves you, you know. She told me."

"I know."

"Then why are you so dismissive to her?"

More beers arrived.

Jason took a long pull on his beer and looked at his friend. There was a deep sadness in his eyes. "I'd marry her in a heartbeat; tomorrow if I could. But I have to do this first."

David shook his head. He thought Jason had his priorities reversed.

"I just want you to know how grateful I am you showed up?"

"Thanks. But I'm not looking for your gratitude. I thought we were going to have a good time. That's what I want. So far, I'm glad I came."

"I think Lillian understands," Jason said.

David gave him a look that stated *dream on*.

Chapter 16
Ala Wai Yacht Harbor

Sunday April 30, 1989

The following morning, Jason and David had raging hangovers. They had just finished washing down *Mataʻi* when Larry arrived. His car was filled with boxes of fresh food that would take them through the first ten days of their trip. The boys brought the provisions onboard and Larry gave them their orders for the day; stow all the food, grease the eggs – coating the shells with Vaseline kept the air out and preserved them for over a week without refrigeration – and had David catalog all the canned goods stored under the floorboards. David now saw the side of Larry that Jason had complained about. Wasn't there already a chart that had been made when they'd first stowed the goods? There was, but Larry wanted David to make his own so that he would know where everything was in case they were in an emergency situation, and Larry suddenly needed a can of beans.

The boat was a mess. Jason was still greasing eggs. David had all the floorboards up in the cabin and half the cans out so that they could be put back according to type, something that hadn't been done originally. In the middle of all this Byron arrived. He was right out of *Miami Vice*—silk shirt and pastel colored pants, loafers without socks, gold chains around his neck, and a tan that was as much from a salon as it was from the sun.

Larry introduced the boys to his brother. After their "hellos" Byron said, "See you tomorrow." With that he disappeared.

Larry ducked back below and demanded, "What have you two been doing all day? I expected everything done by the time Byron arrived. Now he has to spend the night in a hotel. I want everything squared away by five o'clock so Byron, Helen and I can have our cocktails and watch the sunset. You two need to be gone by then, and don't come back until after eight."

As Larry stomped off the boat, the boys heard Byron say, "You said the fucking boat was going to be ready."

"Well, excuse me," Larry replied sarcastically.

The pals looked at each other for a moment and then burst out laughing. They had *Mata'i* shipshape by early afternoon, and David took Jason's car for one last tour around the island. He'd heard about a good Mexican restaurant in Haleiwa and needed one last fix before they sailed to the South Pacific.

Late that afternoon, as the sun approached the horizon and people gathered to watch the "green flash," Jason and Lillian dined together at the at the Royal Hawaiian Hotel's beachside restaurant. Jason couldn't take his eyes off the surf. Lillian didn't really mind. After a class like the one Elizabeth had just given, she loved that Jason could feel the silence and let her digest the new spiritual food she'd been feasting on. They both enjoyed being at the edge of the sand, under a pink umbrella, watching the people on the beach as if they were part of a grand play. People on holiday, especially in a resort like Waikiki Beach, seemed to forget that others can see what they're doing. Perhaps they felt freer to do things they wouldn't do at home because nobody knew them here. Sometimes Lillian and Jason would laugh at the same time, look at each other, and then back to the person who had caused their laughter.

A nice-sized set of waves carried dozens of surfers and outrigger canoes toward the sand. A beach catamaran also got a lift from one of the waves and raced toward shore. A crewman on the bow blew a conch shell horn and shouted for the swimmers to move out of the way. The setting sun turned the whole picture into a post card.

"Do you wish you were out there steering that catamaran into the beach?" Lillian asked him.

"Not really. When the waves are up and the beach is packed, it's kind of hairy."

After drinking in the scenery, Lillian said, "I couldn't live here."

"Why not?"

"It's too beautiful. All I'd want to do is sit around looking at the sea." Lillian realized at that moment that she hated the sea. It had never been part of her life and if she were to lose the one she loved to the sea, it would be medieval.

Jason felt the mood change. "What about Mom's book?" He hated always having his mother linked to Lillian.

"It's coming along." she answered. Lillian felt awkward. She was distracted by a very white family parking themselves on the sand in front of them. She wished Jason were truly free—free of Elizabeth, free of Larry, and free to be her lover. Yet she and Jason had not made love. "Your mom's not a very good writer. She's a wonderful teacher, but to put her teaching into a book is a challenge."

"Will you be here when I get back?"

"I don't know."

"You think I'm being selfish, don't you?" Jason said.

"You know how I feel."

"Do you know how I feel?" Jason continued. "I don't want to leave you, either."

Jason looked away, out to the ocean, and Lillian sensed his

dilemma. She took his hand. "I love you, J.J. Let's get a room here. Who'll know?"

And before he knew it, he was on the bed in the last room that the hotel had available that evening, waiting for Lillian to come to him. *Was she as excited as he was?* Jason wondered. He hadn't expected Lillian's spontaneity. Then he began to have second thoughts. Was this the right thing to do? Should they do this the night before his trip? But this was the only opportunity they had. For the first time he doubted himself. Lillian was his soul mate. He knew that, but he also knew he had to wait until the time was right for marriage. He couldn't bind Lillian until he was fully prepared for their life together. Was he being fair? Would this night ruin everything?

Then Lillian walked into the room and into his arms. Everything changed. They explored each other's bodies tenderly and completely. They couldn't stop giggling. Jason took his time, making sure Lillian felt as much pleasure as he did. She opened a new world for him and took him where he hadn't been before. They exhausted each other and awakened as new people.

Chapter 17
Stanford House

Wednesday Midnight, November 2004

I t had been less than forty-eight hours since Jason was seen in the cancer ward at Marsdan Hospital and he was still trying to make sense of the reaction to that event. He wandered through the rooms of his apartment, going from the parlor to the comfortable family room. He sat at the country table and booted up Lillian's computer. He went on the Internet and typed his name in the Google search box. About a million results came up in a fraction of a second. Jason looked at all the statistics on him—birthdate, nationality, spouse, and education—and shut the iBook in disgust. He looked for the television remote, found it, and turned on the TV set. The channel that came on aired an advertisement about his broadcast coming up on Friday. He couldn't escape the news about himself. He turned the television off, grabbed a hoodie, and left his apartment.

Thomas Parker stood at his post outside Jason's door. When Jason came out, he jumped.

"Let's get a cup of coffee, Tommy." Jason strode down the hall toward the elevator. Thomas followed reluctantly, not sure what he should do. A moment later his earpiece came to life with the voice of the watch captain: "What's going on?"

"We're going to the dining room for coffee."

"The dining room is closed."

"The dining room is closed," Thomas repeated.

The elevator door opened, and Jason entered. "Then we'll open it."

When the elevator arrived on the main floor, Jason got out and walked quickly to the dining hall. Thomas, on his heels, muttered into his mouthpiece and asked his boss what to do. The dining room wasn't closed. The large hall had a dozen people in it. A buffet of pastries, cold cuts, and hot drinks were available for the night shift working in the security and media departments. Jason chose a table away from the others and Thomas sat across from him.

"Who's the watch captain tonight?" Jason asked.

"Terry Dolan."

"Tell him to join us on your little mouthpiece there. I'm surprised he didn't know the dining room is open twenty-four hours."

"I think he's coming in now."

An overweight man in his mid-forties with pasty skin and a shaved head walked quickly over to Jason.

"Sit down. Terry is it?" Jason said.

Terry Dolan remained standing. "You're not allowed to be down here, sir."

"Allowed? Do you know who I am?"

"Yes, sir. Mr. Howell prefers that you remain in your flat for your own safety."

"Is Mr. Howell running things around here?"

"He runs the ISD and I just follow orders, sir."

"Tom, were your orders to keep me in my apartment?" Jason asked.

"I was just told to keep an eye on you because of the heightened threat due to the increased crowds," Thomas replied.

"Are there hostile crowds in here?"

"No."

"Am I in danger? Here in the compound?"

"No."

"Then I'm going to have a cup of coffee and some pie and find out more about young Thomas here before I retire. You may go back to the security bunker, Terry."

Terry didn't leave. After a moment, Jason got up and walked over to the buffet. He poured himself a cup of coffee, grabbed a piece of pumpkin pie, returned to the table and sat down. He told Thomas to get something if he wanted. Thomas looked at both Jason and Terry, got up, went over to the buffet and made himself some tea.

Terry stepped behind Jason and put his hand on Jason's shoulder. "I must take you back to your flat. Please don't make me get physical."

"Take your hands off me!" Jason shoved the table away, stood up, and turned to face Terry. They could smell each other's breath. The spattering of conversation around the room stopped. Jason said very softly to Terry, "You don't seem to get the dynamics of the situation, Mr. Dolan. You work for me. If you want to continue working for me, you'll leave now."

Terry Dolan thought for a moment and then said, "Whatever I do I'm fucked." He grabbed Jason by his shirt, spun him around, and twisted his arm up behind his back. At the same time, he pulled a pair of handcuffs from his belt and applied one part of the cuffs to Jason's twisted arm. Jason bent over in pain and Terry secured the other arm.

Thomas ran back to the table and pushed Terry away from Jason. "What is wrong with you?" he shouted. "We're not running a jail."

"Don't be insubordinate, Parker."

Thomas grabbed Terry's hand and interlocked their fingers, bending Terry's fingers backwards until Terry dropped to his knees and handed over the keys to the cuffs.

Thomas freed Jason, and Jason grabbed Terry's mobile and called Gary.

"Gary, get down to the dining hall now."

Terry hung around for a second, looking to exert his authority, but everybody in the room had already seen what he had done. He walked out projecting a righteous attitude that nobody cared about.

Jason paid no attention to Terry. Instead he learned all he could about Thomas. Thomas had spent five years in the Royal Army with the Queen's Life Guard before he quit to join the St. John Ministries after a riding accident forced him to change jobs.

By the time Gary grabbed a cup of coffee and joined them, Thomas had told Jason his life story.

Gary dismissed Thomas.

Jason could barely keep his voice under control. "Gary, the fucking guy handcuffed me!"

"I apologize for Dolan's behavior."

"Apologize!? Get rid of the creep!"

"He can be overzealous, but he's a good man."

"I don't want him in anyway connected to this ministry."

"Okay, I'll sack him."

Jason looked at Gary, trying to understand when Gary had changed. He seemed more authoritarian than Jason remembered.

"I understand that you and Tony don't want to deal with controversy. But we've always been controversial. And now more than ever you need to understand that the way this Ministry progresses is not up to you."

"I just don't want you to destroy the credibility and the respect you've built."

"Handcuffing me in my own dining room will destroy the Ministry's credibility more than I ever will. The TV conference will explain everything."

"Will you emphatically state that you weren't in the hospital room with those girls?"

"That's not what the program will be about. Besides, the phenomenon of apparitions is relatively common throughout history, and our program will bring many perspectives to it. You shouldn't worry."

"It's what everyone wants to know."

"Everyone wants to know how I heal, and with all my books and videos, and even with private instruction, I'm surprised by how few people catch the secret. We'll give people a sufficient rationale for what they thought happened at Marsdan."

"If you're not going to categorically state that you were not in the room with those girls, I better increase the security for this place. The zealots that want to kill you are not going away."

"I don't give a shit about them."

"You can't be serious. They are the barbarians at the gates. If we don't neutralize them, they will destroy us.

"I am serious. To 'resist not evil' is the core of our work."

"Sometimes you have to confront evil with the flaming sword of truth."

Jason realized that Gary didn't get it. The Sword of Truth wasn't a military weapon; it was the light of the Word that dispelled the darkness.

"I want you to rescind this stupid order to keep me confined to the compound."

"The board will have to rescind it."

"The board has nothing to do with it. This is you, Gary."

"The board voted on it," Gary said.

"The board voted on having the symposium. You and Tony did not. No one is to interfere with my freedom whatsoever. Is that clear?"

Gary was still for a moment, thinking. "I've admired you from the time I regained my sanity and became whole. You are a gift to the world, really a gift. You changed my life and I've credited that to you. And that's why your security is so important to me."

Jason laughed. "What your goon did here tonight shifted the focus of our TV show. You think this won't get out? People won't care about apparitions; they'll want to know why Jason St. John was handcuffed in the dining room of his own headquarters. You and Barbara and all those in the media department will not be answering questions about the nature of reality; not answering questions about healing. You'll have the crowds asking why I was handcuffed. Is he mentally unstable? Is he violent? Do you think that's going to enhance the Ministry?"

Gary looked down at his hands and they were shaking.

"You better make up some story to tell all these people." Jason gestured to those still in the room as he got up. "Make up something good, like this was some kind of test. Tell them I'm not really Jason, but a look-a-like imposter. I'm going to bed."

Jason left Gary sitting at the table with his head in his hands.

After a few hours of fitful sleep, Jason got up. His mind was filled with the rehash of the day, which bothered him more than the actual confrontations. He always thought that he was in control of his mind, but he felt helpless at this particular moment. He believed that he had mastered a level of detachment so that he did not have to relive the events of the past and project them into the future. He understood the mystical principle of now. But could he really maintain that? Was he fearful about this current challenge? Was he fearful of his board and how they appear to have such power over his life? He remembered an Indian guru telling him that there is no fear in the now. Fear only exists in memory—those events in the past that seem to dictate one's current life—or in imagination, which is fear projected into the future.

Mainly he was angry, angry with himself for reacting to what happened today, and for thinking himself above conflict. He hadn't been this fraught since his grand voyage to the South Pacific. Was Tony just another incarnation of Larry, coming back into his life to be purged? How often must he face this type of power? Would he ever be free and able to soar unhampered into the infinity of spiritual creation? Overcoming the barriers of material power had been the core of his teaching and had set him on the road to where he was now. Obviously, he wasn't as purged as he thought.

And now David was coming back, he thought—hoped. Again, his mind ran between the past and the future, bringing to mind images and feelings he thought he'd been rid of for years. Jason still felt that David had betrayed him when he quit the organization and the board. But he couldn't blame David for Tony Bass. He thought that the first words from David would be, "I told you so." Jason knew that this was the typical human response to the dilemma he was in, and he mentally beat himself up for falling into that state of consciousness. Jason had to admit that his ego was raging.

He couldn't stay in bed. He got up, threw on some jeans and a long-sleeved T-shirt, and walked into his parlor. It didn't feel like his home anymore. Thinking about it, it never really did. When he, Lillian, David, Melanie, and Dorothy decided they needed a proper organization, the first thing the board did was purchase this property for their headquarters. Lillian loved London and chose Stanford House to be the center of the world where they all would live and work as one—a new kind of cloister. He liked the idea at the time. So did Lillian. Now he understood why she hated it so.

The arguments kept going on in his head. It wasn't just Gary. They needed the staff. They needed to invest the money and make it work for the Ministry. Ministry? Jason had never been religious, nor did he accept religious dogma and theology as relevant to modern life. Now, he could debate the most learned of scholars about many of the world's sacred texts and point out the differences between doctrine and mystical principle. But that was not what he was about. His mantra was freedom! Ironically, he had become a prisoner of his own creation.

Jason sat before the large windows in his parlor looking out into the darkness. He was in his meditation chair and he started to clear his mind. Although the thoughts and judgments came like Niagara Falls, he struggled to keep them at bay. He kept focusing on the spaces between the thoughts until they slowed down and he found moments of stillness. He settled into his chair and experienced deeper and longer moments of complete mental stillness. But a thought came that jarred him back to the chaos of the past two days.

He opened his eyes and looked down at his arms. They were still on top of the armrest. He got up and walked over to Lillian's chair. He moved it a little; so that it wasn't in the exact place the maid had put it. He didn't want to admit to superstition, but his last few meditations in that room had led to events out of his control. Was there some kind of portal here? He rejected that thought. What he'd experienced was an activity of his consciousness and it was about his quest to know spiritual oneness. That was the foundation of mysticism, oneness—one life, one substance and one love.

He turned on the light. Satisfied with his preparations, he sat in Lillian's chair and it didn't take long to still his mind completely. Jason then entered the deep realm of silence.

Voices talking softly around him caused him to open his eyes. Jason didn't know where he was. He was in a different room. It had wood framed sofas up against the walls and a large Persian carpet on the floor. He saw a kitchen through an open door where people talked in quiet but anxious conversation. Jason couldn't understand the language, but thought they were an extended family—two men, two women, a few children and an older man with a white beard. He closed his eyes again, contemplating his purpose for being there.

Outside the building he heard the popping sounds of gunfire.

He opened his eyes again, stood up and walked into the middle of the room. That movement caught the eye of the two girls in the kitchen. They were in their late teens, and when they saw Jason they jumped.

The men in the kitchen reacted to the girls and also saw Jason. They panicked and pushed their women and younger children into a corner. The older man ran into the living room yelling at Jason. The other men followed and joined the old man, who was in Jason's face. Jason put his hands across his chest in a prayfull gesture.

"I come in peace," Jason said, not knowing what else to do.

Automatic weapon fire exploded outside on the street. And then another blast rattled the windows and sent plaster dust falling from the ceiling. The older man turned from Jason and drove everyone out through the kitchen. One of the girls darted back into the living room, followed by the other girl and the men.

"You're the English healer!" the first girl cried out in accented English.

Everything stopped. The girl's recognition of Jason brought a moment of peace. The men put their arms around the girls, and things seemed normal for an instant.

The mood was broken when more gunfire slammed into the walls and shattered the windows. The girls dropped to their knees. The men blocked the front door just as it exploded into the room, throwing them backwards onto the floor. A squad of British soldiers burst in, ducking and weaving and clinging to the walls just like in the movies.

The old man was again shepherding the rest of the family out the back door.

"Stop!" the first soldier in the house shouted as he ran toward the kitchen. He aimed at the fleeing family, but Jason crashed into him. He missed his shot and shot up the kitchen instead. Chunks of plaster fell from the walls and the cupboards and appliances were destroyed.

Jason grabbed the soldier. "They're unarmed!" he shouted.

The soldier twisted free, ready to shoot Jason, but two of his buddies stopped him.

"What the fuck are you doing here?" one of the soldiers demanded.

"Where are we?"

"Baghdad, you idiot."

"These are just ordinary people, a terrified family," Jason said.

The squad leader pushed his men aside and threw Jason into a chair. "How would you know, you fuck? This whole street is nothing but fucking Al Qaeda." The sergeant turned to his men and shouted, "Search the house for weapons. Secure the people on the floor and find those who ran away!"

"They were little boys and an old man." Jason stood up and the sergeant pushed him back down with the butt of his rifle.

"Shut up. We've been attacked by women in hijabs hiding suicide belts."

"Do you know who've you got here, Sarge?" said the corporal pointing his carbine at the people on the floor.

"Probably some fucking reporter from the Guardian doing a human interest on the poor suffering people of Baghdad."

"No. He's Jason St. John! The healer!"

"The fucking Antichrist. Wouldn't you know he'd be in Baghdad, stirring up trouble?"

The sergeant lifted his C-8 carbine and fired a line of bullets from the floor to the ceiling right where Jason sat. The corporal tackled the sergeant, wrestled his gun from him while screaming at him to stop.

The men chasing the escaping Iraqis rushed back and stopped in shock. The chair Jason had been sitting in was empty. A line of bullet holes had cut it in two.

The sergeant, recovering from his anger, turned to his men and pointed to the chair. "This is fucking insane!"

The corporal cried, "But you shot him."

"We all saw it!" another soldier yelled.

"Then where's the body?" The sergeant walked around behind the shattered chair.

"No. He grabbed me. I felt his body," said the soldier Jason had seized. "You did too! You shoved him into that chair and shot him."

"It was a fucking hallucination," the sergeant said. "You all got that?"

"We've been here too long. We're seeing things." The corporal said lowering his weapon.

Chapter 18

Chester, England

Thursday Morning, November 2004

Lillian woke up early to a gloomy morning. She'd slept in her old bedroom and hadn't liked the fact that after being away from home for twenty-four years her parents had not changed one thing. Everything was in the same place it had been in since she left the Queen's School and went off to the Royal Academy of Dramatic Art in London.

Lillian put on her robe and went downstairs. She stopped on the second-floor landing and peeked through the curtains. The car was still there. It had been there all night. She continued to the kitchen where she put on the kettle. She left the kettle and walked over to the den where Alex had spent the night. She peeked in to check on him. He was sound asleep on the sofa.

The kettle began to sing, and Lillian rushed back to the kitchen before the sound of the whistle woke everybody up. She made a mug of black tea, adding just the right amount of milk and honey, and took her perfect drink into the parlor where she sat in the window seat to catch the early morning light. She looked out the window again at the car parked across the street. It couldn't be from the Ministry. It didn't look like a Ministry car and she didn't believe they had followed her. It wasn't a secret where her parents lived. No. It was someone else. A reporter? Hopefully not some kook bent on assassinating her husband.

Across the room she heard a moan. There, on the sofa, was Jason. Lillian jumped up and ran to him. Jason was pale; his clothes were filled with dust, and his T-shirt was bloodstained, with a line of holes in it from his belt to his neck. She stifled a scream and took Jason in her arms, whispering, "What happened? Are you alright?"

"I need some water," he said weakly.

"What did you do? Can you sit up?"

Jason took a deep breath, and using the back of the sofa, pulled himself up. "What time is it? What day is it?"

"About seven on Thursday." Lillian got up and dashed to the kitchen. There she filled a glass of water and dampened a tea towel. When she returned Jason had his head down and his elbows resting on his knees. She sat next to him and gave him the water. He drank a few sips and looked at her with fear in his eyes. Lillian's first impulse was to cry as she ran the cool cloth over her husband's face. "What's going on, Jason?

"I don't know." He placed a hand on hers and with the other he lifted his shirt where a line of welts the size of fifty-pence coins ran up his torso. There was very little blood and streaks of dirt obscured his tattoos. "I know people hate me, but I've never really felt that hatred until now."

"Where were you?"

"I was told I was in Baghdad."

"Baghdad!?" Lillian tried to keep her distress at bay. She did not want to lose her husband this way.

"I don't know why I'm taken where I'm taken. I've been thinking about that since I first appeared at the hospital. Is it someone reaching out to the Spirit that draws me? Those girls in the hospital were asleep. It wasn't a conscious thing on their part. And I was just in a Muslim house in Iraq."

"Who shot you? Terrorists?"

"No. British soldiers."

Lillian continued dabbing the cool cloth over his chest and the line of welts. The act of tending Jason's fast disappearing wounds, kept her from thinking too much about their situation.

"They're good shots," Lillian said and immediately regretted it. "I mean, how can you have survived?"

"I don't know. I'm in this other dimension, I guess, with my body, and ..."

Lillian threw the towel on the floor and hugged him. She squeezed him and felt his solid flesh in her arms. She kissed his neck and face and tasted his salty sweat. He smelled of fear and dust and gunpowder. "This is too bizarre. I don't think I can handle it."

He hugged and kissed her back, and they both began to laugh and cry at the same time.

"Shush," Lillian said, "I don't want to wake Alex." She caressed his face and then leaned back into his arms.

"When Jesus appeared to his disciples after his Resurrection, according to Scripture, he had the same body with all the wounds of the Crucifixion. What if I enter that dimension of life when my 'instant appearing' occurs? My physical body was in that Baghdad living room and I have the marks of being shot, but nothing happened."

"What if you left before the bullets could penetrate into your chest?"

"Then it wasn't by conscious thought. I had no idea that soldier would shoot me."

"Do you remember him? Could you identify him?"

"Not really." He struggled for the right words. "This phenomenon is more on a feeling level than a mental level. I felt the fear of the Iraqis, but also the longing of that family to protect itself. The two girls were in awe. Their love was incredible. Then I felt the anger and fear of the soldiers. And then, one soldier ... oh, the one that said my name, I felt a wonderful recognition from him, but then the hatred exploded from the soldier who shot me."

"What if all of this is connected to what happened to you in the Marquesas?"

"That was fifteen years ago. Why do you think there's a connection?"

"You've never really faced that experience, J.J. You've told bits and pieces, but I can tell there are parts of what happened that you're afraid to look at."

"I think I've analyzed it from every angle. You don't think I purged all that trauma when I wrote my book?"

"I think you went as deep as you could. Maybe something you overlooked is coming to the surface now."

"I don't think so. This is new. It hasn't any connection to the past."

Lillian shook him, struggling to control her fear and anger. "You said it would never happen again. We had a family meeting. I had to escape from London with Alex, and he's now wondering who you really are. You've got to think about us."

"What do you think I've been hiding?" Jason grew a little angry. "You know me better than anyone. I don't want these manifestations to continue any more than you do. If you think they're caused by some latent curse from a South Seas *tuhuna* ..."

"I never said that." Lillian let go of Jason and turned from him.

"But you've felt this—when we held hands meditating. You saw how easily we just fell into it." He took her hand and brought her back into his embrace.

"I don't know. Something must draw you to these places."

"Those girls wanted to be healed. Baghdad was entirely different. I couldn't sleep. I was furious at Gary. The duty officer actually handcuffed me in the dining room."

"That's ridiculous. Why don't we just leave it all?"

"What would that solve? You know as well as I do that we'd just carry all this with us"

"You know, J.J., your entire experience is an out-picturing of your state of mind." Lillian didn't mean to sound so condescending.

"I guess my mind is a warzone then." He paused and rubbed his temples. "The only way to understand this is in the stillness of that deep peace. But when the peace takes you into another dimension, and deposits you ... who knows where? It's not something I want. What enables me to heal is the oneness and omnipotence of the spirit within me—whatever it's called. It's the same spirit that's in everyone. If this were a universal, transcendental activity, something coming from universal consciousness, it would be harmonious, filled with love, and a blessing to all. Right now, I'm not seeing that. To be jerked here or there because people are thinking about me, or praying to me, is hell!"

"Why one place and not another? Maybe you're being called on to recognize the non-reality of disease or dissolve the hatred and brutality of war." Lillian got up thinking how stupid she sounded trying to be rational. "It's too strange. My tea's cold. You want a cup?"

Jason followed her into the kitchen. "The 'whys' and 'hows' of this are going to take a while to figure out, if they ever can be. What I'm most worried about is my being here and what your parents and Alex are going to think."

Lillian lighted the fire under the kettle again and took another cup from the china closet.

"Dad." Alex stood in the doorway. "I thought I heard you come in. Can I have some tea too?"

Lillian went over to Alex and gave him a hug. "I thought you were sound asleep."

"I heard you guys talking.

"Your dad just surprised me, that's all."

"Just like he surprised Irma?" Alex said.

"Go get your dad a dressing gown. There should be one in the wardrobe in Grandpa's den," Lillian said as she got another cup down for Alex.

"Did Dad do another one of his— 'instant appearing'?"

Jason found a package of muffins in the breadbox. "Alex, why don't you set the table and we'll talk?"

Alex stood there, looking at his parents with a teenage defiance. "I thought we were all going to level with each other. First mom kidnaps me from school and tries to outrun Gary and his goons, but everybody knows where we are, and some strangers have been watching us all night. I'm not stupid."

"No one thinks you're stupid, Alex." Jason gave the muffins to Lillian and she took everything into the dining table. She and Alex sipped their tea in silence.

"It's love that drew me here," Jason said, coming back into the room wearing a robe. "That's got to be the secret behind what's happening, otherwise why wouldn't I return to where I'd started, like the first time?"

"Where did you go?" Alex asked.

"That's not important," his father answered.

"It *is* important. I'm part of this too," Alex insisted.

"The question is, can I control it?" Jason continues. "Can my affection for you keep me here, where you are?"

"Don't use us as an anchor, Jason. As much as this frightens me, I don't want to be the one who prevents some quantum shift in human perception," Lillian said.

"So, where *were* you?" Alex got frustrated at being ignored.

"Iraq," Lillian whispered.

"Holy shit." Alex's language went unnoticed.

"We need to figure out what to do next." Jason reached for more sugar and the tattoos on his arm seemed to glow. He pulled the sleeve of his robe down to hide them.

"Why haven't you ever told me about Uncle Dave and the South Seas?"

"Well, maybe it's time I did."

Chapter 19
Ala Wai Yacht Harbor

Monday May 1, 1989

The sun was just breaching Diamond Head when Larry drove up to his yacht. The *Mataʻi* listed noticeably to port, which was caused by all the gear and provisions that had been loaded onto that side of the yacht to compensate for the upcoming twenty-five-hundred-mile voyage south, most of it on a port tack.

"I think you overdid your storage plan." Byron got out of Larry's car and grabbed his gear

"Once we're underway you'll appreciate it."

Byron followed Larry onto the boat and Larry went below where David was sound asleep.

"How you doing, Dave?" Larry said cheerfully, waking him up. "Ready for our little voyage?"

It took David a moment to compute where he was. "Yes, sir."

"Where's Jason?"

"I have no idea."

"Well, get a move on and find him," Larry ordered. "We have a lot of work to do before our guests arrive."

David staggered out of his bunk, grabbed his toilet kit, and felt Byron's hand on his shoulder.

"Just to let you know, that is my bunk. I'd like you to clean everything off it before you go. And clean your gear from the drawers." He dropped his bag on the deck.

David was about to tell him to fuck off, but it was too early in the morning to argue. Byron gave David a little shake to reaffirm the order and then went topside. David put his things on the port bunk, the one that had the hammock over it filled with greased eggs and packaged food.

When David came back from the showers, Byron was sitting in the cockpit, under the awning, drinking coffee. He winked at him.

Larry had gone to his car and came back with a heavy duffel bag over his shoulder. With one look it was apparent that Larry was a sailor, not a yachtsman. He was wearing what he always wore at the harbor—shorts, topsiders with no socks, a long-sleeve Tahitian-print shirt, and his trademark white safari helmet. It wasn't that he tried to be eccentric; it was just that he was fanatically practical. A pith helmet won out over a canvas hat because pith helmets don't wear out, they shade the sun better, they protect the head from falling objects, and they float. He went into the salon and dumped his load on the settee table. It was a sack full of weapons.

"I need your passports and plane tickets," he told the others.

Byron got up and followed his brother into the cabin and sat at the table. David went forward and found his passport and ticket. "Yours too, Byron."

One of the conditions for sailing to Tahiti was all the crew had to have valid plane tickets from Papeete to wherever they'd come from. Otherwise they had to post a thousand-dollar bond with the authorities when they arrived. The government of French Polynesia wasn't about to let castaways live on the beach.

"Where's Jason?" Larry asked David. "I thought I told you to find him."

David was ready to make an excuse when Jason showed up with a bag of Big Macs and Cokes for everyone.

"Jason. Where's your passport?" Larry shouted.

Jason got his passport and sat at the table with the others. This was the first time that Larry and his crew were together. Larry collected the passports and all the tickets except Jason's. "I'll keep these in the safe in my cabin. Jason, I have your ticket." He looked at each of his crew individually, and David saw, as did the others, that Larry was now completely in command. He picked up one of the rifles, a Winchester 70 bolt action 30-06. He opened the bolt and checked the bore. "Who knows anything about firearms?" Larry looked at Jason and David.

"I'm clueless," Jason said.

"I fired a pistol in the Coast Guard," David replied.

"I guess you'll be in charge of the weapons," Larry said to Byron. "They all need to be cleaned, wrapped in oilcloth, and stowed in these plastic cases. There are a couple of pistols in the bag and a couple of thousand rounds of ammunition." Larry paused and then looked at the boys to see their reaction. "We're going to be on our own for months. There will be no police or government to help us out if we get into trouble, so we need to be self-reliant and prepared for any danger."

"In Tahiti?" Jason said.

Larry just gave him a look that meant "Shut up." He continued, "Okay, then, we'll shove off at one. Jason, take off the awnings and sail covers and stow them in the dinghy. Change out the shore vents for the sea vents, and make sure everything is lashed and secure. Dave, make sure everything in the engine compartment is secure. I want the boat ready to leave when I get back."

Larry got up, picked up the corded, 1960s phone that always sat on the settee and took it ashore. This is the real thing, Jason thought. That phone was like Larry's umbilical cord. Jason watched Larry coil up the cord, unplug it from the shore jack and lock it in his locker.

David squeezed into the engine compartment under the cockpit. It was cramped with little more than a crawl space around the Volvo diesel. To work on the engine meant making love to it. David checked the through hull fitting for the power shaft. *Mata'i* had a folding bronze prop to diminish drag under sail, and a white stripe down the shaft marked where it should be set while sailing. Directly below the helmsman seat, a brake was fitted to the shaft to keep it from moving while under weigh. A three-foot extension rod was attached to the brake handle so the brake could be set or released from the cockpit.

When David finished checking out the engine room, he stopped in the cockpit, lifted the helm-seat and made sure the brake on the shaft was slack. He then continued on deck to help Jason with the sail covers. They stowed them and then changed out the vents. The *Mata'i* was ready for sea.

Byron had made himself a rum and coke, not in the McDonald's cup, but in a crystal tumbler. He watched the boys, taking mental notes. When they finished, Byron invited them to sit with him in the cockpit. No one said anything as they waited for Larry to return with the ladies. This send-off was a big deal for Larry.

Byron laughed, breaking the silence and took a sip of his drink. "Let me be clear, my rum is off limits. It's for medicinal purposes only. I have a bad back and this tends to relax it. So here are my rules. If you boys follow them, we will get along great. I don't do any heavy work; no hoisting of sails or taking in sails in any sort of weather, no pulling on the anchor chain or making do in cramped compartments."

"Do you steer the boat?" Jason said.

"I steer the boat. I don't stand night watches. I don't cook. I will make cocktails and I'll share my rum on special occasions. Most important, I know a lot more about blue water cruising than Larry, though he won't admit it. I've been through hurricanes in the Caribbean and have a good idea what this boat can take. If there's ever a question of what we should do in heavy weather, you guys will side with me. Our trip down is a test. If you fuck up, I'll be leaving in Papeete and you'll have Larry all to yourselves."

The crew had changed from t-shirts into more formal aloha shirts when Larry came back with Elizabeth, Lillian and his current wife, Hellen Graff at precisely 12:40. Helen had a canvas bag containing snacks, champagne, and orange juice. Elizabeth brought books, a Norton Anthology of English Literature for her son and the complete works of Herman Melville for David. Lillian had an armful of flower *leis*. Larry passed the gifts down to the crew's waiting arms and helped the women on board. For a moment the women stood in the cockpit looking at the boat and the men. Lillian broke the awkwardness by giving out her *leis*. Helen Graff, who had disappeared below, came back up with champagne flutes of mimosas and a tray of caviar and blinis.

Larry began. "I'm honored to have my teacher and mentor here to bless this voyage and send us on our way in the knowledge that we are divinely protected. Please enjoy the refreshments while we get the boat ready to set sail. Dave, unplug the shore power and single up the lines."

As David went about his task, he saw Jason and Lillian sitting on the forward cabin roof, leaning against the salon portholes. Lillian was crying and Jason was comforting her. David wanted to be there too, but he left them alone.

Byron poured more champagne and Helen cornered Elizabeth, telling her how she hated entertaining on the boat. Every Sunday she had to make gourmet *hors d'oeuvres* for the *après*-sail cocktail hour. She made it clear that Larry's long absence on this trip would not be a hardship. It would be her celebration of freedom.

David finished getting the boat ready and let Larry know. The skipper waved him off. It wasn't quite time to leave. Lillian was no longer crying, and David went forward and joined Jason and her.

"Thanks for the *lei*." David sat down next to Lillian. "What do you think? Are we going to survive this trip?"

Jason glared at his buddy, and Lillian welled up with tears again.

"I was just trying to lighten things up."

"Neither one of you should go," Lillian said. "Until now it was all speculation. You could still change your minds." She began crying. "I'm going to miss you both ..." She wiped her eyes and regained her composure.

"... And I'm not going to think about either one of you."

Larry stepped on deck and shouted, "Let's get underway!" He looked rather disgusted at the little *ménage à trois* and returned to the cockpit where he fired up the diesel. Jason, Lillian, and David wrapped their arms around each other in a group hug, and Lillian hurried back to the cockpit to join the ladies.

Larry stood at the helm, took one last look around his boat. There were no more preparations to be made and they were ready for sea.

"Dave." Larry waved him over. "Help Helen ashore. She'll take the car over to the gas dock."

David followed Larry's order.

"Byron on the boathook," Larry commanded. "Jason, take the bow, and Dave the stern. Stern lines come off first—we're taking them with us. Jason, undo port side first and then walk us out. And bring the lines."

Jason jumped ashore and waited for David to undo the stern lines. He got them on board cleanly.

"Do you want to raise the main? Just in case?" Byron called back to the cockpit.

"No, I do not." Larry waited for the bow lines to be cast off.

Jason untied the port mooring line, which was cleated twenty feet from the head of the pier on the far side of the storage lockers. He tossed the line to the boat, but his throw was weak, and the rope fell into the water.

"Keep the lines dry, Jason!" Larry yelled.

Jason ran to the other cleat, untied the starboard line, and pulled the bow of the boat toward him so that he could grab the pulpit and walk the boat back.

"We're free!" he shouted.

Larry put his boat in reverse and started backing away from the dock. Jason was supposed to keep the boat straight, and at the last minute, shove the bow away from the dock and jump on board. But Larry gave the motor too much throttle and Jason had to run down the pier just to keep up. He barely had hold of the pulpit, and when he reached the end of the pier, it was all he could do to jump onboard. The other line dropped in the water, and Jason held onto the pulpit. He got a leg over the bowsprit and muscled his way up to the deck.

"Damn it, Jason!" Larry spun the helm to get the boat turning.

Jason gathered in both of the mooring lines that had fallen

in the water, quickly faked them on deck. He headed aft where Byron stopped him at the main. "Undo all but two gaskets and stand by the halyard, just in case."

"Byron, get your boathook back here. Dave, get some fenders aft."

The *Mataʻi* wasn't turning. Instead, she was backing straight toward the yachts berthed across the channel. In a single screw vessel like this one, the spin of the prop tends to swing the stern to port. Since the flow of water wasn't over the rudder, the helm wasn't very efficient. Larry put the helm over to the point where it offset the natural swing of the boat. He didn't want to go in that direction, and without Jason's extra push he couldn't get the bow to turn towards the harbor exit.

"We should raise the main and sail out," Byron shouted.

"Belay that!" Larry called back. "Just stay calm." Larry throttled back, shifted into forward, and swung his helm to the opposite direction. Everyone felt the clank of the shifting gear. Larry accelerated and the motor coughed and quit. He frantically tried to restart it, but it flooded.

"We need that main up," Byron said.

"All I need from you is to shut up and fend us off!" Larry shouted cranking the motor, but it wouldn't turn over. The ladies gathered in one corner of the cockpit. People from the threatened yachts rushed on deck to protect their boats.

"What the hell are you doing, Graff?" a neighbor yelled.

"Fuck! Fuck! Fuck! Come on you fucking bitch," Larry kept saying under his breath. Finally, the motor kicked over. Larry got it in gear and *Mataʻi* moved forward, moments before it would have crashed into a neighbor's boat.

The ladies let out a collective sigh. Lillian approached Elizabeth; she was in tears again. "I have a terrible feeling that this fiasco is but the beginning. Can't you do something?"

"Don't be hypnotized, sweet heart. You're letting this event reinforce your preconceived idea about this voyage. Let go of that concept. Where is the truth in it?" Elizabeth gave Lillian a loving hug and a kiss. "Stop your crying and join me in the Spirit." Elizabeth then turned to Larry who was at the helm a couple of steps away.

"I'm sorry, Elizabeth," he said. "I hate to lose control and I hope you won't hold that outburst against me."

"There's your biggest lesson, Larry. You've got to let go if you want the Spirit to function in you."

"I just want everything to be perfect and harmonious. There's no reason why this trip can't be that. Is that too much to ask?"

"Have you meditated with Jason yet?"

"There just hasn't been time."

Elizabeth went over to Helen and Lillian, having had enough of Larry's alibis. Larry brushed off Elizabeth's snub and chatted up Byron as he motored over to the gas dock. No one said anything about the near miss, but questions about Larry's competence could almost be grabbed from the sky.

Jason and David stood on the foredeck. Larry had jokingly referred to the run to the gas dock as first leg of the journey. David hoped the Jason he'd known as a kid, the one who sat at the feet of the master, was still there. Larry's performance getting underway made him nervous.

Larry pulled up to the fueling station and Jason and David jumped off to handle the mooring lines. Byron helped the ladies ashore, and Larry opened the fuel ports on the boat. The dock attendant hauled over a long hose and topped up the fuel tanks. David brought a water hose over to do the same for the water tanks, but Larry told him to hold off. He didn't like the possibility of getting water mixed in with the fuel. After the fueling was complete and the caps secure, Larry allowed the water tanks to be topped off.

With those chores completed, the men joined the send-off party gathered on the dock. They all stared at the yacht glistening in the afternoon sun. Jason took a deep breath. He was ready, proud of the work he'd done to prepare *Mata'i* to cross an ocean. After leaving the Hawaiian Islands there would be nothing but twenty-six hundred miles of ocean before they reached Tahiti.

Elizabeth gathered everyone in a circle and had them hold hands. She was quiet for a few moments and they all fell into a meditation. Even Byron graciously participated. After the silence, all Elizabeth said was, "Go with God." She kissed each one of the crew. When she came to David, she whispered, "Pay attention."

David gave Lillian a long hug and asked her to write. He had to know how she felt about him. In the few days he had known her, she had changed his life. He would never betray Jason, but he had to know.

Jason and Lillian went off to have a moment of privacy.

"I love you, J.J.," Lillian kissed him. It wasn't passionate but it was filled with agape. This wasn't the moment for passion. "I know you'll be changed when you return. I'll write to you and let you know what I'm thinking. I hope the change will bring greater illumination. The world needs what you have. Never forget that."

Jason hugged her back. "You're my strength. I know that whatever I do spiritually you'll be there. I have no doubt. I love you, too. I'm sorry this trip upsets you so much, Lillian, but I think it's about a greater purpose. I don't know what it is yet, but as soon as I know, you will too." With that he gave her another long kiss and walked over to his mother.

They embraced and she said one word to him, "Listen." Then she kissed him and stepped back. The detachment that David had observed before descended upon them. Their bodies went through the motions of saying goodbye, but the Divine indifference that allowed the Spirit to work was already there in each of them, and David began to understand it for the first time.

The *Mata'i* motored out the Ala Wai channel and Larry raised her sails beyond the reef. The people on the dock waited until the sails were up before they left. Elizabeth nudged Lillian to leave, making her turn away from the yacht to live in the present.

After five hours of sailing, passing Waikiki and Diamond Head and entering the Molokai channel, the *Mata'i* approached the island of Molokai. Larry tacked north to gain some maneuvering room for his plan to sail down the windward coasts of the islands. He wanted to be at least ten miles offshore. The change in course was only for a few hours, but all the weight that had been so carefully stowed on the windward side of the boat was now on the leeward side, and *Mata'i* buried her rail in the stiff wind and heavy sea. Blue water poured down the deck and often into the cockpit. Larry assured his crew it was necessary and better to take the beating now, when they were fresh, than wait until they were off Tahiti. He went back to adjust the Aires self-steering gear and came back to the cockpit to join the others trying to stay dry.

The four men huddled up against the cabin bulkhead—two on each side of the companionway, and still they got wet. The cabin had been secured—the hatch was closed, the companionway doors shut, all the windows and ports sealed, and the air vents turned away from the weather. Below decks it was hot and stuffy. In the cockpit it was hot and wet.

The Aires couldn't keep the yacht on course. Larry had ordered Jason and David to shorten sail three times, and had them try different combinations of jib, forestaysail, main, and mizzen in the hopes of balancing the boat so that the steering gear would work. At that moment he had a shortened jib, a double-reefed main, and no mizzen. The staysail, which was not roller furling, was still attached to the stay but stuffed into its bag. Larry got up again to readjust the Aires to see if he could get it to hold a course, and like every other time he made an adjustment, he cursed the designer and swore that he'd get his money back as soon as he reached port.

No one responded to Larry's cursing. Even making coffee below couldn't be done without cursing. Larry shouted at Jason, motioning to the wind and the sea. "What are you doing about this?"

Finally, Larry got up and pulled Jason with him. "You take the helm. Our course is twenty-five degrees. At one o'clock tack back to one-thirty-five. You have the first watch." Larry then disengaged the self-steering hub from the wheel and went aft and pulled the servo rudder out of the water. He came back to the cockpit and stopped at the hatch to the aft cabin; "Dave, you have the next watch. You better try to get some sleep." With that he opened his hatch and disappeared into his own world.

Chapter 20
Waikiki

Tuesday May 2, 1989

The next evening Lillian had dinner with Elizabeth on the lanai of her apartment. She told Elizabeth her feelings for Jason and David, and about the dilemma she now faced. Elizabeth was not shocked; in fact, she had seen it coming. Her council to Lillian was to be true to herself. But she also told her to be patient and not make any decision in the emotion of the departure. The boys would be gone almost half a year, and the important thing was to keep them in her prayers and meditations.

Then Lillian told Elizabeth that she was going back to London. She had an offer to do a West End play and had come to the conclusion that acting was her true calling. She told Elizabeth that she would never forget their time together, and all that she'd learned by helping her pull the material from her classes into a manuscript. They parted in love, but Elizabeth's detachment from emotion manifested as indifference. Lillian knew Elizabeth loved her, but Elizabeth's impersonal nature rubbed Lillian the wrong way. She remembered how David had misinterpreted that spiritual principle. He thought the St. John family was so cold whenever the problems of life had entered their world. Perhaps they were marvelous healers, but sometimes a person just needed a friend. Where was the line between the emotions of human life and the divine indifference taught by all the mystics?

There had to be a balance.

That night Lillian wrote two letters.

Dear Jason,

I was miserable last night, doubly so because of the night before. I can't stop crying. You're breaking my heart, J.J. I know that sounds selfish. You have such gifts, and I feel we are destined to be together sometime, but I can't wait until that time comes. As painful as it is, I need to set you free to set myself free. It's agony to think of you at sea with Larry. I know you think of this trip as an initiation and that somehow you'll be worthy of your gifts if you survive, but what about those who love you? Don't we have a say in this too? All I can say is that I love you and hope that someday we can look back on these days without regret.

I've decided not to spend any more time in Hawaii. I've been offered a part in a play in London. It's a wonderful new play, so when you return from the South Pacific I'll be in London. Your mother will know where I am. When you are finished with your adventures and ready to seriously continue our relationship, call me.

Until then … Aloha.

Most affectionately, Lillian

Dear David,

I've gone to London to establish my career. I have a part in a new play and I feel it is right to put what I've learned spiritually into my art. I think you should do the same thing. Hopefully your voyage to Tahiti wasn't too bad, but if it was, leave that boat and come to me.

I love you, and I think we would have a happy life together in the arts. Don't worry about Jason. I've already told him I want to be free. I will always love him, but I don't think I could make a life with him. Maybe that voice that said I would marry him meant something other than a physical marriage. I would have never doubted it until I met you.

Please call me as soon as you can. I miss your voice already. All my crying on the boat yesterday was as much about losing you as it was imagining the hell you are going through. Perhaps I'm wrong. I hope I am.

All My Love, Lillian

The next day on her way to the airport, Lillian realized that Elizabeth had been right; she was hypnotized. If she couldn't overcome her attachment to Jason perhaps the mystical life wasn't for her. She had studied Dr. Green since her days at the Royal Academy of Dramatic Arts and thought she had a good grasp of mystical principles. She could meditate and see a change in herself. She had experienced physical healing, but she didn't think she could ever be like Elizabeth. She could not detach herself from her love. At least that was her perception of the St. Johns. That's why she had to let Jason go. Perhaps this experience was necessary for him, but Lillian needed to put aside her spiritual practice and just live her life—though it would be according to spiritual law to the degree she could manage it.

Elizabeth also wrote a letter to her son that day. Without Lillian helping her, she had no desire to stay in Hawaii. She gave notice to her apartment manager in Waikiki and returned to her home in Los Angeles.

Chapter 21

At Sea

May 1989

It took almost two days to reach the Big Island of Hawaii, forty hours of close-hauled sailing with twenty-knot trade winds and fourteen-foot seas. The Aires hadn't worked since the first night out when Larry, frustrated by what he believed to be a flawed piece of equipment, began to blame Jason for the violent weather. Larry had a mind that made those bazar connections seem almost rational.

Those first couple of days set the tone for the whole trip. David was at the helm when the sun rose directly over *Mataʻi's* bow on that second morning. The yacht was approaching the Alenuihaha Channel separating Maui from the Big Island. They were a few points off the wind and Larry had taken one of the reefs from the mainsail. *Mataʻi* had a fine sea-kindly motion as she rose to the top of the swell, splitting its top before riding down into the trough and sending heavy spray back toward the cockpit, drenching the foresail and then rising again.

Larry came topside and stood behind David for a few moments before David realized he was there. David was in the rhythm of the boat, playing with every micro change in wind direction and velocity, keeping the boat at speed while playing the swell. It was a dance, *Mataʻi* was his lady, and the sea and the wind were his orchestra.

"You handle her quite well," Larry said, startling him. "Most racing skippers I know like to beat the shit out of a boat in this kind of weather." David didn't answer as Larry went forward into the salon. He was driving *Mata'i* the same way he would one of the ocean racers that had made his reputation as a helmsman in the international regatta circuits.

Larry came back with a hand held direction finder and took bearings off various landmarks along the windward coast of Maui.

Jason came up on deck and stumbled back to the leeward mizzen shrouds to piss over the side.

Byron came up with two cups of coffee and gave one to David. "Are we going to Mexico or Tahiti? I thought we were supposed to sail south, not east."

"We need to make our easting. I'd rather take it now than have to beat our way into Papeete," Larry informed his brother.

"You're not going to duck through that channel ahead and give us a couple of days' smooth sailing?" Byron said referring to the channel between Maui and Hawaii Island.

Larry looked at Byron as if he was an idiot.

That night, after a monotonous day sailing down the windward coast of Maui, *Mata'i* had left Hana astern and was half way across the Alenuihaha Channel, considered to be one of the roughest on the planet, bound for the Kohala coast of the Big Island. David was back at the helm and he kept his eye on the knot meter. They were still too close-hauled to surf the swells, but their sailing angle had improved the further east they went. Still, the ride was not very smooth. Jason was in the salon cleaning the dinner dishes—a duty only he and David shared— and the diesel had been idling since sunset. Larry insisted that the batteries be charged every night. He and Byron lounged in the cockpit, sipping brandy under a dark and cloudy sky.

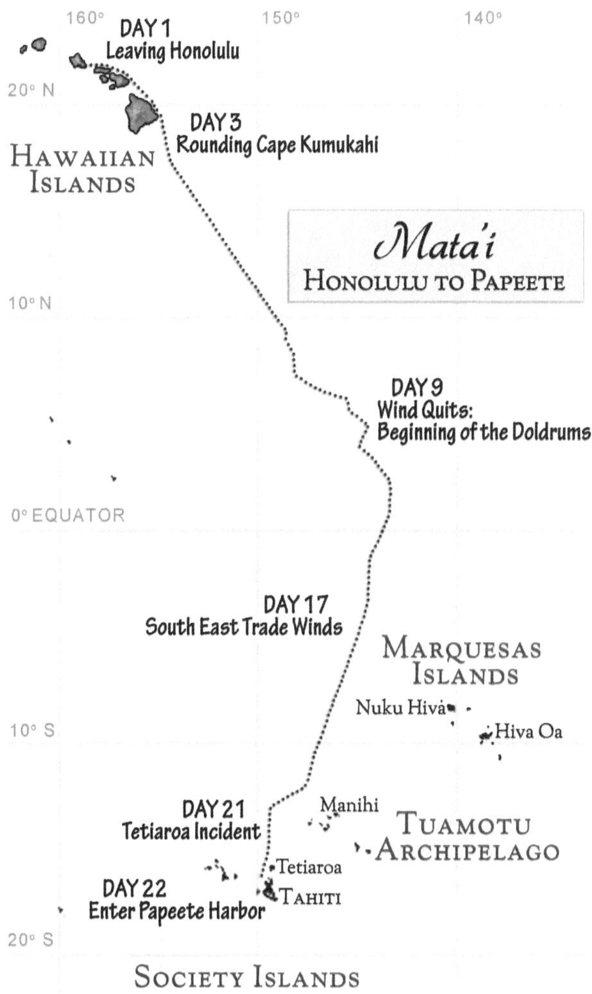

"I was in the 1978 Newport-Bermuda race," Byron said. "Were you with me on that one, Larry? No, I think it was just my first wife and her brothers. We partied all the way down. Can't remember where we placed. But you took the 'Lighthouse Trophy,'" he said to David.

"We had a great crew from the Brown sailing team, and a very nice old Cal 40 loaned to us by an alumnus. He wanted his boat in the race and came along for the ride. I guess it paid off," David said.

"Why the East Coast?" Larry said. "I thought you were a California boy like Jason."

"Just the way things worked out. Two weeks ago I was staying at a fleabag hotel in Barcelona getting my fill of Gaudi."

Jason came up from below and stood in the companionway. "Can we turn off the diesel yet? It's an oven down here."

"What's the reading on the batteries?" Larry said, getting up.

"Both banks one hundred percent."

Larry checked the engine instruments tucked under one of the lounge seats. "Fuck." He tapped on the instrument and then rushed below, pulling Jason into the cockpit so he could get by. "Byron, kill the motor!" he yelled from below. "Shit. Shit. Shit. Jason, get down here!"

Jason glanced at the instruments. "She's overheating," then he disappeared below.

Larry ordered Jason into the scorching engine compartment to discover the problem while he waited in the companionway where the air was fresh. The Volvo was cooled by a heat exchanger, which pumped in seawater to chill the antifreeze running through the engine. Jason discovered a crack in the heat exchanger. Besides being an oven, the engine compartment was cramped. Every time the boat lurched Jason fell against something hot and burned himself. Eventually he sealed the crack with duct tape, which stopped the leak until a more thorough repair could be made when the seas calmed down. After some time below, he came up for air and reported the situation to Larry.

David and Byron thought Jason had been resourceful and

had solved the immediate problem, but Larry was furious. "Who told you to do a fucking makeshift repair? Work done on *Mata'i* is to be done properly at the moment. I don't care what the seas are like. If you put off something like this, or jerry-rig it, you'll pay for it down the road." He made Jason go below, pull the tape off the exchanger, cut a length of copper, and properly solder it to make the repair permanent.

Larry took over the helm and seemed proud of his decision. David noticed that Larry couldn't steer that well. He kept luffing the jib, causing the bow to fall off a swell with a crash rather than slide over the waves as David had done. David looked at Byron, and Byron just shrugged. Was Larry doing that on purpose to make Jason sick, to punish him? Would his pride let him do that, or was he just mean? Byron nodded to David, reminding him what he'd said before they departed: Larry wasn't the sailor he thought he was.

"You're not worried that he'll make a mess of the repair?" Byron finally asked Larry.

"If he does, he'll do it again. The boy's got to learn how to deal with things when they need to be dealt with."

The next day Larry set a course a few more degrees south of east, and Jason and David shook out the remaining reefs in the sails. *Mata'i* fell into a beam reach and showed her speed. Larry was happy on that fourth day. He had planned a fourteen-day trip and provisioned the boat accordingly.

No one in the crew ate much during the rough weather, and now with the boat on a fast reach, Larry begin cooking gourmet meals—at least Larry thought his ham and onion quiche was gourmet. He thought of himself as sophisticated and cultured and tried to make the social occasions—lunch, happy hour, and dinner—a time for stimulating conversation, well-prepared food, and good manners. This attitude also brought out his elitist tendencies. David was part of the club because he had graduated from an Ivy League school. Jason, on the other hand, was looked upon like hired help—more like an indentured servant—and as such was tolerated but not completely accepted. And Jason hadn't been doing a very good job at keeping the weather favorable.

Five days later and eight hundred miles south of the Big Island, *Mataʻi* was drifting, becalmed in the Doldrums, that band around the planet where the North East trade winds met the Southern trade winds and created an area of calm. The lack of wind had started a few degrees further north than Larry had expected and a day or so earlier. Larry fantasized that if his crew were diligent and played what little wind there was, they could slip through the calm belt in a few days. He saw no reason to waste fuel to power across the six hundred miles of windless seas and stifling heat to find the southeast trade winds. His calculations put the boat about five degrees north and one hundred forty-five degrees west. So, Jason and David were set to work while Larry puttered, and Byron drank. The boys cleaned the boat, repaired things not yet broken, and got ready for the southeast trades that were predicted to soon arrive.

The sun was hot, and with no wind the boys pulled up everything that was damp from below and laid it out on deck or hung it from the shrouds and lifelines. *Mataʻi* looked more like a backyard clothesline than a yacht. In the evenings Jason played his ukulele. He entertained the others with *"hapa-haole"* Hawaiian songs he'd learned when sailing beach catamarans out of Waikiki.

Byron began going around naked. He complained that in the hot sticky doldrums even his shorts chafed. Larry joined him in the nudist thing, but unlike his brother, he looked like a withered string bean. Byron was buff and in good shape, even if he did avoid work by blaming his bad back. Jason wouldn't go naked, and David, with his fair skin, couldn't take that much sun and wore long sleeve shirts with his trunks.

Jason spent much of his down time reading. He devoured his *Norton Anthology of English Literature*. He especially liked Samuel Taylor Coleridge's description of the Doldrums in his *The Rime of the Ancient Mariner*.

> *The hot and copper sky*
> *The blood Sun, at noon,*
> *Right up above the mast did stand,*
> *No bigger than the Moon.*

David, on the other hand, spent his time sketching and writing letters. Even Larry laughed at some of the sketches David made of him, but David would not let anyone know to whom he was writing.

As *Mata'i* crossed the equator at approximately 21:37 GMT on May 12th, in keeping with the traditions of the sea, Pollywogs, any sailor who had not crossed the line, were initiated in to the Order of Neptune in a trial by ordeal. This tradition was more than 400 years old, and the sailors of the great sailing ships endured a diverse collection of pranks—all in the cause of appeasing King Neptune. If successful they would become Shellbacks.

Larry was the first on deck to begin the *Mata'i* tradition. He was dressed as King Neptune, naked, wearing a bed sheet for a cape and carrying a coil of rope and a makeshift trident that looked like an oar with some horns attached to it.

Byron showed up next, wearing nothing but a shell necklace, that he said came from King Neptune. He claimed that he had already crossed the equator, and was a certified Shellback, but no one believed him. He sipped his special rum drink and sat in the shade of the awning that had been put up when the boat entered the doldrums.

The Pollywogs, Jason and David, were ordered on deck to begin their initiation. They tried not to laugh at Larry and Byron. Larry order the Pollywogs to strip and asked Byron to tie them up. Byron reluctantly put his drink down and took the rope from Larry. Byron tied the boy's hands and feet together—lingering a bit too long in front of David's genitals. Once they were tied up Larry shoved them overboard. Their initiation was to free themselves and swim back to the boat before it drifted away. Neither David nor Jason thought much about being tied up and tossed into the sea. They laughed at the ritual.

Once the boys hit the water, however, it became apparent that they couldn't float or tread water, and they began to sink. The surface water at the equator was hot; over ninety degrees Fahrenheit, and it grew much cooler a few feet down. As the boys sank into the cold water, they eventually positioned themselves vertically and tried to coordinate their kicking. It didn't work. As the water grew still colder Jason realized that David was beginning to panic. Jason squeezed his hand and David looked at him. Jason closed his eyes and David knew to try and calm himself. Then Jason lifted his knees and David followed. That allowed them to lift their arms and get a good downward stroke to stop their descent. They found a rhythm—knees up, arms up, and stroke down—that brought them to the surface.

As they broke the surface, they gulped a few deep breaths. The sea was without a ripple—no wind—but even so, *Mata'i* had drifted yards away. Larry and Byron were at the rail laughing. Larry saw Jason look his way and waved a cold beer at him. It was surreal. Jason felt so detached from what was happening, like he was in a dream. Then David pulled him close and gasped, "We need to untie our feet."

Jason nodded.

"Fill your lungs. You hold our feet and I'll get the knot," David said.

They took four deep breaths and grabbed each other's ankles. Like contortionists in a fetal position, David kept their feet together while Jason worked on the knot. They tumbled head over heels and used more air than they'd expected to keep the sea from going up their noses. Their heads were in each other's crotches, and they were sinking fast, like a ball tumbling downward. David's dick kept rubbing against Jason's ear. Jason tuned out everything and concentrated on the knot. Finally, he got it untied and the boys jerked out of their restraints. They straightened up and kicked hard for the surface.

After a few panicked breaths, the boys looked around and saw the boat more than fifty yards away. Byron and Larry were no longer laughing. It looked like they were arguing. After Jason and David got their breath, the buddies looked at each other and burst out laughing.

"You had your dick in my ear," Jason said.

"I know. It was the worst fuck I ever had."

"Did nothing for me, either."

Treading water, facing each other, David's eyes were dark with fury. "You think Larry knew what he was doing? He could have killed us!"

"Look at us, though; we went along with it."

"He's psychotic. Lillian warned us. That man is evil."

"What are you going to do about it? Swim to Tahiti?"

"Fuck you. Aren't you pissed?"

The boys struggled to get their hands free.

"When we get back to the boat, I'm going to treat it like a grand joke that we won." Jason pulled the rope and David's hand toward him. "I think Byron was really chewing Larry out."

"Want to bet that he'll turn the motor on and come and get us?" David pulled the rope back to him.

"Not a chance. That would admit that he made a mistake, and Larry Graff never makes a mistake. The knot is on your side."

The boys finally broke free, stretched out into a good crawl and swam back toward the boat.

Jason was just as furious as David, but he could see no benefit in telling Larry off. He couldn't accept that Larry was as malicious as he appeared. Jason knew that Larry was an egotist, but he attributed it to the man's ignorance.

David kept pace as Jason increased his speed. With every stroke, David wrestled with how to extract justice, or at least an admission of stupidity. Fat chance! He probably should let it go and follow Jason's lead in maintaining a sense of civility.

It took a good twenty minutes for the initiates to reach the *Mata'i* and when they got there, they found the boarding ladder hung over the side. They climbed on board and collapsed on the cockpit lounges. Larry and Byron were no longer on deck. The boys were naked, exhausted, and no one was there to applaud them.

Larry came on deck wearing a large smile. "Congratulations. You two now belong to the Ancient Order of the Deep. Well done!"

Byron followed his brother on deck with an armful of towels. Both were dressed as if they were going to a cocktail party. Byron tossed each boy a towel and studied Jason as he dried himself off.

"I'll have that beer now," Jason said to Larry.

"Ice cold beer, coming up." Larry went aft where two wet socks hung from the mizzen boom. The socks were in the shade and the battery-powered fan from Larry's cabin was propped up on the dinghy, blowing air on them. Larry took the heavy socks off of the boom and pulled out two bottles of Hinano beer, handing one to each of the boys. "I've been saving these for this occasion. Surprised you, didn't I?"

The beer was cool.

"Evaporation." Larry proclaimed, smugly.

The boys looked at each other and clinked their bottles.

"Refreshing," David said.

"What a surprise," Jason said. "Cold beer at the equator and not an ice cube for a thousand miles." They saluted Larry with their beers.

"I'm curious, Larry, what was *your* initiation when you first crossed the equator?" David ventured.

He thought a moment. "I was one of a handful of passengers on a freighter heading from Panama to Sydney. The captain had a 'Neptune Ball' and we wore black tie. I drank a lot of champagne."

David got up and went below, mumbling something about getting dressed.

"Nap time," Byron said and followed David.

"I guess you have the watch," Larry said to Jason as he took his fan from the dinghy. "Welcome to the Neptune Club," he said and disappeared into his cabin.

Jason looked around and saw nothing but a flat, mirror-like sea. It was nearly white in the reflected sunlight, and the surrounding horizon made him feel strangely claustrophobic. He felt there was another world out there, just beyond human perception, and it was so close it made reality seem unreal.

The southeast trade winds arrived on their sixteenth day at sea. Larry had planned to be in Papeete by this time, and *Mata'i* was well capable of meeting that schedule. But this is where they were, and Larry set a course of south-by-south-southeast and put up every sail he had. He was happy again and sure that they would make up the time lost in the Doldrums. Everyone checked the knot-meter regularly, especially after gusts of wind, and with the sea still calm, and *Mata'i* well-trimmed, she was doing over twelve knots.

As with all ocean crossings, progress was measured in daily nautical miles. The shortest distance they had made in one day was in the doldrums—thirty-eight miles. At six knots the *Mata'i* would do one hundred forty-four miles in twenty-four hours. If she had averaged that speed for the entire voyage, it would have taken her just under sixteen days to sail from Honolulu to Papeete. *Mata'i* could actually make over fourteen knots with the right sea and wind conditions, and if the current wind held, she could make up some of the lost time and reach Papeete in four days. Larry was hoping to be there in three.

Larry had the guys take a noon sight with their sextants every day. Learning celestial navigation was part of the experience that Larry was providing, and though David had some experience with sextants, chronometers, and nautical almanacs, Jason had not. This was the one time each day when Jason and Larry's relationship was genuine. Jason wanted to learn, and Larry was a good teacher.

Four nights later, on the twentith day, the wind died. A front had moved up from the south and killed the trade winds. *Mata'i* was less than one hundred miles from Papeete and she was becalmed. The morning dawned overcast and still, and it was humid. Larry refused to use the motor to power into Papeete. Byron grew furious as the boat rolled in the swell while the sails slapped back and forth.

"If we turn on the motor now, we'll be in Papeete tomorrow," Byron said as the whole crew sat in the cockpit looking at each other.

"There's a fifty-fifty chance," Larry said, sitting at the helm controlling the boat.

Hours went by. The crew of the *Mata'i* stared at each other, enduring the sickening motion of the boat and the crack of the sails as they popped from one side of the yacht to the other. Larry stubbornly pretended to steer. He couldn't hold a course and with the heavy overcast hiding the sun they were not going to get a sight that day. *Mata'i* had been drifting since four that morning and her last position had put her between Caroline Atoll and Tetiaroa, Marlon Brando's island.

"We're a sailboat, and the diesel is an auxiliary to be used to get us out of trouble. It's not our primary means of power. We leave that to nature and right now nature isn't cooperating," Larry said, looking at Jason. "Shouldn't you be praying or meditating or something?"

"As if that will do any good," Byron said. "I've got a prayer for you: Turn on the god of diesel and let's move."

Larry just stared ahead, perched at the helm as if he were truly sailing.

"Oh, for fuck sake!" Byron cried. "I'm out of here when we reach Papeete." He went below and poured himself a double shot of rum.

The boys went forward and sat on the cabin roof in front of the salon. The last time they were there, Lillian sat between them.

"Are you going to leave, too?" Jason asked David.

"I will if you will."

"I feel like I've made a commitment, and I should see it through."

"You don't owe Larry a damn thing. He's unreasonable and dangerous."

"I wouldn't be staying for Larry. I'd do it to find out what kind of spiritual growth this is forcing on me. I've been so pissed since we left Honolulu, I'm not sure I can even meditate anymore. I've seen people who think they're so committed to the Spirit when all is going well, run from it when things fall apart. They let their instinct to fight, or get the hell out take over. I'm trying to look beyond those feelings and find another way to deal with the situation." Jason looked away, trying to get a handle on his emotions. "I don't know if I'll be successful. If not, then the spiritual life isn't for me."

David put his arm around his friend. "I won't abandon you to that son of a bitch. I might not have much influence, but I'll stay for you."

Larry spent the afternoon looking for Tetiaroa. He thought he knew where it would appear, given *Mata'i's* drift, and where he thought the currents were taking the boat, but he never saw the island. By nightfall he was sure they'd passed it. Still, he wouldn't fire up the motor even though he believed he could see the glow of light from Papeete. Larry was determined to sail into port the next morning.

After a meager dinner of canned food, and the dinner dishes had been cleaned and put away, the boys went forward to their space on the cabin top. Byron was attempting to hold a course. Larry was cussing at the Aires self-steering gear—he hadn't completely given up on it. When there were decent winds, the Aires worked well. Why Larry thought he could get it to work when there was no wind was puzzling. *Mata'i* had been drifting for almost twenty-four hours and everybody had accepted that Papeete was another day away.

Jason was meditating, which made him extra alert. "Did you hear that?" he said.

David turned his head like a direction finder until he was looking to where Jason thought he'd heard the surf. "Yeah. Over there."

The boys went to the rail and looked out into the darkness. The cloud cover was thick and the night dark. Then Jason saw a pale line of white off the port bow and pointed it out to David. "Surf!"

"Larry! Byron! Surf off our port bow!" Jason yelled.

Both men looked to where Jason was pointing.

"Impossible." Larry said, walking to the port shrouds. "We passed Tetiaroa late this afternoon."

A slight breeze drifted over the boat, coming from the direction of the surf, and it smelled like land. The mainsail jibed at the same time that a larger than normal swell rolled under *Mata'i*.

"That's a wave and it's going to break," David said.

"Smell that!" said Byron. He slid off the helmsman's seat and stood at the wheel for better control.

Suddenly it became clear that the boat was about sixty yards off a reef and drifting into the impact zone of the waves.

"Larry, turn on the fuckin' engine before you lose your boat!" Byron yelled.

Larry just stood there, staring at the now apparent surf, and not moving. The boys ran back to the cockpit and David started the vent motor that cleared the bilge of fumes. "Release the shaft brake, J.J."

"I'm starting the goddamn engine now," Byron said shoving David aside. "If we blow up, we blow up."

Jason had the seat hatch raised and was turning the extension into the brake clamp when another swell rolled under the boat and knocked him off-balance. Byron hung onto the helm and pressed the starter button. He shifted the motor in gear and gave it some throttle.

"Wait!" Jason said. "The brake's not off!"

Byron throttled back but the brief turning of the shaft had locked it to where Jason didn't have the purchase to release it.

"Dave, get the brake from below," Larry finally joined the effort to get the boat moving. He took over the helm from Byron.

David ran below, and with Jason working from topside, they were able to release the brake clamp. "We're free!" Jason hollered.

Larry put the boat in gear and gave her some power. The reef was clearly visible, and the boat was still in the crash zone of the surf. Larry was not acting quickly enough. Byron shoved the throttle to max, pushed Larry aside, and then turned the boat ninety degrees to plow through a couple of large swells that were already breaking. Everybody held their breath, hoping that *Mata'i* had enough power to get through the waves before they drove her onto the reef. She did have the power, and the *Mata'i* cleared the impact zone. They were safe, and the crew relaxed.

Byron then declared that they would be motoring to Papeete and demanded a course. Larry brought up his radio direction finder and found two beacons that he triangulated to get them to Papeete. No one said anything about Byron taking over in the emergency.

Mata'i approached the pass through the reef into Papeete harbor at first light the following day. The swell had increased. There was no wind, and large drops of rain randomly fell from the sky. Byron motored the *Mata'i* into the harbor while Larry called customs. At the same time, a fifty-foot sloop backed into the last slot left along Boulevard Pomare. "That's not looking good," Byron said.

The boys were standing on the stern, ready with the mooring lines. "What's wrong?" Jason said.

David saw the situation. "That sloop took our berth. They moor here like the Caribbean, stern to. You just put a gangway off the stern and you're ashore."

Larry came back on deck livid. "That was the last place along the quay. Another boat from Honolulu." Larry shoved Byron out of the way and took over. He turned his boat a hundred and eighty degrees and powered down to where the street turned inland, and the quay stopped. Beyond that was a rock revetment and a bank of grass that made a waterfront park for a few hundred yards until the shore turned into mangrove and mud flats.

"We'll have to anchor off the park," Larry said, maneuvering *Mata'i* to a spot ten yards from the shore.

After the bow anchor was set, the boys lowered the dinghy into the water and rowed ashore, taking a stern line with them. They took the line up the grass and tied it to a nearby coconut tree. Using the tree as a makeshift winch, they pulled the stern of *Mata'i* as close to the shore as was safe and tied her off. *Mata'i* had finally arrived, after twenty-two days at sea.

Chapter 22
Papeete, Tahiti

Monday May 22, 1989

The customs boat arrived shortly after *Mata'i* had set her anchors. It maneuvered alongside and two agents came aboard. Larry had the paperwork ready and spoke to the captain in fluent French. The officer stamped all the passports while his colleague searched the cabin, opened storage lockers and pulled floorboards up from the cabin sole. The sergeant searched the aft cabin while Larry and the captain talked and laughed like old friends. When he came back carrying the bag of firearms, everything changed. The captain felt fooled and demanded an explanation for the guns. Larry argued that they were for protection at sea, but the officer, seeing the thousands of rounds of ammunition, thought Larry was supplying one of the dissident native groups that wanted the French out of their islands. They confiscated the guns and gave Larry a summons to appear before the local magistrate.

As the customs boat pulled away Larry went into his cabin cursing them in French and English. A few minutes later he came back with his shore pack. "Listen up," he said, "I'm staying ashore for a few days. Melanie is here, and we're going to have some private father-daughter time together. I'll straighten out this fucking mess with the *gendarmes* and find a new heat exchanger. I want someone on the boat at all times. Jason, take me ashore and rig something that will make the dinghy more useful."

"I don't get what you mean."

"If I'm ashore, I don't want to have to wait and shout for someone to get me. Rig the dinghy so I can get back to the boat myself. Got it?"

Larry tossed his duffel into *Mata'i-iti*, climbed over the rail into it, and looked back at Jason impatiently. "You coming or what?"

Jason climbed in and looked at Larry puzzled.

"What?" Larry said. "Pull us ashore with the stern line."

This was a scene straight out of *Mutiny on the Bounty*; Larry in the bow with his foot on the rail with Jason working the rope. Larry jumped out as soon as the dinghy reached land and strode off without another word.

When Jason got back to the boat, Byron was standing in the cockpit dressed in his Miami Vice look and clutching his canvas seabag. "What do you charge for a ride?" Jason ignored the question and took Byron ashore. When he returned, he tied the dinghy to a stanchion. David had put up the awning, and the boys flaked out in the cockpit.

The rigging system would have to wait.

The afternoon grew hot and the diesel fumes from the traffic on Boulevard Pomare drifted out to the boat. Someone was yelling from shore. Jason refused to move until David shoved him off the cockpit bench. "We've got company."

Jason rolled off the bench and saw Byron waving, wanting a ride back to the boat.

"I'll do it," David said.

"Then why did you wake me up?"

David shrugged, climbed into the dinghy, and pulled it to shore.

"I thought you were going to rig up some pulley system to do this. I've been here for five minutes," Byron said in a sour voice.

"Well, we've been busy."

Byron stepped in and David pulled him back to the boat.

"Here's the deal," Byron said, climbing aboard *Mata'i*, "I've got a nice room at the Tahiti Nui just up the street on Avenue du Prince Hinoi and thought you dickheads would like to clean up a bit." He gave them a key. "Just fix up the dinghy so we can get back and forth before you go."

The boys rigged a system of pulleys to get the dinghy to and from shore. They grabbed some fresh clothes, and left Byron with a rum drink in one hand and a baguette with cheese in the other. They stepped ashore and staggered down Boulevard Pomare like a couple of drunken sailors. The constant motion of the sea for three weeks made it difficult to walk a straight line on land. It took them ten minutes to reach the hotel and two minutes later they were fighting over who was going to use the shower first.

Feeling revived and like human beings again, the buddies strolled back to the boat through the public market pavilion, a full city block selling everything from fruits and fish to machete's and sparkplugs. They debated whether or not to shop and decided they'd do that later. According to Larry, they were planning to spend at least five days in Papeete, so the guys figured they had time enough to come back. They stopped by the post office where David mailed the stack of letters he wrote on the voyage down. Jason noticed that they were all to Lillian. He was miffed that David was even writing Lillian. For a moment they locked eyes, and each decided not to say anything. Jason asked if there were any letters for them, but the clerk refused to say one way or another. The post office would only release mail to the captain of the yacht.

They left frustrated. Byron was waiting for them at the coconut tree to which the *Mata'i* was tied. He wanted to take them to an expensive French dinner at L'O a la Bouche, a famous waterfront restaurant that was known for serving the best food in the South Pacific. Larry's dictate to not leave the boat unattended was ignored.

On the way to the restaurant they stopped to watch a dance troupe practicing in the park. To a Tahitian, dancing is like breathing—everyone does it. Larry had planned the trip so that they would be in Taiohae in the Marquesas for the Bastille Day Festival in July. He thought the *fête* in Papeete was too commercial. But for the next six weeks dance troupes on all the islands would be practicing the *'upa'upa* and rehearsing for the competitions that would take place throughout the archipelago.

The men watched the dancers for a while. The girls had *pareus* tied low over their jeans. Their hips moved in time with the beating of the *to'ere*, a drum made from a hollowed log and played with short sticks. The drummers varied the rhythm and tone by hitting the log in different places, and the girls matched the beat with their hips. The guys wore *pareus* tied up like Speedos and moved in and around the girls, their knees whirling, answering the girls tempting gestures. The top dancers were guys in grass skirts, their long hair held up with turtle shell combs, and they danced both the male and female parts.

Byron said, "You know, they're *mahu*."

"What's that?" David said.

"Homosexual," Byron said.

"So?"

"Islanders call it the third gender. Most native people respect that social category. It's not put down. *Mahu* are just gay; *rae-rae* are transgender. You'll see *rae-rea* women in most dance troupes.

Shamans, artists and storytellers are many times third gender people. Most of the dancers here are third gender," Byron said.

At the restaurant the conversation drifted onto the topic of native tribes. Byron knew a lot about the Mayan tribes and the Yucatec people of British Honduras, where he had a home. He was interested in how the Polynesians compared to native Caribbean people.

I wonder what would have happened if the missionaries hadn't come to these people? Jason asked.

"There'd have been a lot more fucking." Byron had never talked like this on the boat when Larry was around. After dinner he invited the boys up to his hotel for a nightcap.

They continued talking on Byron's balcony with the honking horns and diesel fumes of Papeete drifting in. Byron had changed into a silk robe and the three of them lounged on the bed that filled his lanai, what the Hawaiians would call a *pune*.

"Let me see your hands," Byron said. Jason and David obeyed. "You can tell a lot about someone by their palms. I can read a palm as well as any shaman or voodoo priestess. A woman in Haiti taught me. She activated my feminine side. All of those animist religions are matriarchal. The pagan part of Christianity is matriarchal through the Virgin Mary. The women have the power and so do those men who have embraced their feminine nature."

The boys looked at each other with a mix of fascination and disbelief. They'd never seen this aspect of Byron.

Byron held David's hand up and turned it front and back. "Dave has the hands of an artist," Byron said to Jason. "They're supple and sensitive." He turned to David, "Your element is water. All that creative energy must express itself through them. I'd never have thought of you as a sailor." Looking closely at

Jason's hand, he continued; "Where Jason here is a man of the Earth … square palms, powerful fingers, almost peasant hands. His element is fire and these hands are meant for transformation." He turned squarely to Jason, and with great sincerity said, "You're impulsive, Jason, and I bet you do something great with your life."

The boys laughed and pulled their hands away.

Byron persisted, not letting them go. "I haven't finished." He moved closer, facing the young men, putting Jason's hand on his knee, and at the same time turning over David's hand. "Don't move, Jason. I'll get back to you. Dave, you have an incredible lifeline, very long with lots of vitality. I bet you're great in bed." David pulled his hand away. But Byron held on, "Come on. Don't be touchy. Your love line is full of emotional trauma. Are you insecure in your love life?"

"Who makes up all of this shit?" David said.

"This is ancient. Protestants discount it. Catholics fear it. Scientist can't really explain it because it's so true. This line is your head … Oh wow! That's great! Deep, sloping, and creative. Uh, oh! Your fate is linked to someone else." David squirmed. "See how it touches your life line?"

Who's he talking about, Lillian or Jason, David thought.

Byron picked up Jason's hand and put David's hand on his other knee. David pulled away

"Keep it there, Dave," he said. "This connects us. Makes the reading stronger."

Byron drew Jason's hand closer and turned it over like he'd done with David. "Jason, Jason, Jason. You've got a very strong life line. If I were a shaman, I'd say you were nearly immortal. You're like Dave with your strength and enthusiasm. You also have a long curving love line. It's deep. You have a very strong love for someone, perhaps you've already met that person, or not, but when you're together you're as one, freely expressing your emotions and feelings. Your head line shows adventure and enthusiasm for life. You're strongly controlled by fate and have the tendency to try to harness it. You can't control your fate."

Byron took both the boys' hands in his and closed his eyes in a kind of meditation. "I can never tell Larry that I do this," he sighed. He pulled them close and hugged each one of them and kissed each one on the cheek. "I want you two to spend the night with me. I want to make love to both of you."

Jason burst out laughing, but David did not laugh. "What the fuck! Was all this just a big come-on?"

"Absolutely not. Everything I told you is true. That's why you are reacting like this. If you do this with me, you'll be free one way or the other."

David got up. "Come on J.J., let's get back to the boat."

Jason sat there. Byron still held his hand. "No. I'll stay a little while longer."

David left, looking at Jason like he'd lost his mind. He was more than disgusted.

When Jason returned an hour or so later, David was in the cockpit, ready for sleep. He turned away, shunning his friend, then rolled back. "How on earth could you do that?"

"Do what?"

"Fuck that dirty old man."

"Aren't you the tolerant one tonight? No compassion. No understanding."

"Why did you stay then? I'll admit Byron is slick. He's been hot for you since we left Honolulu. I never thought you'd actually do it."

"What?"

"But then you betrayed me in high school. My dad thought I was a queer and moved us to Orange County."

"I thought he got a job there," Jason countered.

"You don't remember playing Indian at Camp Josepho and getting busted by the ranger for being a couple of fags?

"Yeah. That was nothing."

"Nothing? Don't you remember the dream, or the vision, or whatever you want to call it? I always thought you conjured that up ... like we were in some rite of passage with a band of Indians. You don't remember that?"

"I remember we were going to meditate and get close to nature and try to experience some kind of mystical union."

"Then where did the Indians come from?"

"I guess that was your experience. I remember we put our costumes on and went up by the spring to see if we could feel the history of the spot." David wasn't getting what Jason was saying.

"I always thought that you rejected me because of what my family believed, that you thought we were a little crazy, and that our religion bordered on being some kind of cult. You were the only one that I could be honest with. Then your dad was so hostile and you all left town. I didn't hear from you for months. I never thought you were a queer. Hell, I got hard-ons riding the bus. I'd carry my books in front of me so nobody would notice."

David laughed, remembering his own embarrassments.

"Fuck you," Jason said.

"No. No. It's not about you. I suddenly understand after all these years."

"I didn't do anything with Byron, Dave. I just wanted to see how far he'd go."

"I've never met someone so out there, so blunt in his sexuality."

Jason was laughing too. "Sometimes I feel like such a stranger on this planet. I don't really understand human relationships. I mean, why is Larry mad at me all the time? I get it, but I don't. I don't meet his expectations, so he wants to punish me. I don't get that. Why would anybody want to punish someone, make them suffer, hurt them? It doesn't do anything for the oppressor."

"Face it, Larry is an asshole,"

"Davy, you're the only one who never judged me."

"Until now, I guess."

"I'm not sure that's judgment. I think we'll always love each other."

David thought a moment, and then had to blurt it out. "What about Lillian?"

"What about her?"

"Are you really in love with her?" David asked.

"Of course!"

"It didn't seem like it in Honolulu, except for the grand public display at the restaurant."

"Are you jealous?"

David couldn't admit that he was. "You kept leaving. You never went to class. I think Lillian felt you didn't care about what she was doing to help your mom."

"How do you know what she felt?" Jason grew serious, as serious as he could be after a couple of bottles of Puligny-Montrachet and a close encounter with a sexual swinger. "I never go to Mom's classes in Hawaii. There's something about that group that turns me off. They don't recognize what I have to offer."

"Are you talking about Larry? Do you want his approval? Jesus, J.J., I thought this trip was about deeper things than that."

"It's about finding out who we are. You just told me something very moving. You've always been my best friend, the one I can share my deepest secrets with. I'm so sorry you misinterpreted that time in junior high, and I'm so happy you're here now," Jason said.

"I'd kiss you, but then I'd have to tell everybody that we're gay."

Saturday May 27, 1989

The end of that week Larry moved back on the boat with his daughter Melanie. She was in great shape, very pretty, and tall like her dad. She had an infectious smile and greeted both David and Jason formally at first, but her handshake turned into a quick hug as if to say, "it's going to be rather intimate on this boat and I want things to be fun and congenial." In everything else – except in her height – she was his exact opposite. Where Larry was stiff and wiry, she was smooth and fluid. Where Larry never revealed what he really wanted, Melanie was straightforward and frank. As nice and polite as Melanie was, Larry was mad and abrupt.

"What did you two do to Byron?" Larry was not really interested in an answer. "Because whatever you did, he left. You two are going to have to pick up the slack."

Larry unlocked the aft cabin and opened the companionway for Melanie. "Come, darling, let's get you settled."

The boys looked at each other and laughed. "Pick up the slack?" Jason said. "Byron did nothing but occasionally steer."

A few minutes later a truck pulled up opposite *Mata'i's* mooring and honked its horn. Larry popped out of his cabin and ordered Jason to bring the repair guy out to the boat. He was lugging a new heat exchanger to install, and some brackets with six jerry cans for extra fuel and water. The man installed the brackets and jerry cans on either side of the forward cabin, and then went below to change out the heat exchanger.

A half hour later another truck arrived and began honking. It was from the market, delivering their provisions for the next three months. Larry said he couldn't count on getting anything from the Marquesas. The boys started stowing the food, but Larry interrupted and told them to leave that for later.

Larry and the boys walked up Boulevard Pomare to the *gendarmerie* to get their papers and straighten out the firearms issue. Larry warned the boys to say as little as possible, noting that they couldn't speak French anyway. However, if they were asked about rebel groups or the purpose of the guns, they were to plead ignorance of island politics and say that the guns and ammo were only there for their protection.

Larry came out of the *gendarmerie* headquarters smiling and totting his weapons. The authorities had had no problem with the guns, however, they did with the ammunition. Larry was allowed to keep one box. Next, Larry led the way to the immigration office. The boys waited outside guarding the guns while Larry retrieved the crew's passports and visas. The last stop was the post office, and Larry went in alone.

David didn't trust Larry and bolted into the building. The clerk handed Larry a package of letters tied up with a string. Larry untied the string and sorted through the mail. He refused two of the letters and handed them back. David thought he saw his name on one.

"Why did you give those letters back?" David was angry and abrupt. "Is that our mail?"

Larry was cool. "It was the wrong general delivery address." He again sorted through the small pile of letters and shook his head. "Nothing for you. Jason has a letter from his mother."

"But you said 'refused.'"

"No. I told her they were in the wrong pile. They were for somebody else." Larry walked past David with the ease of a seasoned liar.

Outside David was on Larry's heels. Jason saw David's rage and dropped the bag of guns on the ground. "What's going on?"

"He refused our letters," David shouted.

"You didn't get any mail," Larry said firmly.

"You're lying!"

Jason ran into the post office and up to the one open window. "I want the mail for Jason St. John and David Walker!" he demanded.

The clerk did that great French put-off by pursing her lips and letting out a gasp of air that meant everything from "fuck you" to "I don't know what you're talking about." Jason reached through the window grabbing the pile of mail near the clerk, only to be pulled back by a couple of security guards. Jason broke free and ran to the bank of phones that lined one wall of the office. It looked like a set from an old movie. Jason fumbled for some change and got an operator on the line.

"I want to make a collect call to Lillian Harvey in Honolulu, Hawaii." He gave the operator the name of the hotel. He heard the hotel clerk responding to the operator, saying that Lillian wasn't there. Jason needed more money to stay on the line. By this time, Larry had entered the post office, hovering over Jason.

Jason put his hand over the mouthpiece; "Larry, I need some change. Please!"

Larry just smiled and pointed to his watch.

Jason yelled into the phone, "I know she's there!"

"The party you want is not there," the operator said and then the line went dead. Jason jiggled the receiver hook.

"Larry, I need change. I need to call my mother," Jason was frantic to know what was going on.

"We need to get back to the boat. Your mother can't do anything for you here." He turned and walked out. Jason was so angry that he ran from the post office all the way back to the boat.

"I always thought he was too immature for this trip," Larry confided to David as David pulled the dinghy to them from the boat. "His mother thought it would do him good, make him grow up, accept his responsibility and service to her Ministry. I can see that he'll never be a spiritual teacher." The men stepped into the dinghy and David pulled the dinghy back to the boat. Larry continued, "The only worthwhile thing Jason had done was to invite you along. With Byron gone, I'm going to need your help." Jason overheard this and watched Larry put his arm around David's shoulders.

Chapter 23
The South Pacific

Monday May 29, 1989

The *Mata'i* left Papeete early in the morning—a week after arriving and two days after Melanie had moved aboard the boat. They took on water and fuel at the commercial pier. The boys hoisted the sails outside the reef and Larry set a course around the north shore of Tahiti, past Point Venus and into the South Pacific. Larry planned to island hop through the flat Tuamotu Archipelago, which meant "the distant islands." But sailors called them the "dangerous islands." Culturally the people there were the same as the people in the Society Islands— Tahiti, Moorea, Bora Bora. They spoke Tahitian, danced the *'upa'upa* dances of Tahiti, and in ancient times, followed the same gods. But they were outliers, far away from the social core of Tahiti, struggling to survive on an archipelago made up of atolls and reefs. The land barely reached six feet above sea level. The trade winds blew over the hardscrabble earth without resistance, and the currents were unpredictable and treacherous. Larry was not going to sail through these islands at night.

With *Mata'i* on a broad reach, Larry estimated a day-and-a-half at sea before reaching the first island, Rangiroa. Jason and David settled into their at-sea routine, which meant trimming the sails and maintaining their course. Larry was mostly tinkering and only joined the boys during social hours. Melanie enjoyed the sail.

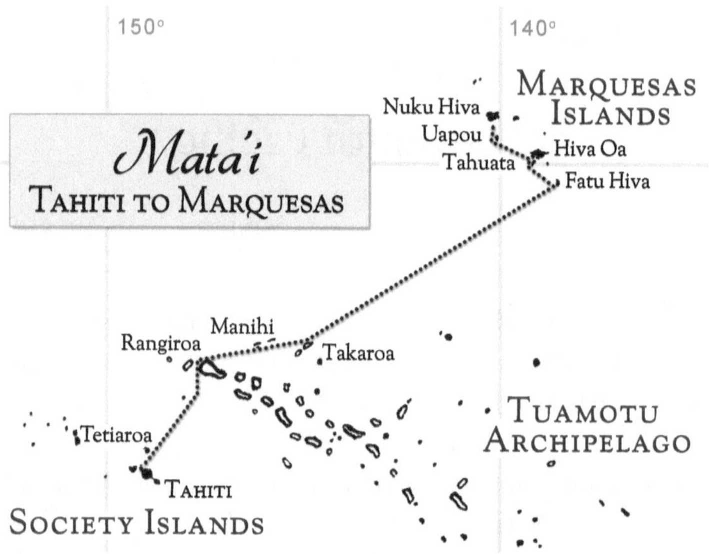

Larry always cooked the main meals. There was a table in the cockpit, and when the weather cooperated, everyone would take their meals there. But that didn't mean the crew would be eating holding paper plates in their laps. No, the table always had a cloth on it, and some sort of centerpiece. Ashore, Larry made the centerpiece out of flowers. At sea, he'd pull together a centerpiece using shells and glass balls arranged in a wooden bowl. Dinners always started with cocktails, and Larry served only French wine with the food.

Melanie enjoyed steering the boat. While Larry was below cooking, Melanie was at the helm, and the boys bombarded her with questions.

"Did you meet any of your half-brothers or sisters in Tahiti?" David and Jason burned with curiosity about Larry and his family. Melanie just smiled.

"I didn't," she said. "I did meet three of Dad's five wives. One was younger than me."

"Everybody in Honolulu speculates about his years in Tahiti. I'm sure the stories are exaggerated, but there are people at the Hawaii Yacht Club convinced that Larry's offspring are Tahitian royalty now ruling Tahiti."

"Wouldn't that be nice?"

"What did your dad do there?"

"I thought you both knew that story."

"Only the rumors," Jason replied.

"Dad's family was wealthy, from Bryn Mawr on the old Main Line of Philadelphia. My grandmother was a Flagler. His upbringing was boarding schools and Palm Beach vacations in the winter and summers in North Haven, Maine. That's where he fell in love with sailing. He graduated from Dartmouth rather young, at twenty, and left to see the world on a steamer sailing from New York to Sydney through the Panama Canal with stops in Havana and Papeete. He didn't like Havana but got off the steamer in Papeete, where he stayed until World War Two."

"Then he saw the unspoiled Tahiti," Jason said.

"Not really. Fletcher Christian saw the unspoiled Tahiti. From then on it was downhill. At least that's my opinion."

"He must have had a few girlfriends?"

Melanie laughed. "Well, my dad's always been curious, except about what I was doing. But he needed to know everything about everything else. So, he learned all there was to know about Tahiti, including the language. He already knew French. Of course, he loved many women. He got married to a princess from one of the chiefly families. I'm sure he never told my grandparents."

Melanie looked at Jason and David like the reporter she hoped to be. "If this is boring, stop me. I only heard this story last week.

My mother won't talk about him. Frankly, I have a hard time relating to him."

"Didn't you see him growing up?" Jason said.

"Not much. He got into all that Dr. Green crap and mom couldn't stand those people."

The boys looked at each other and started to laugh.

"I'm sorry." She realized that perhaps she had hit a nerve.

"No, it's so honest. It's wonderful," Jason said. "Go on."

"I didn't know Dad had so many friends in Tahiti. He and I visited James Norman Hall's widow a few days ago and saw where the *Bounty Trilogy* was written. Mrs. Hall treated him like a son. Did Dad make you read the *Bounty Trilogy*?"

"I'm on the last book," David said.

"I guess he found his paradise," Melanie continued. "He had a son. He said he tried to work with the territorial president to create some kind of economy for the islanders—his major at Dartmouth was economics—but the war came along, and he returned to the states."

"I never knew any of this," Jason said. "He doesn't like to talk about himself."

"You've got that right," Melanie said. "He never said boo to me until I got here and all of sudden, he never shut up."

"And then what happened," David said.

"He received a commission in the Navy and after a couple of years in San Diego he was sent back here. He was second in command at the big allied supply base on Bora Bora. He gave me a whole history of World War Two as well. Want to hear that too?"

"I've nowhere to go," Jason said.

"Bora Bora was beyond the reach of the Japanese. War matériel from San Diego to Hawaii to here, and from the East

Coast through the Panama Canal could move without danger from Japanese planes and submarines. The base supported the campaigns to take back New Caledonia and the New Hebrides. It had seaplane runways, fuel—seven thousand men—so I guess it was a big responsibility."

"I bet his family was happy to see him back."

"No. His wife and child had drowned in a boating accident. Their boat sank in a storm while sailing from Moorea to Papeete. Nobody knew how to reach Dad, so he didn't find out until he got back."

"That's horrible," David said. Jason could see that David was readjusting his opinion of Larry and what he had suffered.

"Well, he became one of those rogue South Pacific officers Michener wrote about in *Tales of the South Pacific*. He drank way too much. He started a black market in war surplus and had a fleet of schooners sailing the islands. He probably ran a few spies too! When the war ended, he had a legitimate trading company that supplied islands from Rarotonga to Samoa and throughout French Polynesia. But he said he was miserable. All he could think about was his lost family."

"What about the Navy? They couldn't have liked what he was doing," David said.

"I don't know. He never mentioned any problem with the Navy. He was honorably discharged in 1946, when they closed the base in Bora Bora. Two years later he sold his business to his Tahitian partner. I don't think he ever wanted to come back. He went to New York and became an investment banker."

Larry came on deck with a tray of hors d'oeuvres. "Are you giving away all my secrets?"

"Dad, you never told these guys your history. How come you never told me until last week at the hotel?"

"It doesn't mean anything. What's human history worth, anyway? I'm not that person. Haven't been for decades. You've only known me since I met Dr. Green. His teaching changed my life. I admit I can't always live up to the ideal, but I'm trying to live up to that now."

"But your story is a great adventure. You *should* tell it," Melanie said.

"Bollocks on that. The greatest adventure is discovering your spiritual nature. You should ask Jason about that."

"Is there something going on here that I need to know?" Melanie asked.

"We're out to discover ourselves," David said. "You know, face adversity to discover the depth of our character."

Melanie didn't like being excluded. "What's my role in your little drama?"

"That's still to be determined" Jason said. "Perhaps you're the witness."

"I hope this isn't a Greek tragedy," she replied.

Larry's *hors d'oeuvres* were excellent: a *poisson cru* on slices of baguette. He baked a Tahitian snapper in coconut milk and served it with island sweet potatoes and a leafy vegetable similar to spinach. Comparing this with the first night out of Honolulu was impossible. The angle of sail was smooth broad reach with a gentle quartering sea—it was like being on a cruise ship. The *al fresco* dinner in the cockpit, with a warm fair wind was the kind of experience everyone wanted to remember. The setting sun over the transom turned the ocean into a golden highway, one without markers, seemingly infinite in its reach. The waxing moon was three-quarters full and already a few degrees above the eastern horizon.

Maybe Melanie was the civilizing quotient Larry needed. Maybe now this was going to be the voyage that Jason had sold to David in Europe? David liked *this* Larry. And he liked Melanie, too.

Chapter 24
Rangiroa, Tuamotu Archipelago

Wednesday May 31, 1989

After two days and nights at sea, *Mata'i* sailed through the Avatoru Pass into the lagoon of Rangiroa, and continued down the leeward shore of the main *motu*, Tahitian for "tiny island," and dropped anchor near the Tiputu Pass. The captain and crew dined ashore that night and while Larry talked to the village chief about the weather and politics, the boys encouraged Melanie to tell them more of Larry's history. She was a good story teller, and the boys were captivated by more than just her story telling.

Melanie confessed that she had never been very close to her father. Her parents divorced when she was two and her mother could not let go of hating Larry. It wasn't for anything particular; it was just a general hatred.

"Dad worked for J. P. Morgan in New York during most of the '50s. He married again and in 1959, quit his job, bought a classic Sparkman & Stephens schooner, and took his new wife back to Tahiti."

"Did you know her?" David said.

"No. I don't even know her name. They ended up back in Bora Bora, where Dad formed a hotel company with his former partner from after the war."

"Was she a Tahitian?" Jason asked.

"I don't think so. I think she was a New York socialite. Dad wouldn't talk to me about that time. He divorced whatever-her-name-was and sailed his schooner solo to Hawaii where he met my mom."

"You were born in Honolulu, then?" Jason and David looked at each other, both having the same questions on their minds.

"Yeah, in 1968. I graduated from Punahou School and just got my journalism degree from Arizona State. What else do you want to know?" Melanie was growing resistant.

"I'm sorry. You're just so fascinating." David said.

Melanie looked at the boys, took a breath, and decided to go on. "Mom and I kind of raised each other. She came from a *kamaaina* family, deep roots in the islands, and Dad loved that. Then he found those spiritual books and no longer cared about anything Mom liked. I barely saw him, and we lived in the same town, except in the summers when he made me spend every August on the *Mataʻi* in Hanalei Bay in Kauai with his new wife Helen. I think Helen always hated me."

David nodded his head in understanding. His parents divorced and he saw Melanie's struggle.

"Really? I can't see that in Helen. She was so kind to me," Jason said. "And, she really practiced forgiveness around Larry."

Melanie didn't want to get into that relationship. "I think the reason we didn't go to Bora Bora and the Leeward Islands is because of bad feelings down there. I know Dad says it's because he didn't want to sail against the wind, but I don't believe it. This whole trip was to show me the islands, so why not those?"

"You dad is obsessed by the Marquesas," Jason said. "All he talked about while preparing the boat was getting back to those islands before they got ruined by tourism and everything. That's why he didn't want to go to the Leeward Islands."

"I don't know," Melanie answered. "I think his partner was arrested for being a subversive."

"Why do you think that?" David said.

"My mother, of course. I think there were a number of Tahitians on many of the islands that wanted the French out and were arming themselves. Maybe it had to do with atomic testing, or something. And I guess he got in trouble with the government."

"Like he did in Papeete?" David laughed.

"Anyway, here we are now and where's Dad? Off talking politics with the local chief."

"If your mom wouldn't talk about it, why do you think there was something subversive going on?" David asked.

"Well, this Tahitian came up to Honolulu when I was fourteen. I've always been nosey, and I overheard him begging Dad for money."

Jason laughed.

"Yeah. You know how Dad feels about money." Melanie grew serious. "Well, the man left angry, shouting that Larry would get it. It scared me. Island people have long memories. Then he left for Mexico."

"That's a lot of speculation just because Larry wouldn't fund someone's trip to Mexico," David said.

"I know. I've got to watch that if I'm ever going to be a reporter. But when I asked mother about it, she said I was better off not knowing. She could be right."

The next day the captain and his crew spent relaxing, anchored in the lagoon and looking for pearls.

Chapter 25
Manihi, Tuamotu Archipelago

Friday, June 2, 1989

The fifth day out of Papeete, the *Mata'i* pulled into the quay at the atoll of Manihi. Larry had planned to pass Manihi and spend the night at the next atoll along the route, to be closer to the Marquesas, but the winds picked up and shifted to the east. Larry made the decision to duck into the safety of Manihi in the afternoon when the island was abeam. He didn't want to push his luck with the weather. The way the wind was acting, Larry didn't think they'd make the next island until dusk, and to approach the pass after dark was too dangerous.

There were no other boats at the quay so *Mata'i* tied up to the concrete wharf. The current through the pass was swift, almost four knots, and the boys doubled up the mooring lines. Larry ordered his crew to stay with the boat while he found the village leader to announce their arrival. Custom and protocol required visiting yachts to register with the local government representative—show their papers, sign the mayor's logbook, and pay proper respect to the village chief.

Mata'i spent the night at Manihi and left the following morning heading to Fatu Hiva, the southernmost Marquesan island, about six hundred miles away, an estimated four to five-day sail. The wind kept pushing the boat further north, so Larry tacked and spent the day sailing south-south-east hoping the front would pass quickly and they'd catch the returning trade winds and ride them up to Fatu Hiva. That didn't happen.

Larry's mood changed with the weather. It was overcast, windy and hot, and the new tack took the boat toward the atoll of Takaroa, a dangerous island that had a history of eating ships. After sailing most of the day and making less than fifty miles toward the Marquesas, Larry decided to pull in to Takaroa before dark. Again, the *Mata'i* moored along the wharf in the pass where the current was strong, and the guys doubled up the lines again.

Chapter 26
Takaroa, Tuamotu Archipelago

Saturday, June 3, 1989

E verybody was tired and Larry put off reporting his arrival at Takaroa until the morning. He was in no mood to cook dinner and he retired early to his cabin. David threw together some pasta and he, Melanie, and Jason ate in the salon at the settee as the wind picked up to gale force.

"Larry made the right decision," David shouted over the wind singing in the rigging. *Mata'i* struggled to be free of the wharf, and even with doubled up lines and large fenders she banged and rubbed along the quay.

"Dad's not going to sleep tonight with all this going on. He's so attached to this boat that every time it groans, he feels pain."

"Let's make sure we're well moored and everything is battened down. I don't want anything to come apart or break," Jason told them.

He and David went topside and put the sail covers on the main and mizzen sails. They checked the sheets of the roller-furling jenny, turned the air funnels away from the wind-driven rain, and made sure that nothing loose was left on deck. Jason strapped an extra line over and around the dinghy cover and took off the wooden sail from the Aires wind vane. David pulled the servo rudder out of the water and strapped it up. When they finished, they sat down at their favorite spot on the fore cabin roof and watched the storm build.

You guys are going to get wet." Melanie said, but she sat down next to the boys. "Wow, Dad has a nasty temper, doesn't he?"

"He can be unreasonable at times," Jason said.

"You know, when shit happens, I don't want to have to choose between you two and Dad. In fact, you guys probably know him better than I do. Coming on this trip was a hard decision. My mom was totally against it. But I thought, if I'm going to be a journalist and all, it might provide some good material. I guess I'll have to figure out how to deal with adversity."

David guffawed. "You might get to learn how to do that!"

"More like practicing forgiveness," Jason said.

"I never understood how important that was until I took your mom's class," David said.

"I'm not into that spiritual stuff. When I think about it, I'm stunned Dad ever got into it. It's so unlike him," Melanie said. "Hope it's not like all his other passions: Once he knows all there is about it, he moves on. If it doesn't benefit him, he'll drop it."

"You can't fault him for trying. Something in his consciousness drew him to find a deeper meaning to life," Jason said.

Sunday, June 4, 1989

A gale blew through the night, and the next morning dawned gray and stormy. It was the seventh day out of Papeete, and Larry wanted to move on, but because of the storm, he couldn't. Two more yachts limped in to Takaroa that morning. The crews told of towering seas and winds that tested their sanity. Larry didn't like hearing this and believed their stories were highly exaggerated. He held to the belief that someone spiritually in tune could alter weather, and inclement weather should never limit human endeavor.

Larry kept asking Jason what he was going to do about the delay. With every stormy hour, Larry became convinced that Jason was turning out to be useless. If he'd wanted just a crewman, he could have picked up some surfer off the beach to steer the boat and man the sails. That would have been much cheaper than supporting Jason for months—feeding him, teaching him the skills of a blue-water sailor—one who could find his way around any ocean, know the stars at every latitude, and survive any storm. But with Jason and his advanced spiritual consciousness on board, there were not supposed to be any trials and mishaps.

Larry set the boys to work and went ashore with Melanie. Jason and David did some caulking, sanded some peeling paint, and resealed the aprons around the main and mizzenmast.

David couldn't figure out why Larry thought Jason could alter the weather.

"Solomon Green did some experiments with his close students regarding the weather. In one of his books he writes about a hurricane that had been approaching Palm Beach back in the 70s. Based on the biblical statement that ten righteous men could save a city, Dr. Green thought that if enough individuals could bring into realization the presence of God, nothing destructive could take place where that consciousness of peace existed. And it worked. A group of students meditated to realize the Presence and the storm dissipated and changed direction."

"So, what's going on *here*?"

"Larry isn't interested in God for God's sake. He's interested in having God do something to make *his* human experience better, like fair winds and sunny skies for this trip. That's not how it works."

"So why even pray?"

"You're right. Praying to a god out there to change a human condition is useless. If God is one, and God is omnipotent, there can't be anything *but* God. The moment you have God and a storm and people who want the storm to stop, you fail. To succeed you can only have God."

"But isn't that the way you pray?" David said.

"Yes, but I'm not doing a very good job of it. Maybe subconsciously I'm looking for results just like every other human being. I know that won't bring about a spiritual change. I don't care about the weather. It's not like we're a cruise ship with a schedule to keep. The first principle in spiritual healing is to stop judging—good weather, bad weather—what does that have to do with Spirit? So, either I'm no good at this or there is some other reason for all this suffering."

"Perhaps one of the reasons is that Larry is an asshole."

"What's that statement about God's rain falling on the just and the unjust?"

"Are we just victims of fate, then, in a godless world?" David asked.

"The block is obviously in me," Jason said. "Larry hasn't a clue. He thinks I'm some sort of magician who can miraculously make the crooked places straight. But I don't see that as the point of spiritual illumination. There's got to be more to that than just creating a harmonious human condition."

Monday, June 5, 1989

The next morning the sky was brighter, and the winds had dialed down a couple of notches. They were still blowing from the wrong direction, though. Larry wouldn't say where he and his daughter had been the night before. Melanie just said they'd been to a settlement across the lagoon to visit some of her dad's old friends.

That afternoon two more yachts limped into the pass and tied up along the quay. One, a state-of-the-art maxi yacht sailed by a group of teenagers, flew the flag of the British Virgin Islands, a well-known tax haven. Larry was convinced they were drug smugglers even though they claimed they were delivering the Dutch-built ketch to her owner in Sydney. The other yacht looked barely seaworthy. She flew an American flag and was sailed by a young hippy-looking couple with two small children. Larry was equally mad at them for risking the lives of their children, and he didn't like that the quay had filled up. The next yacht fleeing the storm would have to anchor in the lagoon.

That evening the visitors joined the islanders in the community hall to watch the village dance troupe practice for the Bastille Day *fête* on July 14th. They practiced an *upa'upa* called the *'ote'a*, a line dance with girls on one side and boys on the other. The islanders played a collection of drums. Some were five-gallon Wesson Oil tins, others conventional snare drums, but the main rhythm came from the *to'ere*, the small hollowed out log played with short sticks. The noise that reverberated off the concrete walls of the hall was deafening.

In Tahitian dancing, the hands tell the story. The men's hands invited the girls to have sex, and the girls' hands teased and rebuffed. That night, the visitors joined the natives in their dance which began with two lines of dancers, men in one line and woman in the other, all facing in the same direction. As the rhythms changed, the lines turned so that the girls and boys faced each other. At that moment everyone chose a partner and began courting with their hands. The girls rapidly moved their hips, causing their grass skirts to ripple in waves from the waist to the ground. The guys moved around the girls, flashing their knees in and out, inviting the girls closer.

Melanie attracted the best-looking guy in the line. His smile could have been on a poster enticing Western women to lose it all on his island. He moved around Melanie like a bee to honeysuckle. He came in very close and when Melanie grew hesitant, he took her hips in his hands and got them moving with the beat.

Jason drew the prettiest girl, as he always did, and David attracted the oldest woman dancing. Jason tried to get into the soul of the dance, but the girl was a tease, giving just so much to the foreigner and then withdrawing, leaving Jason frustrated. David's partner, on the other hand, was the *kumu*; the master and she guided David into feeling the deeper meaning of the dance, which was not just sexual but also spiritual.

When the tease was at its height, the drummers changed the beat to one that was slow and sexy. Then everybody moved closer—the girls with their arms overhead enticing the boys to come near as the guys extended their arms around the girls, as if hugging them but not touching. Every movement was a pantomime of seduction.

Just when things got really hot, the drummers would change the rhythm again and everyone would move apart and return to their respective lines. Then one couple would come out into the center and show off their moves.

When the *'ote'a* practice ended and the dancers had a few minutes to cool off, the musicians traded their drums for stringed instruments—banjos, ukuleles and guitars, and began playing Western music. They loved to waltz, and soon all the island couples were spinning formally around the room like they were at Belvedere Palace in Vienna.

The *kumu* invited David outside. Jason and Melanie were both dancing, so David followed the older woman out into the cool night. She took him to a patch of mangrove near the lagoon, her arm around his waist so that they bumped hips as they walked. They stopped by a picnic table and the woman kneeled in front of David, taking hold of his hips and swinging them in the figure eight movement of the *'ote'a*. She had him continue the hip movement and then took hold of his knees and moved them from side to side instructing him to keep his hips moving at the same time and pretend like he was climbing steps.

"She's teaching you the proper way to do it," came a voice from the beach. Two island men, David's age, walked up smoking cigarettes.

"She's the best teacher anywhere. Takaroa always wins the *fête*," the other man said.

The woman looked up at David and smiled. She was missing half of her teeth. She moved her hands back up to David's hips and started undoing his pants.

"She also teaches men how to pleasure a woman," the first man said as the woman unzipped David's fly.

"She taught both of us," the other man said proudly.

David pushed the woman away and zipped his fly. "Fuck," he said as he walked back to the *Mata'i*.

Tuesday, June 6, 1989

On the ninth day out of Papeete, Larry organized an excursion to a famous shipwreck on the northern end of Takaroa. He hired an outboard motorboat to take him and his crew there, and when they returned that evening, tired and exhausted, they found another boat rafted to *Mata'i*. Larry was furious. That skipper should have anchored in the lagoon. The idea of people tromping over Larry's deck to get ashore was an unforgivable insult. Larry boarded the offending boat and pounded on the cabin hatch. Nobody was there and it was locked up tight.

David checked the name on the transom. "She's *Cozy Cup* from Liverpool."

"Well, she can't raft to *us!*" Larry said.

He returned to the *Mata'i* and stepped ashore, walking down the quay looking for the owners of *Cozy Cup*. His crew followed him. They didn't like the idea of people tramping over their boat to get to get ashore any more than Larry did. Larry found a crewman from the French boat on deck and said in French, "Do you know anything about the boat that's rafted to mine?"

"Not a thing," the Frenchman replied.

"Where's the rest of your crew?"

"They're off with one of the natives to see a pearl farm. The ladies think they can make a deal."

"Who let them raft to my boat?" Larry said.

"The mayor came down to the dock when he saw them sail into the passage. You were off to see the wreck, so he tied them to your boat and then they all took off across the lagoon in the mayor's skiff."

That sounded strange.

"We'll have to move them," Larry said.

"I don't think they're from England," the Frenchman said. "And they off-loaded some crates into the mayor's skiff before they left."

That did it. "We're leaving," Larry told his crew. "Get the boat ready." He turned to the Frenchman and asked if he'd help move the English boat into *Mata'i's* place at the wharf. The Frenchman cautioned that the storm was still raging, but Larry didn't care. He told the Frenchman to beware of the island chief.

Jason looked at David questioningly.

But Larry pushed them to get the *Mata'i* ready to leave. They hadn't much time. The tide was slack so there was very little current in the passage. David took off all the sail covers and reassembled the self-steering gear. Melanie combined the jerry cans of water and took the empties ashore to fill at the community cistern. Jason lashed the cans of extra diesel to the racks that had been installed in Papeete. He attached the staysail stay to the deck and bent on the sail and ran the sheets but left the sail in the bag. If Larry wanted to use that sail all he'd need to do was attach the halyard and hoist it.

When *Mata'i* was ready to leave, David boarded the English boat and Jason untied her from *Mata'i*. Larry, at the helm, had the Volvo idling. Jason tossed the mooring line to the Frenchman on his boat and the guys pulled *Cozy Cup* forward until she could be temporarily rafted to the French boat. Then Larry showed why he was considered one of the best sailors in Honolulu. With Melanie onshore handling the spring line, Larry powered forward against that line, which swung the stern away from the dock. When he had cleared the boat behind him, he told Melanie to get onboard and then neatly backed away into the channel.

With the help of the Frenchman, David and Jason hauled the English boat into the space left by *Mata'i* and secured her to the quay. Larry then pulled alongside, and the boys jumped aboard their boat as Larry accelerated toward the open sea. The Frenchman shouted at Larry to reconsider, given the storm, but Larry ignored him.

"I want the main up now with a double reef, and then unfurl twenty percent of the jenny," Larry ordered as he opened up the throttle.

David and Jason went to work and *Mata'i* left the safety of the channel and sailed into the raging ocean. It was dusk. Melanie stood by her father as they beat their way into fifteen-foot swells. Larry was unusually quiet as he gaged the wind and found his course. He told Jason to take the helm, hinting that he was responsible for their situation. He kissed Melanie on her forehead and went below. Those on deck were surprised by his sudden departure.

"He was too angry to curse," David said.

"That wasn't anger," Jason said. "It was fear."

"I don't understand what's going on," Melanie said.

Chapter 27
South Pacific

Wednesday June 7, 1989

Morning dawned grey and blustery. Squalls, heavy with rain, and strong wind gusts assaulted the boat. The weather wasn't behaving as Larry had planned. The wind kept pushing them further and further south, but they needed to be going north. By that afternoon, Larry was so frustrated sailing in the wrong direction that he decided to tack to another wrong direction. Larry calculated the new tack could bring them closer to where they wanted to go if the wind shifted. David was at the helm when Larry ordered him to tack. Jason went forward to help the jib around the staysail. Melanie handled the sheets.

As the yacht came into the wind, a massive wave slammed into *Mata'i's* bow. The boat dove into a deep trough. The deck dropped out from under Jason, leaving him dangling in the air. Jason kicked and searched for something to hang onto. Just as he was coming down, the deck came up, buckling Jason's knees. A jerry can tore loose and hit him in the side. Jason stumbled backward, to the leeward rail, hit the lifelines with the back of his legs, and cartwheeled into the sea.

Melanie screamed.

What happened next was a blur. David didn't complete the tack. He kept the yacht into the wind, common procedure for a man overboard. He ordered Melanie to slack the sails. Throughout all of this, David kept his eye on Jason and was relieved to see him wave, knowing that Jason was okay.

Jason lost sight of the boat when he dropped into a trough but found it again when he rose to the crest of a wave. The wind blew flurries of froth across the warm water, and panic hadn't hit him yet.

Larry ordered David to fall off.

"Do that and you'll kill Jason," David yelled back to him. Larry pulled him from the wheel. Melanie watched in horror, not knowing what to do. She had the slack mainsheet in her hand. The steep swell had *Mata'i* bucking like a hobbyhorse.

"If we stay heaved-to we'll drift down on Jason!" David shouted, struggling to get back to the wheel. "Melanie, throw over the pole and life ring!"

"No! We'll be dismasted!" Larry shoved David aside and completed the tack.

David jumped onto the aft cabin, grabbed the lifesaving gear, and leapt overboard with it. "Don't sheet in!" he yelled back to Melanie.

Melanie struggled with her father, trying to pull him off the wheel. In doing so the boat jibed and the mainsail shifted violently from one side to the other with a deadly crack. The jib caught in the staysail stay and suddenly the yacht was on her side.

Jason watched David jump into the sea with the man-overboard pole and tried to keep his eyes on that. He saw *Mata'i* knocked down in the violent jibe. This was it, Jason thought. This was his initiation, to die at sea. He wasn't in a panic and he had no anger. Life, he realized, was eternal. Nothing would change. He wouldn't have this body, but he'd still be who he was.

On the *Mata'i* Larry was almost crying. "I'm going to lose my boat." He struggled to stay on his feet as the deck reached an eighty-degree angle. He cursed everyone and everything. Melanie stood frozen in fear, hanging on to the mainsheet to keep from sliding into the sea.

"Sheet in the fucking main!" Larry shouted at Melanie as he swung *Mataʻi* back through the wind in another jibe. The boat popped back up and Melanie pulled in the sail as fast as she could.

David blindly swam to where he thought Jason was. He kept his eyes focused on where he thought his buddy would be and paid no attention to the yacht. If *Mataʻi* was still afloat when he found Jason, so much the better.

On the next crest, Jason saw the *Mataʻi* right herself and saw Larry at the helm. Melanie was handling the sheets and as a result, the boat was recovering. The main went in tight as Larry swung into the wind and when the jib began flapping free, Melanie rolled it up with the roller-furling gear.

Jason dropped back into a trough and when he came back up he saw David on the crest of the next wave. Shouting would be useless; voices couldn't be heard for more than a few feet. Jason could see the flag on top of the overboard pole and swam toward that. The boys met when the next large swell lifted them both up, Jason from one side and David from the other. They grabbed hold of each other at the crest. Jason was exhausted and David gave him the life ring.

"Are you okay?" David shouted at his friend.

"Yes," Jason shouted back.

"Now what are we going to do?"

"Wait for the boat to come around."

"You think that's going to happen?"

"There's a fifty-fifty chance." They both laughed, and then coughed when they were hit in the face with a breaking wave.

Larry maneuvered *Mata'i* through the gale and put his boat perfectly upwind from the guys. Again, his seamanship came to the fore. Melanie obeyed every order with the sheets, and the positioning of the boat relative to the boys in the water was textbook. Larry used the flag on top of the overboard pole as his mark, and even with the high seas and having only the mainsail for power, he brought his boat next to the boys and they scrambled on board with the next swell.

Jason collapsed in the cockpit. "I owe all of you my life. Thank you."

Dave pulled the emergency gear onboard and Melanie gave him a hug. "Thank God for you!"

"I'm glad you two are okay," Larry said. "Let's get back to sailing. Next stop the Bay of Virgins."

Larry brought *Mata'i* back to the course he wanted and reset the sails. He seemed very pleased that the wind had shifted to give them a decent sailing angle to the Marquesas. Melanie had noticed something change in her father in the midst of the crises and felt that perhaps now she could get to know him.

David looked at Jason and wondered if he should tell him what an asshole Larry had been or let it go. Judging by Jason's response to being rescued, David saw how grateful he was and that he'd apparently chosen to forgive Larry. David wondered if he could do the same.

Chapter 28
Chester, England

Thursday Afternoon, November 2004

Lillian and Alex sat at the small game table in the parlor staring at her parents, Lloyd and Nancy Harvey, who seemed to be in deep thought. Lloyd, a thin ascetic type, was a law professor at Chester University, and an honored solicitor. Nancy, always the good wife and a beauty like her daughter, was there to support her husband.

Finally, Lloyd broke the silence, "So Jason allegedly does what? Astral travel, or something like that?" He was also a deacon in the Anglican Church, and had always been very conservative.,

"He just meditates and disappears," Alex told his grandfather. Lloyd gave him a look as if to say children, even thirteen-year-olds, should be seen and not heard. "It's true. I've seen…" Alex stopped—not because of his grandfather's glare—but because he thought this should be kept secret from his grandparents, too.

"Even in your church, Dad, you accept a spiritual realm," Lillian said. "Even if you personally don't believe it, your church accepts miracles and angels and a transcendent reality that alters the commonsense notion of existence."

"Are you putting Jason on the level of Jesus Christ, or are you saying that he's an angel?" Lloyd said. "Give me a break…"

"Do you think he's a fake, Dad? He's sitting in your den."

"He's like all those other evangelicals who are in it for the money." Lloyd never approved of Jason. He opposed Lillian marrying him, he had always rejected New Age thinking, and was appalled that Jason was in his house at this moment.

Lillian struggled not to react and blow up at her father. "Jason has the gift to heal. I've seen it. I've experienced it. He thinks everybody has the same ability. Maybe that's a fault, but all he's ever wanted to do is show people that they don't have to suffer the ills of the world. What's wrong with that?"

"Why does he need a mansion in the heart of London with all those people saying that this is right and that's not? He's creating another church, another religion."

"That's a mistake we're trying to correct."

"By appearing out of the blue and causing hysteria?"

Father and daughter stared at each other like adversaries in a courtroom. Lillian, the acclaimed stage actress, versus the gaunt academic, skilled at convincing judges that his was the correct argument. Alex had never seen this kind of exchange before in his family, and he liked it. Maybe he should follow his grandfather into law.

Nancy cleared her throat and got everyone's attention. "None of this addresses the situation at hand. How do we explain Jason being here and where did he come from?"

"It's ridiculous that Jason is not in this conversation, Father." Lillian nodded to Alex who ran out and brought Jason into the discussion.

Jason entered the room filling out one of Lloyd's dress shirts. The sleeves were too long, and he still wore his jeans covered in Iraqi dirt. He was barefoot and completely inappropriately dressed for this family. Lloyd was appalled at Jason's appearance.

There wasn't a seat for him at the table.

"How on earth do you just *appear?*" Nancy could barely hide her anxiety.

"I can give you my theory."

"How can we stop you?" Lloyd said. "You can appear wherever you like."

"Would I ever appear at your house looking like this, Lloyd?"

Alex pulled an ottoman to the table and gave up his seat to his dad. Lloyd wouldn't give Jason the benefit of the doubt.

"Lillian, Alex and I have struggled with this since it first happened, and I'd welcome your input in dealing with this problem."

"So, you think it's a problem?" Lloyd said.

"Of course, I do. It goes beyond what I'd ever planned to teach in my healing courses."

"You can't teach people to heal," Lloyd replied. "They're not like you, freaks of nature."

"Father! Don't make this personal."

Lloyd wouldn't be interrupted. "For the rest of us, all we want is to suffer through this world with some dignity in hopes of a better one to come. But if you're the new messiah, enlighten us."

"There's no need to be hostile, Lloyd," Nancy said. "We're family and that's a fact. Just deal with it."

Lillian burst out laughing. "I've never heard you stand up to Dad." Her mother's glare quickly shut Lillian up. Even though her mother looked like a pensioner, albeit a beautiful one, with her permed white hair, she was tough as steel.

"Well then, you don't know me very well. You think your father and I have survived forty-five years of marriage without some push and pull?"

Jason broke the tension. "I'm not a messiah, Lloyd, and I have no explanation for this phenomenon that I experience. But in theory, if there is a transcendent dimension of life and it coexists with the physical reality, someone with a spiritually developed consciousness can shift between these two worlds."

"Who's to say there're not three or four or five?"

"There can be an infinite number if you accept God as infinite. But in the same way that physical disease disappears in the presence of a spiritually realized individual, can't that same person have a similarly boundless experience? As Mrs. Eddy said, 'I am at once the center and circumference of the universe.'"

"She's a heretic!"

"Even in your church you accept God as omnipresent. Couldn't someone in God-consciousness be omnipresent also? Or appear somewhere in seeming violation of physical law."

"I've read the accounts of St. Theresa of Avila levitating," Lloyd said, "and she tried resisting it. Why don't you just resist it, if you're such a healer?"

"My whole life has been built on not resisting physical belief or limitation. It's the only way to heal."

Lloyd left the room, and quickly returned with St. Teresa's book *The Interior Castle*. "I see you've been reading this," he stated holding up the book.

"You have a wonderful library, Lloyd."

"Do you know what made her a saint?"

"Her union with God."

"No, her resistance to rapture, Jason. Man isn't supposed to know or feel the things of God. To look upon God is death. That's what you're playing with Jason—death." Lloyd slammed the book on the table defiantly.

"If you're such a scholar on St. Teresa you can't dismiss her autobiography." Jason closed his eyes, recalling a passage; "In her own words, I quote, ... *'Occasionally I have been able to make some resistance but at the cost of great exhaustion. At other times resistance has been impossible: my soul has been borne away, and indeed as a rule my head also, without my being able to prevent it. Sometimes my whole body has been affected to the point of being raised up from the ground.'"*

"Every airy-fairy guru who claims they can levitate refers to that passage as if it were fact," Lloyd said.

"I'm not claiming that as fact, Lloyd, but it helps explain how I got here."

"What do you mean?"

"I was here this morning when you got up. No car. I didn't walk..."

Alex jumped up from the table, ran to the front window, and peeked out through the curtains. "Mom, the car that followed us here is gone!"

"Hallelujah!" Nancy got up and followed her grandson to the window. "Perhaps they've given up trying to crucify you, Jason."

"I wouldn't bet on it," Lloyd muttered.

"We should go," Jason said.

"Why? What purpose will it serve going back to that prison before we have to?" Lillian joined her mother and son at the window.

"I have the TV symposium tomorrow," Jason reminded her from the parlor. "I hate to ask this, Lloyd, but I need to borrow a pair of shoes and a jacket."

"Can I come?" Alex implored.

"Sure." Lillian and Alex walked back into the parlor, and Lillian took Jason's hand. "How do you feel about that? Are you up to it?"

"All I can do is be myself."

Lillian bit her lip, put on a brave face, and embraced her family. She saw her parents in all their tradition and drew Alex and Jason close to her.

"I guess we better hit the road then," Lillian said.

Lloyd stood next to Nancy as his daughter and her family left. He looked sternly at Lillian, assured in his righteousness. Nancy, torn between husband and daughter, remained at her husband's side. They looked like Boaz and Jachin, the pillars in King Solomon's Temple. They were the strength and stability of God's promised kingdom, upholding that tradition on earth.

Chapter 29
Stanford House

Thursday Afternoon, November 2004

Barbara Buchanan, her Jamaican assistant Jimmy Powell, and a handful of interns, dressed the studio for the TV symposium scheduled for the next afternoon. On the platform, six armchairs were set up in a semicircle and Barbara didn't like what she saw. Two of the chairs were a little bit different. "Let's use six identical chairs."

"Ok. I'll have to get them from the boardroom, but this was all I could find down here," Jimmy replied.

"It's going to be all knees and crotches in a long shot. Everybody's got to be equal. What about a table?"

"I thought Mr. St. John liked to get up and move around."

"I want Mr. St. John stationary for this. We must have a curved conference table somewhere. I want this to look like the UN."

"Okay." Jimmy visualized the set. "We can do a semicircle with the cameras in the middle. That way they'll be looking at one another and we can have name plaques in front of each speaker."

"Good," Barbara said. "A neutral color on the skirt; not green or white or red. Have an oak veneer on the top and let's use table mics, not lapels. What about the background?"

One of the interns showed Barbara a sketchpad with ideas for the backdrop. As Barbara flipped through the drawings the intern said, "I kind of like the collage with all the religious buildings and symbols. The other one I like is the picture of

London at night. It would make it look like they're sitting in a window, overlooking the city."

"No religion. We're not a religion and this is not about any religion."

Jimmy said, "How about we just do a paneled wall, like a library? This is a meeting of scholars, right?"

"That's it! Let's bring in the table and chairs from the boardroom and have the set convey an academic feel," Barbara said.

"Why don't we just broadcast from the boardroom?"

"No, it'll feel too much like a Ministry event. All these people are used to television studios, so they'll be more comfortable here."

Chapter 30
On the Road, England

Thursday Evening, November 2004

That evening Jason St. John drove his family back to London in the Range Rover. He was dressed in one of Lloyd's old tweed jackets and wore a pair of his ill-fitting shoes. The Three Musketeers were intact. He took the secondary roads, picking the A41 to Whitchurch and Wolverhampton, skirting Birmingham, Coventry, and Bletchlery. They came into London from the west, through Aylesbury and Uxbridge.

They arrived at Stanford House around midnight and found the crowds surrounding the Ministry headquarters rather quiet. Lillian opened the gate to the underground garage with her remote, and Jason parked the Rover without being stopped by a guard. Lillian roused Alex from a fitful sleep in the back seat, and the three of them walked to the main elevator.

"Think we'll get back to the flat without being seen?" Alex asked, looking at all the cameras.

"We've a fifty-fifty chance." His family groaned at the cliché Jason had used ever since his return from the South Pacific.

They rode the elevator without incident and startled a dozing Thomas Parker. "I thought you were... and Mrs. St. John, you're supposed to be in Chester."

"They called. I just went down to help them with their things. I didn't think I needed to wake you." Jason gave Thomas a playful punch. "No one will know."

Jason searched Lloyd's jacket for his house key before Lillian realized he didn't have one and pulled out her key to unlock the door.

"How long have you been out here, Tom?" Jason asked.

"Since four this afternoon. They've got me twelve on and twelve off."

"So, you've pulled the night shift all week. I'm sorry about that," Jason told the young man.

"All part of my job."

Lillian and Alex entered the apartment and Jason pulled Thomas aside. "I like the way you handled things in the dining room last night. I appreciate someone who can grasp a situation and make a reasonable decision. I don't think you saw me leave to help Lillian and Alex..."

A light started to dawn in Thomas, awakening him to what was going on. "Oh. I had to use the loo."

"Don't worry about it," Jason said as he slipped into his apartment.

Chapter 31

Stanford House

Friday Morning, November 2004

"**S**o the St. Johns came home together last night and Mr. St. John was with them. How did that happen? Mr. St. John never left his apartment." Gary said to a perplexed Thomas Parker. They were in Gary Howell's spartan office. The young security guard stood at attention under Gary's stern look. Thomas was mute.

"Come with me." Gary took Thomas into the ISD command center. The shift captain sat on a raised podium in the middle of the room watching the array of monitors for the forty-eight cameras on the property. The day crew filled a half-a-dozen workstations. Gary pulled a man from a workstation and made Thomas sit behind his monitor. "You have a plum job, Parker, an easy one. All you're required to do is let the watch captain know when Mr. St. John leaves his apartment. So how come Mr. St. John was with his family when they returned last night?"

"I'm not sure what you mean, sir. I had no advance knowledge of their return. They just showed up at the door with their bags."

"When did Mr. St. John leave the apartment?"

"I don't think he did." Thomas realized what had happened and quickly added, "At one point I had to use the loo."

Gary brought up the footage from the surveillance camera outside the St. John apartment and started narrating the events for Thomas. "After Dolan's little fuckup in the dining hall, Mr.

St. John returned to his apartment and you were outside his door until zero two hundred hours." Thomas nodded. "Then you were relieved by ... Mr. Beaumont." Gary sped up the video. "Beaumont had four breaks during his shift, which were either covered by Mr. Cook or by a dedicated video surveillance. You came on at sixteen hundred yesterday..." Gary slowed the video down, "...took a ten-minute rest at eighteen hundred, a twenty-minute break in the dining hall at twenty-two hundred, and another scheduled break at midnight, just after the St. John party arrived. You had an unscheduled break at twenty-three-thirty and didn't notify the video controller."

"That's when Mr. St. John must have left. I just had a sudden call. I'm sorry."

"But Mr. St. John didn't leave the apartment, Parker."

"That can't be."

"It's happened before. We're just waiting for the fallout."

That afternoon Jason St. John politely listened to Tony Bass as Tony went over the bullet points that needed to be addressed in the symposium. They were in the Ministry's media center, a state-of-the-art sound stage.

"Be sure to stress that apparitions are common throughout the world and there is nothing supernatural about them. Hell, people see the dearly departed all the time. I had a friend who hated funerals because he always saw the person who'd died there—usually laughing! Tony was giving Jason his best sales pitch. When Jason didn't react, Tony became serious. "Just stick to the bullet points and you'll do fine. Don't go into mysticism. This is not the forum for that."

"I will put the Marsdan affair in a context that will give the religious people a plausible explanation for what had happened and show the secular world how common such things are," Jason said as if the statement had been rehearsed many times.

"I'm counting on you, Jason." Tony left the studio. "I'll be watching from the control room," he called back.

Jason looked from the script to the stage. A semicircular UN-style conference table was on a dais, and two of Barbara's assistants reworked the large floral arrangement on the floor in front of the table making sure that no wayward flower disrupted the cameras angled at the participants. Two cameramen glided their cameras around the floor, hitting marks that the director in the control room noted on his console. A third camera would be dedicated to the moderator, the broadcast reporter Theodore Spencer. The backdrop was a wood-paneled wall, so that the setting would create an academic tone.

Barbara changed the seating arrangement at the conference table once again. "You need to be in the center, Jason," she said, "This is all about you."

"Where will Spencer be?"

"He'll be on the floor. I want him to be free to move around when he asks questions and moderates the conversation."

"So, this *is* going to be a conversation."

"You authorized this, Jason. You're the one who's going to put apparitions and the Marsdan incident in proper perspective, so everyone gets it." Barbara tapped her earphones. "Why don't you take your seat? I've just been told that the panelists have arrived."

"I'll wait here. I want to greet them as they come in." Jason took one last glance at his script, folded it, and stuffed it in his pocket.

Upstairs, in the St. John apartment, Lillian, Melanie, Dorothy settled on the sofa as Alex turned on the TV set and tuned in the channel. "This is cool," he said as he found a place between his mom and Melanie.

"It's necessary," Dorothy said, reaching over to pat Alex on the knee. "People have to hear the truth."

Lillian hoped Jason wouldn't go too far.

Melanie, ever the atheist, said, "I don't believe in miracles, but I know what I've seen, so this will be interesting to say the least.

Jason remained just inside the door to the media center's studio as Rabbi Levinson entered, the first to arrive. He shook Jason's hand and gave him a fatherly pat on the back. Levinson was in his late sixties, a little overweight, and had wiry gray hair. "Don't know why you're doing this, but it takes a lot of guts."

Catholic Cardinal Richards and Anglican Bishop Eastman were right behind the rabbi, talking intently. They had worked together on many ecumenical counsels and liked each other. The cardinal was tall and thin. His scarlet hat and piping seemed to outline his lanky frame, and at age seventy-three he was badgering the younger bishop. The bishop was approaching sixty and had dyed brown hair combed over a receding hairline. They both greeted Jason cordially, but the cardinal was more intent on making his point with the bishop than he was in engaging Jason.

Sheikh Qamarussaman followed the Christian prelates and Jason greeted him with the traditional greeting of peace, "*as-salamu alaykum*." The imam, in a simple suit under a white *taqiyah*, or robe, kissed Jason on both cheeks and thanked him for including him on the panel. He was forty-one, closest to Jason in age, handsome, and had very kind eyes.

Theodore Spencer arrived last, with Reverend Cyrus Germaine, who was all business and ready to begin.

After the guests had taken their seats, Barbara began her countdown. The panelists all put on their "television" look and Jason closed his eyes briefly in meditation. The last five seconds were silent, with Barbara counting of the seconds on her fingers, and then Theodore Spencer was on.

"Welcome, ladies and gentlemen around the world, to this very special broadcast from the St. John Ministry's Media Center on the Nature of Apparitions. What are they? Who sees them? Are they ghosts? Here to answer some of these questions are representatives from the five major religions in Britain, and our host, Mr. Jason St. John. Seated from my left is Reverend Cyrus Germaine from Hope Chapel, representing the Evangelical movement."

Reverend Germaine nodded and smiled like a politician.

"Sheikh Tariq Qamarussaman, Imam of the London Central Mosque, and our representative from the Muslim faith."

This elicited a polite nod from the imam.

"Bishop Walter Eastman, our Anglican representative."

The bishop offered up a smile and wave.

"Cardinal Lionel Richards, the Catholic leader here in London."

The cardinal gave a quick three-finger blessing.

"And Rabbi Aaron Levinson of the West London Synagogue, one of the oldest in the city."

The rabbi treated the viewers to a casual salute.

"And, in the center of the group, who I'm sure you all recognize, is Mr. Jason St. John."

Jason smiled at the camera and looked a little like Daniel in the lion's den.

"After the startling news a few days ago that Jason St. John appeared to a young girl at Royal Marsdan Hospital," Spencer continued, "and healed her and the other girls in the room of cancer, the world would like to know if Mr. St. John actually transported himself by some transcendent means to the hospital, or if the girl just imagined seeing him—thereby experiencing an apparition. On the one hand consider this statement from Albert Einstein: 'It is entirely possible that behind the perception of our senses, worlds are hidden of which we are unaware.'"

Ever the showman, Spencer paused, letting the weight of his words sink in.

Tony, in the control room, nodded his approval. This was beginning the way he had hoped.

Spencer continued; "People all over the world claim to have been visited by holy people sacred to many of the world's religions. The Virgin Mary at Fatima, Our Lady of Guadalupe are two that come to mind. Millions of people a year visit the Grotto of Massabielle in Lourdes in hopes of being healed. Is this just a Catholic phenomenon? Do other religions accept holy visitations from their saints and gurus?"

Spencer took a breath and looked right at Jason. "Are these apparitions, or can people—living or dead—appear out of thin air? And if they can, for what purpose?"

Spencer had been approaching Jason during that speech and stopped at the desk, less than a foot from Jason's face. "Mr. St. John, did that girl at Royal Marsdan Hospital see an apparition, or were you actually there?"

Jason took a moment before answering, letting a calm infuse him that he hoped would be perceived through the camera. "What is real seems rather obvious, but is it? We accept what our senses tell us without much question. We expect others to see what we're seeing, and often what we accept as real is illusory; a mirage being the most common example. My healing courses are based on a reality that does not give power to illusion, no matter how real it appears or how many people see it. My courses are based on the premise that there is a universal unity to all life, in mystical terminology, *oneness*, and those programs show that the spiritual essence of all life is omnipresent, meaning filling all space."

"That's not in the script!" Tony yelled into his headset. "Tell them you were not there!"

Gary, who was standing right behind Tony, watching what the directors and sound engineers were broadcasting to the world, said, "I told you you couldn't control him."

"Damn it, Jason! Stick to the script!" Tony was so focused on Jason he barely noticed Gary.

Gary didn't like any of it.

On the floor of the studio Barbara got the message from Tony and motioned to Jason to "cut it," but Jason ignored her.

"When I experience spiritual consciousness, I'm not in time and space..." Jason made air-quotes with his fingers when he said time and space. "I'm in the now moment, one with the universal presence that fills all space. We all can experience that. We have that ability within us if we would take the time to develop it. If I'm in the present moment and still enough to be aware of the universal consciousness, and another person, for whatever reason, is receptive to that same consciousness—remember, from the mystical point of view there is only one—either of us could experience the presence of the other and perceive them to be real."

"So, you're saying that you were not there? And what that girl saw was an apparition?"

"I have no idea what the girl saw. I'm just giving you a spiritual principle."

"If the girl saw you as an apparition," the cardinal asked, "wouldn't that put you on the level of our Holy Mother?"

"I don't think we're talking about the same thing here," Jason answered.

Spencer turned to the Catholic leader; "Are all apparitions the appearance of saints? Cardinal?"

"God sends the Virgin Mary to help people have faith. She is the most common vehicle He uses because she has the authority, as a mother would, to gently discipline and cajole her children to do the right thing, to bring them into the arms of the church, where they are safe. I don't think Mr. St. John has that purpose."

"Let me pose the same question to Rabbi Levinson. Are all apparitions saints?"

"Mr. Spencer, we don't have the tradition of holy visitations in Judaism. The closest we have to that idea are angels, which function to help man do the will of God."

"Would you consider Mr. St. John an angel?"

"The healing talent is a gift from God, so in that context you could say he is an angel. I believe his books and courses are based on a spiritual premise..."

"But they have nothing to do with God, Rabbi," Reverend Germaine interrupted. "He does not mention God, or Jesus at all, and assumes that we all can perform magic like he does."

"When is healing magic and when is it spiritual?" asked Spencer.

"Only God can create miracles." Germaine was adamant. "Man, with all of his scientific education, can only treat symptoms."

"Would you say all healing is spiritual?" Jason asked.

"Nothing happens without God. He knows even when a

sparrow falls. He knows the number of hairs on your head. It's foolish to think that a mere man can change anything. True healing is an act of grace."

"Would you say, Reverend Germaine," asked Bishop Eastman, "that the absence of healing is the absence of God? Does God turn his back on the prayers given for children suffering and dying of cancer?"

"God is a righteous judge. Unfortunately, there are sinners who will not experience divine grace until they repent."

"Sheikh," Theodore Spencer said, turning to the imam, "do Muslims believe God can heal?"

"Like all the Abrahamic religions, we believe in the oneness of God, *Allah*, the all-powerful and all-knowing. If it is *Allah's* will, it will happen. If it is not *Allah's* will, it will not happen. We are taught to do *Allah's* will by obeying the Holy Koran. The pain and suffering in this life is rewarded in the afterlife to those who have done the will of *Allah*."

"Is there nothing to relieve the evils of the world?" Bishop Eastman asked.

"Bad things happen to good people," replied the sheikh. "It is not for us understand the ways of the Divine. Look at the Prophet Joseph ..." a nod to the rabbi, "a man all our religions honor. He was betrayed by his brothers and sold into slavery. But the Hand of God was with him and he saved Egypt from starvation. Had he not been a slave, Joseph would not have fulfilled his destiny—or *Allah's* will."

"Well said. But we are drifting off our subject of apparitions. What is your teaching on that subject, Sheikh Qamarussman?" asked Spencer.

"We are closer to our Jewish friends there. We don't have saints who appear to people. We believe *Allah* can send prophets to Earth to deliver Divine Messages, but it's a rare occurrence for our people."

"Cardinal Richards, why doesn't the Catholic Church heal?" Spencer asked.

"We've had many healing miracles in the church. Even today, with technology and a godless pop culture diverting our young from the church, prayers are answered, and people are saved. You know our Lord performed only thirty-seven miracles. The Church is not about healing mortal bodies, it is about saving souls."

"Reverend Germaine, what about healing in your faith?"

"Only Jesus heals. We have healing services where we invite Jesus to enter our hearts to bless us with His healing power. When He graces us with His presence, we have witnessed many miracles. But Jesus was very specific about how this happens. He said, 'I am the way' and 'only through Me can you enter the Kingdom of Heaven.'"

"He was speaking as the Christ!" Bishop Eastman reminded Reverend Germaine.

"Absolutely! Jesus is the Christ."

Bishop Eastman continued; "When Saint Paul said, 'I can do all things through Christ' he was speaking about the Divine Spirit within him, not Jesus."

"If we do not personally accept Jesus as our Savior, that Divine Spirit is not part of us, Bishop!"

"That's right!" said Cardinal Richards. "Man is born a sinner, and until he's baptized, and has the stain of original sin removed from his soul, he will not see the face of God."

Jason slowly shook his head and looked down at the table so the camera couldn't catch the sadness in his eyes. "Can you describe the Kingdom of Heaven and is it attainable here on Earth?" Jason said without looking up.

"I'll quote our Master," said the Bishop: "'The Kingdom of Heaven is within you.'"

"So, if you can access that inner kingdom, have you entered heaven?" Jason looked up at Bishop Eastman and glanced at the others around the table.

"No. No. No," said the Cardinal. "Without intersession, without a spiritual guide, the individual would be lost. We can only know God in a state of transubstantiation, when the body and blood of Christ is made flesh in Communion and comes alive in the faithful."

"The outward act of Communion is a metaphor for our inner commitment to the Christ, to letting the Christ be born in us spiritually so that we may live a Christian life," stated the Bishop.

"You are leaving out our Jewish and Muslim friends," Jason replied. "Isn't there a universal spirituality that can be accepted by all?"

"They have to accept Jesus, or they will never enter heaven." Reverend Germaine couldn't control his zealousness. "But in the last days, in the final battle between good and evil when Lucifer is defeated..." a pointed look at Jason, "the redemption of the world will be achieved by the Second Coming of Christ, through which all people will be saved, including our Jewish and Muslim friends, and Christ will reign forever and ever."

Spencer stopped a moment before saying anything, looking at the rabbi and the sheikh for signs of anger.

"What if the world doesn't end?" Jason said. "Shouldn't we be more concerned with making the world a better place to live for everyone today? Wouldn't it be more beneficial to obey the

Sermon on the Mount and love our enemies, forgive seventy times seven, and turn the other cheek?"

"That's not possible for human beings. Christ was talking about the Kingdom of God when he said that," Reverend Germaine informed the others.

Jason looked directly at Germaine. "The instructions from Jesus were to "Resist not evil." It's in the Bible. It's the basis of all healing. You should study how Jesus healed. Nowhere in scripture does Jesus call upon God to heal someone. 'What did hinder you?' He knew there was no power in the illusions of this world. 'Judge not by appearances.' 'Greater works than these shall you do.'"

"He was not referring to the average man!" Germaine argued.

"Then to whom was he referring?"

"He warned us against the Great Liar who would come and do miracles and lead the world to destruction." Germaine looked pointedly at Jason.

"Actually, Reverend Germaine, that was Paul's and John's thinking."

"What you do is evil. It's the Devil's work leading the faithful away from the truth."

"I simply teach people how to have dominion over their lives. We'll never have peace when we judge one thing good and the other evil. It's only when we have an ecumenical view of life and society that we can begin to practice what religion teaches. I believe everyone at this table accepts the oneness of God. So how can one God be so different to so many people?"

"There is no dispute about the oneness of God," Sheikh Qamarussman stepped in. "There are differences in our approach to *Allah*, but that is all about man, not *Allah*. *Allah* is unchangeable."

"To quote Rabbi Maimonides from the thirteenth century," Rabbi Levinson added, "*the only image of God is man, living and thinking man, and that man acts as the image of God only through worshipping the invisible or hidden God alone.*'"

"Well, that's rather esoteric," Spencer said. But the Rabbi wasn't finished.

"If Jesus alone was the messiah," Rabbi Levinson talked over Spencer, "Christ to use the Greek word, why then hasn't there been peace on Earth for the last two millennia? That's the promise of the Messiah. It is more important for us to find our individual connection to God alone, in our hearts, than to bicker amongst ourselves."

"Again, we're drifting off point," Spencer said. "Let's get back to apparitions, and visitations of holy people. Many people claim to see spirits, dead people, ghosts... Are apparitions a Catholic phenomenon? Can non-Catholics experience them?"

"Or are they relevant to anyone *but* Catholics?" Reverend Germaine added.

"Every reminder to put God first is relevant to all mankind," replied the cardinal. "That the Virgin appears mostly to Catholics is because of our special relationship to Her. Her blessings touch not only those who see her but spread beyond those ordained by her presence to the whole world."

"Using that reasoning," Spencer said, "perhaps that girl, being so aware of Mr. St. John as a healer, brought about an apparition of him instead of someone else."

"I don't think a parallel can be drawn there. With all due respect to Mr. St. John, he doesn't have the status of the Virgin Mary."

"For one thing, he hasn't been dead for two thousand years," said Rabbi Levinson. The cardinal took that as an insult. The others suppressed a chuckle.

"What do we really want to discover here?" Jason said. "The world has a hard time accepting how natural transcendental healing is. There seems to be only two accepted paths to alleviating pain and suffering: the scientific-medical path, or the path of miracles. I don't perform miracles, and I have always invited the scientific community to watch my healing practice and put what happens into scientific terms. To even use the word *spiritual* for what I do is not completely accurate because that has a religious connotation. There are nonmaterial ways to affect our material world, and those ancient practices take on the patina of the supernatural, even though they're a natural part of life.

"Recent research on the historical Jesus revealed that there were many messiahs during that period of the Roman Empire, and also many healers. To categorize the healings Jesus did as miracles elevates them beyond the normal and gives Jesus special power. Why him and not the other healers throughout the empire? There're some who stigmatize what they can't do or don't understand. To make a judgment about whether or not I appeared to those girls in the flesh is irrelevant. To judge me good or evil according to my work only benefits the judgmental and their supporters; it cannot change the healings people have had, or the principles behind those healings— principles *everyone* is capable of grasping."

Reverend Germaine jumped up and turned to his colleagues on the panel. "That is the greatest blasphemy ever broadcast to the world! You should all condemn this man. He insults all people of faith by denigrating our Lord and making himself a god. '*And I stood upon the sand of the sea and saw a beast rise up out of the sea, having seven heads and ten horns, and upon his horns ten crowns, and upon his heads the name of blasphemy.*' Revelations chapter thirteen, verse one

"Reverend Germain! Please…" Spencer interrupted.

Germaine barreled on; "St. John is a surfer, having risen up out of the sea, and his every healing is blasphemous. Even his name is blasphemous! He is not a saint! It's an outrage that we're in the presence of the Antichrist."

The reverend leaned over, pounded on the table, making sure the camera was on him, and gave the world his famous look of righteous indignation.

Spencer drew the camera to him and addressed Jason. "Mr. St. John, I heard you were shot yesterday. … In Baghdad. Would you please comment on that?"

The panel jumped to their feet, all shouting in disbelief.

Spencer continued while Jason retreated into his long-practiced attitude of divine indifference.

"This will be on the news tonight," Spencer said directly into the camera. "British soldiers reported seeing Jason St. John in Bagdad, yesterday, in Sadr City, in the house of Iraqi insurgents. He was shot and then disappeared."

Tony Bass bolted for the phone, never taking his eyes off the television monitors. At the same time, Gary shouted a stream of invectives into his handheld radio and ordered all security personnel to the highest alert.

Barbara signaled her director to cut the video feed. A moment later she heard Tony shouting in her earphones, "Keep it rolling. Mr. St. John needs to respond. It can't be left like this!"

The rest of the panel were standing around Jason, waiting. Jason, still seated, closed his eyes to the chaos to gain some peace.

"This is not about apparitions, or angels, or people hallucinating," Theodore Spencer shouted. "It's about you, Jason St. John! Who are you? What are you doing?"

Every eye was on Jason as he sat very still. The people staffing the media center begin to feel the serene atmosphere Jason created in meditation and quieted down.

"Keep the cameras rolling," demanded Reverend Germaine. "The world needs to see this blasphemy revealed." He hovered over the group like a prosecutor demanding justice.

The cameramen maneuvered to get closeups on Reverend Germaine, Theodore Spencer, and Jason. Not one camera caught Bishop Eastman sitting down next to Jason and putting his hand on top of Jason's. The Bishop pulled away in shock when he felt the hardness of the table and realized that his hand had fallen right through Jason's. Jason was in a deep silence, and the Bishop quietly said, "Jason! Jason!"

Jason opened his eyes and raised his arms for attention.

"Even now this deceiver demands recognition," Germaine shouted. "Don't give him a platform to spread his lies. Turn from evil and let Christ enter your lives."

Bishop Eastman composed himself, not even hearing Germaine, and realized that his life had just changed.

Barbara, talking into her headset, took over the direction. "Keep camera one on Spencer and camera two on Mr. St. John. I'll queue you when to cut."

She blasted the reporter: "Mr. Spencer, are you going to moderate or let this conversation devolve into a shouting match?"

"I'm waiting for a response from Mr. St. John."

"After sandbagging him like that you expect a legitimate response?" Rabbi Levinson said. "My response to you could not be broadcast."

"Rabbi. Reverend." Jason stood, motioning for his guests to be seated. All but Reverend Germain did so. Germain had his hands on his hips and watched Jason like a schoolyard bully.

Jason ignored him. "Cardinal, Sheikh, Bishop, as you all well know, there are elements in our society that have no other purpose than to accuse, denigrate, and try to invalidate anything that doesn't conform to their own beliefs and personal agenda. I fully understand Reverend Germaine's passionate faith and would never insult his views. I would not insult the tenets of any of your religions. But the religious establishment has seldom accepted what hasn't conformed to its dogma."

Jason walked around behind his guests. One camera stayed on him, and the other followed Germain, who was like a dark shadow attached to Jason. "I rarely address the public's reaction to what I do," Jason continued. "The people who come to my rallies and study my healing principles do so of their own volition. I might have a large media presence, but I've never solicited money nor advertised my material. People who have been helped by my programs keep their experiences private. Yes, I have done public healing, but they have been demonstrations for the scientific world to show that nothing supernatural or beyond the laws of nature takes place. That being said, if the religious world is offended by this kind of healing, spiritual healing if you will, then they must deal with it."

"That's it!" Germain shouted. "I will not be insulted by this charlatan."

"Sit down, Reverend!" Barbara used her best Oakland street voice. "You are not in charge here."

Germain would have left, but he didn't want to be the only one. When he saw his colleagues waiting to hear what Jason had to say, he sat down.

"The religions of the world cannot be the sole interpreters of an invisible reality..." Jason could put people at ease when he explained esoteric ideas. "... especially when the scientific world is exploring what used to be the sole domain of religion—the relationship between matter and mind and consciousness. Mysticism can no longer be defined in terms of religious belief. Now, as they did with Copernicus, the religious leaders need to adjust their dogma; just as the Church eventually adjusted to the fact that the Earth revolves around the sun and not the other way around. Was religion destroyed by that fact? I ask you, would the religious world be destroyed by the revelation of an inner Spirit, an inner Presence and Grace within each of us? Think how life would change if people knew about the spiritual dimension of reality in which all humanity truly exists as spiritual beings? What Mr. Spencer is asking me—who am I?—is what we all should be asking ourselves. What others say about me, or claim I have done, affects only their personal experience. Did those children who saw the Virgin at Fatima have any effect on the Virgin? No. She endures as an ideal in faith, untouched by those who have had their lives altered by seeing her. So, to all of you out there, be skeptical. Your beliefs and your judgments form what you experience. Don't let what you believe hide the truth. Jesus said it two thousand years ago, 'Know the truth and the truth will set you free.' You have to experience the truth for yourself. Nobody else can tell you what it is. Don't accept at face value what *anybody* says. What does it have to do with you?"

Barbara signaled for the director to cut the broadcast and walked over to the panel.

"That's it?" Theodore Spencer said. "No time for rebuttal?"

"I don't think you'd have a rebuttal to that." Barbara took off her headset and stood by the door to wish the panelists goodbye.

Reverend Germaine stormed out of the studio, followed by Cardinal Richards and Sheikh Qamarussman. Bishop Eastman and Rabbi Levinson remained behind, lending their support to

Jason.

"Prepare for the lions, Mr. St. John," the rabbi said. "If they still crucified people today you'd be first in line." Jason shook the rabbi's hand and gave him a pat on the back.

Bishop Eastman took Jason's hand and squeezed it. "I'd like to learn more about what you're doing."

Jason just smiled.

The audience in the St. John apartment were on their feet as soon as Theodore Spencer reported that Jason had been shot, in Baghdad. Melanie gave Lillian an accusing look. "You know about this?"

Dorothy shut her up. "Not now, Melanie. Let's hear what J.J. has to say."

Lillian and Alex put their arms around each other in a protective embrace while they listened to the final moments of the broadcast.

When the screen went to the St. John Ministry's logo, the ladies and Alex let out a pent-up sigh. Melanie and Dorothy started talking at the same time, but Lillian stopped them with a gesture. "I think we all need to let what was said be weighed by our understanding of spiritual reality. What is rumor and what is true? Who's behind that ambush? Tony? Spencer? Please think about what we can do to keep J.J. safe."

"I need to know if what Spencer said is true?" Melanie wasn't leaving until Lillian leveled with her.

Dorothy took hold of Melanie's arm and said, "I think we need to let Lillian and Alex be alone." She gently tried to get Melanie to leave with her.

Melanie pulled away. "I know what J.J. can do, Lillian. Please. How can we help if we don't know the truth?"

Lillian sat back down on the sofa with Alex next to her. "J.J. showed up in Chester yesterday morning. He was dirty, disoriented, and his shirt was bloody. Yet he was fine. When I asked where he'd been, he said he was told Baghdad. We all drove back last night."

Dorothy and Melanie said nothing. They were in deep thought as they left.

Jason entered a few moments later and joined his family on the couch. Alex thought his father had nailed it; told it like it was. If people were too stupid to get it that was their problem. He was proud of his dad.

Jason was depressed. His true intent had been to make his appearance at the hospital so boring that people would forget about it. Now he was a "super hero," the incarnation of Thor, or Zeus, or a half-human-half-god like Prometheus, appearing to his followers to change the nature of mortal life. To the people who hated him he was more of a flashpoint than ever. The last thing he wanted to do was retreat into a cocoon from which he and his family would never break free. Was this the death of his message to the world? Even the tenderness and affection of Lillian and Alex loving him, holding on to him, and hugging him, did nothing to lift the black cloud that engulfed him.

Barbara and Gary met in Tony's office later that night. They sat across Tony's conference madly making notes on how to deal with the crisis. The crowds outside carried on their verbal war; some chanting Jason's name while the detractors tried to drown them out with chants of Lucifer and Antichrist.

"I never knew that apparitions were just a Catholic thing," Barbara said, just to say something.

"Fuck apparitions! Where did that bastard Spencer get his information and is it reliable?" Tony gave Gary a disappointed look. Gary had failed to keep ahead of this news.

"This story can't be substantiated," Gary argued. "I don't know how he can run it on television without verification. Remember, Spencer latched on to this story from the get-go. Why would you give him any credibility?"

"Because he has the highest ratings on television," Tony said, trying to figure out Spencer's motive. "He lies. He'll lie to keep his ratings up, but what does it do for him to make Jason into something supernatural? The sad thing is that people believe him. The real question is what is this going to do to the Ministry?"

"No, the question now is how do we protect Jason." Gary said.

"You think Jason is really in danger? Really in need of protection?"

"Spencer's given us the scenario we've been trying to avoid."

"We deny it and turn the tables on Spencer; prove him to be no better than the National Inquirer," Barbara offered.

"That'll just feed his need for publicity."

"Why did we invite him in the first place." Gary faced Tony. He wasn't going to be the fall guy.

"You gave him the script. You assured me he'd go along with this if he had an exclusive." Tony reminded him.

"Is Spencer that well connected?" Barbara mused.

"We need to meet tomorrow, with everybody—Jason, Lillian, everybody," Tony said standing up. "We need to put our heads together. Jason must realize the predicament he's put us in."

The others took the clue and headed for the door.

"One second, Gary," Tony said.

Gary waited while Barbara left.

Barbara felt a prejudice she had rarely felt at the St. John Ministry. Tony and Gary were circling the chauvinistic wagons. She realized that even with all the teaching of oneness, fear brought out a tribal, exclusive attitude in people, and she marveled at how easy it was for men to revert to their base conditioning, even men who were supposedly following the spiritual path.

Tony walked over to his desk and sat on the edge of it. He didn't invite Gary to sit. "Jason is a tumor eating away at this ministry. Now, more than ever, we need to control the public perception of what we are about, and to do that we need to control Jason. And Jason should now understand that more than ever.

"I think I've got a good start on mitigating the situation, if that's what you want." Gary stayed in the middle of the room, watching Tony process his next move.

"I want what's best for the Ministry." Tony sauntered over to the windows and looked out onto Collingham Gardens. "What we discussed down there is more important than ever. You said that your military friends would be all over Jason if they thought he could disappear and reappear somewhere else. Is there any doubt now?"

"Is that best for the Ministry? If it could be proven that Jason was in Iraq, and that he was shot and that he lived, we'd have our religion," Gary said.

Tony turned, and walked back toward Gary. He saw a zealot standing in front of him. He wondered who was manipulating whom? He had believed that Gary would be the faithful lieutenant but not take over.

"Thank you, Gary," Tony said.

Gary paused a moment, projecting an attitude of power, and then walked out. That moment troubled Tony. Gary's vision would destroy the Ministry, and it would destroy it in a way that left Tony with nothing.

After Gary shut the door, Tony picked up his phone and dialed the Home Secretary, David Plunkett, someone he'd done battle with over the years. The man, however, always took his calls. Tony told him that St. John Ministries would cooperate in every way in an investigation into Mr. St. John's supposed appearances, if the government thought there might be national security issues involved with his behavior. He made a second call to Child Protective Services and said that he believed that Alex St. John was in danger because of his father's paranormal incidents.

Chapter 32
Fatu Hiva, Marquesas Islands

Saturday June 14, 1989

Having survived the storm and with the crew intact, it took another seven days of favorable wind and seas for the *Mata'i* to reach the southern-most Marquesas island. The golden light of the afternoon sun bathed the fjord-like Bay of Virgins on the island of Fatu Hiva. The crew had never seen an island so lush. Coconut trees grew out of the cliffs lining the bay, and the dramatic rock formations guarding the valley looked like carvings of the native gods—fierce and protective of this paradise. It was the seventeenth day out of Papeete, and the Marquesas Islands were what Melanie, David and Jason had hoped to see.

Larry dropped anchor a short distance from the rocky beach, joining half a dozen sail boats in the bay. Soon after they'd set their hook, a native canoe with three boys and a girl paddled out to the yacht bringing fresh fruit—bananas, papayas, breadfruit, and more. The crew was still cleaning up the boat after the rough crossing, and Larry wasn't in the mood for guests, but the teens tied their canoe to *Mata'i's* transom and boarded anyway.

They were all smiles, and after they had given Larry their gifts, they sat in the cockpit playing homemade guitars and banjos. The girl did a small dance on the aft cabin roof to welcome the *aoe*, the Marquesan word for "stranger." They were so innocent and pure that Larry's objections melted away. The crew were enthralled by the first Hiva people they met. They sat in the cockpit and ate bananas while Larry tried to talk to the teenagers in Tahitian. The Hiva kids didn't understand that language, and when Larry switched to French, they refused to speak to him. David thought that strange. Later he would discover that the natives had shunned a yacht in the bay flying the French flag. Where *Mata'i* was greeted with fruit and song, the people on that yacht had none.

The Polynesians are a diverse people that spread across the Central Pacific from Hawaii in the north to Aotearoa (New Zealand) in the south. Its western limits are the Fiji Islands— some of which are Polynesian, but most are Melanesian—and the eastern most island is Rapa Nui (Easter Island), home of the monumental stone sculptures. The major island groups have their own language and culture, and all experienced European and American colonialism in different ways. The Marquesan people differ significantly from the Tahitians. Though politically part of French Polynesian, their relationship with the French had been much more strained than that of the Tahitians. Outside of missionaries, few Europeans would venture that far away from Tahiti to set up trading outposts or settlements. The only outsiders who saw a profit in these isolated islands were the Chinese. They would go where the Europeans wouldn't.

The island kids saw that *Mata'i* was from Honolulu, and one boy smiled and made gestures of driving a car while making car sounds. Yet there were no cars in Hana Vave, nor anywhere on the island. The boy made it known that it was his dream to go to Hawaii. That same boy kept staring at David. Even though David had tanned up some from his first pale days in Honolulu, he still was not very brown. He had dark hair all over his chest. Finally, the boy staring at David sat next to him. Everything seemed funny to these island kids who couldn't stop giggling. At last the boy next to David couldn't resist his curiosity any longer and reached over and ran his hand over David's hairy chest. The other three teens froze, waiting for David's reaction. David laughed and then likewise rubbed the hair on the boy's head, at which point the natives rolled on the deck in glee. They were all now friends for life.

Sunday, June 15, 1989

The next morning Larry cooked banana pancakes for breakfast and the same native kids came back as captain and crew were finishing the meal. Larry invited them onboard and offered them some pancakes, which they tried but didn't like. Through sign language and now a little French, Larry told his crew that the natives wanted to give them a tour of their valley. There was a wonderful waterfall at the end of it, and the views from the ridges surrounding the bay were spectacular.

Larry, Melanie and Jason wanted to take the hike up to the waterfall, but David didn't. He had not been able to let go of his resentment of Larry's behavior during the storm, and it had festered in him ever sense. Every time he looked at Larry, he saw a coward willing to sacrifice one of his crew for the sake of his boat. Jason understood that David could not tolerate Larry. He could sense the hatred crawling up on his friend like a giant spider, wrapping its black legs around his body, mind, and soul.

"Come with us, Dave. This is why we're here," Jason told his friend.

David declined again. Larry was going and David wanted to be alone. Jason and Melanie climbed into the native canoe, and when Larry saw how low it was in the water, he changed his mind and stayed on the yacht with David.

The hikers landed on a rocky shore—many of the bays in these exotic islands had no beach—and Melanie and Jason helped the natives pull their canoe above the high-water line. They walked through the typical Marquesan village. It had a Chinese store, a community center that served as a school and a church, and a government building that flew the French flag. The Chinese store usually had a generator, which, on many similar islands, might be the only power the island had. The stores stocked everything the village needed, from spark plugs to Spam to beer. The Chinese store in Hana Vave was about a mile from the landing, at the end of a muddy lane lined by row after row of coconut trees.

From the village it took another thirty minutes to hike through the jungle to the falls. Melanie and Jason were told by Larry to wear long pants and long-sleeved shirts if they didn't want to get eaten up by the bugs, and they were glad they did. They stayed on the narrow dirt path winding through mahogany trees, a variety of palms and the ever-present creepers like philodendron that crawled up most of the trees. When they reached the falls, they stripped down to their bathing suits and dove into the cool, fresh water of the fall's plunge pool. They shouted and splashed each other, and ducked beneath the surface, holding their breath as long as they could. The freshwater took away the constant salt itch they had endured at sea. It also washed away the feeling of being subject to Larry's control.

Melanie couldn't stop laughing and Jason could tell that she had seldom felt this free in her life. The natives loved it too. They took great pleasure in offering this joy to the foreigners visiting their paradise.

Larry turned on his charm and persuaded David into going ashore by offering to buy him a beer. Larry seemed to need his companionship, and David suspended his judgment for the moment and went along. They found a table under the thatched awning of the Chinese store and ordered two beers. The beers were the last two on the island, according to the merchant. The trading steamer was due any day, but nobody knew when because of the bad weather.

"Did he raise the price on us?" David asked.

"Probably. He's Chinese. In the past, when we ended up following the steamer, the natives were all drunk and eating Spam. I like it better when the natives are out of beer and canned goods and live like true natives."

That statement revealed another dichotomy in Larry's character, David thought. Larry was a racist, yet he'd married a Polynesian woman and loved the people. The two men sipped their beers and watched a native woman in a Gauguin type *pareu* sweep the dirt in front of her thatched house.

"When I sailed these waters with my second wife back in the '60s," Larry said, "you couldn't trust the natives up here. They'd rob you blind, and if you weren't careful, they'd kidnap your women. Marquesans hate the French almost as much as they hate the Tahitians. They're completely different from the Tahitians, and they stubbornly resisted the change brought by the colonialists. The Church was brutal in converting them and it needed the backing of the army to do the job. I'm here now, hoping to find some cultural awakening, like what's been happening in Hawaii."

"I'd like to find Gauguin's pink beach," David said.

"I can show you his grave."

"We're stopping there?"

"It's the government center for the southern Marquesas. The leaders on these minor islands, like Fatu Hiva, just want to collect entries in their logbooks, but someone from the government will inspect us in Atuona, where Gauguin's buried, I'm sure. These people like to think of themselves as a separate country. Did you see the past entries I made in the logbooks at Rangiroa and Manihi?"

"I did. You're obviously really well-known in those waters."

"Maybe notorious is a better word. But it's been a long time."

Larry took a pull on his beer while looking intensely at David. He had turned up the charm. David felt Larry was attempting to win him over, and he resented that. But David was willing to listen, given that they were virtually married to the boat and voyage.

"I want to explain to you what happened when Jason fell overboard," Larry said. "I seriously thought that to maneuver the boat in that weather would break our mast."

David didn't say anything but thought that Larry had revealed something important; that he cared more for his boat than for Jason.

"I respect your seamanship, David," Larry continued, "and know you've survived some very heavy weather. You have the right instincts."

David nodded. "So does Jason."

"I just froze," Larry interrupted. "I couldn't think straight. The last thing I'd want to do would be to lose Jason at sea, or any of us for that matter. But Jason makes me so furious that I want to make him suffer. He's never had to work hard for anything important. Everything's been handed to him. There's been no trial by fire."

"How would you know?"

"All the great spiritual masters have suffered," Larry continued ignoring David's question. "It's what drove them to overcome the material. Why doesn't God favor those who work hard and study all the time and pray without ceasing instead of giving His grace to someone who doesn't even care about it?"

David didn't say a thing. He had to force himself not to leave.

Larry's face was tormented. There was a brief crack in his ego and David felt Larry's desire to understand what Elizabeth St. John taught. For a moment David could see why Jason had admired Larry, so open to the Spirit, yet at the same time living through his senses and by his wits; a man struggling to conform to an idea of what makes someone spiritual, and yet filled with judgment toward those who don't measure up. David realized that Larry had a strong concept of how a spiritual person should behave and Jason did not fit that image. Did Jason feel the same way now? David didn't know.

"I was asked to leave these islands twenty-two years ago," Larry finally continued. "Petty bureaucrats with delusions of power ruined my business, my marriage... and my life. But I bless them. They thought they were doing what was right, what was in the best interests of the islands. They were colonials who had no awareness of the people living under their thumb. French expats were not what these islands were about. But, like I said, I blessed them. Without that shaking up, that taking from me all that was good and beautiful, I would not have found the depth of soul that I have now."

David finished his beer, shook the can to make sure it was empty, and wished there were more.

"It was painful" Larry said. "It took years, but now I'm back, in peace, in love, forgiving and compassionate. Jason needs to face his demons. He doesn't even know how deeply attached he is to this world. I thought this trip would show him another side to life, show him how simple and fulfilling it can be without all the adulation and reverence for the heir apparent to his mother. But he's asleep. He can't see what I'm offering."

"Maybe he does, maybe he doesn't. I don't think you know him that well, Larry." David said.

"Oh, believe me, I know him," Larry said in the most egotistical way. "But who am I to change him? I've given him the opportunity, but he'll have to rise to the occasion. I'll keep giving him opportunities. This is my gift to you kids, and I'm going to enjoy it. Just say 'thank you' once in a while."

David had a hard time not reminding Larry that they all had paid in one way or another for the trip. Jason worked on the *Mata'i* for three months without pay, and David had used the last of his European money to cover his food and board.

"Basically, I just want to enjoy our voyage." Larry finished his beer and pulled an air horn from his bag. "Give two blasts on that and I'll bring the dinghy ashore," he said.

He got up and headed back to his boat.

A few minutes later Jason and Melanie came down the trail from the waterfall holding hands. David saw them and looked away, stunned. He didn't want to intrude on their moment by watching them. He thought of Lillian, and how often Jason seemed to abandon her.

Then Melanie and Jason saw David and walked over to him.

"Any beer left for us?" Jason said.

"Last one," David said. He dismissed the hand holding as not meaning anything serious.

"Was Dad here?" Melanie said, noticing the air horn.

"Yeah. He'll come and get us when we're ready."

Monday, June 16, 1989

The next day, Larry wanted to putter around the boat and relax. When he found out that his crew was planning to go the highlands, Larry became professorial.

While David and Jason loaded the dinghy, Larry said, "It was here on Fatu Hiva that Thor Heyerdahl came up with his theory that the Polynesians were originally from South America. He thought the Marquesan temple sculptures were similar to those of the Incas. His *Kon-Tiki* expedition was to prove that. But his idea that the Polynesians had drifted from South American in crude rafts was discredited by the voyages of the Hawaiian sailing canoe, *Hokulea*. Up until the late seventies Europeans wouldn't believe that native people had the skill to settle the Polynesian islands. But they were wrong."

Finally, the crew were able to shove off and took the dinghy ashore. They pulled the *Mataʻi Iti* above the high-water mark on the rocks. The village was quiet. The villagers went about their business in another world from the *aoes* from the yachts. Their needs were simple, and the abundance of food was all around. Their houses were neat, and the walkways always swept. Their priorities in life were singing and dancing; everything else was secondary.

Melanie, David and Jason grabbed their rucksacks and headed inland. The trek to the highlands took a couple of hours climbing a switch-back trail to reach one of the promontories overlooking Hana Vave Bay. As they left the valley the air became cooler and there were fewer bugs. In the highlands the trio found a grassy pasture. They explored the meadows. Melanie found a bleached goat head stuck on a tall stick. The views of the bay and coastline were spectacular.

"This is fabulous," Melanie said. "I'm imagining myself in Eden. Everything is beautiful. Everything is warm. Everything is... well, it's paradise! I hope we stay here a week. I can see why Dad wanted me to see this."

They unpacked their picnic and spread out one of Larry's tablecloths. Sitting around on top of this island, they were completely removed from the yacht, and the sea, and all the challenges below. Up where they were on top the world and everything about it was peaceful.

"I'm sorry you got stuck with Larry," Jason said to David.

"Oh, we had a great time. The last beers on the island." David's sarcasm wasn't lost on the others.

"You've got to forget what happened at sea," Jason said.

"I know. I can see where he's coming from. I'm okay."

"Where *is* he coming from?" Melanie said. "I can't figure him out."

"I never imagined he could be so mean," Jason said.

Melanie and David laughed. Melanie said, "Are you kidding? You never knew he was mean? He's always been mean. It's just that he's so much meaner now."

Jason laughed too. "Your father can't stand not being in control, and under pressure he loses it."

"That's not all of it," David argued. "He's trying to atone for something that happened a long time ago. That's why he's so zealous in his spiritual work. He's so compartmentalized that to face his sins is agony. I assume that's why he's making this trip. I just hope he can keep it all together."

"Are you two finished psychoanalyzing him?"

"Just trying to be helpful," David replied.

Melanie got up and walked to the edge of the cliffs. The yachts looked smaller than toys in the bay below. "Oh damn," she said.

The boys got up and followed her gaze. A French naval vessel had pulled into the Bay of Virgins and had dropped anchor just seaward of the yachts.

"Dad won't like that."

Larry had the boat ready for sea when his crew returned from their excursion. He wasn't willing to share his paradise with the French Navy. He wasn't curious about where Jason, David, and Melanie had been, or what they'd seen. His dark mood was back.

They pulled the dinghy onboard and left as soon as Jason and David could get the anchor up. By midnight *Mata'i* was miles to sea, Fatu Hiva now a memory. The Milky Way stretched across the sky from the southwest to the northeast and Scorpio sat in the west. To the Polynesians the Milky Way was a great shark and the scorpion was Maui's fishhook.

Chapter 33
Tahuata, Marquesas Islands

Tuesday, June 17, 1989

Mata'i reached Tahuata in the morning and sailed into Vaitahu. A red-roofed church stood at one end of the cove and the tin-roofed houses spread out from there. The mountains rose gently from the lee shore, and the terrain was dryer, with yellow meadows between the valleys dense with jungle. And the water was exceptionally clear. Three yachts were anchored off the beach. Larry saw the yachts anchored in the bay and European people on the beach. That whole picture turned Larry off, and he tacked back out to sea.

"What now?" Melanie was videotaping the beach and turned her camera on Larry.

"I think Gauguin's pink beach is just up the coast," Larry said in to the camera. "Let's play there and forget all these strangers."

Two hours later *Mata'i* inched close to a pristine beach. The aquamarine water was so clear that twenty feet looked like two. Jason took a continual sounding, measuring the depth moment by moment. He was sure they were going to run aground. When the *Mata'i* finally dropped her hook, she was just a few feet from shore. Dense coconut trees framed a quarter mile of pink sand, and every one of the crew felt like they were the first people on Earth. Larry kept the dinghy in its chocks, and as soon as the stern anchor was set, to keep the boat from swinging on to the sand, all four denizens of *Mata'i* dove overboard and swam to a beach that had no footprints. The rest of that day was spent in the water, snorkeling and exploring. It was so salty and buoyant it took no effort to float.

While Jason watched a cowrie make faint tracks in the sand, and contemplated picking it up as a souvenir, he thought about how great Larry's gift was to bring them here. This was how Larry expressed love; by sharing his vision of paradise. Jason decided to leave the shell in its natural environment.

Melanie felt guilty making footprints in the sand but got over it. She made sand angels instead of snow angels, and later, Jason and David built sand tikis at the waterline. When not in the water, the three of them lounged in the cockpit while Larry tended to one of his never-ending projects. The *Mata'i* was Larry's most enduring relationship.

Melanie and David had bought a couple of native banjos in Hana Vave, and Jason showed them some Tahitian riffs on his ukulele.

The sunset turned Gauguin's pink beach golden and at long last Larry looked happy.

Chapter 34
Hiva Oa, Marquesas Islands

Sunday June 25, 1989

A tuona, the major town on Hiva Oa, fronted a beautiful beach with strong waves, making it unsuitable as an anchorage. The yachts, and the trading vessels calling on Atuona anchored in the adjacent harbor of Tahauhu, where there was a wharf for the steamers and a small pier for the tenders from visiting yachts. A fleet of sailboats were tightly packed in the small bay when the *Mata'i* arrived. She anchored near the pier.

Larry went ashore alone, taking the passports and the yacht's papers expecting a quick clearance. Instead, he returned a couple of hours later with a French *gendarme* who thoroughly searched *Mata'i*. Larry wasn't happy. Most yachts were given a cursory look at their papers, not a thorough inspection of their personal goods. Larry showed the *gendarme* the guns and what little ammunition they had left in an effort to keep things aboveboard. Larry had convinced David, in their talk at Hana Vave, that his previous activities in French Polynesia had been forgotten. But David saw that he was wrong. He was no friend to the French, and they seemed to have a long memory.

When the *gendarme* left, Larry told his crew that the next day they were to have lunch with an old friend and then tour Ta'aoa Valley to see an important archeological site and swim under another waterfall. At the moment, David wasn't interest

295

in tomorrow. He was anxious to get off the boat to spend time with Paul Gauguin, alone, before the sun got too low. He excused himself and took the dinghy ashore.

David walked along the revetment on the east side of the anchorage to a narrow road that went over a hill, separating the harbor from the town. When David crested the hill, Atuona spread out below him, a town of about a thousand people nestled under a thick canopy of coconut trees. The white sand beach was fringed with breakers, and inland toward the base of the hill was the cemetery. David imagined Gauguin walking here, and it dawned on him how remote this island was. Eighty-five years ago, it was at the end of the Earth. Gauguin was looking for a pureness in life, the guiltless race, that noble savage uncorrupted by modern man. He sought a people untouched by industry, people without masters and serfs, people free from Western belief. He sought paradise on Earth, but he didn't find it. The priests had gotten there first.

It was not hard to find the artist's grave. Someone, perhaps Gauguin himself, had carved his name, like his signature on his paintings, into a black lava rock and painted the letters pink. At the head of his tomb were two of his ceramic *tikis*, and behind his headstone a frangipani tree bloomed. The afternoon sun sent rays of light, like a spotlight, through the clouds that illumined the tree. David stood in awe before the tomb, filling his mind and heart with all that Paul Gauguin had wanted to tell the world. Yes, there were colors in nature like the colors he painted. There were pink beaches and green skies and lavender clouds. David saw the people he painted walking the streets and sitting in the meadows. But this was no paradise. There were devils everywhere, in the cobalt shadows lurking behind the mango trees. There was no joy. No amount of genius could pierce the landscape to the heart of the people, because their collective heart had been stolen. The soul of the islands was nowhere to be found. This was France with exotic foliage and a different colored skin.

Monday, June 26, 1989

Larry roused his crew at dawn. Melanie came on deck first and sat at the cockpit table where Larry had laid out the boat's weapons. The boys came up from the salon, followed by Larry carrying an armload of cereal boxes, which he stacked on the table. His crew had no idea what he was up to.

"That's rather cheesy keeping all that food hidden," Melanie said.

"You wouldn't want to eat this," Larry replied. He opened the boxes and dumped the contents on to the table. To his crew's amazement, there were hundreds of rounds of ammunition hidden in the corn flakes. "Here's the deal. I want you guys to match the ammo with the weapon."

Larry left and quickly returned with a canvas sail bag and an armful of towels. His crew was still puzzling over the guns and the bullets scattered among the corn flakes. "Don't dilly-dally. This is important. When you're done, wrap the weapons and ammo in the towels and put them in the bag. I'll make breakfast."

Larry disappeared below and his crew began to separate the ammunition from the cereal. David made little armies of rifle bullets standing upright. Jason had companies of shotgun shells, and Melanie had platoons of thirty-eight and forty-five pistol rounds.

At ten o'clock Larry took his crew and the weapons ashore in the dinghy. He tied *Mata'i Iti* to the pier and they walked up to the beat-up Toyota pickup truck waiting for them. Jason threw the sail bag of guns in the back and he and David climbed in after them. Larry and Melanie jumped in the front with the driver.

"Larry's not a very stable man," David said, as they left the harbor and headed inland on a rough road. "He told me some bizarre things when you and Melanie hiked up to that waterfall on Fatu Hiva."

"I don't want to get into that, Davy. We don't know what's going on and it's probably for the best."

"You think Byron knew Larry had a clandestine agenda and that's why he left?"

"I doubt it. I think he lost all respect for him when he wouldn't motor into Papeete. And ... I don't think he could take two more months without sex." They both laugh.

"For some reason Larry wanted to explain why he reacted the way he did when you fell overboard."

"I've already cleared myself of that."

"Don't you think it's odd that he would tell me, justify himself to me and not you?"

Jason just shook his head. "That's Larry. He doesn't confront things well."

"He told me he just froze. He thought the weather would tear the boat apart if he heaved to. Melanie forced him to do it when I came after you."

"Dave, I know all that. I could see what was going on."

"No, it wasn't the boat; it was you. He told me he wants to make you suffer. He thinks you've never had to work for anything in your life."

"Sounds like he's talking about himself."

"Larry thinks spiritual masters have to go through a trial by fire, that they have to suffer to overcome the material world. He thinks he's doing all this to make you deserving of your spiritual gifts. He's crazy, J.J. And what do you think he's going to do with these guns?"

"He told me the people up here rely on hunting as much as they do the trading steamers, and the French make it very hard for them to buy rifles. They have a hundred percent tax on guns. He's just helping them out."

"Why didn't you tell me this when he first brought out the guns in Honolulu?"

"It didn't cross my mind. You're making a big conspiracy out of nothing."

"Well, he scares me."

Both of them fell silent as they drove through the center of town and into a valley. The truck pulled onto an expansive meadow of emerald grass in front of a wooden house with a large veranda where three men and a woman waited for them. The woman, about Larry's age dressed in a pink muumuu and looking like the subject of a Gauguin painting, ran down the stairs to Larry, tears wetting her face. She was large, and her dark hair, adorned with flowers, was piled on top of her head like a crown. Larry jumped from the truck before it had fully stopped and ran to her, hugging her tightly, then waltzing her around while kissing her tears.

The boys got out of the back of the truck and the driver grabbed the bag of guns and took them to the men on the veranda. Larry opened his arms and beckoned for Melanie to join him. She looked at the boys, shrugged, and then went to her father. The woman, Ama, embraced her and sobbed, creating a three-way hug.

Jason and David watched, surprised by the passion between Larry and the woman. They both wondered who she was. The men on the veranda came down and introduced themselves; they were Ama's sons. They spoke English and were from Bora Bora.

Inside the house, while everyone dined on fish and suckling pig, plates of vegetables and bowls of fruit, Larry forbade talk of the past—no reminiscing and no personal histories. This was a celebration of the moment, filled with food and exotic drink. They talked about what life was like on a small island. They talked about the sea. They questioned why some people lived happy lives and others didn't. Larry would switch into Tahitian at times and Jason, David, and Melanie would speculate about what subject had prompted the switch. Was Larry talking about them? Was he talking about the Bora Bora connection? Was he hiding something?

After lunch Larry and his crew said their good-byes and headed on to Ta'aoa and the famous disappearing waterfall located beyond the Road of Men. It was a long one-hour drive over a twisting rutted road. The boys bounced around in the bed of the pickup, unable to find a comfortable position. The road clung to the rugged terrain, sometimes leaving little room between the jungle rising on one side and the cliffs falling into the sea on the other. When they finally reached a remote bay, at the base of the Road of Men, they parked on a grassy meadow near a stone church. A few houses fronted the meadow. They couldn't drive any further.

The guys were bruised and dizzy from the trip. While Larry and the driver were clarifying their route to the waterfall, David rolled out of the truck bed and stumbled across the grass to the beach. He let the waves wash around his legs. He had sailed on two oceans, survived storms and the Gulf Stream and had never gotten sick, but the ride to the Road of Men had him puking over the side of the truck. After David regained his equilibrium, he went back to get Jason, but Jason was still curled up in the truck bed.

David climbed into the truck and put a hand on his friend's back. "What's wrong?"

"I feel terrible," Jason said weakly.

Melanie joined the boys and didn't like the way Jason looked. "Oh, Jason, are you okay?"

Jason got up and struggled out of the truck. "I think it was just the ride."

Larry walked over and looked at Jason. "Bollocks. Let's go and have some fun."

"He doesn't look good." Melanie said to her dad. "Why make him go if he doesn't feel like it?"

"Because he'll never be in this place again and he shouldn't miss the experience."

David put his arm around his buddy and said, "You sure you're alright?"

"Yeah," Jason picked up his knapsack, and everyone but the driver headed for the Road of Men.

The driver jogged across the green to a thatched house with some tables and chairs out in front and joined a handful of men drinking.

"I think I'd rather follow him," David said.

Larry scoffed.

"I thought he was our guide," Melanie said.

"No, it's just us," Larry took the lead and set a fast pace. "I know the way and it would be nice if you kids were a little more appreciative."

The rutted avenue embodied the clash of Western colonialism. It was lined with stately palms and cut through a village that had been abandoned for generations. Nothing was left but the grand building sites called *paepae*, which spread out on either side of the road. Each platform, about three feet high and thirty feet square was made from hand-hewn lava rock. Beautiful crafted stone steps led up to a terrace that would have held a number of well-built wood and grass structures—a large common house for family gatherings, a cooking house, an eating-house for the men that would have been *tapu* (forbidden) to the women, and numerous sleeping houses. Extended families had lived together—couples in their own sleeping quarters; children, siblings and cousins all, sharing the large common spaces, and sleeping with whomever would have them.

Shading the *paepaes* were tall breadfruit trees which had multiplied to form a dense forest where the only open space was the road and the *paepae*. The Hiva tradition dictated that when a child was born, the family planted a tree for the child, and that tree, with its life-giving fruit, belonged to that person forever. But forever wasn't forever on the Road of Men. The jungle had taken over the *paepaes*, covering them with roots and breaking down the stone. Whatever had caused the people to leave their homes had left a miserable atmosphere. Whatever horror had happened there still lingered and David felt like he was an unwelcome guest at a funeral.

"You know why this village was abandoned?" Larry wiped the sweat from his brow. He was breathing heavily as the road narrowed and they climbed into the valley. It was a rhetorical question.

"The Catholic Church destroyed these people. It was a slow strangulation of one culture by another." Larry was in his teaching mode again. "The Hiva gave up the will to live. Before the missionaries, the people had attained a perfect balance between the land and the population. There was a season of harvest and renewal called the *matari'i* when all conflict was put aside and the clans from all the valleys mixed. Traveling performers went from valley to valley inviting people to join their troupes. They satirized their rulers, pilloried the rich, and enticed the brightest and most talented to join them. They danced, performed mock battles, and chanted the genealogy of their ancestors. They kept the culture alive and had sex without boundaries."

"Isn't it always about sex." David said.

"Those villages that didn't participate in the *matari'i* became ingrown and weak, and the missionaries were able to take over."

As they reached the end of the lane, they came upon a *takai'i me'ae*, an ancient temple platform filled with large stone *tikis*. Larry climbed onto the *me'ae* and stood next to one of the *tikis*. "Melanie, take my picture." Larry put his arm around a life-size stone sculpture. Melanie snapped away as her father went from one god to the next. Some had fallen and Melanie got shots of Larry resting his foot on the head of one of the gods.

Jason sat on the steps of the *me'ae* and clutched his stomach. David squatted next to him and felt strange too. The atmosphere was very dark and heavy. It was as if something bad was going to happen, and it overwhelmed him.

"I don't think I can make it to the falls." Jason was obviously in physical pain.

David empathized with friend. "I've never felt anything like this, either. What's going on?"

"I don't know." Jason groaned.

Larry and Melanie were ready to proceed up the valley. Larry nudged Jason with his foot. "Let's go. We've got a good mile to the falls."

"You guys go on. I can't do it," Jason said.

"Come on! You're not going to let a little discomfort ruin our hike. Put some spiritual consciousness toward it." Larry stared at Jason disapprovingly. Jason had grown pale and was sweating.

"I'll stay here with J.J.," David said. "He doesn't look too good."

"Bollocks. Stick with us, Dave. This might be your last chance to see the most famous of Marquesan waterfalls."

"Go," Jason said. "I'll wait for you here, Davy."

"Really?" David reluctantly got up.

Leaving Jason at the temple, Larry, Melanie and David forged their way through the jungle, following the stream. With their machetes, they hacked at the creepers and hanging roots blocking their way. After a half hour of hiking, the valley narrowed into a tall gorge and the stream disappeared. Still, the roar of the waterfall echoed off the walls of the towering cliffs. They stopped at the entrance of the gorge and saw the soaring falls but not the river carrying away the water. It had disappeared. There wasn't even a dry riverbed—nothing but the jungle and the chasm before them.

Larry pointed to a little totem of rocks someone before them had constructed. "We can't go through there yet," Larry said.

"Don't tell me you're superstitious?" Melanie answered. "You rushed us to get up here, now we have to wait while you appease some native god?"

"Don't be so critical. We should respect the native tradition."

"Like putting your foot on a tiki?" Melanie continued.

"It's not the same."

"I thought the Hiva here were Catholics," David said.

"Only on the surface."Larry began foraging for his own rocks. The kids helped, and in a few minutes, Larry had built a totem of rocks bigger and taller than the one they had stumbled upon. "This has to be right. These cliffs are notorious for falling rocks. We don't want them falling on our heads.

Once through the ravine the gang hiked up a sloping meadow that ended at a small pool at the base of a thirty-foot cliff. Small rivulets of water spilled over the cliff but the two-hundred-foot waterfall roaring above could not be seen.

Larry laughed at Melanie's confusion. "One of the great deceptions of the island—the phantom waterfall!"

David examined the pond before them. It was still and he couldn't find anything that showed where the water escaped. It was amazing. Thousands of gallons of water poured out of the mountains, and all they saw was a dark pool at the base of a damp cliff. The river had been swallowed by the terrain, an eerie collection of grassy mounds, steep jungle walls, and the narrow box canyon that hemmed them in. It was unsettling. The jungle was strangely silent, no birdsong, no rustle of life in the underbrush. Gauguin's devils hid in the shadows of the vine-clad trees, warning the *aoe*—foreigners—not to delve too deeply into the mysteries of the Hiva lands.

"Anybody going to take a swim?" Larry stripped down to his underwear. David was spooked and didn't want to go into the water. Melanie wasn't in the mood. Instead, she took photographs from every angle.

"Jeez, I can't take you two anywhere." Larry dove into the pond. The dark water hid what was beneath the surface and Melanie half expected her father to come up with a bloody head, if at all.

After his swim, Larry wanted to climb to the upper falls, where they could feel the water and solve the mystery of where it went. Neither Melanie nor David wanted to do that, so with his mood turning sour Larry agreed to head back and see how Jason was doing.

They found Jason on the *takai'i me'ae,* lying in a fetal position next to one of the *tikis.* They had been gone almost two hours, and Jason looked worse and had difficulty breathing. David helped his friend to stand. Jason could barely walk back to the truck.

"I think J.J. should ride in front," David said to Larry.

"That's out of the question. He's not sick, and he doesn't deserve to be coddled." Larry got into the truck and began blowing the horn. The driver ran back to the truck. He was drunk, and Larry insisted on driving. Melanie hopped in the truck bed with the guys.

Driveling back, they kept to the high road that dipped into each valley. They avoided Atuona and took a more direct way to the harbor. All this time Jason mumbled about *tuhunas* and curses and some kind of native ritual. He was delirious and kept calling out Dr. Green's name.

As soon as they reached the boat, Larry had David haul in the dinghy and raise anchor. It was dusk, and Larry wanted to get to the other side of the island by morning. After *Mata'i* cleared Tahauku Harbor and sailed into Atuona Bay, Larry gave David the course and went below. They were to sail around the west side of the island, along a coast of high cliffs, where the large swells came from behind and pushed the boat forward like the impatient hand of Neptune.

It was a disturbing night. Jason grew sicker. Melanie and David attended to him in the cockpit between turns at the helm. The following wind and sea made *Mata'i* skittish. The Aires couldn't handle the wind at this angle, and it took a lot of skill to keep the boat on course and not jibe the mainsail. It was on this leg that Melanie proved herself to be a first-class sailor and helmswoman.

Jason went on about shamans... about taking the people back to the old gods... those gods still had power... people must remember... they must restore the third gender, the artist, the tattoos, the dances that brought the land alive, and the chants that soothed the *haka-iki*. He rambled on about *tuhunas—Tuhuna Up'e, Tuhuna O'ono, Tuhuna Mata Tetau, and Tuhuna Patu Tiki*, and Melanie wrote those names down. She was worried about Jason and put aside her fear to follow her journalistic curiosity. She was curious about those words and wanted them for reference when Jason regained his lucidity.

David was also in conflict. From what he had taken away from Elizabeth's class only a few weeks ago, he should be able to dismiss Jason's ranting as being without spiritual substance, therefore without power. But seeing his friend suffer so much, David couldn't do that. He still had a deep feeling of dread from the hike. It was as if they were entering a valley of death.

Tuesday, June 27, 1989

Mata'i sailed into Hanamenu on the leeward side of Hiva Oa about ten o'clock the next morning and dropped anchor a few yards off a gray sand beach. Larry went ashore alone, as usual, but this time he was nervous. He needed to meet someone at the behest of Ama from Atuona.

David put up the awning over the cockpit while Jason lay with his head on Melanie's lap. She dabbed his forehead with a cool cloth and massaged his temples. They were wondering why no one else had gotten sick—they had all eaten the same food.

"Me thinks J.J. is over acting." David said.

For a sick man, Jason was rather lucid. "I think I tuned into something primal. I can't say it was spiritual, but it definitely was not of this world." Jason took the cloth from Melanie and wiped his neck and under his arms. "I think that there are layers of reality and given the right circumstances you can experience a nonmaterial realm that isn't spiritual or pure. I think there are souls who have not moved on, for one reason or another, probably a strong attachment to something earthly in their immediate past."

"Do you believe there are ghosts and spirits?" Melanie said.

"I guess that's as good a label as any." Jason said. "It's the world of the spiritualist and I don't think it's a fantasy, not after yesterday."

David tied off the last cord of the awning and sat down next to Melanie.

"I felt very strange up at that waterfall." David said. "And Larry suddenly got superstitious."

"Dad would never make some sort of a pagan shrine. That was so weird. And the falls, Jason, they were mind blowing. Where did all that water go?"

"Do you think native superstitions have any power? I mean, do you think someone with a Western mindset can be harmed by evil spirits or angry ancestors if he doesn't believe in them?" David asked.

"No." Jason said decisively. "We're too rational, scientific. On the other hand, look what happened to the men who opened Tutankhamen's tomb; they all died horrible deaths."

"Evil is evil," Melanie said. "It's not supernatural, it's just a fact of life. Evil people exist just as do evil circumstances. I wouldn't put a spiritual connotation to it. People have been praying to get rid of evil since the beginning of time and it hasn't worked. It's just something we live with."

Melanie took the cloth back from Jason, dipped it into a bucket of water, and wrung it out.

"Do you think there's a way to keep evil from affecting you? Do you think building that little shrine at the mouth of the gorge was foolish?" David said.

"I wouldn't have done it. But Dad thought it was necessary and we went along with him."

"What if rocks had fallen after you'd built the shrine?" Jason asked.

"You could say the shrine was useless, or you could say you didn't do it right. Basically, this kind of debate is stupid. No one can prove that the so-called spirit world or psychic world has any effect on our world, or if it even exists," Melanie replied.

"I guess what happened to me at the temple was a psychotic incident, nothing to do with spirits or island curses?"

"Or someone drugged you," Melanie said. "Do know what *Tuhuna O'ono* means?"

"No."

"I took notes while you were delirious, and that's something you said."

"Yeah, you did." David said. "So, what you're saying, Jason, is that your illness was psychotic episode, or you were drugged, or was it an island curse?" Turning to Melanie; "Did you feel strange in the gorge and up at the falls?"

"I did. But all kinds of things spook me. It doesn't mean that I believe in evil spirits or angry ancestors. I didn't like walking through that gorge because rocks could have fallen on us. If they had, I wouldn't have thought it was caused by the spirit world. It would've been gravity, and if I'd been hit on the head it would've been my bad luck."

"So, life is just a matter of luck?" Jason said.

"You can be careful and take precautions," Melanie told him.

"Like building a shrine?" David smiled.

"Let me ask you this," Jason said. "Do you think there is just one set of laws for all that exists?"

"Not at all. There are all sorts of laws for all kinds of disciplines," David replied.

"I mean, is there one supreme law? Something that's not affected by any other law?"

"Are you trying to bring God into this?" David said.

"I'm just wondering if there is such a thing as grace, and if it can lift someone out of all these other states of existence. Is *anything* omnipotent?"

"You are dragging God into this," Melanie said.

Jason took the washcloth and laid it over his face.

David said, "If Larry expected you to be a talisman and make this a pleasant trip, it hasn't worked."

"I guess it's my fault I got sick," Jason mumbled through the washcloth. "Melanie, can you massage my temples again?"

Melanie took the cloth back from Jason and slapped him playfully on the chest with it. "You like all the attention, don't you? The cool water on your forehead, the head massage, that's all you've been after the whole time!"

Jason sat up laughing. "Let me massage your neck."

Melanie laid back and put her head in his lap. He wrung out the cloth, folded it, and draped it over her forehead.

David had not noticed the affection growing between the two. How had he missed the clues? The *tamure* dancing at

Takaroa? Walking back from the waterfall at Hana Vave hand in hand? Maybe Jason was like this with all the girls. Maybe the nonchalant detached attitude with women was his secret.

David got up to go below but Melanie grabbed his hand. "Don't go. We haven't finished our conversation," she said. David sat down next to Melanie's feet. She raised her legs and motioned for him to move closer, and when he did, she put her legs on his lap.

"So why do you think your dad treats J.J. so poorly?" David said.

"Don't know. My mom taught me to live by the golden rule; treat others the way you want to be treated. The jury's still out on my dad."

"Will that protect you from evil?"

"If I treat everyone with love and respect, more likely than not that is what I'll get back."

Jason piped in. "What if we exist within another parameter but are unaware of its existence or laws?" Melanie and David weren't with Jason on this one.

"Don't be so dismissive," he continued. "I'm serious. What if our world of conflict is imposed upon us by our beliefs? What if there's another dimension within this world that includes all life, but only a few people are aware of it? And in that dimension, what if there were no opposites? All who lived there lived in total harmony. Would you want to find that dimension?"

"You're talking in hypotheticals. If there were such a place, that was completely harmonious, of course I'd like to live there," Melanie said.

"It does exist, Melanie," Jason said, "All the great spiritual lights have described it."

Melanie sat up and looked at Jason and then David. "I'm an atheist. I don't believe in Jehovah any more than I believe in Zeus or Athena. The world is random. Shit happens. We have to learn how to deal with it and not always try to change it. I've read some of Dr. Green's books. Dad sent me a whole library of them. Perhaps there is a Christ consciousness. Perhaps all life is spiritual on some level. There are many unexplained things in this world, but for me, it's all about how people treat each other. Can you forgive?"

Melanie kissed both of them—Jason on the lips, David on both cheeks— and disappeared into the aft cabin.

Larry returned to the boat late that afternoon with fish, taro root, heart of palm, and breadfruit poi. He didn't disturb his crew, who were napping, and set about cooking one of his gourmet meals. Larry put a fresh cloth on the table in the cockpit and arranged a centerpiece from protea blossoms from shore and pieces of coral. When dinner was ready, he called his crew on deck. They were impressed with his meal and the beauty of his table. They also appreciated his good mood.

Larry had a whole new plan and was excited. There was a rarely performed ceremony happening in nine days on Ua Pou. "One of the most insane rites of passage in the world," he told his crew. "And one that might lead to the renaissance of the Hiva culture. They want me to film it."

"That sounds great," Melanie encouraged.

"Does that mean we have to leave soon?" David asked. "It'd be nice to be in one place for a while."

"Jacques, the man who lives here, is a hermit," Larry answered. "I have to see him again, so at least another day. He was part of the independence movement I got involved with in the mid-sixties, and I'm the first person he's talked to in five years. It took me all morning just to get him to come out of his hiding place."

"What did he do?" Melanie glanced over at Jason, who looked under the weather again. In truth, Jason had begun to feel like something was coming over him, the way it had at Atuona. But he avoided Melanie's inquisitive gaze and said nothing.

"He wanted to help the Marquesans restore their culture," Larry continued. "We thought we could do this through tourism. He thought of Melville's novels and his descriptions of the cannibal people, and Tommo falling in love with Fayaway, where the sex was innocent and yet there was danger from the ferocious islanders. We thought that we could attract a certain type of tourist who'd delight in this kind of adventure. I know it sounds bizarre today, but we thought we could sell it. He researched all the Hiva music and dance and we made a business plan based on his discoveries. He thought the original culture could recover from their spiritual genocide. Obviously, the French didn't. The colonialists still had the attitude that these people were savages who needed to be subdued. Otherwise their primitive ways would destroy the civilization that was given to them for their salvation."

After a moment of bemused silence, Melanie and David howled with laughter. "That is the most ridiculous thing I've ever heard," Melanie said.

"Not great marketing," David added. "Come to our islands and get eaten by cannibals."

"No, no, no. That was his problem; he saw things differently from most people. He was brilliant. But now, who knows? He left his research with the elders of Hakamaii and I guess in the past few years they've restored one of the most incredible rites of passage in the world. Nobody has filmed it. Hell, very few outside the island have ever *seen* it! This will be the highlight of our trip. He wants me to document the whole thing."

Wednesday, June 28, 1989

Larry spent another day at Hanamenu gathering every piece of information he could from his hermit friend Jacques, and Jacques gave him an introduction letter for the ruler at Hakamaii, where the ritual was to be performed.

"They have the ceremony every year when Venus is overhead as the sun sets. That's in eight days. It'll give us enough time for me to show you Ua Huka," Larry told his crew as they gathered around the cockpit table for another gourmet dinner that night. "I think this is why we're here."

Chapter 35
Ua Pou, Marquesas Islands

Tuesday July 6, 1989

After sailing from Hiva Oa to Ua Huka, where Larry and his crew had spent a few days of pure sightseeing, the *Mata'i* made the one day crossing to the island of Ua Pou. It was mid-afternoon when they sailed into Hakamaii, a small native settlement on the southwest side of the island and found that it had no safe harbor. The treacherous anchorage was open to the sea. A jagged rock took up one side of the cove, and there was no beach, just basketball-sized boulders lining the shore. A concrete boat ramp was the only place to land, and a row of canoe sheds stood on either side of the ramp. The anchorage was deep, and the sea surged up the boulder shore with great force. To be safe, Larry had to anchor his boat more than fifty yards from the "beach." Once the *Mata'i* was anchored, two teenage boys wearing traditional loincloths, their bodies sparsely tattooed, launched their canoes. Each boy stood in his canoes and paddled out to *Mata'i*. They ferried Larry and his crew to shore, expertly riding the surge up the boat ramp, timing their landing so that their passengers stepped out onto dry concrete when the water receded.

Larry clung to his ever-present satchel. As usual, Larry wore his long sleeve Tahitian print shirt, pith helmet and shorts. He made sure he had his introduction letter to the *haka'iki*, or chief. He checked his video equipment in his bag. The younger crew brought with them their cameras, recorders, and sketch pads. It was very hot and still, and the kids wore only their bathing suits; Melanie's was a small bikini.

On shore, Larry and his crew were greeted by two fully tattooed men, also wearing traditional loincloths. They escorted the crew of the *Mata'i* inland, past the canoe sheds, across the grassy commons, with a *tohua*, a sacred dance space, at its center. The sides of the valley were steep and close, and they pinched into a gorge not far from shore. A rutted dirt road came through the gorge into the settlement. This was the first place *Mata'i* had anchored that had no church, and the attitude was different, aboriginal. No one wore Western dress. The children were naked and the women bare breasted. Very few Westerners visited this valley.

It didn't take long for Larry and his crew to reach the *haka'iki's* home. The wood-framed house stood on a tall *paepae* overlooking the village and had a large, thatched roof lanai in front. Four tattooed bodyguards made Larry and his crew wait outside the residence while the chief's *tuhunas*, or priests, chanted a welcome to the *aoes*, or foreigners. When the chant finished the *haka'iki* came out and greeted each of the visitors by pressing his forehead to theirs and exchanging breath. Larry gave the chief the message from Jacques at Hanamenu, and the *haka'iki* invited the *aoes* into his house.

Larry and his crew sat on finely woven mats on the darkly polished wooden floor. Also, in the room were the elders from the settlement. A *haka'iki* servant ladled *kava* from a large bowl into the guest's cups. *Kava* was a native intoxicant made from the root of the *ti* plant. Melanie took a sip of the brown liquid and didn't like the taste. The others politely sipped the drink. Larry and the elders talked in French, while Melanie recorded everything on her Walkman and noted her impressions, like a good reporter, on her steno pad. David busied himself sketching and tried to understand the French being spoken. Jason meditated without closing his eyes and looking obvious. He wanted to sense if there was some underlying atmosphere that the island shamans had created, like what had happened to him on Hiva Oa, that might affect him and what they were doing there. He felt nothing out of the ordinary. The elders, high priest, and keepers of the sacred rituals felt the atmosphere of Jason's meditation. The most sensitive of the priests even saw an aura around him.

As the afternoon wore on, the people from the yacht drank more kava and ate the *haka'iki's* food. Two young women watched the *aoe* from behind a fretted screen. When Jason laid eyes upon them, their exotic beauty entranced him. David had a strange sensation come over him, too, one that he tried to dismiss. It felt evil and disturbed his sketching. He poked Jason to indicate he should stop looking at the girls.

"Those are my daughters," said the *haka'iki* in broken English, interrupting the story he was telling Larry. "They are in seclusion until the ceremony tonight."

"They're beautiful," Jason murmured. His voice seemed distant as he took another sip of kava. David prodded him to pay attention. Jason turned his gaze to the *haka'iki*. The chief had been fixated on Jason since he entered the room. He not only examined every part of Jason physically, but probed him mentally and psychically too. The elders had been doing the same thing and watched Jason slide from a self-assured introspection into the shadowy mental condition being created in preparation for the ritual.

At that moment, the *haka'iki* brought the young people into the conversation. Larry translated the French and relayed that the ancient ceremony they were going to witness that night had almost been lost because of the oppression of the Catholic

Church and the French military. "The priests saw everything in terms of sex. They banned dancing because it was lewd. They thought our dress was vulgar. They forbade men and women to bathe together in public. They believed tattooing was the work of the devil, and they outlawed drinking kava because it was an aphrodisiac."

David looked at Jason, grinning, and flashed the *shaka* sign. He pushed aside his Baptist conditioning and embraced the atmosphere of the coming ritual.

"But Hakamaii was spared the plague of the Christians," Larry went on, doing his best to keep up with the chief. "We were remote enough to keep the priests at bay. But without a church we were not allowed to mingle with the other communities and our village nearly died. Twenty-three years ago, Larry's friend Jacques, saved us. He brought new people to the valley and fragments of our old chants. Our population began to grow, and people came to see our ceremonies. Now we are famous—or infamous; the old rituals are not accepted by all."

Outside, at dusk, a bonfire was lit in the commons and the villagers began their feast. The crowd swirled around the *tohua*. People gorged on food—sweet succulent meats swimming in exotic syrups—as they searched for a place to sit and watch the ceremony. The *haka'iki's* men walked through the crowd ladling kava into the coconut bowls of the spectators. Torches gave off the only light, and young people, many who had traveled from other Hiva islands, poured through the gorge to join this most sacred festival. Everyone was adorned with flowers and greenery. And *Larry filmed everything.*

David stood watching the crowd and he couldn't help feeling that what he saw was sinful. It was indulgent, hedonistic, and he grew uncomfortable with the vibe. Jason roamed around like he was at a cocktail party, looking very detached, like he was in a dream. The *haka'iki's* men gestured for David and Melanie to join the circle forming around the *tohua*. All of the Hiva boys wanted to touch Melanie's white skin and she was forced to shove intoxicated young men off of her. She dropped her camera in her small, crossbody bag and found a seat next to David.

"I wish I'd put my T-shirt and shorts in here," she said, placing her satchel between them. Jason staggered over to his shipmates and sat down next to Melanie. He had a full bowl of *kava* in his hands and a glazed look on his face. He was overly friendly, talking to the nearby native girls, who had no idea what he was saying, but laughed and talked back to him like they were old friends speaking the same language. Melanie turned away from Jason and held on to David.

"What's gotten into Jason?" she asked.

A troupe of drummers strode onto the *tohua* and beat out a fast, ancient rhythm, grabbing everybody's attention. Then twenty female dancers surged into the sacred circle. Bare breasted and wearing feathered crowns, they kicked up dust as they danced around the *tohua*, moving around the clusters of excited natives, enticing them with their sexuality. Grass skirts undulated as they followed the beat with their hips. The *'upa'upa*—the fast gyrating of hips and abdomen—exploded in front of the spectators.

The rhythm changed and the women moved to one side as a line of male dancers entered the circle. The leader was covered in vines and thrust a spear out in front of him. He wove through the other dancers as if hunting, leading his men around the circle toward the women. In the line of men were two dancers who carried a boy tied to a pole as if he were a pig. As the hunters moved through the crowd, the women ran in mock terror until one girl, exceptionally beautiful, stepped in front of the leader and held up her arms. The drumming stopped and for a moment everything was still as the hunter and the girl stared at each other. Then she began a slow, seductive hip movement and lowered her arms in a beckoning fashion. The drummers picked up her rhythm and the hunter dropped his spear in surrender. The passion grew as the rest of the women who had fled returned and found men to seduce.

The dancers went through the moves of sexual foreplay and followed the drummers' every rhythm until the drums stopped. The dancers stood in place, panting. The drums began again, and the dancers walked around the circle, men in one direction and women in the other. One woman stopped in front of David, grabbed his arm, and pulled him up. She placed her hands on David's hips, showing him what to do. A sexy young guy pulled Melanie from the crowd and did the same; soon she was gyrating her hips in a figure eight to the rhythm of the drums. All around the circle dancers were pulling new people onto the *tohua*. The Hiva people knew the movements. The beauty who had danced with the hunter chose Jason. The beat picked up, and the dancing created clouds of dust.

Larry caught it all on film. He was zooming in on Melanie when her dance partner reached around her back and cut her bikini strap with a piece of shell. Melanie tried to hang on to her top, and at the same time, shove the boy away. Larry dropped his camera. He ran up to help Melanie, but the young Hiva man gave Larry a shoulder check that knocked Larry to the ground. Then the kid grabbed Melanie and pulled her from the circle. Larry charged the boy, seized him around the waist, and tore him away from Melanie, still desperately clinging to her top. David rushed over to help.

"We're leaving. This is going to get ugly," Larry put his arm around his daughter, protectively, as they shoved their way toward the landing. "Get Jason."

David pushed his way back through the crowd to where he'd last seen Jason. Jason and the Hiva girl were gone. Dave struggled on through the mob, heading toward the far end of the *tohua*, toward the *haka'iki's* house. A Hiva boy, much larger than David, grabbed David from behind and pinned his arms to his side. The boy began kissing David on the neck. David struggled but couldn't break the boy's grip. At that moment, the girl he'd been dancing with staggered up to him and pulled down his shorts. She was naked. The boy let go of David and chased the girl, who ran away laughing, loving the game.

David took a step in the other direction but tripped over his shorts. Another girl ran over and jumped on him. They stumbled around in a cloud of groping kids. After a month at sea, David was aroused. The girl grabbed his cock and wanted to pull him on top of her right there. It was not the time, nor place, and David had to rescue Jason. Duty, and all his Baptist conditioning forced David to shove the girl away. She ran off and David pulled up his trunks and cinched them tight. He spotted Jason and the gorgeous dancer stride up the hill, leaving the commons. David ran after them. Before he could get close, however, two of the *haka'iki's* guards blocked his way. He yelled after his buddy, but Jason didn't look back. The guards pushed David into the frenzied circle. A moment later he heard the air horn blaring from the landing. He reluctantly raced back to shore.

Larry had managed to get Melanie out of the circle and to the boat ramp. Protecting his daughter from handful of oversexed adolescents, he blew the horn again. He needed David there to bring the dinghy. David shoved his way through the crowd and moments later showed up.

"Where the fuck is Jason?" Larry shouted.

"I couldn't get to him."

"Forget him. Swim out to the boat and bring back the dinghy."

Not again, David thought. "We can't leave him."

"You'll never find him in that madness. He's probably been taken away by now anyway."

David just stood there, torn. Jason *had* been taken away.

"For the last time, Dave, we need a way out of here!" Larry said. "These people won't take us back to the boat.

David looked at Melanie and she nodded for him to do as her father said. She was terrified.

David dove into the water. It was dark and the flickering light from the bonfire and torches danced over the waves. The drums grew louder, and he swam faster, feeling like Tommo in Melville's novel *Typee* escaping from the cannibals. It was a long swim, with the surge taking him this way and that before he finally reached the boat.

On shore, the *haka'iki* cornered Larry, and the boys bothering Melanie melted back into the circle. He begged Larry not to take Melanie from the ceremony. She wouldn't be hurt. And besides, the wild melee was all part of the preparation for the sacred ritual that Jacques wanted Larry to film. But Larry was now enraged.

"It's my fault, Melanie." Larry held his daughter close, wary of the bodyguards gathering around the *haka'iki*. "I should have asked more questions before I gave the *haka'iki* that note."

"What did the note say?"

"I'll tell you later. Right now, we need our dinghy. Where the hell is David."

David climbed on board *Mata'i* and lowered the dinghy. He'd barely caught his breath as he lowered *Mata'i Iti* over the side, unhooked the tackle, and started rowing back to shore. Then the drumming stopped. When he reached the boat ramp a squad of armed men had surrounded Larry and Melanie—native warriors gripping wooden spears. David could see nothing modern in that picture. The men looked like the savages Melville had described. David rode the back of a swell up the boat ramp and grounded the dinghy as close as he could get to Larry and Melanie. He jumped out as the water began to recede and held onto the painter, keeping the dinghy from drifting back out to sea.

"Turn it around," Larry ordered.

David did as he was told and wondered why they weren't all taken captive. Was the *haka'iki* afraid of Larry?

"You're making a big mistake," Larry shouted, still speaking French. "That boy isn't the one we thought he was. You'll kill him and destroy any chance you have of reviving your culture."

The *haka'iki* was in Larry's face as a phalanx of warriors closed in on them. "The elders and *Tuhuna O'ono* met him. They disagree. He *is* the one," the *haka'iki* shouted back at Larry. "You tested him. He meets all the requirements. He has the gifts."

"He's not Polynesian!" Larry argued.

"You said he was prepared. He knows the *Kumulipo*. He's the best candidate we've ever had for the *atua* ritual. That's why you came. Those were your orders from Hiva Oa."

"Bring Jason back to our boat tonight, before it's too late."

"It's already too late. Let your daughter and the boy stay. We will open their souls."

David could tell from the shouting that Larry had used Jason in some cruel way. Larry had brought them to this primeval place, and now Jason would complete the ritual without Larry filming it.

Larry turned from the *haka'iki* and stepped into his dinghy. One of the *haka'iki's* men handed Larry his camera. Larry helped Melanie into the dinghy, and on the next surge David pushed them out and rowed back to *Mata'i* in the blackness of a moonless night.

As soon as they were on board the yacht, Larry brought out his guns, the Winchester and the Colt. He didn't want to talk about their situation, but Melanie and David insisted on it.

David understood French better than Larry had realized, and he now confronted Larry with what had been said. "Jason was the chosen one? He was the best person for the *atua* ritual? The ritual that would kill him? You were planning Jason's death!" Melanie was horrified. David grabbed Larry's rifle from the cockpit and scampered aft to climb into the dinghy. "I'll find him."

Larry blocked his way. He grabbed the rifle with a speed and force David didn't expect from an old man, popped out the magazine, and put it in his pocket. "Sit down."

Melanie jumped up and stood next to David, facing down her father. "What were the other guns for? Are you hoping to start a revolution?"

Larry shrugged. He forgot how timid Melanie's generation was. Don't make waves; just take care of me. "How disappointing you two are. You have no idea what it costs to be free."

"You can't play with Jason's life like this."

"This is no game, Dave. Those people don't care about us. Hell, they don't even like us."

David left the cockpit, grabbed his swim fins from the lazarette, and dove into the water. He looked up at Melanie, hoping she'd join him.

"You do this, and they will kill you." Larry stood at the rail hoping to block his daughter from diving off the boat. "They will rape my daughter and keep raping her until she's pregnant, and they'll hold her hostage until she has a baby."

David looked toward shore and dozens of men stood ready to launch their canoes. Behind them was a frenzy of lovemaking and shouting.

"This is insane," Melanie cried. "We can't leave him."

"He's already dead." Larry moved to embrace his daughter.

Melanie let out a sob and pushed her father away. He grabbed a shroud to keep from falling overboard. He stared back to the shore and saw men carrying canoes to the boat ramp. "We need to get the anchor up without a sound. You two do that now."

"Everything is a lie with you," Melanie cried, beating on her father's back. "You think you're doing good. You think you've enabled J.J.'s rise to glory, or some such shit. Oh fuck. You're an idiot!"

She crumpled onto the deck, hung over the rail and vomited.

David looked to shore. A growing fleet of canoes pointed toward them. Machetes flashed in the firelight. "Do they have guns?"

"I doubt it. Not from me, anyway," Larry would not take his eyes off the natives.

David climbed back onboard and put his arm around Melanie. He'd never felt so trapped or useless in his life. "Maybe we can wait them out here. They wouldn't come on the boat. We can see what happens in the morning."

The drums began again, this time a threatening war rhythm. The frenzy was no longer lustful; it was dangerous. The men lining the shore began slapping their bodies and chanting a *haka*, something all Polynesian people did before attacking.

"I'm serious. Get the anchor onboard now. They can't know we're leaving, so no winch, no motor, no noise until we're free."

David and Melanie went forward pulling up the anchor hand over hand. Slowly *Mataʻi* moved to a position directly over the hook. Larry kept an eye on the shore. At the first sign of canoes being launched toward them he was prepared to fire up the diesel and take the boat out. But Melanie and David couldn't pull the anchor off the bottom. It was stuck.

Larry quickly realized this. David slipped over the side, even though he was a poor diver. Melanie knew that he could not clear his ears and if he dove deeper than fifteen feet he'd be in great pain. Melanie started to slip over the side to help, but Larry grabbed her, holding her back.

"I said for Dave to free it. Melanie you stay on deck." This order was in a whispered shout.

Things became more aggressive on shore; the warriors began pounding on their canoes with their paddles. It was a terrifying sound. On David's first try he only got halfway to the bottom before his ears screeched. When David got back to the surface Larry said, "Be a man, Dave."

David fantasized swimming ashore and hiding in the jungle and rescuing Jason—it's better to lose your life for a friend, but there was Melanie looking over the rail at him. His second try got him closer and he could make out what was hanging up the anchor. On the third try, with his ears screaming in pain, he was able to pull one of the flukes out of a hole and untangle the chain from a large rock. He gave the anchor line a tug, to signal Melanie, and a few seconds later the anchor and chain were free.

He drifted to the surface, tasting blood in the back of his mouth and wondering if he'd ever hear again. Melanie secured the anchor. As soon as Larry saw David grab the gunwale, he started the motor. As David climbed on deck he glanced toward shore where the men began to push their canoes into the water.

The first canoes hit the water with their outboard motors running. More canoes followed.

Larry put *Mata'i* in gear and powered toward the open sea with the throttle wide open. The yacht was not nearly as fast as the canoes with the outboard motors, but they had a fifty-yard head start. Larry gave David the helm and went aft with his Winchester. He took the magazine from his pocket, shoved it into the rifle, and chambered a round. He braced himself on the backstay and aimed at the lead canoe.

Just as he was about to fire Melanie screamed and shoved his rifle toward the sky. "You are not going to kill anybody else!" The shot fired into the air and Larry shoved his daughter aside and took aim again. But the islanders had turned back.

Larry yelled at his daughter. "Don't you ever interfere with what I'm doing. Ever!" He set the safety on the gun and returned to the cockpit, Melanie on his heels, yelling, "You tell me what was in that note now!"

After catching his breath and letting the adrenalin diminish, Larry spoke in a very measured manner. "Jacques told me that the people of Hakamaii were going to revive the ancient initiation ritual and that I should record it." He paused. "That's what was in the note I gave the chief. He told me not to be shocked, that it was just a reenactment."

"You're a fucking nutcase jeopardizing us like this! And for what?" said David standing at the helm.

"For the greater good! Jacques told me I'd understand when I saw the ritual." Larry picked up the Colt from the cockpit seat and automatically popped the magazine and checked the ammunition. He shoved the clip back in the handle of the gun and shoved it into his pocket. This was so professional and so unthinking that David wondered what other secrets Larry had kept from them.

Melanie was outraged. "You knew this was going to happen to Jason?"

"I thought we were going to see a performance. That's all. We thought we could help them restore their power, their *mana*. Perhaps that would have mitigated some of the damage done by our forefathers. I expect Jason will rise to the occasion."

"You're such a fucking liar." David's anger rose to where he was out of breath. "You said J.J. was not the one! You brought him down here for this, didn't you? All that bullshit about J.J. calming the sea was just a ruse. You were covering something up! What?"

"You don't have the consciousness to understand. I thought Jason did, but once we were out to sea, I knew that he didn't. There are things these people can do that are mind-boggling. All the sex and stuff is meaningless. Granted, they want to expand the gene pool, but that's easy. What the Hiva people truly want goes back to when the gods visited this planet. All spirituality comes from that source, and these people have a direct connection to it. I know that. If Jason really were the chosen one, these people would make him a new messiah, an *atua* man—if he survived the initiation. But I don't think he is and there's nothing I can do to save him. His fate is with the *Tuhuna O'ono*."

Melanie screamed at the top of her lungs. She was no longer his daughter. She would bring charges of murder against him. Her mother was right; he ruined everything he touched. She warned him never to talk to her again. Larry grabbed the rifle and took his weapons below to his cabin. Melanie stood over the companionway shrieking at him as Larry closed the hatch.

David drove the *Mata'i* straight out to sea, motoring at ten knots into a five-foot swell and traveling directly away from the valley. When Melanie had finished her rant, David asked her to take the helm. She did and he set the sails. When the sails were drawing, Melanie killed the motor. David went into the salon and studied the charts. He came back on deck and said, "Keep the island to the left and when we clear it, it's due north to Taiohae."

"I hope the fucking French Navy is there. They can save J.J. and then execute Larry."

As Larry and the *Mata'i* sailed away from Ua Pou, Jason and the dancer staggered up the east side of the valley with a horde of people, all intoxicated and full of lust. They entered a meadow ringed with ancient *paepaes* and towering breadfruit trees. Scattered around the meadow were woven mats for lovemaking. The Hiva girl striped off her headdress and leis and pressed her breasts against Jason's bare chest. If she could have crawled under his skin, she would have.

Around them, other couples copulated while still standing. She removed Jason's shorts and pushed him down on the nearest mat. Nothing but lust filled their minds. Jason would have this girl without a thought. Lillian was a world away, and his desire in the moment was all that mattered.

Before they could begin their lovemaking, however, the *tuhuna O'ono*, the sacred priest, and three of his acolytes separated the couple. This was not the person to receive Jason's seed. The girl, terrified of the priests, fled. The priest put a drug-soaked cloth into Jason's mouth, and he became limp. The holy men dragged him to a *me'ae* at the edge of the meadow overlooking the sacred valley. *Tapu* sticks forbade any but the priests to enter.

Tiki images of the Hiva deities stood at the corners of the *me'ae*. *Atea*, the father of the people, stood on one side of the altar, and *Atanua*, his wife, stood on the other. A wind blew over the open temple as the priest laid a listless Jason on a thick bed of smooth mats in the middle of the sacred space. Jason tried to get up, but the combination of the drug and kava semi-paralyzed him. The *Tuhuna O'ono* lit a brazier under the altar and in the soft light of the coals Jason saw ten girls sitting around the images of their gods. They were all naked. Some were just entering puberty.

The priest began chanting and one of the girls was brought to Jason. She began arousing him. While kava relaxes the body, and is a mild aphrodisiac, the *Tuhuna O'ono* squeezed another potion into Jason's mouth from a small sponge. It was a powerful sexual stimulant made from ginger type roots and tree bark. Jason was hard in a few seconds. The girl, at this point, took his penis into her and danced on top of him until she felt him ejaculate. The *tuhuna's* assistants watched and pulled the girl away as soon as they knew she had his seed. Before Jason could collapse, the priest moistened his lips with the drug sodden sponge. By the time the acolytes brought over another girl, Jason was ready again.

Through the fog of the intoxicants and the rhythm of sex, Jason became aware of his primitive self. The pleasure of sex tied him to the physical and the chanting hypnotized him into believing he had a duty to perform for these people. Part of his mentality traveled through their Hiva myths, into the time of their gods, and he saw the Hiva path into the spiritual. It was filled with conflict. Heroes needed to be created to fight evil. Men needed to be infused with the power of the gods to vanquish the dark forces, the demons and devils that brought suffering to these people. But this was not his path.

Another part of his mind brought peace. It assured him that his soul, his true self was the same substance as the earth and sea and heavens above. Pleasure spread across the universe like waves rolling over an atoll. His inner grace knew no boundaries. It filled all space leaving no opposite, only one life, one love, one self. He felt the oneness of the others. He let *It* take over, until his mortal-self surrendered to infinite consciousness. He was without opposite or conflict, beyond myth, and entered a state of omnipresence. With all the power, conflict, and domination being inflected on him, he realized he was being raped. Yet he had to include the Hiva people in his prayer of spiritual oneness. He had to forgive their animalistic rituals. Forgiveness detached him from the physical and released him from the psychic connections being forced upon him. The more he let *It* take over, the less he struggled both mentally and physically. Without love there could be no physical bondage, and he felt no love. He held onto the knowledge that forgiveness would heal the terrible guilt to come and reveal the reality of who he truly was.

He had sex all night, impregnating eight of the highest caste girls in the valley.

Chapter 36
Nuku Hiva, Marquesas Islands

Wednesday, July 8, 1989

Six hours after leaving Hakamaii, just as dawn was breaking, the *Mata'i* sailed into a crowded Taiohae Bay, the capital of the northern Hiva Islands. Melanie pounded on the aft cabin hatch, but Larry was still fuming and didn't answer. David maneuvered the boat to the west side of the bay, away from the thick cluster of yachts around the jetty, and Melanie dropped the anchor. As soon as the anchor was set, David lowered the dinghy and started the motor. He needed to go ashore and tell the authorities that Jason had been kidnapped on Ua Pou.

Larry, hearing the anchor drop, came on deck. He was in a foul mood and saw David in the dinghy. "You better take all your gear if you go ashore because you're not getting back on this boat."

David had his wallet, slippers, and T-shirt; what else did he need? He certainly didn't need anything from Larry. "I guess I'll take my passport and plane ticket then."

Larry went back to his cabin and returned with David's papers.

"I thought you had more backbone." Larry handed him his papers.

"You're the coward, man. Do the right thing. Get the authorities involved. This is a kidnapping."

Larry laughed. "Jason willingly went with those girls... No, happily! Besides the French won't go near Hakamaii. They think it's cursed."

"I'm not getting back on your fucking boat unless it's to get Jason."

"Dave," Melanie pleaded. "He's serious.

"I guess this is it. Goodbye, Melanie. He's going to rot in hell."

Melanie was torn between David and her father. "Larry be reasonable. How are we going to get the *Mata'i* back to Honolulu without a crew?" She could no longer call him Dad.

"I've made that crossing alone, before you were born, in a boat more difficult to sail than this one.

"So, you'd leave me too?"

"If it came to that." He watched his daughter poised to get in the dinghy with David. "I made this trip for you. It's the best gift I can give you. I want to complete it with you—and Dave."

"But not Jason?" Melanie was disgusted.

"There's nothing I can do for him. I wish I could, I really do."

Melanie sensed a tinge of regret in her father. Maybe this was as close to an apology as he could muster. But it wasn't enough.

"Why would I ever want to stay with you?" Melanie climbed over the side joining David in the dinghy. Did David see a moment of anguish flood Larry? He couldn't tell.

"Somebody's got to bring the fucking dinghy back," Melanie took control of the *Mata'i Iti* and drove David to shore.

"You don't have to go with him. He's quite capable of sailing back by himself."

"I know." Melanie started to cry. "But he's not really that tough."

"Please, Melanie, help me find J.J.

"I can't do this. I can't do this anymore."

Melanie dropped David on the beach near the *Temehea Tohua* monument, quickly turned the boat around and left him. She was still crying and didn't say good-bye.

The weeklong Bastille Day *Fête* had started. There were hundreds of people wandering up and down the road between the center of town and the school. All kinds of stalls lined the road. Some were elaborate bamboo structures with thatched roofs, others were store-bought tents, and many were just mats spread out on the ground. And everything from woodcarvings and print fabrics to musical instruments and food was for sale. David passed a tattoo artist—the only one on the road. He was giving a tourist from one of the yachts a native design on his leg. David stopped to watch for a moment. He couldn't help himself. One of the reasons he signed on to this voyage was to see some Marquesan tattoos. He had studied them in his Arts of the Pacific class in college and he saw in their curving, floral designs a hint of Antonio Gaudi. He was disappointed so few natives wore them. Perhaps they still were not accepted by the French.

David reached the government house feeling a little guilty that he had interrupted his mission to rescue Jason by watching someone being tattooed. When he entered the administration building, it exuded as festive an atmosphere as the street. Musicians were singing and strumming their instruments in the foyer. The clerks wore flower leis. David asked to see the governor and was told he was in Papeete. "He's too French," one clerk said laughing, wearing a head lei made from petite mountain ferns.

David told her he needed to rescue his brother from Ua Pou, and she very sweetly told him she couldn't help. When David mentioned that he was at Hakamaii, she turned and walked into her office, slamming the door. The others in the foyer moved away from him like he was contagious.

David left, heading back to the heart of the festival, all the while scanning the bay for new boats. He saw the *Mataʻi* leaving, motoring out and pulling the dinghy. So, this was it. He was alone like Melville, but Melville hadn't landed in the midst of a *fête*.

David needed to find a way back to Hakamaii. He was less than six hours away with the right boat. His first thought was the wharf. Perhaps there was ferry service between the islands. He checked out the kiosk at the end of the wharf. No ferries for two days. He looked in to chartering a boat, but there were none. David then headed back to the main drag, desperate to find someone who would take him to Hakamii. He discovered that name was toxic.

It began to rain heavily and didn't let up. The people on the road and in the stalls hardly noticed. Umbrellas came out, more tarps went up, and the festival shifted into high gear.

Like on Hakamaii, the night brought out the primeval in the celebrations. The pavilion, just off the park where the *Temehea Tohua* monument stood, was packed. The excitement was high. A trio played a mix of "Island Pop," the islander's take on Western pop songs, and local *meles*, ancient chants put to music. On one level it was entertaining, but emotionally, the dances and chants touched something basic, something frightening. To David they were savage. Were these ceremonies the way societies survived? Did celebrating ancient sacrifices to appease fierce gods perpetuate a culture? Did it make people feel safe, connected? How could one celebrate sacrifice and maintain one's humanity? Who chooses the sacrifice? And if *you* are the sacrifice, does your blood give humanity its nobility? David was bombarded with these thoughts as the first dance began. It was the pig dance; the same one David had seen at Hakamaii. It made the hair on his neck stand up.

The next group to perform was a troupe from Atuona, and David believed that their *kumu* was the woman he had visited there. In his current state of mind, he wasn't one hundred percent certain, but then her sons came onstage, and David knew for sure that it was Ama. Their troupe was mostly female, and their dance was graceful and melodic. Their costumes blended Tahiti with Hawaii, and their movements told another story—a story of love and caring. Was this also traditional, the *yin* and the *yang* of Hiva culture? On the one hand there was hunting, sacrifice, and survival, and on the other, love and compassion?

When the dance ended, David made his way backstage. Many people crowded around the Atuona group and the performers struggled to get away. David had to push his way in to get Ama's attention. At first, she didn't recognize him. David could see her wondering why this white man wanted to get so close to her, and then her face lit up in recognition. She threw people aside and hugged him warmly.

"Where is Larry and his charming daughter?" she asked.

David told her he wasn't getting along with Larry at the moment and that he needed a place to stay for the night.

She patted his hand. "Not to worry. Nobody gets along with Larry." And she ushered David out with her troupe.

Ama and her sons had a bungalow at the Pearl Lodge, just a ten-minute walk from the pavilion. Did she know Jason's fate? According to Larry she was in on the ordeal, but she showed no sign of awareness about the ritual. She wouldn't let David tell his story until they were on the lanai of her bungalow and David had a glass of wine in his hand. When he'd finished his story, she embraced him and held him tight.

"Your friend is in the bosom of the gods. We cannot change our fate. You must move on."

David freed himself from her hug and was repulsed by her attitude. "This is not J.J.'s fate. This was a conspiracy by a bunch of old farts wanting to rekindle something that's been long dead." He put the glass of wine down untouched and left.

"I will save your friend," she called after him, and he heard her telling her sons to find Jason. She caught up to David outside and laying a hand on his arm, stopped him. "Even if we had lured your friend to the ritual under false pretenses, the *mana* surrounding Larry and his loved ones would not allow his destiny to be diverted." She explained *mana* as Larry's spiritual power, which he had always had. He had lived in the islands all those years and everyone there knew his *mana*. The French were afraid of him, and some of the *tuhunas* feared him, but it would be their death to plot against him. David realized this was why the *haka'iki* didn't go after Larry.

These people believed the unseen world was as real and as powerful as the seen world. To the modern person it's all superstition, and fake. But in many parts of the planet the unseen and the unworldly is more powerful than the visible, and the shaman and the priest are more powerful than the king and the ruler. Jason would never call that world spiritual, David thought. To him the divine was without opposite, omnipotent and good.

"If Jason completes the initiation," Ama went on…

If he survives, David thought…

"He will become the *Atua Man*, god incarnate, and he will be recognized as the new *Tuhuna O'ono*. The *haka'iki* would bring him here to announce the new beginning of the Hiva people, and their connections to the gods."

David didn't take any of this seriously, except that his best friend could be dead. Hiva gods, fate, and destiny were woven into these people's lives like the fibers in a matt. He had to concentrate to hear what Ama was telling him.

"He will be here tomorrow night, introduced to the people as their new *tapu chief* and *tuhuna O'ono*. If he is alive."

Chapter 37
Ua Pou, Marquesas Islands

Wednesday, July 8, 1989

The same morning, while David watched a tourist being tattooed at Taiohae, four men, *tuhuna patutikis*, masters of tattooing, were covering Jason's torso and limbs with their traditional designs. Jason lay on his back in the middle of the high stone platform. The girls were gone, not allowed to watch this sacred work. There was nothing modern in the *me'ae*. The tattoo instruments were traditional—bone and mallet and charcoal ink. The native clothing was made from bark cloth, not Western material.

Jason awoke from his drug induced sleep, slapping at his body where the *patutiki* artists were working on him, as if he were swatting at mosquitoes. He shouted and struggled to get up, but the men shoved him down, with one man putting a knee on his chest. To Jason's horror he was being made into a Hiva man of high rank. The *tuhuna O'ono*, the master of the ritual, rushed over with a sheep's bladder filled with *kava*. He shoved the nipple of the kava pouch into Jason's mouth. Jason gagged, struggling to fight them off. After they had forced the drink down his throat, Jason relaxed and couldn't move. The *patutiki* practitioners turned him onto his stomach and proceded to work on his back, chanting while they formed their designs.

The tapping of the ink into his skin sent Jason into another state of mind. In this altered mindset, he could perceive the patterns being etched into his body. He saw the might of the sea in wave-like patterns intertwined with the symbols of the turtle, the whale, and the spikey fins of the *a'ahi*. He felt the life of the land surge with the shapes of the fern, and the taro and the breadfruit. He became aware of these images through the minds of the *patutiki* artists. As they tattooed, they prayed, each to the god they represented. The most powerful *tuhunas*, the high priests, worked around his lower torso, the place in his body where his *mana* originated. They directed the *tuhuna patutikis* to carve, in thick black ink, semblances of the pantheon of their gods. The images were as contemporary as they were ancient, and their purpose was to connect Jason to these people, to this island. Jason wasn't being made a Hiva man, they were making him an embodied god—an *Atua Man*.

Jason didn't need tattoos to connect him to the gods. He already knew his relationship to the divine. He had already experienced his unity with his fellow brothers and sisters. He did not need tattoos to connect him to the life of the planet or tell him how he should live to keep harmony and abundance flowing into the world. Dr. Green came to him, imparting a message: neither human good nor human evil is real. The source of life is beyond human comprehension. Remain detached and be free.

Chapter 38

Nuku Hiva, Marquesas Islands

Thursday, July 9, 1989

David got up at sunrise with Ama's words in his mind; "I will save your friend." That night, desperate for hope, he had believed her. Now, beginning his second day in Taiohae, he doubted her. He had slept on the *lanai* of Ama's room at the Pearl Lodge, and he left before any of the others woke up. It had rained all night—a hot, tropical deluge that made the road along the strand a muddy bog. It was now up to David to save Jason. No one else could or would.

Sloshing through the mud he made a mental list of what he thought he knew. It was the last day of the native competitions, a part of the Bastille Day Festival. The highlighted performance that night would feature the Ua Pou dancers. Were they already here, in Taiohae, or were they arriving later? He had watched one troupe from Ua Pou practicing the day before and he couldn't imagine they were the final act. If another group was arriving, David wanted to be at the wharf to meet them. He had convinced himself that Jason would be among them. David hoped Ama was right, and that Jason would perform with the troupe. Even if the ritual had damaged Jason, if his mind was gone and he was a babbling idiot, David wanted to pull his best friend out of this mess. He loved Jason more than he'd ever realized.

David hung around the wharf all morning. He sat on the edge of the jetty watching the children jump into the water. It began to rain again and that seemed to increase the joy of the kids swimming in the bay. They wanted him to play too, but he wouldn't. This reminded David of the way he and Jason used to play as kids. It was too painful watching them, and he left to get something to eat. He bought some fried breadfruit from a vendor and drank a warm orange soda. No boat had arrived from Ua Pou.

Late that afternoon David headed back to the Pearl Lodge to talk to Ama. He needed her positive spirit. He wanted another shot of hope, someone to hug him and tell him it had all been a dream. Ama was the only contact he had in this remote corner of the Pacific, but even that was a stretch. She was the one who had originally drugged Jason to make him a candidate for godhood. How could that even be considered rational?

David suddenly had a vision of why so few white people lived in these islands. Unless you were part of the culture, there was nothing to do. The foreigners all sought some sort of paradise, and when it never appeared, they grew complacent, apathetic, and then they couldn't escape. Eventually they died here, like Paul Gauguin. That wasn't going to be David's fate, and hopefully it wasn't already Jason's.

When David returned to the hotel, he learned that Ama and her boys had checked out. Another betrayal. His only hope now was that Jason would be one of the dancers.

That night David got to the pavilion early and found a seat in the front row. If Jason was going to show up, he would find him. The dancers from Ua Pou were the last act, and David didn't see anyone from Hakamaii in their company, not the *haka'iki* nor his servants, and definitely not Jason. As the crowd left, happy and content, David sat alone in the bleachers until they shut off the lights. That was it; he was defeated.

He walked back to the Pearl Lodge and took a room for the night, pulling out the trusty American Express card that he hadn't used since Europe. It was hard for him to fathom that he'd been in Barcelona in April and three months later he was stranded in Taiohae, his best friend missing and perhaps killed. David ordered a bottle of whisky sent to his room and drank until he passed out.

That night, in his sleep, Jason came to him bathed in an unholy light. He brought the sounds of *haka*—warriors slapping their bodies and shouting insults at unseen enemies. Jason was in the front line, beating himself. Then it all dissolved in a fog of nothingness.

Chapter 39
Ua Pou, Marquesas Islands

Thursday, July 9, 1989

A moon rose over the valley, peeking out between the clouds. After two days of intensive work, Jason's body had been covered in the swirling designs of a *tapu* man. Jason knew a *tapu* person was sacred. He held the wisdom of the people and could not be approached. The uniniatiated who ventured into his presence to learn the mystery of life would die. Jason's body now warned people to stay away. The only ones allowed close were the *haka'iki* and the high priest. They would come prostrate, bringing food and *tapa*, and in return they would hear the will of the gods through Jason's voice. After the final phase of the ritual Jason would be the *atua*, god incarnate on Earth.

When the planet Venus reached its summit, the village elders, in their ceremonial dress, formed a circle in the center of the *me'ae*. Musicians and dancers chanted and performed in front of the sacrificial altar overlooking the sacred valley. Two warriors—temple guards—brought a naked and kava-intoxicated Jason into the middle of the circle. The moment he saw the stone alter he tried to get away. The strong men held him tighter as the *haka'iki*, wearing his chiefly regalia, led his naked daughters up to Jason. The *haka'iki* tied his oldest daughter's wrists to Jason's, while the younger daughter aroused him. Jason resisted, squirming and kicking as much as he could with two huge guys holding him.

"You must," said the *haka'iki.*

The older girl, tied to Jason, kissed him and begged him with her eyes to fulfill her.

The *haka'iki* and the elders squeezed in closer, encircling the couple. And the music swelled. When Jason was fully erect, the young girl slipped out of the way and the *haka'iki* took hold of Jason's penis and slipped it into his daughter's vagina. Once Jason was inside her he couldn't stop. The girl's father and the other elders—relatives all—embraced the pair. They needed to experience this union too.

When Jason reached climax, they knew that their princess was impregnated. The elders moved back, and the girl collapsed in ecstasy. Jason was breathing hard, like he had run a race. The guards untied him from the girl and Jason immediately tried to escape. The men had anticipated this and seized Jason, forcing him back into the circle where the younger daughter waited. The *Tuhuna O'ono's* acolytes bound them together and wrapped them in white tapa—their finest native cloth. The attendants of the high priest then carried the couple through a phalanx of warriors, to the stone alter while the dancers and chanters called on the gods to join the ceremony.

As much as he tried, Jason couldn't move. It took six strong men to lay him and the girl out on the stone and hold them down. The senior acolyte handed the *Tuhuna O'ono* the ceremonial knife and the high priest approached the altar. As the *Tuhuna O'ono* began the ritual, and the chanting grew quiet and reverent, a white bird flew into the temple and landed on the *Tiki* of *Atanua,* the wife of the Creator and the progenitor of the people. Immediately the *Tuhuna O'ono* fell to his knees. He raised his arms and the warriors unwrapped the couple. The girl ran to her sister. She had been saved by a sign from the gods. But Jason was forced back down and pinned to the stone by the temple guards. He was on his back and his heart beat rapidly, uncontrolled.

The *Tuhuna O'ono* raised his ceremonial knife again, and this time made a shallow cut from Jason's neck to his navel. He waited for the blood red line to grow. Panic rushed into Jason's mind as the pain pushed into his brain. Yet something kept thundering from the fringes of his mind, *oneness, oneness, oneness!* He had experienced oneness with the Creator, that which never changes, that which always exists as the individual expression of the Divine. He had experienced immortality at the bottom of Makaha Bay in Hawaii. And, he had experienced mystical union through Dr. Green. His life was not his; it was the life of the Creator living through him and *as* him. Nothing could alter that.

The *tuhuna* made a second cut, and a profound stillness came over him, something so powerful that his body calmed, and his mind became silent. He was in the Divine Presence, and the actions of mortal man had no effect on him. Jason seemed less dense, lighter, and pulsed with energy. The priest made another cut, and Jason began to disappear. The more they cut, the more ethereal he became, shifting from matter to energy. The other *tuhunas* began chanting wild desperate sounds, calling on their ancestors to help. The Hiva nation needed his heart, but it was not theirs to take. Before the ceremonial blade reached his heart, Jason had become pure energy and had disappeared.

Friday, July 10, 1989

The following day Jason found himself lying on the beach at Hakahau, the popular tourist port on the opposite side of the island from where the ritual had taken place. Hakahau was famous for the gigantic granite spires, the main attraction of the island, that rose up over the village like a primitive cathedral. Jason was naked and covered in tattoos. He was drowsy and confused. Had it been a horrible nightmare? After looking at his body, and all the tattoos, and the long red cut from his neck to his stomach that was fast disappearing, he knew it hadn't been a dream. Now he had to confront his current situation. Where was Larry and the *Matai'i*? How was he to find them? Where was he going to get clothes? How was he going to get along with his life after what had happened?

As Jason stirred, trying to get his bearings, a Canadian fellow nudged him with his foot, wanting him to move. Jason looked up at the Maple Leaf cap and scowling face and groaned. More tourists from the anchored yachts wandered over, wanting him to get off the beach. One man who spoke French shouted at a group of natives nearby to do something about this bum. Another person tossed Jason a light jacket to cover his body.

Jason got up, wrapped the jacket around his waist, and staggered over to where the natives were. The Hiva people didn't mind his nakedness, but his tattoos terrified them. An old woman warned her people to stay away from him. Somehow their language was in his head and he asked them, "Have you some clothes?" A teenage boy wearing a Rolling Stones T-shirt— the one with the tongue falling out of Mick Jagger's mouth— went up to Jason and said in English, "I have some clothes. I live right over there.

Chapter 40
Nuku Hiva, Marquesas Islands

Friday, July 10, 1989

It was the third day since Jason's abduction, and David awoke hung over and depressed. He had a vague recollection of Jason in his mind. It was raining again, and Taiohae was a swamp. He saw no way to get to Hakamaii, and he sure as hell wasn't going to stay in these god-forsaken islands.

David really couldn't blame the turn of events on Jason, but they did seem to follow the same pattern every time he hooked up with him. Jason was like the god Shiva, destroying the plans made by humans until they learned not to plan but to live in the moment. All of David's depression was due to the fact that he was mourning the loss of his best friend. The hope of the past couple of days, with Ama's assurances that Jason would show up, evaporated like rain puddles in the sun. Everything was futile. David's willingness to abandon all rational thought, in the fantasy that he could rescue Jason, left him longing for an order he could understand. This was an upside-down world that he could not navigate. He accepted the fact that Jason was gone and checked out of his room. A taxi arrived, the only one on the island, and drove him to the airport.

The village was as hung over as David was. There were four more days of partying, dancing, and sporting contests leading up to Bastille Day. The craft booths would be in full swing by the afternoon, and all this gaiety further depressed David. It took over an hour to get to the airport in the rain. The flight that day to Papeete was filled so David bought a ticket for one departing the next day. He drove back to Taiohae and hung out at the wharf watching more people leave than arrive. He was beginning to believe that Larry was right. Jason was already dead.

David had lunch at the Pension Moana Nui. The name made him nostalgic for Hawaii. He lingered over a glass of wine, looking out to the bay, when he spotted *Mata'i* motoring in at top speed, towing her dinghy. David threw some money on the table and raced down to the wharf. By the time he got there, Melanie had already anchored the yacht and carelessly tied up *Mata'i Iti* to the pier. When she saw David, she ran into his arms. She was frantic—Larry was deathly sick. He needed a doctor.

"Dad insisted we see these *tikis* in Taipivai." She burst into tears.

After what he'd experienced with Larry on Hiva Oa, David could picture the whole thing: Larry's arrogance, his belief that he was somehow connected to the Hiva people and yet be immune to their beliefs, the rightness of his mission—all that infuriated David.

"Did J.J. show up?" asked Melanie.

"No. I tried everything."

"I'm sick and tired of being manipulated by Larry and all his bullshit," she grumbled as they headed to the infirmary. "Even now I can't feel sorry for him."

David took Melanie's hand. "Maybe this is your dad's karma."

"Dad was so gross." She shuddered at the thought. "He said, 'who wouldn't want to die that way, having sex with a bunch of gorgeous little island girls? There're a lot worse ways to go than fucking yourself to death.'"

David pulled her close and held on to her.

"He's such an asshole, but I don't want him to die." She released herself from his hug, and they continued on toward the infirmary. "He browbeat this little kid for directions, and we found the overgrown trail where the boy said the *me'ae* would be. We hiked about half a mile and came upon *kapu* sticks, just like in Hawaii. I didn't want to go on, but Dad made me. It was the biggest *me'ae* I'd ever seen, breathtaking, the size of a football field. We climbed onto the platform and went up to the altar."

Melanie stopped, as if she was about to faint.

"I don't have to know."

"I need to tell someone. It was awful. I got sick. The altar was covered in blood."

They were almost to the infirmary. "You don't have to say any more."

Melanie walked ahead of him and entered the infirmary. "Dad put his fingers in the blood," she continued. "He thought he could tell if it was animal blood or human. It was just stupid, his stupid curiosity, wanting to know everything. He laughed. He rubbed it between his fingers, smelled it and announced it was a pig. We headed back and Dad was in a triumphant mood, the conqueror of superstition. When we got to the village, he was breathing hard. By the time we got to the boat he could barely climb onboard. I got him into his bunk, but he couldn't move and now he's struggling to breathe."

They waited a few minutes in silence for the doctor. David understood Melanie's rage. Was this nightmare ever going to end? The doctor came out with his little black bag, and the three of them headed back to the *Mata'i*.

David and Melanie waited in the cockpit while the doctor examined Larry. It was not unusual for doctors to go out to people's yachts to treat someone. When he was done, he kept his face neutral. "Where did he fall ill?"

"Taipivai. We'd hiked up to see the *tikis*."

The doctor sighed, not sure how to tell Melanie and David this. "He's dying and there's nothing I can do."

"Come on!" David didn't believe the doctor. "This looks like some kind of respiratory problem. Certainly, you can do something."

"I've seen this with a native before, never with a European. I'm sorry."

Melanie rushed into Larry's cabin, and David followed, leaving the doctor wondering how he was going to get to shore. Larry struggled to draw air into his lungs. David hated to see anyone suffer. He turned away, but Larry grabbed his hand, gasping, "Heal me, Dave."

David held onto Larry's hand for a moment and then laid it back on Larry's torso. "I can't. I'm not Jason."

Melanie began to cry again and ran up to the cockpit with David on her heels. "He must be oxygen starved," she said. "Help me get him to the infirmary."

"I need to get back," said the doctor insistently, looking at David. There was nothing more he could do. "You'll need to get the harbor master to bring out a gurney."

"Can you do that for us?" Melanie asked.

The doctor shrugged—maybe yes, maybe no. "But he'll die anyway."

David flopped down on the cockpit seat and put his head between his knees. The doctor could swim ashore for all he cared. His ticket to Papeete hung out of his pocket. He was in agony. "Why on earth would your dad think I could heal him?"

"I don't know what to do, Dave."

The doctor stood irritably by the boarding ladder, thumping his fingers on the stanchion.

"Please," she implored David, "help me. I can't do this alone."

David reluctantly got up, brought the dinghy around and helped the doctor down the ladder. He kissed Melanie and took the doctor to shore.

Saturday, July 11, 1989

David sat alone in the cockpit of the *Mata'i*, watching the sunset send shafts of light onto Taiohae Bay. He had not been successful in finding a launch or a gurney, so Larry was still on board. Melanie was with her father in the aft cabin. The *Mata'i* wasn't shipshape: there was no awning over the cockpit in case of rain; the dinghy was tied off and not onboard; and *Mata'i* swung on just one anchor, not the way Larry liked. Melanie and David were in no mood to do anything on the boat. But who cared about all that crap anymore? David and Melanie had spent the whole day on the yacht hoping Larry would improve.

No one was hungry. David poured a glass of wine, but it tasted foul and he tossed it overboard. He still thought Jason could be alive, but in what state? David could commandeer *Mata'i* and sail back to Hakamaii, given that Larry was in no condition to stop him now. Besides, David was still furious with the bastard for leaving Jason. Larry had brought all this on himself, so why should he feel guilty about wanting to find Jason? Larry had left! He wouldn't be in Taiohae if he hadn't fallen sick. No, the only right thing to do would be to sail back to Ua Pou. Would Melanie agree after all she'd been through? She could stay with the boat. He'd go ashore alone; Larry still had his guns.

Sunday, July 12, 1989

At sunup David was flaked out in the cockpit. It had been a horrible night, filled with guilt and self-recrimination, but David awoke ready for action. He would take the boat to Ua Pou. He looked into the aft cabin and Melanie was sleeping soundly. He couldn't tell if Larry was asleep or dead. He pulled the dinghy around to the boarding ladder, got in and rowed a few yards before starting the outboard. David tied the *Mata'i Iti* to the pier, climbed the steps to the jetty and noticed that a cruise ship and a trading steamer had arrived during the night.

At seven o'clock in the morning the town was alive and bustling. The islanders had set up their stalls for the tourists, and the merchants expecting cargo crowded the foot of the jetty as stevedores hauled carts of goods to the vendors who were waiting with their trucks. It was a different crowd from the festival crowd celebrating the *fête*. It was a mix of people—natives getting on with everyday life and tourists arriving to celebrate the last couple of days before the Bastille Day ceremonies. David made his way up the jetty to the market to grab a quick croissant and coffee. He found the market overrun with tourists. He bought half a dozen croissants and headed back to the dinghy.

David heard someone call his name. He looked around but didn't see anybody he recognized. Then he heard his named shouted again. It sounded like Jason's voice. Again, David didn't recognize anybody. Then someone grabbed him by the shoulder and turned him around.

"What is wrong with you? Don't you know your own name?" Jason gave David a bear hug. David was speechless. Jason smelled like diesel fuel and old hemp. He wore dirty jeans, a chambray work shirt, and heavy boots. His hair was greasy and clung to his neck and he had a four-day-old beard. David hugged him back and began to cry, it was such a relief to see him.

"Are we going to finish our voyage, or what? I see *Mata'i* anchored off the jetty."

David composed himself. "You asshole."

David turned away, his face still streaked with tears. "I tried to find you in that fucking orgy." He then turned back. "I saw you walking away with that dancer. I called your name, but you didn't answer. Then Melanie was attacked, and Larry just fucking abandoned you. I'm so fucking sorry."

Jason pulled David back and hugged him again. In that moment David felt something new, something powerful. It was what he had felt with Jason as a kid, only now it had matured. Something flowed between them that David had never felt. It wasn't physical but filled him with a love so strong and pure that all his guilt and sorrow vanished. He was washed clean by the power in Jason's embrace and felt the freedom that came with true forgiveness. David knew this feeling could not be the result of a *tuhuna*. It was the triumph of spiritual awareness over material belief, and that had nothing to do with a native ritual. David knew that Jason had entered a new dimension of consciousness. And he now understood his part in all of this. He was the witness, and he saw the power that his recognition brought. It was the reason they had been together their whole lives.

Jason released David. "You have nothing to regret, my friend."

They looked at each other for a moment, and then David said, "I think Larry died last night."

"Bollocks," said Jason mimicking Larry. "Where's Melanie?"

"She's on the boat."

"Then what are we doing ashore?" The two of them ran to the wharf.

As they sped out to the *Mata'i*, David wanted to know what had happened at Hakamaii, but Jason wouldn't talk about it. Instead, he wanted to know about Larry's death.

"A curse was put on him," David replied with a straight face.

"That's ridiculous."

David tied the dinghy up to *Mata'i*, and the boys climbed on board.

Melanie was in the cockpit weeping. When she saw Jason, she flew into his arms. "He's gone," she sobbed. She hugged Jason so tight that he could hardly breathe. He gently pushed her away and, at the same time, embraced her with his eyes. Her relief came with a shudder, and she sat back down on the cockpit bench. Knowing her father was dead, she shook her head at Jason, and the tears came again. Jason went aft and descended into the owner's cabin.

David sat down next to Melanie and put his arms around her. He held her until she stopped crying. Then David felt an incredible peace come over him. It wiped his mind of all thoughts and filled him with joy. At first, he started to resist it. Why would he feel joy at someone's death? But he found he couldn't resist it. He didn't judge the feeling; he didn't question it. He just accepted it as the grace of God. David hoped Melanie felt it too, but he didn't look at her for fear of losing the moment.

Melanie shook David from his meditation and pointed to the aft cabin. An intense light radiated from the portholes and the passageway. They grabbed hold of each other and waited. The light grew, like a musical chord reaching climax, and then it was gone. All that was left was a pale blue glow.

Jason came out and sat across the cockpit from his shipmates. He smiled. "He's fine. Asked me what the fuck I was doing here. I told him we had to finish our voyage."

"This is crazy." Melanie jumped up and went in to see her father.

"I've got to get out of these clothes." Jason kicked off his boots and stripped off his shirt and pants. For the first time David saw that he was covered in native tattoos – front to back, shoulders to ankles. They looked like they had been there for years. There was no redness around the ink. David knew that in native cultures the tattoos were powerful talismans, portals to another world where death and life coexisted in a different dimension. These same tattoo designs had shocked and intrigued the early European explorers of the Pacific. They were one of the elements that began a debate as to what was civilized and what was savage, and that debate continues to this day.

David started to comment, but Jason raised his tattooed arm, "I'll tell you later." Jason ducked below to find his own clothes.

As David looked back at the island, the images of the past couple of days flooded his mind, like the tattoos covering Jason's body. Everything he thought he knew had been destroyed here, in the Hiva Islands. He knew nothing. Right, wrong, good, evil; it no longer made any sense. Jason had just healed the man who wanted to kill him. Could all sins be forgiven? Were they now going to sail home to civilization and pretend nothing had changed? He wasn't sure he could do that.

Melanie came back on deck. "Dad wants to go home. Are you guys ready?"

Half an hour later the crew had the dinghy stowed, the anchor up, and *Mata'i* was sailing out of Taiohae Bay under a sunny sky. They left the *fête* before the finale on July fourteenth, Bastille Day.

They sailed away from the crowds and the people hoping to glimpse a bit of native culture. They had more than fulfilled the purpose of the voyage, but in ways no one had anticipated.

It took all day to sail around the west side of Nuku Hiva to Anaho Bay. They had the place to themselves. The deep bay was a perfect anchorage with flat, pristine water and a crescent of white sand. There was no permanent settlement, only a few shacks for fisherman, and the land was lush with coconut trees.

They stayed there a week, eating fish they had caught, picking pamplemousse, hiking the ridge behind the bay, and snorkeling the one untouched reef in the island chain. They played music and began to heal.

PART III

Chapter 41
Honolulu – Los Angeles – London

August 9, 1989

Ala Wai Yacht Harbor

The *Mata'i*'s arrival in Honolulu was a microcosm of the trip in general, with Larry back to his old tricks. Before reaching Honolulu, Larry didn't want to toss overboard the remaining *pamplemousse* they had gathered at Anaho, so David, Melanie, and Jason peeled and segmented what fruit was left and put the pieces in plastic bags. Larry reasoned that without the skin the fruit couldn't be denied entry. It was another of Larry's make-work miscalculations. All the plastic bags were confiscated. Jason was beyond commenting on Larry's blunders, and Melanie laughed in disbelief. But David told Larry off in front of the inspectors. He let fly with all of his frustrations and anger at Larry's behavior while Larry tried to eat as much of the fruit as he could.

Larry hadn't radioed his wife Helen of his arrival, and when the agricultural inspectors left, Larry took his shore phone from his storage locker and plugged it in. He still had a dial tone and called Helen, leaving a message that they had arrived. He retrieved Jason's log from the aft cabin and tallied up the last few pages of expenses and told Jason he owed him $832. David and Melanie were outraged. Jason just laughed. The crew gathered up their gear and called a cab. Melanie invited them to stay at her mother's house for a few days, leaving Larry alone on the boat.

David declined Melanie's offer to stay with them and found a cheap hotel in Waikiki. He needed to be alone to reflect on what had taken place. Jason spent three days at Melanie's mother's house. He sat by her pool, drank gallons of iced tea, and tried to figure out what to do next. He thought about Lillian constantly. He called his mother in Los Angeles and found out that Lillian was in London. Elizabeth wouldn't tell him any more than that. Melanie couldn't share anything about Larry with her mother, and when her mother questioned her about Jason, she wouldn't answer those questions either. So, Melanie's mother left the kids alone and went on with her life. Melanie spent most of her time with her high-school friends, away from her mother, her house, and Jason.

Every time Jason looked at his body, covered as it was in tattoos, it brought to mind the horror and insight of his Hiva ritual. On the sail home the tattoos hadn't bothered him—being at sea on the *Mata'i* made them seem natural. Larry could barely look at Jason, though. For all his supposed love for the islanders, he couldn't get over his bigotry that tattooed people were lower class and stupid. The tattoos made David cringe, because he felt the pain, both emotional and physical, that had come with them. Melanie, on the other hand, thought they were cool. Now, back in the States, Jason viewed them as symbols of a culture he wanted nothing more to do with. He felt disfigured and he worried about how Lillian would react. Would she still love him?

In the backyard of Melanie's mother's Kahala house, Jason reflected on what had happened to him and struggled to find some kind of rationale for his reactions to the rituals on Hakamaii. He had reacted like a normal man during the sexual rites, yet the whole situation disgusted him. He felt like he had been raped. He prayed none of those girls would bear his child, but the thought of having children pleased him. Eventually he understood how Spirit had embraced him until he was so united in oneness that the physical dimension dissolved, saving his life on the sacrificial altar. Would that ever happen again? Had he fulfilled what every mystery school required of a master—the death of the mortal self for the immortality of the spirit? Would he be living in a resurrected state of consciousness? He didn't know. It was all a jumble of ideas and theories and physical sensations that, if pulled together into some semblance of reason might reveal a greater spectrum of life.

Jason knew that life was not just a product of matter. If it was, he could not have escaped the psychological manipulation and drugs of the *tahunas*. Life was an expression of the unseen reality of individual being. Without the mental conditioning imposed by the relative reality of Newtonian physics, any physical condition could be changed. If Jason could get others to believe what he had experienced in the spiritual realm during that horrendous ritual, perhaps he could change the perception of humanity. Jason had escaped from death, and it confirmed the mystical principle which stated that a person consciously realizing the oneness of infinite consciousness is untouched by material cause and effect. Human belief never enters the mystical dimension. Jason firmly believed that the hundredth-monkey effect was true. He felt that an idea in consciousness, when accepted by enough people, could change the way humanity saw the world. There had to be a critical mass to everything, and perhaps sharing his experience in Hakamaii would start that ball rolling.

For David the trip seemed like an interruption to his life. He would never forget the experience, yet there was much about the voyage that he wanted to forget. He questioned everything. Could he even go back to whom he was before he got the telegram in Barcelona that began it all? Jason had warned him that it might be a life defining experience, and it was. But as much as David loved Jason, he didn't want to be involved in Jason's life anymore. He made a mental note to "say no" to any and all requests by Jason St. John.

On their third night ashore, Jason, David, and Melanie had dinner at the private Outrigger Canoe Club, thanks to Melanie's membership. There was a touch of sadness in the air. Watching the sunset, the three friends realized how much the South Pacific had changed them. Jason, usually blunt and outgoing, was reserved and thoughtful. David, who had always deferred to Jason now demanded to know where he stood with his friends. If they weren't as close as they were, David would have just drifted away. But he needed clarity to move on. Specifically, he wanted to know if Melanie and Jason loved each other. If they did it would free Lillian up for him.

"Are you going back to Lillian?" David asked, rather bluntly. He looked at Melanie for her reaction. David was sure Melanie had fallen in love with Jason.

Melanie pointedly examined her drink.

Jason laughed. "Do you want to duel me for her?"

"You're an asshole, you know that?"

Jason reached across the table and took hold of David's arm. "You know I love her... And I love you." He turned to Melanie and said, "And I love you."

Now Melanie laughed. "You two are the closest people in the world to me, but at this moment I've lived with you both long enough."

"You're not in love with J.J.?"

"No, Dave, I'm not. And I'm not in love with you either." She pushed her chair back from the table. "Jesus Christ, you guys, has three days ashore rotted your brains?"

David turned to Jason, "What are you going to do?"

"I don't know, Dave. I really don't know. I need time to figure it all out."

"What about you?" Jason looked at Melanie.

Melanie glanced at her shipmates, "I need to go somewhere where I can think and maybe find a rational explanation to what we all experienced."

Jason stood up. "I've got to get out of here, too."

Melanie wandered over to the seawall and stared out to sea. David and Jason joined her. She was crying softly. The boys put their arms around her.

"I love you two so much, but I don't think I ever want to see you again," said Melanie.

The trio stood there for a few moments until Jason said, "I'm going back to L.A. Want to come with me Dave?"

David pulled away. "No." He kissed them both and left.

Melanie kissed Jason on both cheeks, in the French manner. "Good luck," She said and left.

Jason was suddenly all alone.

Melanie couldn't stay with her mother any longer and refused to get into the "I told you so" battles with her about Larry. She also needed to get out of Honolulu, but she didn't want to go back to the Mainland. Having witnessed her father laid flat from a curse, and then resurrected, threatened all that she had believed. Had he actually died? What did Jason do and who was he really? She was still an atheist, but it was now necessary to put the recent bizarre events into some sort of rational order.

Her solution was on the island of Kauai. It meant asking something of Larry, which she didn't want to do. Larry had some land on Hanalei Bay, a couple of acres on the west end of the beach with an old cottage on it. Melanie wanted to use it for a few months and Larry was happy to please his daughter.

Finding a reason, an explanation for what she had seen, was all that mattered to her. Jason had told her that she was to be the witness; but what exactly *had* she seen? Melanie began ordering every book she could find on the paranormal, mysticism and quantum theory. Soon books were arriving daily that filled every corner of her cottage. Most people went there to vacation, to play on the beach, to drink and eat and make holiday friendships. Melanie shunned all that. Her world became a mix of religious beliefs battling the quantum physicists and the materialists. After a couple of months, she became known as the Hermit of Hanalei. Her friends left her alone, and when she did emerge from the cottage ten months later, she decided to start a tour business. She discovered that she loved showing people her island and making money. In that respect, she was her father's daughter. She found a niche in the tourist industry and became very successful—successful enough that she didn't have to ask her father for anything again. And, she would not talk about her hermit period to anyone.

Los Angeles

September 1989

David bought Jason a plane ticket to Los Angeles. On the flight over the Pacific Jason thought about how to tell his mother about his experiences. She had told Jason that it would be an initiation, and that he must pay attention. Of course, she was right.

Elizabeth had her assistant pick Jason up at the airport and bring him to her Wilshire Boulevard apartment in Westwood. Elizabeth wasn't expecting her son to be as changed as he was. When she opened the door, she almost recoiled from him. And Jason hadn't expected his mother to react in the way she did.

After Jason had showered and was settled, mother and son sat down to talk. However, Elizabeth wasn't interested in what had happened in the South Pacific. She didn't want to hear about the adventure at all. She was only interested in how her son had grown spiritually. What principles he had practiced, and how had they furthered his understanding of the spiritual realm? If he had had a negative experience, then she was sorry and saddened, but the past was over and done. There was no discussion of justice, because she wasn't interested in karma. Her power lay entirely in the "now moment."

Jason asked about Lillian. Elizabeth had received one letter from her after she had settled in London, but nothing since then. She gave Jason Lillian's address, but her detachment made Jason wonder what had happened between them. He attempted to talk about David and Melanie, and how Helen never showed up at the boat, but she was totally disinterested. She had known that Helen wanted to divorce Larry, and pronounced, "He never got it anyway." Why then had Jason suffered Larry's abuse? Why had Elizabeth sanctioned this trip if there was no chance for Larry to realize the spiritual presence? Jason needed some understanding, some emotional comfort from his mother, but Elizabeth was in her detached mode, indifferent to human appearances, including Jason's distress. When Elizabeth continued to probe what spiritual insights her son had gleaned, he couldn't tell her. At this point he felt his mother would take his experience, judge it, and put her interpretation to it. He wouldn't let that happen.

The next day at breakfast, Elizabeth told her son that he could not stay with her. She had important work to do and assistants coming in daily. He could spend a few nights in the spare bedroom, but he needed to look for a job and find a place to live. She gave him a thousand dollars to get started, and Jason felt the connection between them cut. It was probably time for that to happen, but it still hurt, coming when he was so vulnerable. But she had been a good teacher, and Jason concealed his feelings and kissed her on both cheeks. He was free.

As Jason cleaned up the breakfast dishes, Dorothy Delany entered the apartment using her key. Elizabeth shouted from the adjoining room that she would be there in a minute, and Dorothy should pick up from where they had left off the day before. Dorothy was like an aunt to Jason and gave him a warm hug and kiss. She wanted to hear all about his voyage, and what he had learned. The difference between her caring and his mother's indifference almost made him cry. He told her he was going to write a book about it, and that excited her. What a different response from his mother who had remarked, "What on earth would you have to say?"

London

January 1990

Lillian had left the Pacific, and her life there far behind, both in her mind and geographically. She was now fulfilling her dream and performing in a new play, Charlotte Keatley's *My Mother Said I Never Should* at the Royal Court Theater in London. The play was bold and edgy. Lillian's character was one of four women in a multigenerational story about women and female relationships. The play explored what it meant to be female at various times in the twentieth century. Lillian's character was a product of the sixties, a hippy girl with a baby that she gave to her sister to raise. In a strange way, playing this role gave Lillian insights into her complex feelings about the two men she loved. She took great cathartic pleasure kicking and screaming on stage, letting out her frustrations for her audience to see.

It also gave her the independence she craved. For her entire life, people had wanted to control her. Lloyd, Lillian's father, had never approved of her acting, and he had completely rejected her spiritual study. Her mother, Nancy, loved her creativity but would never contradict Lloyd. And Elizabeth had been grooming her to become Elizabeth's clone. As much as Lillian loved Elizabeth, she couldn't put on the persona that Elizabeth deemed necessary to be seen as spiritual. Moving back to England had been the right choice. It freed her from the arrogance of the American exceptionalism she had witnessed in Jason, Larry, and so many people she had encountered in the States. For the first time in her life she was happy to be in England, and in control of her destiny.

Lillian had also chosen not to date. This was not to say that she wasn't having fun with her colleagues. She became very adept at fending off the guys who just wanted a roll in the sack. But she couldn't help wondering what had happened to Jason and David. Were they back in Honolulu? Had the trip been successful? She had a stack of letters from David describing their trip from Honolulu to Papeete, and Larry's behavior. She could have written them herself from what she had perceived about Larry. And there was nothing from Jason but a kitschy postcard of a Tahitian dancer in a grass skirt and coconut shell bra with him wishing she were there.

Lillian splurged on a two-bedroom flat on Jermyn Street and signed a year's contract for the apartment. Even though her salary was quite good, it was a gamble. If the play closed early, she would have to take in a roommate. But the play was a success. It was nominated for a number of Olivier Awards, and though Lillian didn't receive a nomination herself, she gained a lot of recognition and her contract was extended as a result.

Jason and David entered her mind less and less and she doubted she'd ever see either one of them again, until, in February she received the following letter:

Dear Lillian,

You were right. I have to say that first off. Larry Graff was a monster. I won't tell you all that happened in this letter because I'm writing a book about the experience. I know I've changed. My mother could hardly look at me. But I think there is a new spiritual revelation unfolding in me. I've dedicated myself to bringing it forth. I have missed you so much. You are my spiritual rock, and you are my only love. Dave said that I treated you terribly in Honolulu. If I did, I'm so sorry. I was unaware of how it all looked. I can't take you away from your career. I saw your picture on a magazine cover at the supermarket and you looked so happy. How could I ask you to leave that? I would never do it. For the time being I'm stuck here in LA. Please be patient with me. We are destined to be together. After all I've gone through, I know that more than ever. I just don't know when it will be. How can we get together?

Wait for me, my love. Give me hope.

Forever yours,

Jason

Lillian read the letter over and over. At first it made her cry, then it made her mad. Why had it taken him so long to write? Jason had a way of burdening people with his gifts. What was she supposed to do now? She had spent most of the past year holding on to her ideal concept of him, even treating their separation like a death, and now the same old Jason was knocking on her door, telling her to wait because he wasn't ready to come in yet. Hadn't he received her letter? Jason's letter made her think it was strange that David hadn't written her either since they had returned to the States. Had Jason put David off? She was more confused than ever and did not like it one bit.

Honolulu

January 1990

After Jason's departure, David stayed in Hawaii. He found a job teaching art at the University of Hawaii. His degree from Rhode Island School of Design was in ceramics. At the university he met a group of young native Hawaiians intent on establishing more sovereignty over their land. David joined their movement and celebrated when President George H. W. Bush ordered the Navy to stop bombing the island of Kahoolawe. He decided that his artistic talent should be in support of Hawaiian cultural values and reflect a contemporary vision of traditional Hawaiian art. What if the ancient Hawaiians had had modern tools and access to clay and all the materials available today? What would they have created?

His experiences in the South Pacific supported his reimaging of designs not seen for many, many decades. His being a white man put off some of the *kanaka maoli*, Hawaiian natives, but others appreciated his insight and ability to teach kids starved for a cultural touchstone. Hawaii became the muse that allowed his art to flower. His students, both at the university level and at the grammar school level—he also taught kids at the Honolulu Academy of Art—inspired him. And he gave them an insight to their culture as Tocqueville had done for the United States. He dated a lot, mainly brown skinned girls, and fell for a part Hawaiian girl of exceptional beauty; yet in the back of his mind there was always Lillian. He didn't let the irony of settling in Hawaii and becoming involved in the native culture bother him. He was nothing like Larry.

Los Angeles

July 1990

Jason was getting by in Los Angeles. He lived on a boat in the marina, surfed, and drove a taxi to make ends meet. He was writing his book. One of the black drivers at his company, invited Jason to his predominately black church. He thought Jason was struggling to find himself and asked Jason if he'd ever heard of Dr. Solomon Green. Their preacher read from Dr. Green every Sunday. Jason attended services the next week. They sang. They danced. The minister, Barry Washington, broke through traditional Christian dogma and taught a truth that Jason understood. And he had never felt such love.

When the minister overheard Jason talking to some of his congregation about mysticism, he thought Jason was a natural teacher. Jason let Reverend Washington know that he had studied with Dr. Green, and the reverend asked Jason if he'd give a class based on Dr. Green's books. Jason eagerly accepted, and for the next few months he poured himself into his classes and the sharing of his mystical consciousness.

Then, almost a year after Jason had returned to the city, the classes he taught had grown tremendously, and people came up to him and shared how his classes had healed them. On top of that, Lillian wrote Jason to say that she had landed the female lead in a big American motion picture with a star director she admired and costars she was in awe of. Her contract included a bungalow in the Hollywood Hills for six months and a large salary. Before she knew it, she was in Los Angeles. She told Jason to wait until she got settled into her bungalow before getting together. Jason, having waited so long, thought that was ridiculous. He didn't seem to realize that Lillian had waited just as long.

At last they met at a café on Sunset Boulevard. Jason wore a long-sleeved shirt buttoned at the neck though it was a hot day. He hadn't told Lillian about his tattoos. When he saw her he cried. Lillian felt such a relief at seeing him, she too released her pent-up desire. They embraced for a long time, kissed each other deeply, and went from tears to laughter many times. Nobody noticed. This was Hollywood.

They talked the whole afternoon. Jason told Lillian all the things he couldn't tell his mother. She cringed and cursed at some of the incidents, and when Jason finished his story, Lillian felt like she'd been on the voyage with him. She was curious as to why Jason didn't answer her letter. That opened up the incident with Larry refusing mail at the post office in Papeete and brought about more cursing. Lillian didn't show how relieved she was that Jason hadn't read it. Jason had changed, and all she wanted now was to be with him from that moment on.

Jason and Lillian lived for six months in a fantasy relationship. She had a house in the Hollywood hills and a driver to take her to work, and Jason was "house sitting" a forty-foot sloop in Marina del Rey and giving meditation classes on Venice Beach. She wanted him to move in with her, but he wouldn't until he could afford to. They went to parties together and someone would always corner Jason and tell him their problems. By the time the person had left, Jason had missed most of the fun and the person looked renewed. Lillian hated that. Lillian thought Jason had been taken advantage of and that he was always too willing to give of himself.

The first draft of Jason's manuscript was not well received by those Jason thought would like it. His writing professor at UCLA had recommended several editors but they all rejected it. His mother hated it—no surprise there. Reverend Washington thought it was a pack of lies. He didn't want Jason teaching in his church anymore. Lillian was stunned; it made her cry, and it filled her with so much love that she wanted to take Jason into her arms and never let him go. It also frightened her.

The moment of truth came when Lillian's contract was up, and she needed to return to London. If they were to have a life together Jason would have to come to London. It took all her willpower not to beg him to come. It had to be his decision. Jason knew this and didn't know why he was afraid to take the step. Was there still ego and conditioning that assumed he had to be the breadwinner? Could he not let Lillian shine and be in her shadow? Wasn't the point of all he went through freedom? He chose love over ego.

January 1, 1991

Lillian and Jason were married on the sand at Venice Beach under a clear sky and warm sun. David flew over from Hawaii to be the best man, and Dorothy stood with Lillian. It was bittersweet for David to see Lillian, but he had to stand up for Jason. Elizabeth was out of town lecturing and members of the meditation circle were there to celebrate the nuptials. The next day the couple flew to London and Lillian immediately called her parents with the news. Lloyd Harvey wouldn't speak to his daughter or new son-in-law.

David felt abandoned when Lillian and Jason left. Now things were settled. There was no more dreaming that Lillian could ever be his. Now he could go back to his life in Hawaii and be true to his promise to not ever again get involved with Jason's life. Dorothy put him up for a couple of days and he visited his parents and sisters in Costa Mesa. But California was no longer his home.

On his flight back to the Islands David read a draft of Jason's book. Everything about it was true. He'd been there. But was the world ready to go that far beyond everyday reality? He wrote Jason that if he found an audience for the book he'd be taken on the ride of his life.

The other person Jason left a manuscript with was Dorothy Delany. She had finished her project with Elizabeth and thought Jason had a real gift. She offered to edit it and Jason turned his baby over to her.

London

September 1991

Alex St. John was born in London on September 13th. Elizabeth St. John couldn't make it to England to meet her only grandchild. Lillian's mother came, but not her father. He would not be in the same room with Jason. He had made peace with his daughter, but he couldn't accept an American, much less a near heathen, as his son-in-law.

In the next twelve months everything changed for Jason. His mother died unexpectedly. She had informed her secretary that she would be leaving her mortal body that morning and not to disturb her. At the end of the day, the secretary found Elizabeth St. John slumped back in her chair with a smile on her face. Jason realized that she had finally made her demonstration. There was no memorial service, per her request.

Dorothy Delany came to London bringing condolences and news of Jason's inheritance, which could only be used to further Jason's spiritual development. She also brought contracts from major publishers competing for the right to distribute *The Undiscovered Land*. Jason gave that right to a British firm and that company arranged book signings and seminars all over the world. People were healed, and Venice Beach, where Jason had started a meditation circle, became a mecca. Jason's followers began to form their own meditation circles. People wanted pictures of Jason to pray to. Dorothy, Lillian, and Jason saw that this had to be controlled or it would take them all to hell.

Jason called David and Melanie to see if they wanted to join them and figure out how to harness the energy that was being generated by Jason's work. He caught Melanie at the perfect time. She had grown tired of showing people around Kauai and had sold her business. Her father had died in a hiking accident that summer, and she needed a change. Jason was offering her the kind of challenge she needed. David, who had promised himself at the end of the South Seas trip that he would never again be part of a St. John adventure, felt compelled to accept. He was not on a tenured track at the University of Hawaii and hated the annual employment dance—like a lottery—where the instructors all waited to see who would be rehired for the next term. David had landed a few important commissions for hotels and the government, but they were not enough to live on in high-priced Hawaii. And, this was not a typical St. John adventure; this was about showing the world what David had already witnessed. It had to be done to justify what had happened in the Hiva Isalnds. So began the first incarnation of St. John Ministries.

Chapter 42
Stanford House

Saturday Afternoon, November 2004

Tony sat at the head of the large conference table in the boardroom waiting for the others to arrive. He finally felt the situation regarding Jason appearing out of the blue would get sorted out. With the revelation of the Baghdad episode in last night's broadcast, he was confident that his agenda for curtailing Jason's activities would pass the board's vote. In addition, he thought that all board members would agree that the telecast was a disaster. It had opened the ministry to the kind of criticism and scrutiny he was trying to avoid.

Dorothy Delany arrived early and joined Tony at the conference table.

"I hope you now realize the gravity of our situation." Tony stood as Dorothy took her seat. "We can't allow Jason to put himself in any further situations that would violate the public trust or bring ridicule to our organization.

"The more you try to resist this, Tony, the more power you give it. It's one of our principles. You should know that."

Tony smiled smugly. "I'm sure you'll vote for the best interests of the organization. You know that we're greater than any one person, even Jason."

Dorothy smiled back at him. "I'm aware of that." Tony figured that Dorothy was in Jason's camp no matter what.

Gary came in with Michael Condon, the Ministry's treasurer. Michael had missed Tuesday's meeting where the agenda was discarded because of the news about Jason appearing to the girls at Royal Marsdan Hospital. If he had known, he would have abandoned his meeting with a hedge fund manager who was only in London that day. He did catch Friday's telecast of Jason trying to explain apparitions and getting gobsmacked by Theodore Spencer. There was no way he was going to miss this meeting.

Melanie and Barbara were right behind Gary and Michael, and Michael held the door for them. He gave Melanie a flirtatious kiss when she passed, but just nodded to Barbara. Tony watched, not liking the informality. He had carefully calculated the support for his plan to limit Jason's activities within the Ministry, and he didn't like surprises. He counted Michael firmly behind him and didn't appreciate Melanie flirting with him. Then they sat next to each other whispering and then laughing. Tony figured Melanie to be the swing vote. Maybe Michael was bringing her to his side.

Barbara shared the latest figures from the ratings agencies for the television broadcast. They were stunning. Nearly one hundred and ten million people had watched Jason and the religious leaders, rivaling the Super Bowl in viewership. The numbers showed that many more people supported Jason than opposed him, even though Saturday's headlines were screaming about Jason and Baghdad. Investigations were sure to follow. Barbara murmured that she wished she could have sold advertisements.

"Barbara." Jason said, entering with Lillian on his arm, "You sound like you're running a political campaign."

"It's important to know where we stand with the public," Barbara took a seat next to Dorothy.

"Our standing with the public, according to the headlines, is precarious," Tony responded.

Jason pulled out a chair opposite Tony at the foot of the table and Lillian took the seat next to Melanie, squeezing her hand. Tony looked at his directors, so many people on one side of the table and empty seats on the other. He hoped it wasn't an omen as he opened the leather-bound portfolio in front of him. He looked at each person mentally calculating how they would respond to his proposal. His gaze rested on Jason. Every organization Tony had run was turned on a meeting such as this. He had restructured many companies in his business career, and the pivotal moment often dealt with telling the founder of a company that he had lost the support of the board and would be retired from day-to-day operations. In the case of Steve Jobs and Apple, that board actually fired him. Tony would love to fire Jason, except that he was the product.

"Do you have an agenda, Tony? I didn't receive one if you did."

"No, Jason, your behavior both in Marsdan and the rumors about Baghdad have prompted this meeting and that's all we'll be talking about."

Jason looked at his board. Like Tony, he took a mental note of who supported him. "Let me say this, before Tony proceeds. Those who've been with me from the beginning..." looking at Dorothy, Melanie and Lillian, "... know that what's taken place this week isn't any more outrageous than the healing that happened at our early rallies. If Dave was here, he'd tell you how the press followed us into the ocean at Malibu after our first public demonstration at the UCLA Jonsson Cancer Center. They kept yelling, 'Is it true?' while Dave and I were surfing."

Tony cleared his throat. This wasn't the time for Jason to reminisce.

"I get it, Tony. I just want all of you to really think about what you do today. People were just as shocked by that healing as they are about what's being broadcast today. Please, listen to your inner voice."

"This isn't a hostile move, Jason. It's about the future of the Ministry. Just look outside and think about your impact on the world. I understand there are demonstrations occurring outside our healing centers around the planet. You no longer have the luxury of doing what you want. You're responsible for all those people who've embraced your message."

"Wait a minute! You're talking like a prelate of the Roman Curia. Are we a nonprofit organization or have you created a church? Is this a board of directors or the office of the inquisition?"

"Jason, you're out of line and out of touch. You're not just some televangelist..."

"I'm not even a minister!"

"You're someone who has healed thousands of people. Are you so stupid as to think you can live a normal life and do all of that?"

"Where are you going with this, Tony?" Melanie asked.

"The mission of our foundation," Tony continued in his most businesslike voice, "is to teach and facilitate inspirational healing. To that end, Jason has been instrumental, and his books and courses will be studied for generations. But at this moment, with what he's been doing, he's no longer an asset for our work."

"Are you firing me?" Jason couldn't believe he was actually enjoying this.

"I can't fire you, but I can prevent you from harming our foundation."

Tony looked around the table, assessing reactions from the others, but there was no response. "I propose the board restrict Mr. St. John in the following manner: no public engagements, no speaking to the press, and no more personal classes."

At that moment David barged into the boardroom with Sir William Boyd, the trust's solicitor. "What do you want him to do, disappear?"

"What the fuck are you doing here?" Tony shouted, losing his composure. "This is a closed meeting!"

"Nice to see you again, Tony," said David sarcastically. "Do you think all those people are out there because of the board of directors? I bet most of them don't even know you exist."

Melanie shoved her chair back, rushed into David's arms and gave him a longer than appropriate kiss. Michael watched with an amused look. He was the newcomer here, though he'd known Melanie since Harvard Business School. She was the one who had persuaded Tony to hire Michael when Tony became CEO. He thought it funny Melanie had never mentioned David in a way that warranted such a kiss.

Lillian smiled at David like she would to an old lover and took hold of Jason's hand. She squeezed it and gave her husband a kiss.

David freed himself from Melanie and gave Jason a warm hug. Jason couldn't help enjoying Tony's loss of composure.

"Thank you, my friend."

"You could've called sooner."

Sir William addressed the board: "According to the foundation charter, David Walker has a permanent seat on the board. Nothing can change that. If he quits and wants to come back, he can do that. You should know that, Mr. Bass."

Barbara motioned for David and Sir William to sit. David sat next to Jason wondering why it had taken so long. Seven years meant nothing. And that it took a crisis to get the two men back together was just stupid.

"We asked David to return and resume his seat on the board," stated Lillian. David couldn't help staring at her. Jason noticed, but made nothing of it.

"Shall we continue the meeting?" Jason asked.

"I don't think it would be productive after such a dramatic entrance." Tony had cooled down a bit. "Perhaps we should reschedule for..."

"A year from now?" Jason interrupted. "I think we need to put our cards on the table. You were proposing to forbid me from appearing in public, speaking to the press, and there was one other thing I didn't get."

"Teaching," Dorothy said.

"We're trying to preserve the St. John name and what it stands for. I think the board has every right, no—a duty—to do all it can to maintain the credibility of the foundation. To do anything less would be a breach of our responsibility as officers of this trust. Jason, I'm sorry to say, you are longer relevant to this ministry."

Jason burst out laughing.

"And how do you propose to enforce this, Tony? Lock us up in our flat?" Lillian asked.

"It's nice to see you participating after all these years, Mrs. St. John." Tony's sarcasm was softened with a genuine smile. "But this is about Jason, not about you and Alex." Tony looked at the old group—the four people who had been through so much together, and his resolve hardened. They all had to go. He couldn't do anything about Melanie at the moment, but he could the others. "Before we formally entertain the issues before the board, I move that Lillian St. John, Jason St. John, and David Walker be recused from this vote. They have not participated in prior discussions and are not fully informed of the issues."

"We've been *living* the issues." Lillian's anger flared.

"Do I have a second?" Tony looked around the table. Gary seconded the motion. "All in favor?"

Tony, Gary, and Barbara put up their hands. "All opposed." All the others raised their hands. "I guess the measure is defeated," Tony admitted.

"I have a proposition for the board." Jason nodded to Lillian who handed out written copies of what Jason was going to say. "I will resign from this Ministry if the following conditions are met: The board will transfer to me ten percent of the assets of The Foundation. If anything should happen to me it will endow Lillian and Alex a lifetime income, the amount to be decided upon when the other conditions have been met. Neither the board nor The Foundation will interfere with my work from this point forward, and any benefits from that work will be solely mine. The Foundation will provide me and my family adequate security for us to live freely wherever we choose until it is mutually agreed that the security is no longer needed. And finally, my whereabouts will be kept confidential."

No one said a thing. Lillian and Dorothy closed their eyes in meditation. Melanie looked around to see how her colleagues were reacting. Tony glared at Jason.

"Otherwise," Jason continued, "I'll go back to my regular schedule and our Ministry work will continue as normal."

"As if there's anything normal about Ministry operations after what you've done," said Tony.

"I'll leave that up to you. I'll recuse myself from that vote," Jason told them.

"I won't," Lillian announced.

"It's a long flight from Honolulu to London," David began, "and before I left, I had Sir William fax me the charter for our little group here. Our mission statement is very clear: 'To explore the mystical nature of reality and reveal the natural healing capacity of those in touch with their transcendent Self.' It also states that a director can be removed by a two-thirds vote if their actions are shown to undermine the purpose of the foundation."

"This is ridiculous!" Tony shouted. "If you think any of us here are trying to undermine the foundation, you're off your rocker, David! It's Jason who's putting the Ministry in danger; we're trying to preserve it."

"I move we postpone the vote until Monday," Melanie said. "And I'd like to say something. Jason's work is evolving, as it should. He has always stretched the boundaries of conventional thinking, and it's easy to ride into the future on what's been done in the past. But you should know that's not what Jason, or this foundation, is about. We've never been in the healing business. If we as an organization think we can heal, or that the world needs healing, we've missed the point."

She nodded at Jason, and he smiled. "We're in the *revealing* business. Our whole mission is to reveal the spiritual nature of life. Then we let Spirit take over. I've seen things with Jason that none of you will ever know. In the South Pacific I told him I'm an atheist, and maybe I still am. But I've seen what this other dimension, this invisible reality can do if people get out of the way. Tony, you're really getting in the way of Jason's next step. Again, I move we postpone this vote until Monday."

"I second it," Dorothy said.

"All in favor?"

The vote was unanimous.

Chapter 43
Collingham Gardens

Sunday Morning, November 2004

The morning was bright but cold, and the sun reflected off one of the never-ending jets that flew into Heathrow. The garden was getting ready for winter. Only a few leaves clung to the deciduous trees while the lush conifers and hollies were already bracing for the first snowfall. One last rose blossom stood tall and red in the bare garden.

Jason, Lillian, Melanie, and Michael sat on a large blanket taking in the sun, enjoying each other. They watched David and Alex kick a soccer ball around on the lawn. Lillian leaned up against her husband who enjoyed seeing his best friend play with his son. There was so much affection between the two of them, and it made him tear up seeing Alex so happy. But he kept anxiously looking up at the leaded windows of the residence floor of Stanford House, drawing his attention away from what he loved most. "I think we're being watched." But nobody was at the windows.

"I thought you'd be impervious to that kind of scrutiny by now." Melanie had a knit cap pulled down over her ears and leaned against Michael in the same way that Lillian leaned against Jason.

"Jason might be impervious to it, but I hate it," said Lillian.

"No, I feel something more than just the standard spying."

"Darling, this week started out malicious and has grown outright hostile." Lillian leaned over and gave Jason a kiss on his neck.

Jason watched Alex run under a highflying ball, stop it with his chest, and then kick it with all his might toward the rear garden wall. Alex then raced David to the ball. The two crashed into each other, got their feet entangled and fell in a heap. At first David thought he'd hurt Alex, but Alex laughed, jumped up, and continued after the ball.

"It's so good to have Davy back," Jason said.

David got up, jogged over and flopped down between Melanie and Lillian. The four original board members were back, and they were happy to be together again. There was a moment of comfortable silence between them, no agenda, no demands, just the contentment of being united in *The Now.*

David broke the silence. "Jason, let me see where you were shot?"

Jason ignored him.

"What do you think they're doing?" Jason couldn't help staring up at the executive apartments.

"I could care less what they're doing." Melanie followed Jason's gaze. "Tony's all bluff and bull.

"There's nothing to see, Davy."

"This isn't the right time, Dave. Give him a break." Lillian kept her eye on Alex, dribbling the ball at the far end of the garden.

"Don't tell me Alex has never seen his father naked?" Melanie pressed.

"Not very often."

David sat up. "No biggie, J.J. I'm on your side. I love you. I wouldn't be here if I didn't." He gave Lillian a kiss and winked at

Melanie. Melanie patted Michael's leg. He'd get use to the four of them.

Jason pulled away from Lillian and stood, still fixated on the apartments. "No wonder Dr. Green warned us all against organizing. I'm so grateful having you all here with me, but in this beautiful moment together we can't escape those up in the tower?"

"The tower?" Melanie mimicked. "You sound like you're writing a horror movie."

"This is a horror movie. What could be more horrible than to know the truth and have the rest of the world call you crazy?"

No one had an answer and Jason walked over to the lone rose, retreating into his contemplations. For the past decade his life had been about discipline. It had been about proving the principles of spiritual oneness and teaching those principles to the world. But it seemed the world didn't care. People wanted to be healed, but they didn't want to break out of their conditioning and discover their spiritual nature. That was too much work— too great a sacrifice. Jason was tired. He was fed up with being judged and vilified. He'd like to scream and cry and strip off his clothes so the world could see his marked-up body. He'd like for the world to realize that he too was a human being who could be hurt. He wanted to lash out at his enemies but knew that to join the battle was death. Evil must be seen as the Buddha saw it, attached to the opposite end of the same stick as good, where both conditions dissolved in the realization of spiritual oneness. After all, it was an invisible spirit that did everything; he just opened up to it.

Alex came running back and collapsed onto David's lap. He tossed his ball to his father standing at the edge of the group and Jason tossed it back. But the ball bounced off Alex's fingers and David caught it, holding it over his head. Alex tried to knock it out of David's hand but instead hit him in the face. David threw the ball back to Jason and shoved Alex off his lap. Jason took the ball, bouncing it on his knees and then kicked it high in the air. He pulled his son up off the blanket. "I'm better at this than your Uncle Dave, you know."

Jason raced after the ball with Alex in pursuit. Father and son spent a few minutes passing the ball back and forth, and when Jason had the ball, he dribbled it down the path before kicking it back to the friends on the blanket.

"This is why we have a male dominated world." Melanie deflected the ball to David who tossed it to Alex who fielded it with his feet and then kept it in the air by bouncing it off one foot then another.

Jason dropped onto the blanket and let his head rest in Lillian's lap. The tension was gone. Perhaps the anger too. "The principle behind what people think they see is basic metaphysics. It's human conditioning. If you look through rose colored glasses, you'll see a rose-colored world. The reality is, there is only one substance, but it appears to us through our physical senses, and our conditioned beliefs."

"It sounds like you're appearing to people and it's not just their imagination or an apparition?" Melanie said.

"I'm not going to say one way or another. Not that I don't want to share what I think will be the next step in the evolution of spiritual understanding. But at this time, I don't want any of you to have to lie on my behalf."

"We've been to hell and back with you, J.J., and now at this point you're trying to protect us?" said David.

"Perhaps I've become a little more insightful and compassionate." Jason sat up.

"Guys, it doesn't matter!" Lillian wanted to move forward. "We all need to put our heads together and come up with a plan."

"Ok. What takes place when you go into deep meditation?" Jason looked at each one of his friends, who were actually more than friends—they were his spiritual family.

"As the old metaphysical cliché says, 'you become absent from the body and present with the Lord.'" Lillian chuckled.

"You mean *you* don't even know what he's doing?" Melanie looked at Lillian in disbelief.

"I think we listen to Jason and not ask questions," Michael said, wanting to expand his awareness of the nature of the Ministry.

Lillian smiled a thank-you. Alex drifted back to the group, sitting between his parents.

"What do you think happens to your body as you go into a really deep meditation?" Jason looked around waiting for anybody to answer.

"It comes under spiritual law," said Alex.

"And what is the foundation of spiritual law?"

They all answered; "Oneness."

"And omnipresence," Jason added. "Transcendent consciousness exists only in the now, so when a person realizes that now principle, he or she is at once here and simultaneously everywhere or anywhere. There is no time *or* space. We've all experienced that to some degree. But there is usually such a strong coupling with the physical that we can't get free. No matter how deeply we let go and touch our spiritual essence, our bodies keep us coupled to the physical. But what if that last limitation was dissolved? What if we became physically *uncoupled*? What would happen to us? Would we float around bodiless? Or would we have the form we identify with but be so loosely connected to a particular time and a particular place that we truly experience the Divine moment?"

An aura came over Jason like the auras that appear at many of his healing rallies when he was completely in tune with the spiritual realm. Alex felt it. He loved the atmosphere when his dad was teaching or meditating. It was his conditioning. He'd seen it often at the healing rallies when he was little.

"Humanity has always stretched the limits of what's possible," Jason told them. "Our bodies are the last frontier, and the limitations of time and space will be looked upon like the belief in a flat Earth. But the world will need a quantum leap in its ever-changing perception of reality before that can happen. Once something has been demonstrated, once it's been witnessed, the nature of reality changes, and then people accept the new normal. A hundred and fifty years ago it was just as bizarre to think people could fly in big silver birds. You are the only ones I trust with this knowledge, but I'm stuck. I don't know what to do. I don't know where to go with it."

Everyone remained quiet, lost in contemplation. "Let's pray the board votes for Jason's proposal," said David.

"And what if they don't?" Lillian didn't like being negative, but this was where she was at the moment.

"Then I'll continue my schedule and force Tony to stop me."

"Why are we speculating? Nothing has happened yet. The board doesn't vote until Monday and I'll be part of that vote. Is this what you really want, J.J.?" David asked his friend.

"I want what I proposed."

David shook his head. "How much thought have you given that? What if the board releases you and you're on your own? Do you think the world will forget about you? Is there any place to hide that you'd want to live? And what about Lillian and Alex? What about school? I don't want to sound negative either, but are those options really that great?"

"I just want to get out of this mess, to go back to some sort of normalcy." Lillian's voice cracked with emotion. "I hate the organization and their presumptions over our lives, like we're commodities they're selling."

"Unfortunately, you are," Melanie said.

"Then we'll discontinue the product." Jason looked around to see if anyone else thought that was funny.

"What, you'll disappear and not come back?" David didn't realize the ramifications of that statement, given what Sir. William had told Jason and Lillian.

Lillian gasped at the thought of it. Alex moved over to sit next to her. He was alarmed but put on a brave face.

Lillian looked directly at Jason: "Remember what Sir William told you. If you disappear and there is no body, Tony and the board could control Alex and me for the rest of our lives."

"I know that. I would never abandon you. When all this talk about apparitions or my appearing or disappearing gets lost and becomes old news, we'll approach the board again and find a way to live more freely."

"I thought you said you couldn't control the instant appearing," Alex stated.

David, Melanie and Michael all looked at each other and realized that Alex had just confirmed the truth.

"How would you stop?" Melanie said.

"I'd stop meditating."

"Right, like you'd stop breathing," Lillian cracked.

"This is ridiculous." Melanie used Michael's back as a support and stood. "J.J. has unlimited options. He's not restricted by the board or by anything on the planet."

Lillian looked at her with a glimmer of hope.

"What power does Tony think he has over J.J.?" Melanie continued. "Money? The trust owns J.J.'s name and his intellectual output. So what? There's a lot of support out there for J.J. that the board can't touch. Then there's security. Again, security can be bought anywhere. There's no legal way the board can stop Jason, or Lillian, from buying a ticket to Hawaii and leaving this very moment."

"I don't think I can just run away from this or the board," Jason said.

"Why not?" Lillian demanded. "You don't owe them a thing."

"Hell. I'll give you and Jason some land on Kauai and we can start another Taylor Camp. I'm sure Alex would love living in a tree house."

"I think the question for you, Jason, is do you want to work through this organization that you've built, or walk away and start over?" David asked.

"There's a truth that states any obstacle to spiritual unfoldment is either healed or removed by the Spirit, as long as the initiate stays out of the battle. As much as I'd love to move to Hanalei, if I just walk away without resolving this problem, I'll just have to face it down the road."

"Do you think you're going to heal the board?" Lillian's pointed question made Jason look deeper into the situation. Could Jason 'heal' the board when they believed they were in the right? Could he heal a headache? He knew that if he thought there was a problem, and a healer, and the Spirit—three separate elements—he'd already failed. He knew better.

"Touché," Jason said. He knew there was only One. And that meant that harmony and freedom already existed.

Jason got up and continued, "Shall we all go to Kauai for the winter?"

Chapter 44
Stanford House

Monday Morning, November 2004

All the directors except Jason were present in the boardroom when Tony Bass called the meeting to order at precisely nine o'clock. The vote was by a show of hands. Those in favor of Jason resigning were Lillian, David, Melanie. Those opposed were Tony, Gary, Barbara, Michael, and Dorothy.

Lillian and Melanie were shocked by the outcome. Melanie looked at Michael accusingly. He just shrugged and Tony smiled.

Dorothy stood, put an arm up, and stopped Tony from gaveling the motion into the record. "I want what I have to say put into the minutes."

She looked at Lillian with a sadness that revealed her inner struggle. "I would not remain on this board or be part of this Ministry without Jason. I could not bear to think what would become of it solely under the control of Tony. It would lose every ounce of enlightenment it has. I believe Jason can hold it together if he's allowed to continue what he's been doing. He needs your support, Tony, not your condemnation."

Dorothy returned to her seat. Tony slammed down the wooden disc he used as a gavel, and stated for the record, "The motion is defeated. We will continue our schedule as planned. Jason has a healing assembly at the Royal Albert Hall tomorrow night. He has master classes this afternoon, I believe. I totally agree with Dorothy that any new work be kept confidential until such time as we can properly present it to the public."

Tony adjourned the meeting.

Melanie walked over to Dorothy furious at her. "How could you betray us like that?"

Dorothy, having picked up some of Elizabeth St. John's detachment, said, "You'll understand someday, dear," and walked away.

Lillian and David hung around in the foyer as Melanie stormed out, giving Michael what they call in Hawaii 'stink eye.' The other board members returned to their jobs.

"What now?" Lillian said.

"I'm going to the British Museum to do a little research," David announced.

"I guess I'll just go upstairs and see if my husband is still there."

When Lillian returned to their apartment, Jason was at his computer writing. He could tell by her attitude that the vote had gone against them. He got up and gave his wife a hug.

"It's alright. We'll figure this out."

"Dorothy voted against us."

"Really? Did she give a reason? Of course, she did. She always has a reason."

"She didn't agree with Tony but wouldn't trust Tony running the Ministry without you."

"Okay. What about us? Let's go out to lunch. I'd love some Indian food. We can walk down to Bombay Brasserie."

"Get serious. Let's hold hands and just disappear together." Lillian kicked off her shoes and collapsed into her meditation chair.

"I am serious. I've got my wig and glasses. I can put on my fat suit like we used to do when we wanted to go out incognito."

Jason left for the bedroom and found the extra-large suit that went over the bodysuit Gary had bought him a year ago, which he had only put on once before.

Lillian followed him into the bedroom. "I don't have a disguise. People will recognize me."

"Fine. You're meeting your girlfriends for lunch and I'm your bodyguard."

"I've got a fat bodyguard?"

"Why not. Let's try it." Jason stripped down to his underwear and stepped into the bodysuit. Lillian started to laugh and couldn't stop. Jason began laughing too and they both fell back on the bed in hysterics.

They barely heard the knocking on the front door. "I'll get it," Lillian told her husband, and then looked at the rolls of foam-fat engulfing Jason and cracked up again.

She opened the door on Thomas Parker and Gary. "Is Jason dressed?" said Gary.

"Yes. Why?"

"Two government men are here to see him, on official business. They're waiting in the main library." Lillian felt Gary's concern.

"I'll get him."

She shut the door and returned to the bedroom. Jason had size forty-six pants on over the fat suit and was bent over, looking for the right size shirt in his dresser. She laughed again because the suit was anatomically correct and the suit's butt crack reminded her of a plumber who'd worked for her parents when she was a girl.

"There are some men from the government that want to see you. They're waiting downstairs. I don't think you should wear that, though."

Jason entered the grand foyer of Stanford House wearing a black turtleneck, khaki trousers and boating shoes. He crossed the foyer and opened the carved doors to the library. The men in cheap government suits stood up and Jason shook their outstretched hands. They seemed genuinely pleased to meet him and showed him their identification. They were from MI5, the state security service and had a warrant requiring Jason to come with them to Thames House for questioning. Jason wanted to run upstairs to get a jacket and his wallet, but the men wouldn't let him. They took him directly to their SUV in the garage and drove away.

Chapter 45
London

Monday Afternoon, November 2004

Thames House

J ason was alone in a chair in one of the interrogation rooms at the MI5 headquarters. He could tell that a group of men were watching him from behind a mirrored wall. An older man entered the room, senior interrogator Jason assumed, and sat opposite him at the metal table.

"Mr. St. John," the man began, "you are not being charged with a crime. The purpose of this meeting is to ascertain the reliability of reports that you appeared in a terrorist house in the Baghdad area while British soldiers were engaged in anti-terrorist operations there. Would that be a correct statement?"

"As I told you before, I will not answer any questions until I've consulted with my lawyer, Sir William Boyd."

"This is not a criminal proceeding. You are not entitled to legal representation. What were you doing in Baghdad? Why were you in a terrorist's house? Were you shot by British soldiers?"

Jason didn't answer.

"We can play this game for a long time, Mr. St. John. We just want to find out the truth. I find the report that you were in Baghdad three days ago hard to believe, but I have to verify it one way or another. The sooner you cooperate, the sooner we can all get back to business."

"And what business is that?" Jason said.

"The business of keeping this country safe from terrorists. Are you a terrorist, Mr. St. John? Is your preaching just an elaborate cover? Help us out. Prove us wrong."

The interrogator walked out. Jason mentally debated whether to meditate and establish the Peace but decided that would be putting his pearls before swine. Then again, if he could slip into that dimension of oneness he could disappear and be free. The words "agree with thy adversary" came to him. This was just another form of material power that couldn't touch him—unless he resisted or fought. His human agenda could always be changed and if he maintained his dominion and remained calm and detached, nothing important would be lost.

Hours later, well after dinner according to Jason's stomach, two men Jason hadn't seen before entered the interrogation room. Spiritual facts and inspiration were running through Jason's mind: "Be at peace." "Do not resist." "Love your enemy." The same interrogator followed the younger men into the room.

"Please take off your sweater and pants," the older man ordered.

Jason started to resist but decided against it. He pulled his turtleneck over his head and removed it and then undid his pants and stepped out of them. He could feel the shock when they saw his tattoos. They ordered him to remove his undershirt, and he did. Very few people had ever seen the scope of the tattoos that covered Jason's body. The guards stepped back, almost like they had been accosted by the tribal images. Their reaction was visceral. It was as if they subconsciously understood what the tattoos meant, and the icons were as toxic to these Brits as they were to the native Hiva people.

The lead inspector warily examined Jason's torso, afraid to actually touch his tattoos, and found no sign of gunshot wounds.

Embarrassed, the inspector told Jason to get dressed. "We have you on a twenty-four-hour hold, so you will be spending the night," the inspector said as he left.

"On what grounds?"

"Aiding and abetting terrorists," he called back.

"Are you out of your mind? I demand to be released immediately."

"I'm sorry sir," one of the younger inspectors said, taking hold of Jason's arm. Jason wondered where Sir William was, and realized there was nothing he could do at that moment. He followed the man into the heart of Thames House where he was locked up for the night.

King's College School

Monday Afternoon, November 2004

Alex was called from class fifteen minutes before school ended. He thought it was another security situation and picked up his backpack assuming he wouldn't be coming back. One of the school secretaries took him into the foyer of the headmaster's office where a middle-aged man and woman waited for him. They identified themselves as being from Social Services and showed Alex a court order authorizing them to take him into custody to examine alleged abuse at Stanford House.

Alex refused to go. He started yelling and barged into the headmaster's office. "This is all fake! I've never been abused!

The headmaster put down his newspaper; the headline read "Jason St. John in Custody at MI5." He looked at the warrant and told Alex he had to comply with the order, but he would ring his mother and things would get straightened out very quickly. The male social worker dragged the still resisting Alex from the office, as the headmaster, shaking his head in disbelief, phoned Lillian.

Hope Chapel

Monday Afternoon, November 2004

Gary Howell sat in Reverend Germaine's office. A stack of flyers for the St. John Royal Albert Hall Healing Assembly, scheduled for the following night, laid on the Reverend's desk. Gary was waiting for a response. He thought it was ecumenically important for Reverend Germaine to witness a healing demonstration.

"You say you want to save souls," he continued while Germaine studied a flyer. "Here's your chance. Why not send your followers to see firsthand what a St. John Healing Rally is all about? Maybe you'll be surprised by what happens."

"You don't see the light, do you? He's lied to you from the beginning. He's the devil. I don't need any more evidence to support that," Reverend Germaine told Gary.

"Doesn't it say in Second Thessalonians that the breath of the Lord will put an end to him? Wouldn't the presence of your congregation there be that breath? You said that in your healing services you call on Jesus to enter the hearts and minds of your people. Couldn't He enter the heart and mind of Jason St. John? You said Friday night that you have seen many miracles. I'm inviting you to put aside your concept of Mr. St. John and see for yourself, not just on television but in his presence, where you might feel something extraordinary."

"You've been sent on a fool's errand. I don't understand why you're here when I've so publicly challenged your guru. Jason St. John can do nothing for me or my congregation."

"In the beginning Mr. St. John reached out to the medical profession, which was probably more skeptical and hostile to what he does than you are. We want to extend the olive branch to you, Cyrus. Come and see what a healing meeting is like. Nothing can change the truth. If what you believe is true, Mr. St. John wouldn't have the power to change that. What are you worried about, that you'll lose your flock?"

Reverend Germaine looked at Gary with contempt. "You and your kind are so arrogant, Gary, so sure that you're right. You come here and insult me and my religion by inferring it isn't true, and you expect a civil response? You're as evil as your master. The sooner that evil is eliminated the better off mankind will be." He dumped the flyers for the assembly into his wastebasket and walked out on Gary. "My secretary will show you the door," he said without looking back.

Stanford House

Monday Evening, November 2004

Sir William opened the door of the St. John's apartment and let David in. Lillian was furiously pacing around. Sir William tried to calm her. Melanie and Michael had come to some sort of truce.

"Child Protective Services took Alex from school today. They had complaints that he was being psychologically abused living here at Stanford House," Melanie said to David as he entered the parlor.

"What about J.J.? I just heard that he was at state security?"

"Who told you that?"

"Some damn reporter. They were filming me on my way over here."

"This is Tony's full-court press," said Lillian. "No one else has the contacts or the clout to get these agencies to do something like this."

"It's diversionary," Michael replied. He paused a moment not sure his opinion would be welcome. The others waited, so he continued, "We would do similar things in the investment world; make a problem over here, while you get to your target over there first. So, what's the target? What is Tony afraid of? The assembly tomorrow?"

"J.J. disappearing?" Melanie said.

David turned to Lillian. "How does J.J. conduct his rallies today?"

"That's it!" she shouted. "They want him to sit behind a table and disappear. They want to blow this whole thing up. If Jason disappears, they take over everything. Nobody's left and they step into the driver's seat. Alex and I are screwed. Their concern about the credibility of the Ministry was a bluff. Tony wants to create a religion."

"What does this have to do with sitting behind a table?" David wondered.

"That's when J.J. travels. Alex and I have seen it. J.J. enters such a state of spiritual unity, I mean the atmosphere is incredible, and he begins melting into his environment, for lack of a better term. He pointed out to us that there is a lot of space between molecules, or something like that. The solid state of matter dissolves. I wish I could explain it like he did. I'm not sure if he can disappear if he's not completely still."

David started pacing and thinking. "Then we'll make sure there is no table or chair. Can J.J. do a healing rally walking around like he used to?"

Lillian gave David a big hug. "That's it. We've only had Jason sitting behind a table recently. It seems people quiet down faster that way, but we never did that in the beginning."

"But how would anybody know that's how Jason travels?" Melanie asked.

"I don't know." Lillian sat in her meditation chair. "But it seems obvious, in a way."

"Can J.J. walk around and do healings?" David said.

"Absolutely."

Sir William finished a call on his mobile and put the phone in his pocket. "That was the commissioner's office. They're bringing Alex back as we speak."

Lillian jumped up from the chair and gave David another strong hug. "Thank God! What about J.J.?"

"He'll be out tomorrow, I'm told." Sir William eyed Lillian in David's arms. She gave Dave a quick kiss and pushed him away, feeling slightly embarrassed.

Chapter 46
Royal Albert Hall, London

Tuesday Afternoon, November 2004

G ary and his team met with the staff of the Hall and went over the security for that evening. The Metropolitan Police were to control the crowds and secure the streets. People were already queuing up. Since it was an open assembly, and no tickets were required, the Hall ushers were instructed to seat people by section and not allow them free reign of the house. Each section needed to be filled before moving on to another.

Gary supervised the placement of the table on the dais. With his usual attention to detail, Gary marked where Jason would sit and chose a leather wing back chair from what was offered by the hall. He made sure his staff knew exactly where to place the chair and let them know that the table would be covered in flowers. He went over the sound system with the engineers, making sure the microphone would be hidden in the flowers, and told his security personnel where to stand for the optimum crowd control. When he finished with his staff, he walked to the elevator by the stage door pulling a wheeled case behind him.

An Albert Hall security guard stopped him. "Where are you going with that?"

"I'm moving some special sound and video equipment to the back of the hall," Gary replied.

"Mind if I look inside?"

Gary laid the case on the floor and opened it. It looked like a typical audio/visual trunk; the inside held microphones, booms, and tripod and camera equipment in foam receptacles. "We like to have our own record of Mr. St. John's events. I have a box on the Grand Tier. It would be easier for me to set it up now than this evening."

The guard gave the equipment a cursory inspection and stepped aside.

Gary continued, "We have some special cameras that will capture the heart and soul of Mr. St. John's talk tonight. Thanks."

Gary entered the elevator and exited on the Grand Tier. He pulled his case down the curving corridor, finding the box he had reserved and unlocked the door. Inside the box he closed the curtains that separated the reception area from the seats. He set up a tripod and using a mono scope lined it up with Jason's chair. He marked the position of the tripod on the floor, collapsed it and put everything back in his case. He secured the case and left the box, locking the door behind him. Gary walked around the Grand Tier, coming back to his people setting up the stage.

Chapter 47
Stanford House

Tuesday Afternoon, November 2004

It was a joyous moment when Jason walked into his apartment. Lillian let out a happy cry and ran into his arms. Everyone he loved was there, which took some of his anger away. Alex dropped his mobile and joined the family hug. Melanie and David applauded. He acknowledged them all as he made his way to his bedroom. "Thank you, guys. I'll be back in a minute. I just have to wash MI5 out of my hair."

When he returned to the great room everyone except Alex and David were on their phones. Jason stepped out into the hall where Thomas Parker was stationed.

"Hey, Thomas, how're you doing?"

"Fine, Mr. St. John."

"Did you get in trouble the other night when we all came back from the country?"

"A little. Nothing really. Don't worry about it." Thomas was flattered by Jason's attention.

"Mr. Howell doesn't always see the bigger picture. Listen, I need a favor. Can you get me a list of the phone records of all the calls coming in and out of the compound right after the broadcast?"

Thomas hesitated.

"That's alright, Thomas. I can get it from Gary." Jason gave him a pat on the back and went back inside his apartment.

The adults were still on their phones. Alex was showing David his battleship game on his Nintendo when Jason walked up to his son and put his arm around him. "I heard you had a trying day yesterday, too."

"I don't understand why people are so crazy," Alex said.

Jason ruffled his son's hair and gave David a friendly arm punch and a look that meant thanks... and *here we go again*.

"Don't even try," David responded.

"Melanie's going to be interviewed this afternoon on the Norton Graham show," Lillian announced to the group, closing her phone. "Once we let it out that we were willing to talk about our work here, everybody wants an interview."

"Well, tell them I'm canceling tonight." Jason walked into the center of the room.

"Why would you do that? We're turning this whole thing around."

"Because I'm tired. Because I'm not going to fight Tony."

Lillian went over to Jason and gently took him in her arms and held him close. The buzz in the room quieted down as the others felt a transcendent peace descend upon them. They were together for only one purpose, to recognize this atmosphere, knowing that by doing so they would throw open the doors to the hidden life within. The stillness nearly took their collective breath away. Finally, Jason broke the silence. "You're so wonderful staying by me and coming so far to support this work. I suppose we do make a difference, but sometimes the ignorance and self-interest can be overwhelming. That's the big, hypnotic trap, believing that there is power in the material world that needs to be overcome. Thank you for breaking the hypnotism."

"Will you go ahead with the program, then?" said Melanie.

"Yes."

Chapter 48
Royal Albert Hall

Tuesday Evening, November 2004

The police had closed Kensington Gore in front of the Hall and a sea of humanity spread across the street to the Albert Memorial. People congregated around the building and down the steps to Prince Consort Road. Jason and his motorcade entered from the east, turning off Prince Consort Road onto Kensington Gore before driving up to the stage door. Alex sat between his mother and father in the back seat of their Jaguar sedan. For the most part the crowd was quiet and orderly. Some people around the Albert Memorial chanted Antichrist slogans, but most everybody was there to experience the consciousness Jason brought to these rallies.

David called Gary over to the stage entrance as one of the Hall attendants showed Jason, Lillian and Alex to the headliner's dressing rooms. Melanie and Michael followed them, and David asked Gary to take him to the stage. "Jason's decided he's not going to sit. He'll be standing and walking around," David told Gary. "And the table with the flowers should be behind him.

"I wish you'd told me that sooner," Gary complained. "We'll need to adjust the receivers and re-equalize the room for sound."

"It's what the boss wants."

"But he always sits behind a table. I'm not sure he can create the proper atmosphere unless he's stationary."

"Don't worry about that, my man. I've seen him quiet fifty thousand people in an arena just by walking on stage and standing there. I thought you got your healing at one of his arena events."

Gary wasn't going to argue with David. He'd make the changes and adjust things accordingly, but he didn't like it. He didn't like David. What he'd heard about the early days sounded chaotic to Gary. He was convinced you needed order and structure to heal, and that's what Tony had brought to the Ministry. And, he couldn't forgive David for abandoning the Ministry when Jason needed him the most. Granted, Gary had been healed at an arena event in Washington D.C. but that had nothing to do with David. And David coming back now really ticked him off. What entitled him to have a say in the direction the Ministry would take? By supporting Jason in his out of this world adventures he would kill the Ministry.

The men walked onto the stage. The choirs behind them were empty, and rows of potted palms lined the back of the stage blocking the view from those sections of the hall. Two stagehands joined Gary, and he told them how to rearrange the furniture.

David politely thanked Gary and said, "When do the doors open?"

Gary checked his watch, "In about thirty minutes."

"Any fundamentalists coming?"

"A few hundred, I expect, from the reports I'm getting."

"Are they going to be a problem?"

"I don't think so. I'm making sure they're spread out and not sitting together."

"I'm glad I don't have your job. See you later."

David left the stage and joined Jason's party in his dressing room. Jason was meditating and Lillian and Alex were holding his hands. The others were quiet but had their eyes open. When David entered Melanie got up and took him aside.

"I have such a negative feeling. I don't know why."

David gave her a warm hug and she melted into his arms. Michael looked down at his feet.

"This feels like Hakamaii," Melanie whispered.

"I hope not." David pushed Melanie back, holding on to her arms and looking into her eyes. "You know, until J.J. gets out there and takes them through his mind exercises, it's chaos. All those people with their expectations and fears and who knows what? They'll calm down. Be patient. Have you been able to get still?"

"No. Every time I get to a point of opening, I'm bombarded with negativity."

"I guess things are more charged since the TV show."

Melanie hugged David again. "You're the rock." She went back to Michael just as the assistant stage manager knocked on the door, opened it, and called "ten minutes."

"Why don't you guys go on out and get your seats?" Jason said. "I want to be alone the last few minutes."

They all got up and left without saying anything.

Lillian and Alex sat in the first row of the stalls, next to the railing and facing into the arena. The others sat behind them. David leaned over and whispered in Lillian's ear. "Where's the rest of the board?"

Melanie tapped David on his arm to get his attention. "Dorothy never comes to these events. She can't handle the crowds, and Barbara and her crew pick up the live feed at the studio. I thought Tony would be here though, it's right in our backyard."

David sat back in his seat and patted Melanie's knee. "You feel better?"

"No, not really."

"I'm a little nervous too. Haven't been to one of these things for years."

The buzz in the Hall began to quiet down as the time for Jason to appear drew near. Many were there to experience the stillness and feel the peace that came with these events. Many did not expect to be healed or didn't need a healing. Rather, for them it was a rare opportunity to be with someone in such a high spiritual state and have that soul connection. Others did have problems and expected Jason to solve them. They weren't sure how he'd do that, but many said that after being at a St. John rally their problems disappeared. Some felt the moment when a healing took place. Others didn't realize they'd been healed for days after. Then there were those who came to scoff. Often, they were changed but they never admitted it.

Finally, Jason came out and was handed a wireless microphone by a stagehand. He stood in the middle of the stage, the flowered covered table and a wall of areca palms behind him, and waited for the room become quiet. When he had the audience's attention, he felt the invisible presence rise in him and a great peace filled the Hall. He smiled. This truly was his calling. He took a moment to look into the eyes of those standing close to the stage. Many were young, and hungry for the experience, wanting to be filled with the invisible essence of Spirit. They wanted to let go of their persona and experience the incorporeal One, united as the heavens were united in the void of space—no more you, and me—just one.

"Good evening." Jason brought his hands together in a gesture of Namaste. "I'm going to be asking for your help tonight." A murmur rose from the audience, and then was replaced by a stillness.

"I know you think I'm here to help you, but that's not true. My presence at a healing rally is for one purpose only and it is *not* to give people healings. That is something I cannot do. What I *can* do is realize the spiritual oneness of all here in this auditorium. Those of you who have read my books know what that means. The universe is perfect in its creation. The infinity of creation, from the planets to the forces that keep them aligned to the smallest expressions of life, all of it is perfect. It is all in harmony. It exists in this moment. Nothing exists outside of this moment. The past doesn't exist. The future doesn't exist. All existence is now, and it is perfect."

The audience began to feel the stillness and grow quiet. Jason honored that quietness before continuing.

"If I know this completely, if I have brought my mind and body into the harmony and perfection of this moment, everything conforms to its original state of grace. When I understand that creation is one, one substance, one cause, one life, and I experience that oneness completely, I am there in that consciousness. I am one, and I feel the presence, the consciousness, that is both the Creator and the Creation. I am the perfect manifestation of life in a particular form. I would like all of you to experience that with me." He paused for a moment to let that idea sink in.

"All of you have concepts of me, but I am just a man. And as much as I try to see through them, I have concepts of those around me. Concepts lead to judgment, and judgment leads to conflict. This past week I have been in the center of a conflict. People have said that I can take my body and transport it instantly from one place to another. Is that possible? Perhaps. Someday when we learn more about the nature of matter, and we are able to bring matter under the dominion of the mind, we might experience a greater freedom. To do that, though, the mind has to be free of concept so that through it, we, the incorporeal beings that we are, can see how *one* we are. There is not me onstage and you out there. That is only the appearance of this moment. In reality, there is the infinite nature of life experiencing its essential self as individual expressions of life and realizing that its purpose is in its expression.

"Quantum physics shows us that matter is based on observation. Without an observer, and remember we are one in this endeavor, matter does not appear. When the observer is conditioned, the matter he or she experiences carries that same conditioning. If we all join together to disregard the appearances in front of us, me up here and you out there, the belief that I am different from you, that I have some special abilities or that I have been given a divine gift, all that will be revealed as false. You are as spiritually endowed as I am; just realize it. If you do that, and contemplate our essential unity, then you will be helping me dissolve this conflict."

"Heresy!" someone yelled from the audience.

"We are not a religion. We are talking about the nonphysical reality of life."

Jason began to walk around the stage. He took in all fifty-two hundred people. "Healings," he continued, "are not miracles. They are bringing into harmony that which is out of balance because of human belief."

"Only Jesus can do miracles," another voice shouted.

David scanned the audience to see if he could spot the hecklers, but the Hall was full. The people standing in the prom-pit were spellbound. Most of the people in the stalls were still. The boxes were full, and he scanned the tiers encircling the hall. Even the Royal Box was occupied. But next to it, that box was empty, and the curtains behind the chairs were drawn.

"Where's Gary?" David leaned forward, speaking over Lillian's shoulder.

"He's around. He's always moving around the edges. If the hecklers get too intrusive, he'll find them and escort them out." Lillian was distracted, watching Jason, and trying to get a sense of his state of mind. He didn't seem thrown by the hecklers.

Jason continued, "Every culture, and every era has made magicians or gods out of their great sages. Most were like us here in this hall. They were seekers of truth, and, for one reason or another, they discovered the grand secret—that creation is spiritual, or to put it simply, nonphysical. When the secret is known, and the physical sense of a person changes because of that truth, that person is separated from the crowd. If an individual frightens authority, he or she is either co-opted by the powers that be, or they are eliminated. Saint Teresa of Avila was said to levitate. The church locked her in a cell. After Moses learned the name of God, he came down from Mount Sinai and found his people had made a golden idol to worship. An incorporeal God was beyond their comprehension. Jesus said that 'I am the Christ' and became the Son of God to the exclusion of the rest of mankind. All of us are the only begotten sons and daughters of God."

A roar of protest came from the evangelicals around the hall.

"What's he doing?" Lillian cried, turning around to the board sitting behind her. "He never talks like this in public." She took hold of Alex's hand.

David stood up and searched the audience again. Most of the people were on their feet. Some were booing and shouting epitaphs, others were trying to quiet things down. The noise grew deafening.

Jason raised his hand for quiet. "I am not the messiah nor the Antichrist. The St. John Ministries is no more a religious organization than the Ministry of Justice. Those who want to create a religion around what I do are misguided and wrong. Be skeptical of those who tell you they can heal you, or make you happy, or take away your suffering. I have never said that. If you have the impression that I have, coming from those around me, they don't know what they're talking about. From this moment on I renounce the St. John Ministries and all who work there. They no longer represent the truth of my work. My work is, and always has been, to teach humanity how to be absolutely and unconditionally free.

"Look at our literature. It's all about teaching you, *you*, how to achieve an understanding of your spiritual identity. That is your ultimate freedom. That is healing..."

At that moment Jason jerked and collapsed on to the stage floor. The Hall instantly became hushed. Lillian and Alex jumped up. David bounded over the railing and ran onto the stage. Lillian and Alex immediately followed and all three surrounded Jason. David cradled his friend and then Lillian screamed! She saw blood and tried to keep Alex back. Melanie vaulted over the first row of seats and ran to her friends. The audience began to murmur, especially those in the front, and then the entire hall erupted in chaos. The rest of the board members rushed on stage and encircled Jason.

Gary Howell disassembled his rifle in the rear of the box on the Grand Tier, put his tripod and the deadly components back into the sound equipment case and closed it. He left the box and ran down the curving hall toward the stage pulling his kit behind him. He stashed the trunk with the rest of the audio gear and dashed toward the stage.

On the stage, David shouted, "Where's Gary!" Lillian sobbed prostrate over Jason. David handed Alex over to Melanie, who guided the hysterical boy away from his father. The Albert Hall guards secured the stage, and the Ministry people gently pulled Lillian off of Jason and covered his body with coats and jackets.

"Where is fucking Gary!" David shouted again.

At that moment Gary pushed his way through the mob gasping and out of breath. He saw Jason and dropped to his knees as if shocked. "Oh my God! Oh, sweet Jesus."

Chapter 49
Hanalei Bay, Kauai

December 25, 2004

The press reported every nuance and theory about Jason's murder in the ten weeks that had elapsed since his death. Half the press blamed the religious right. The other half would make no judgment until an arrest had been made. Speculation was rampant on the television talk shows about who murdered Jason and why. They also asked, was Jason St. John really the Antichrist? Or was he in fact a Christ figure who suffered a modern-day crucifixion?

Jason's closest friends were gathered on Kauai where that debate was a world away. There, on Hanalei beach, things were quiet. Melanie owned a beautiful estate on the west end of the beach, away from the Princeville resorts. She had invited Lillian, Alex and David to join her and Michael for the Christmas holiday. David insisted on staying in a hotel until Melanie persuaded him to move in with the rest of them.

Christmas dinner was a beautiful affair with a Hawaiian touch. The buffet was set on a sideboard carved with Hiva designs. A large painting of Larry and Melanie hung over the buffet. It showed them posed on a promontory overlooking a tropical bay where the *Mata'i* was anchored. They toasted Larry with glasses of Cristal champagne and burst out laughing.

"If my dad were here, he would have made a breadfruit *poi* and a *poisson cru*," Melanie declared as they lined up to fill their plates. "To Larry and J.J."

"That's Anaho Bay, our last stop before we sailed home," David told Alex.

"It was heaven," Melanie added.

They all filled their plates and sat down to dinner. The afternoon sun sent shafts of light through the clouds. Typical of the Hawaiian winter, it rained most of the day, but now the clouds had parted to give the island another spectacular sunset.

"Dad said he'd tell me about his initiation when I was old enough. Does anybody know what happened?" Alex asked.

David looked at Lillian who said, "Your Uncle Dave knows. Maybe this is the time."

"Your dad had been gone for three days and everybody thought he was dead. Not just us," he gestured around the table awkwardly, "but the islanders who knew about the ceremony. I had a plane ticket home. I thought that finding him was hopeless. Then the *Mata'i* sailed back to Taiohae and Melanie came ashore crying that Larry was dying. The French doctor was useless. He said we needed a *tuhuna*; that Larry was dying of a curse. Then your dad showed up and healed him."

"But that doesn't tell me anything about the initiation."

"Let me say this. Besides having had his body covered in tattoos in forty-eight hours, your dad was given mind-altering drugs that were supposed to reveal the secrets of the Hiva people to him." For some reason David couldn't tell the story the way he wanted to. Alex was so hungry to know, and words seemed so inadequate.

"Like LSD?"

"No. The main intoxicant was a drink called *kava*. We all drank it. But your dad was given something else. They told me it opened your mind, but it also was a strong aphrodisiac."

"What's an aphrodisiac?" Alex said pronouncing the word syllable by syllable.

David turned to Lillian for guidance.

She just smiled at him. "You're on your own."

"Did he have sex?" Alex continued. "Do I have any brothers and sisters there?"

"You take over," David told Lillian.

Lillian continued, "I don't know, honey, if you have any siblings, or not. They did force your dad to have sex. But he told me that his biggest lesson was learning the difference between the physical and the spiritual. The sexual part wasn't as traumatic as other parts of the ritual. I mean, you came into our lives with all the joy and anticipation every normal couple experience. It was the psychic initiation that troubled him the most, but it was also the experience that gave him the greatest insight into the nature of reality."

"What do you mean by psychic initiation?" Alex was a great Harry Potter fan and had pictured his dad in some kind of great magical battle. "Did those people have wizards?"

"Their priests were shamans. I guess they were like magicians. But they didn't succeed in what they set out to do. They wanted your dad as a human sacrifice…"

"What! Were they cannibals?"

"I don't think so. But your father escaped their knife."

"How did he do that?"

"You know. You've seen it."

"Was he doing instant appearing back then?"

"I don't know what took place. Their belief in good and evil couldn't penetrate the consciousness your dad had developed. He saw through those beliefs into the omnipotent nature of spiritual reality. He wasn't scared of that world—well maybe he was to a degree—but he knew not to fight the forces set against him. That allowed him to be enough detached from his body that they couldn't complete their sacrifice in the way they wanted. I think he experienced a oneness so complete that their beliefs, their gods or whatever they thought they were going to make of him, were completely powerless. That's why your dad was so threatening to the fundamentalists. Without evil they have nothing to fight."

"But why did he have to die?"

Lillian got up from the table and walked over to where her son sat and embraced him. They had done all their crying in the days and weeks after Jason's murder, but finding the answer to Alex's question might never come. Everyone at the table waited for Lillian to continue, but she just shook her head sadly.

David stepped in: "I loved your father, Alex, and I love you too, so I don't want you to take this as a criticism. You're so young, but you're also an old soul. You know what that means?"

"I guess."

"Your father was so advanced in his perception of life that he wouldn't ask that question. He understood the eternal nature of life, and he demonstrated his incorporeal self. Are you with me?"

"You mean his instant appearing?"

"No. It was so much more than that. He showed the world that life isn't confined to physical form. And he showed that his body was as transcendent as his soul. He gave me a great gift in the Marquesas, you know. He gave me an embrace that shifted my whole perception of the world." David stifled his tears. "He told me that I had nothing to regret. You have nothing to regret, Alex. I'm sure he'll always be with you."

"But was he tortured?"

"Not in the way you'd think." David had to hold it together for Alex. He walked over to Lillian and Alex and joined in their embrace. "He suffered because we weren't with him, and he might have missed a chance to make things right with Larry. It angered him that Larry had judged him and that he had reacted to that judgment. When he finally got free and found us, we thought Larry was dead."

"But how did he get away?"

"I don't really know. All I know was that he was there on the shore in Taiohae after Melanie's dad had died."

Alex looked up at the picture of Larry and Melanie on the wall as the pieces of his family's relationship began to click in his head.

David continued, "J.J. wanted to see Larry and told Melanie and me to wait outside his cabin. While he was in with Larry, Melanie and I could feel something extraordinary happening. Just like you've felt in your dad's classes. Then the most amazing thing happened. We heard Larry and your dad laughing, and there was this bright light that came from the cabin. When they both came out on deck Larry said, 'Let's go home.'"

Melanie knelt down next to Alex and caressed his cheek. "So, the idea that your dad's healing gift was the product of some South Seas voodoo was entirely false. In fact, the change of relationship between your father and my father was amazing. We sailed back to Hawaii in a state of bliss. At one point a school of whales began riding our bow wave. J.J. went forward and sat on the bowsprit to watch them more closely. Coming off one wave, our bowsprit went slightly under water. At first J.J. stood up so his butt wouldn't get wet and when he looked down, a whale was right under him. On the next wave he didn't get up and when another whale showed up, he rubbed its back with his feet. That was communicated to the pod and soon all the whales were lining up to get their backs rubbed. We all took turns riding the bowsprit and massaging the whales."

"I wish I could do that someday," said Alex.

Lillian sobbed. David held her and she put her head on his shoulder. Alex got up and hugged them both. David said; "I'm sorry. We shouldn't be telling stories about J.J."

"No," Lillian replied. "This is what I need. I got so jealous when you three returned and you had that shared experience. I could feel the spiritual reality of it, but I missed being there."

"You didn't miss a thing," Melanie kissed Lillian on her cheeks and wiped away her tears. "Why go through hell when you can gain the truth through grace? You had J.J. in your life for fourteen years. You got the best of him. You saw him in his most giving state. Count your lucky stars."

Epilogue

Though Jason's funeral was public and there was no doubt about his death, people still thought he lived. There were many sightings of him with various leaders and he was seen by whole groups of people so it couldn't be said that those sightings were hallucinations. The board never commented on them.

The murder changed the organization completely. Thomas Parker had actually copied the phone logs like Jason asked and had turned them over to the police. He hadn't trusted anybody at the Ministry. The police found a connection between Tony Bass and the calls to various government agencies confirming that Tony was indeed trying to undermine the purpose of the foundation. The board voted him off by a five to two margin. A week later Gary Howell killed himself. Today the trust is back in the hands of its founders.

The End

Acknowledgements

Many people gave their time and expertise to make this book what it is. I thank them all.

SANDRA KNIGHT, my muse, partner and best friend went through every draft, questioned every unclear sentence, and made sure this was the best read possible. I am most grateful.

CHRISTINE WAGNER was a champion of this book from the first draft. She has read, corrected and coaxed from me the most creative way to say what was said. She's the best.

SUNNY CHAYES loved the story early on and made sure the story conveyed the message I intended it to. She was extremely helpful in getting the book out to publishers. I'm so grateful for her help.

There were many people who read early drafts, gave notes, and generally encouraged me to continue on. They were Marty and Liz Parker, Wendy Thomas, Beth Halter, Ann McCoy, Laurie Parker, Anne Dillon of the New York Book Editors, and many others.

A special thanks to the person who wants to remain anonymous yet was instrumental in getting the book edited.

For more background on the story and photos from the Marquesas Islands go to **www.theatuaman.com**

For more information on contemporary mysticism go to **www.alohamystics.com**

About the Author

John Stephenson

Praise for John's book:
Fullness of Joy
A Spiritual Guide to the Paradise Within

"John Stephenson is an amazing and unique man who has expertise in so many areas. Aside from teaching the spiritual wisdom of Joel Goldsmith, he is also a sailor, surfer, artist, sculptor and scriptwriter. As one of the most committed individuals I know who lives and tastes life to its fullest, John Stephenson writes with authenticity, sincerity, honesty, inspiration and conviction ... he truly walks his spiritual pathway."

Gerald G. Jampolsky, MD

"In his book, *Fullness of Joy*, John Stephenson, a truly inspirational teacher has given us the 'keys to the kingdom.' He clearly outlines the steps to a life free from physical limitation, financial limitation and emotional limitation. Can you think of a greater gift? I can't."

Raymond Wagner,
Motion Picture Executive

www.ingramcontent.com/pod-product-compliance
Lightning Source LLC
Chambersburg PA
CBHW050856130726
47900CB00013B/60